The Secrets of Harry Bright

Joseph Wambaugh

LONGMEADOW
— **HALL** —

Published in Large Print by arrangement with
William Morrow and Company, Inc.

British Commonwealth rights courtesy of
Michael Joseph Ltd.

Set in 16 pt Plantin.

ISBN 0-681-40121-4 (Longmeadow Hall)

This Large Print edition produced exclusively for
Longmeadow Hall, 201 High Ridge Road,
Stamford, CT 06904, by G. K. Hall & Co.,
Boston, MA 02111.

This one is especially for Dee

This time my thanks for the wonderful cop talk goes to officers of the San Diego Police Department, San Diego Sheriff's Department, National City Police Department, Palm Springs Police Department, Riverside County Sheriff's Department and Desert Hot Springs Police Department
and
to the many desert rats who kindly provided so much extraordinary local color
and
to my editor, Jeanne Bernkopf, for her superb work.

For this my son was dead, and is alive again; he was lost, and is found.

—Luke 15:24

Prologue

THE SECRET

The single-engine Cessna 172 was a tiny blip on the radar screen at San Diego's Lindbergh Field. Air-traffic controllers also watched another blip, PSA Flight 182 en route from Los Angeles. Suddenly the impossible: two blips merged.

Nothing was ever heard from the Cessna. It fell like a shotgunned dove. The last official communication from the PSA pilot said: "Tower, we're going down! This is PSA!"

There followed a seventeen-second silence, but the voice recorder carried the pilot's final words: "This is it, baby. Brace yourselves."

There was yet another message on the recorder found that Monday morning in 1978, after the country's worst domestic air disaster to date. The message was a version of the declaration most often uttered on deathbeds as well as on all the battlefields of life. A child cries out to a parent. The final words on the voice recorder: "Ma, I love you."

Many North Park residents thought it was a monster quake. They waited in terror for aftershocks. Then a firestorm and a mushroom of black fuel smoke turned terror to panic. Some now thought the prediction had been fulfilled: San Diego *was* among the first of Russian targets!

The explosion launched 144 human beings and parts of human beings from the airplane like rockets. The first policeman on the scene had no idea how to begin contending with fires raging, and people screaming through the streets, and smoke obliterating everything. He later said that it was like the old Warner Bros. cartoon where the walls of houses bore gaping holes in the shapes of people. The young cop ran inside a one-story stucco home struck by a human projectile. He found a man shrieking at a naked headless woman lying in his wife's bed. When his hysteria subsided, the man suddenly cried, "Wait a minute! That's *not* my wife! My wife doesn't have tits that big!"

He was correct. An airline passenger had been blasted through the wall of the house and landed precisely on the bed recently vacated by the wife who was one of the many people fleeing in panic.

The only "crash survivor" to be taken to the hospital was a woman covered with gore found lying dazed by the disaster site. She was sped away by ambulance, and when they washed off the blood and mangled flesh, and treated her for shock, it was discovered that she had been a passing motorist whose car windshield was suddenly demolished by not one but *three* flying bodies. She had skidded to a stop and leaped from a car suddenly crammed with limbs and torsos, bursting skulls and exploding organs. The patient was found to be physically sound. She wasn't even bruised.

That first young cop on the scene saw quite a few things that would cause recurring nightmares and unwanted memories, but none more vivid than the kneeling man. He wore a pair of athletic shoes, baggy khakis and a San Diego Padres baseball shirt. At first the young cop thought the kneeling man was a corpse robber. Then the cop saw a police badge pinned to the shoulder of the Padres sweatshirt and believed that the kneeling man was an off-duty policeman trying to help out. The young cop was about to ask him to check the burning homes for injured victims when he saw that the kneeling man was studying something on the ground. The man just stared through eyeglasses, nodding up and down to focus through bifocals.

When the young cop got close enough to look for himself, he yelped and turned away. Then he gathered himself and called to another smoke-blackened cop who was heading toward a burning home with a commandeered garden hose. Both policemen approached the kneeling man cautiously. The kneeling man moved a few inches as though to obstruct their view, as though he was guarding his find. Then the cops saw it clearly. First one cop, then the other started to giggle. Soon they were cackling and losing control. They were doubled up and roaring just as an outraged news photographer saw them and snapped a photo. The wire services scotched the picture when later at the command post the cops were able to explain the circumstances that provoked the seemingly ghoulish outburst.

Afterward, they were not able to locate the kneeling man. On reflection, they weren't even sure that the badge on his baseball shirt was a San Diego Police Department shield. Whatever the kneeling man might have learned would remain his secret in the years to come.

Chapter 1

THE MACHO LIZARD

Across the globe there are two narrow belts 25 degrees north and south of the equator where the movement of winds and oceans prevents rain clouds from penetrating the earth. The sun, without cloud cover below, is free to suck the moisture from earth, plants, animals. The night sky in such places is very clear, and it turns suddenly cool when the ground heat bounces back to the heavens. The daytime baking and night cooling of the earth's floor creates formidable winds. Where mountains exist, the rising hot air is replaced by cool air from the mountains that funnels down the canyons and dries the land even more.

In former times such places were thought inhospitable to ordinary human beings, but then nobody ever said that ordinary human beings lived in Hollywood. It was probably the excess of the good life during Hollywood's Golden Age that pushed them out there, just two hours drive from Los Angeles but a world away.

People who lived their lives like they were hot-wired to Caddy convertibles, people who

5

claimed to wear cocaine on their genitals to *stay* hot-wired, found that for the first time in years they could actually uncoil. The desert possessed magic.

At first some of them didn't see it. The desert looked forbidding and hostile, but pretty soon the enveloping mountains stopped seeming like slag heaps. The mountains took on noble shapes, elegant lines. The movie stars talked of subtle desert pastels and ever-changing light shows. Cloud shadow from feathery cumulus banks spangled the mountains and hills with light and dappled shade. A movie star could sit by poolside or in a natural hot spring and watch the shadows magically swirling in color, and the coral, scarlet and purple cactus blossoms and wild flowers flooding the foreground. The foothills were so covered with verbena that they were called the Purple Mountains. And then there were the nights, cool nights when movie stars would gaze at real ones. The dipper burned like a strand of diamonds on a sable cloak.

So Palm Springs provided a refuge, a sanctuary between pictures. They all came: Gable, Lombard, Cagney, Tracy, Hepburn, the Marx Brothers, even Garbo. And no matter how fearful they might be about Time, those people who had to remain changeless, the desert had an answer even for that. The warm dry climate soothed arthritic pain, bursitis, lung disorders. Everyone started feeling more vigorous, playing tennis and golf, swimming, cavorting like Errol Flynn.

There were endless surprises. Mount San Jacinto's peak at dusk was backlit by the sun setting over the Pacific. It gave the thrilling impression that *just* west of the mountain was the city, the searchlights of Grauman's Chinese, The Pantages and The Egyptian theaters. The drooling mobs with their pencils and notebooks and flashbulbs seemed to be *just* on the other side. It was all so comforting it allowed them to relax and play like children. The mountain was backlit for *them* by The Great Gaffer in the sky. They were safe. They could rest because reassuringly close, ever waiting in the lights, was Hollywood.

Then of course after show biz found sand and cactus to its liking, land developers invaded the desert like Rommel's panzers. They started in Palm Springs and eventually spread south to Cathedral City, Rancho Mirage, Palm Desert, Indian Wells, La Quinta. The Coachella Valley was blitzkrieged.

It appeared that absolutely nothing could halt the country club and resort developers. Those big cat tractors would challenge Godzilla, they said. But one of Godzilla's little cousins slowed them down a bit. Apparently, certain portions of the Coachella Valley provide the last chance for a tiny endangered creature called the fringe-toed lizard. He's an unremarkable little fellow with overlapping eyelids, fat belly and snowshoe scales for sand dwelling. Yet he has become the environmentalists' best hope for slowing the momentum that Hollywood started so long ago. But some of the richest and most famous people on earth own real estate in the fringe-toed lizard's bailiwick, so gamblers aren't betting much on the little reptile.

Today there are at least fifty golf courses in the Coachella Valley and over two hundred hotels, and the low humidity condition in the desert has been forever altered by colossal raids on the underground water table.

But there are parts of the valley that aren't amenable to raids by big cat tractors. One of them is the little town of Mineral Springs, about ten miles out of Palm Springs. The reason is simple: wind. Desert wind that could drive ten thousand wind turbines. The Mineral Springs Chamber of Commerce calls the winds "therapeutic breezes." The residents call them gale force.

There's little sand left, the residents say. It's been blown clear to the Salton Sea. The wind can make it rain pebbles and stones like a desert hailstorm. Cars left with windows open need to be pickaxed, they say.

But in 1978 the good people of Mineral Springs decided that wind or no wind they wanted some of the tourist bucks from their neighbors on the other side of the valley. After all, their mineral water spouting from the ground at 180 degrees Fahrenheit was pure,

8

and didn't smell like rotten eggs as does most mineral water. In fact, it was so clean that they wanted a federal grant to study the phenomenon of odorless hot mineral water, until it was pointed out that the smell is probably blown away before it can *reach* the nose.

The townsfolk decided that if their small city was going to be taken seriously it needed among other things its own police force, so they decided to take applications for a chief of police and eventually settled on a fourteen-year veteran of the county sheriff's office. Paco Pedroza had also been a sergeant with the Los Angeles Police Department for nine years prior to that, and had moved to a desert climate hoping to arrest his daughter's chronic bronchitis.

The town of Mineral Springs thought it could get by with a three-man police force until its new chief pointed out a few territorial problems. Mineral Springs, being remote, yet easily accessible to the rich desert resorts, was the home of more chemists than Cal Tech, but they were all amateurs. The lonely windblown desert canyons were full of Cobras, an outlaw motorcycle gang that made its living by brewing vats of methamphetamine. If there was an ideal place for speed labs this was it. The ether smell of "crank" or "crystal" was blown halfway to Indio the second it escaped the lab. There was no danger of cops literally nosing their way into a lab as in ordinary neighborhoods. So there were a lot of Harley hogs and chopper bikes in or about the town, and they did more business than the Rotary Club.

In addition to the crank labs, Mineral Springs, with its low-cost housing, was also an ideal spot for most of the meat eaters who flock to rich resort communities to feed on tourists. It had two halfway houses and a de-tox center for the ex-cons and "reformed" dopers and alcoholics of the Coachella Valley. The only mansion in town had been built by a pimp who ran thirteen girls into Palm Springs during the height of the season to work the hotels. An early reputation for a laissez-faire life-style also brought a nudist colony, and the nudist colony brought hordes of hang gliders, which often crashed in the treacherous winds. It was not an easy town for cops in that the ex-cons, bikers, crank dealers, Palm Springs burglars, nudists, robbers and pimps, horny kite pilots, dopers and drunks didn't necessarily want a police force of any kind.

Paco Pedroza needed savvy cops, and they had to be the right kind to make it in these parts, being ten miles from the closest police jurisdiction where there might be help available.

He gave each cop he hired over the years the same admonition: "I gotta have people with street smarts and moxie but they also gotta have somethin *more* important: diplomacy. When you're out there all alone and no help on the horizon you gotta be able to *talk* people into doing it your way. Remember one thing: out

10

here you ain't got no *'or else'* at your disposal."

And Paco gave each cop he hired (except the lone female, Ruth Kosko) the same warning: "I won't hassle you about the weapons you carry. We got M-fourteens in your car with a clip a thirty that you can fire in three round bursts. You can carry forty-four magnums, or forty-fives with as hot a load as they can stand. You can carry nine millimeters cocked and locked, if you need more rounds. You can wear a Whammo wrist rocket or you can stash a backup derringer up your ass if it makes you feel better. I ain't gonna hassle you about the iron you carry even if it looks offensive. And there ain't much of a dress code. I won't worry about a shoeshine since the sun'll melt it off anyway. I won't worry if you catch a few winks sometimes on a graveyard shift if you got to. I have just a few rules for my cops: no drugs and no thieves at no time. And no booze on the job. And no aberrant sexual behavior inside the city limits with anybody under the age a forty even when you're off duty. And that's about it, far as rules."

The last one was because the 150 single-parent divorcees and widows who lived in the mobile-home park (which the citizens called Mid-Life Junction) were driving the chief bughouse. They came every month to the city-council meeting with a ten-page list of what was wrong with the town and figured that the police chief was responsible for most of it. Paco

Pedroza, who admitted to being a sexist pig, figured that all those waitresses and manicurists and hairdressers who lived in Mineral Springs but commuted to jobs in the resort towns were suffering from the fact that available women greatly outnumbered men except during the height of the tourist season when the conventions hit the desert. So he encouraged his cops to do "P.R. work" at Mid-Life Junction by attending their coffee klatches. But his cops were mostly young dudes, and the burnouts at Mid-Life Junction looked to them even older than they were. After the press began calling a particularly dangerous strip of desert highway "Blood Alley," the cops started calling Mid-Life Junction "No-Blood Alley."

When Paco Pedroza got the call from Hollywood Division of the Los Angeles Police Department informing him of a possible hot new lead in a cold but notorious desert murder case that had touched the town of Mineral Springs, he promised total cooperation to the boys from his old alma mater. Then he hung up and posted a notice to his eight man and one woman police force that they would be receiving guests from planet Hollywood, after which he had his secretary and clerk, Annie Paskewicz, draw a picture of a coiled desert sidewinder with a caption that said: "We don't give a shit *how* they do it in L.A.," which he attached to his incoming file basket.

Paco Pedroza dragged his overweight body

12

up the steps to the roof of the police station/ city hall/jailhouse, stripped off his mustard-yellow aloha shirt and groaned at the sight of his gelatinous pecs which seemed to fall a quarter of an inch a year.

"I oughtta have our Hollywood guests bring me something black and lacy and *big* from Frederick's," Paco groaned to his sergeant. Then Paco squeezed one of his hairy breasts, dropped into a battered lawn chair and said, "That's *it*. I'm way past a training bra. No more burritos for this Mexican."

Coy Brickman, at forty-one, was ten years younger than Paco, several inches taller, and looked taller yet in his blue uniform.

"They think a pair a big town cops can clear a no-leads seventeen-month-old case?" Coy Brickman tore disgustedly at a meatball sandwich he'd got at the town's only deli, washing it down with a quart of orange juice.

Paco settled back, letting the desert rays have at his bronze belly and said, "Wonder if they'll send any a the dicks I used to know?"

"You don't clear a no-leads, seventeen-month-old case very often," Coy Brickman repeated.

"So?" Paco shrugged, closing his eyes. "They can have a week in a Palm Springs spa getting a facial, a body wrap and a blowjob. Speakin a which, what's the wind look like?"

"Therapeutic breeze," Coy Brickman said, watching the dust devils and whirlwinds forming in the valley.

Paco Pedroza sighed and said, "A breeze in this freaking town could blow the nuts off a ground squirrel. Bring me a snack next time ya drive by Humberto's."

"Three, four chicken tacos okay?"

"Make it four," the chief mumbled, never opening his eyes. "*With* frijoles. One thing about this freaking wind. You learn to fart silently and nobody ever knows."

And while Paco dozed and his sergeant ate an early supper of ersatz meatballs on the roof of the police station, a Mineral Springs wino named Beavertail Bigelow was 86'd from a gin mill for picking a fight. A grimy wrinkled desert rat who looked as though he'd lurched into town with his bedroll lashed to a double-parked donkey, Beavertail drank a fifth of gin, they said, every day it didn't snow in town, and never went home when the cops told him to, and respected authority about like Sacco and Vanzetti.

The cops wished that some night when he was sleeping it off on a table at the oasis picnic ground, a flash flood would wash the son of a bitch clear to Indio. But he was a true desert rat. He hated people, understood hostile environments and could survive fifty megatons at ground zero.

Beavertail Bigelow was sixty years old, weighed less than 130 pounds, was chinless and watery-eyed, and was described as having shoulders like Reagan — Nancy that is. He got his sobriquet from the flat oval cactus of the same name that proliferated in the Coachella Valley, a species that looked harmless but bore minute barbed hairlike spines. The saying went, "You think the little wimp's spineless till you press him."

As darkness fell so did Beavertail Bigelow, onto his favorite table at the oasis picnic ground. He was ten fathoms deep in a Beefeater slumber when a tall dark figure hoisted him up and hauled his carcass toward a waiting car, which roared toward the highway to Twentynine Palms.

There was a diner on that highway where a bus driver made regular rest stops and lots of passes at a counter waitress. The unattended bus was parked in the light by the road sign, but no one saw the dark-clad figure carrying his shabby bundle. Beavertail Bigelow was found thirty minutes later on the back seat of the bus when his snoring woke two marines on their way to their base. He got kicked off the bus, minus his cowboy hat, and had to hitchhike back to Mineral Springs, therefore adding bus drivers to the list of things he hated.

By the time Beavertail reached the outskirts of Mineral Springs the rising sun was smacking him in the eyes. His cerebellum was fogged by gin fumes and his soggy cortex was giving conflicting orders to his ravaged little body. All those millions of marinated brain cells were firing aimlessly. Beavertail Bigelow was parched and confused.

He decided to cut across a mile of desert directly to the oasis picnic ground where there was a water fountain piped from a natural spring. He kept his mouth clamped shut and breathed through his nose to keep the mucous membranes moist, but his narrow skull was already heating up. The sun was just above the horizon but soaring fast, and throwing purples and pinks and crimsons and blues across the Santa Rosa Mountains.

Beavertail realized that the gin was accelerating dehydration like crazy. The marrow in his bones was sizzling. Might as well stick a blow dryer in his mouth as drink a fifth of gin and start trucking across the desert, he thought. Then he decided that if he had lots of money like Johnny Cash or Liz Taylor and Liza Minelli and all the other rich cocksuckers that came to the desert to get cured at the Eisenhower detox clinic, he wouldn't be out here at the crack of dawn staggering around. He was only in this goddamn pickle because he was poor.

Beavertail was now about tired enough to accept help even from a cop if he spotted one, but he figured they were all sleeping in their patrol cars somewhere, the lazy pricks. He had to pull himself together and take a breather, so he wobbled toward a honeypod mesquite, the shade tree of the desert. It was about thirty feet tall, a dramatic species with rounded crown and rough-textured bark.

He scared a roadrunner who leaped from behind a spray of desert lavender and zoomed off, his topknot fluttering. The scented flowers and strong mint aroma attracted swarms of bees, but this one was beeless at the moment so Beavertail squatted beside it, careful not to disturb a large jumping cholla. The slightest touch of the cactus' joints will shoot you full of barbs, yet birds nest in it. *Another* desert mystery.

As Beavertail squatted like a Morongo Indian, getting crankier by the minute, he spotted a banded gecko lizard doing a few pushups on a little sand drift. The gecko shot Beavertail Bigelow a mean little glare and tossed off about five more pushups for effect. The "pushup" movement is thought to be a display of territorial dominance, and this four-inch reptile was so full of anxiety he was into his third set.

Suddenly, the lizard took a bluff step toward Beavertail Bigelow and squeezed out three *more* pushups, though by now his little tongue was lolling from exhaustion and his eyes were sliding back in his skull.

Beavertail got very curious. The desert rat creaked to his feet and braced the lizard like a gunslinger. "You ain't no fringe-toed, you little cocksucker," Beavertail told the gecko. "I can kick your ass and who cares?"

With that, Beavertail Bigelow tried to give

17

the gecko a swift kick, but since his brain cells were firing at random he only kicked desert air. Beavertail sailed over the sand drift, landing flat on his bony spine. He let out a yelp and was answered by a musical plink. He thought at first that the sound was a spinal disk blowing, so he gingerly pulled himself to a sitting position.

He figured the little cocksucker lizard had jammed on home until he saw what the lizard had been guarding. The asshole *was* home! He'd been living inside his treasure, which was now the property of Beavertail Bigelow by virtue of superior size. It was a funny-looking ukulele.

Beavertail picked it up, dusted it off and saw that it was in one piece. How the hell did it get here? Fell off a passing truck probably. He could clean it up and take it to a pawnshop he knew in Cathedral City, where there were no cathedrals but lots of secondhand joints and so many gay bars that desert barflies would say, "Are you married, fella, or do you live in Cathedral City?"

When at a later time, lawmen would reflect upon how a notorious Palm Springs murder case was methodically deciphered by seemingly random discoveries, they would find undeniable that a growing evidence chain was forged by a very macho lizard.

Chapter 2

THE PAYOFF

President Ronald Reagan had not yet arrived at the Century Plaza Hotel to await election results, but half a block away on Avenue of the Stars, Sidney Blackpool was making a call at an office suite when he saw two men standing beside a limousine. They wore three-piece suits and button-down shirts and striped neckties and shiny wingtips, but despite the duds they didn't have the gee-whiz look of a George Bush preppie. For one thing their arms hung funny and they both looked about as lighthearted as Jack Nicklaus lining up a putt on the eighteenth.

Sidney Blackpool was never comfortable walking past Secret Service agents, but had had several occasions to do so in the past twenty-one years when bigshot politicians came to town. Like most policemen he didn't think that Secret Service agents were *real* cops, so he wasn't altogether relaxed when he had to stroll by with a Smith & Wesson under his coat. Regular cops could spot a plainclothes dick in a minute, but he always feared that one of these guys might eyeball the gun bulge and give him a John Hinckley brain massage with the butt of an Uzi before he could identify himself.

They didn't call him Black Sid for any reason related to his appearance. In fact, his hair was sandy brown and gray mottled, and his eyes were pale green, and he had the kind of freckled flesh that seemed to invite a keratosis every time he played a round of golf without sunscreen lotion.

"A skin-doctor's dream," his dermatologist told him. "Keep it up, and by the time you're forty-five you'll progress from something that sounds ugly, like keratosis, to something that sounds pretty, like melanoma."

People always asked if he got his nickname from being a Dirty Harry, black-glove cop, and he'd explain that policemen love monickers and when your name is Sidney Blackpool you just naturally become Black Sid. What he didn't tell them was that "Black Sid" reflected his cynical demeanor, a look that said doomsday couldn't come soon enough. Nor did he say that he drank *lots* more than his share of Johnnie Walker Black Label Scotch — ergo, Black Sid.

Sidney Blackpool was not kept waiting by the foxy secretary at an art nouveau desk shaped like an oil spill. She certainly had no trouble spotting him for a cop, and asked, "Sergeant Blackpool?," the second he entered the office.

The detective was about to make himself comfortable and maybe see if she was as friendly as she looked when she said, "Oh, you don't have to wait. Mister Watson's expecting you."

20

Victor Watson's office was not quite as overdone as the palace at Versailles but it did have a Louis XV parquet floor. And there were terra-cotta urns and Chinese pots on that floor, and Italian rococo mirrors, and a J.M.W. Turner oil painting on the wall, and polished granite tabletops, and a lacquered desk, if it *was* a desk, that looked like one of those ten-thousand-dollar numbers that're supposed to combine form and function but look like an organ pulled from the belly of a dinosaur.

Sidney Blackpool was looking for Victor Watson in all this loopy art mix when a voice from the adjoining salon said, "In here, Sergeant Blackpool."

The smaller room was a sudden relief. It was orderly with nubby upholstery and wood, real wood, and rough tactile accents. It was a man's room, and the desk top of polished granite reflected the pupils and irises of the suntanned smiling man behind it.

"Doesn't that office make you want to puke?" Victor Watson said.

"Who designed it, Busby Berkeley?" the detective said dryly.

"My wife did, I'm afraid."

"She only forgot a singing waterfall," Sidney Blackpool said, shaking hands with the older man and being beckoned toward the camel sofa.

Everyone knew who the "wife" was even if they'd never heard of Victor Watson. She was at one time a top star of feature films and was

21

now experiencing a comeback as a nighttime soap opera killer-bitch.

There were two crystal tumblers and an ice bucket on the simple oak cocktail table, but there was nothing simple about the Ming-dynasty figural group resting beside a full bottle of Johnnie Walker Black Label.

Victor Watson looked at his wristwatch, Patek Phillipe of course, and said, "Late enough for a drink, Sergeant? You're almost off duty."

"I don't worry about duty," Sidney Blackpool said. "Only about my liver. Four o'clock's late enough."

Victor Watson sat beside the detective and poured three fingers of Scotch into each tumbler, then added two ice cubes to both drinks. He was so tanned that his crow's-feet crinkled dead white when he smiled, as chalky white as his hair. His hands were delicate and they too were covered with white hairs.

"Tell me," he said, "do you resent being sent over here to humor some millionaire about a seventeen-month-old murder case?"

"Not as long as he buys the drinks, Mister Watson," Sidney Blackpool said, eyeing the older man over the edge of the glass.

Victor Watson shifted his weight on the sofa, adjusting the crease in his Nino Cerruti pleated pants as he did so. His outfit included a brocade vest, which was back in style (at least in Beverly Hills and its environs) after a fifty-year absence, and kiltie Italian slip-on loafers.

22

Then he saw the detective's cynical green eyes looking him over and said, "When I'm in my downtown offices in the financial district, I don't wear clothes from a Paris boutique."

Sidney Blackpool managed a halfhearted smile and continued to drink without comment. So far the guy had apologized for his wife's goofy taste and his frog clothes designer. Still, he was paying for the drinks.

As though he read the detective's mind, Victor Watson freshened the drink and said, "You're not *about* to ask me how I knew you drink Johnnie Walker Black, are you?"

Victor Watson chuckled and those polished granite eyes got a bit less riveting. "A childish trick I know, but things like that impress the idiots around this town. I asked your lieutenant when I called your office, and he asked your partner."

"My partner's on vacation. Won't be back for a couple of weeks."

"Of course, I was told that. He must've asked somebody in your office."

"It's okay with me," Sidney Blackpool said, and the Scotch was warming his belly and throat and if this kept up he might start to tolerate this guy.

"How old're you, Sergeant?" Victor Watson asked.

"Forty-two."

"I'm only fifty-nine years old and you thought I was sixty-nine."

"I didn't say that."

"It's okay; I know how I look. Life hasn't always been so nice to me. When I was nineteen I spent two days as a guest of your department. I was selling sandwiches from the back of a truck to the garment workers downtown and I got a few tickets for being parked in a red zone. I couldn't afford to pay them and one day one of your motor cops ran a make on me and put me in jail. The judge told me fifty dollars or three days. I didn't *have* fifty dollars. That Lincoln Heights was one shitty jail. I got in three fights to save my virtue."

"Did you save it?"

"For a while," he said. "Then I married my present wife and backed one of her movies and got myself gangbanged every day by the studio *goniffs*."

Sidney Blackpool caught himself guzzling, which was what he had promised himself he wouldn't do the last time he failed to quit drinking. Well, shit, if you *have* to listen to some industrialist's life story . . .

"Help yourself," Victor Watson said, and the detective poured generously.

"People think I made my money in land development," Victor Watson continued, sipping with restraint. "High tech is where I hit it big. I have a tenth-grade education but I can sell anything: rags, cars, junk, land. You name it, I can sell it."

By now, Sidney Blackpool was drifting. The

sun was filtering in the windows from the west, and twelve-year-old Johnnie Walker was making fifty-nine-year-old Victor Watson seem like an old pal.

"Fame is what works around these parts," Victor Watson continued. "Lots of guys who make *Forbes* magazine get snubbed by every snotty maître d' in town. If you want to be where it's at you have two choices: buy a sports franchise, which is the second crappiest business in the world, or get into movies, which is the most crappy. I discovered a third way and married a famous movie star. We get the tables in her name. My picture gets taken when I'm with her. I go to parties because of her. Now I can go anywhere I want and eat cold potato soup and everyone knows me. Do you play golf?"

"As a matter of fact," Sidney Blackpool nodded.

"We'll play sometime. I like the Bel-Air course. I belong to half a dozen clubs but I don't get a chance to play much. What do you know about my son's murder?"

The guy could shift gears without a clutch, and before the detective could answer, Victor Watson said, "You may have read that my boy disappeared from our Palm Springs home last year and was found murdered out in the desert near a blister of a town called Mineral Springs."

"I never read whether they caught the . . ."

"They didn't," Victor Watson said, and just

25

for a second those irises flickered. Then he stood and walked to the window, gazing at the sun falling toward Santa Monica.

"I'm wondering what I can do for you," Sidney Blackpool said.

"Your department's *got* to get involved, Sid," Victor Watson announced, with just a touch of fervor. "I'm not bad-mouthing Palm Springs P.D. or anybody else. But it's been seventeen months and . . ."

Victor Watson was not a man to lose control and he didn't. He smiled and returned to the sofa, sitting down beside the detective. "It's come to my attention that my boy may have been in Hollywood the day he died. It could be that the events leading up to the murder in the desert emanated from Hollywood. In that case, Hollywood Division of the L.A. Police Department becomes the proper agency to join this investigation, right?"

"Hold on, Mister Watson." Sidney Blackpool didn't like this a bit. He had enough cases without being drawn into a cold Palm Springs homicide with a guy like this applying the torque.

"Listen to me, Sidney," Victor Watson said, leaning toward the detective. "I know it's stretching matters a bit to draw you in, but I need to keep this investigation going. I don't know where to turn. All the goddamn money I gave the Republicans the last four years, yet the F.B.I. dropped out within three days. And

26

the Palm Springs P.D. was finished in six months. Oh, they still call me but they don't have leads. And my son, my boy, he . . ."

"I suppose I can maybe make a few calls, Mister Watson," the detective offered. "After you tell me about the new information that makes you think Hollywood's involved."

"I was thirty-six years old when Jack was born," Victor Watson said. "My daughters were already in high school when he came along. My first wife was probably too old for child-bearing, but it worked. Did it ever. He had an I.Q. of a hundred and forty. And he was a talented piano player. And he had the sweetest golf swing you have *ever* seen. . . . Tell me, do you know about depression and despair?" Without waiting for an answer Victor Watson said, "I can tell you that despair is not merely acute depression. Despair is *more* than the sum of many terrible parts. Depression is purgatory. Despair is hell."

The detective almost sent the Ming-dynasty figurine spinning off the cocktail table, he snatched at the Johnnie Walker so quickly.

Victor Watson didn't notice. He just kept talking in a monotone that was getting spooky. "Do you know how a man feels when he loses his son? He feels . . . incomplete. Nothing in the whole world looks the same or *is* the same. He goes around looking for pieces of himself. *Incomplete*. And . . . and then all his daydreams and fantasies go back to June of last year.

27

Whatever he's thinking about, it's got to precede the time he got the phone call about his son. You see, he just keeps trying to turn the clock back. He wants just one more chance. For what? He can't even say for sure. He wants to communicate. What? He isn't sure." And then Victor Watson breathed a sigh and said: "The ancient inherited shame of fathers and sons."

"I'd *like* to help you, Mister Watson." Sidney Blackpool was getting unaccountably warm. He unbuttoned his collar, removed his necktie and shoved it into his coat pocket.

"Hear me out, Sid," Victor Watson said quietly. "It's important that I lay things out . . . well . . . methodically. It's how I am. He isn't able to answer his phone at first, the father of a dead boy. Especially since so many people think they have to call to express condolences. One friend calls four times and finally you speak to him and he says, 'Why didn't you return my calls? I want to *share* your grief.' And you say to him, 'You dumb son of a bitch. If you could share any part of it, I'd give it to you! I'd give it *all* to you, you stupid bastard!' And then of course I lost that friend."

Sidney Blackpool made a mental note, as though it were a crime confession, that Victor Watson had switched persons three times before he was ready or maybe *able* to start telling it in the first person.

"Then for several weeks, all I could think about were the bad moments. I couldn't

28

remember the good times, the good things we had together, Jack and me. Only the problems. Only the bad times. You know something? Booze used to make me silly and happy. Now I hardly touch it because it makes me morose and mean. Can I freshen that?"

"Yeah." The detective began massaging the back of his neck. He was starting to get a headache at the base of his skull. It was more than warm. It was *stifling,* yet he could see the papers on the polished granite desk top fluttering from an overhead air register.

"On June twenty-first of last year, my twenty-two-year-old son Jack went to Palm Springs after his last term at U.S.C. He went alone but was going to be joined by his fiancée who was a senior at U.C.L.A. He was there two days and two nights and then he was gone. So was my car. I keep a Rolls-Royce there because I sometimes fly to Palm Springs from LAX instead of driving. Our Palm Springs houseboy found the car missing and by the second night he got worried and called us. Jack was found two days later in the desert, in some godforsaken canyon near Mineral Springs. He was shot through the head and the car was burned with his body inside."

"Was he . . . uh, was he . . ."

"Yes, he was already dead when they torched the car."

"They?"

"He, she, they. Whoever. At first the police

29

thought there was some sort of accident where he ran off a dirt road down into a canyon and the car caught fire. But at the autopsy they found that though he was totally burned, the inside of his lungs were hardly scorched. And there was very little carbon monoxide in his blood. And then they found a thirty-eight-caliber bullet in his head. I brought in another pathologist and he concurred. Jack was shot and was dead or dying before somebody burned him.

"The F.B.I. called it a straightforward murder, maybe a kidnapping and murder, but not within their investigative jurisdiction. The Palm Springs police've pretty well given up. I thought about hiring private investigators but I know the difference between movie private eyes and real ones. Even if I could find a good one, no police agency gives the time of day to private investigators."

"So how does the L.A.P.D. get brought into this?"

"It's the best thing that's happened to me for a while," Victor Watson said. "On Monday I got a notice from my Hollywood Rolls-Royce dealership that it's time to bring the car in for service. There was a note attached saying they'd neglected to bill me for a tire purchased on June twenty-first of last year. That's the day Jack disappeared! Of course I ran straight to the Rolls-Royce dealer, and the service manager identified a picture of Jack. My boy was *there* that afternoon in the Rolls and ordered a tire because his was going flat."

"You notify Palm Springs P.D. about this?"

"Yesterday. They thanked me, of course. They said they'd make a follow-up call to the Rolls-Royce dealer. That means they'll be told the same thing I was told and they'll file it. But look, the crime may have *originated* in Hollywood. Jack may have met someone here or been kidnapped here or picked up a hitchhiker here or . . ."

"This is a lotta supposition, Mister Watson," Sidney Blackpool said, restraining himself from going for old Johnnie Walker yet another time. "This case belongs to Palm Springs P.D."

"But they're out of ideas. And I've already publicly offered a fifty-thousand-dollar reward for *any* relevant information. You have a big department, Sid. More facilities."

"Look, most murders and most crimes in general are solved by the art of conversation, not the science of forensics. It's *their* town. They know who to talk to. I can't walk in there and make a case outta nothing."

"There's an answer there. I *know* it! In the desert cities there're lots of unsolved murders. Maybe you can add something fresh."

"Resort cities're transient places," the detective argued. "There could well be lots a uncleared murders. That doesn't mean the police aren't competent."

"A *fresh* look at it, that's all I want from the

L.A.P.D. Somebody shot my boy and burned his body. Somebody left him there for . . . Animals had gotten to him. Coyotes, skunks, buzzards, I don't know. Desert animals."

"You really can't hope for justice after this much time's passed, Mister Watson." Sidney Blackpool succumbed and went for the Johnnie Walker Black, but he only poured two ounces this time.

"I know, Sid. I don't want justice."

"Well, whadda you want?"

"Revenge, of course. A sliver of revenge."

"Revenge. And what from me?"

"Identify the killer or killers even if you can never make an arrest. Even if there isn't proof beyond a reasonable doubt to satisfy a district attorney."

"And what're you gonna do?"

Victor Watson got up again and paced back and forth in front of the window. Now the sun was nearly gone and his tanned face took on the color of a bruise. He said, "I recently watched a documentary where Jane Goodall got herself in a tizzy because one of her mother apes had *et* one of the neighbor ape's babies. She didn't know after all her years of research that they were capable of human cruelty. Hell, that's no discovery. The *real* discovery'd be if the neighbor mother'd waited for the killer to go to sleep and then bashed in her skull. That's what sets man apart from other primates. Not the crap about us being aware of our own mortality. What sets us apart is our capacity and *need* for revenge."

"You wanna have the killer smoked, is that it? This is a job for Charles Bronson, not me."

Victor Watson turned toward the detective, and now under the track light he looked like an old man. His eyes and cheeks were hollow in the shadow. He said, "Don't be silly. I'm not a criminal, but I have enough money to punish people in lots of ways. I can get my own kind of revenge without physically harming anyone."

Suddenly a bolt of headache pain hit Sidney Blackpool like a slap shot.

"It wouldn't make you feel better, Mister Watson," the detective said, feeling clammy. His armpits were soaked.

"It won't help his mother. She's accommodated the grief. Mothers can do it. I've tried everything: psychotherapy, religion, Zen. Nothing diminishes my rage. I just know *you* can help me. Intuition's made me what I am."

"Me? I'm one a several guys working homicide at Hollywood Station. I happened to be sent over to talk to you because nobody else was handy."

"I asked for *you*," Victor Watson said.

"You asked for *me?*"

"I made a few inquiries about the homicide teams. If it'd turned out Jack could be traced to our home in Bel-Air that day I would've done the same at West L.A. Station. Or Beverly

Hills if he'd been seen there. I would've tried to pick the man I needed from whichever agency that could justify getting into the case."

"And what'd your *few inquiries* reveal about me?"

"You're a very good investigator and you drink Johnnie Walker Black and you play golf. I thought the golf was an omen. I belong to a country club in the desert and I can get you onto any other course you want to play. Take your clubs."

"You think my department's gonna let me drop my workload and run to Palm Springs, just like that?"

"Take one week from your accumulated overtime, Sid. Take your partner. I've learned that his vacation isn't up for ten more days. The two of you'll have a suite at a first-class hotel. You'll like it. I have copies of every police report here." Victor Watson tapped his desk drawer. "You can read them at your leisure and do some investigating during a hell of a nice vacation. Your lieutenant said it wouldn't be a problem."

"This isn't sensible."

"You're the best man available to me at this time and that *is* the God's truth."

"How'd you meet my lieutenant?"

"I help sponsor the police olympics and the police-celebrity golf tournament, and I intend to back your chief if he decides to retire and run for mayor. I was given an introduction by an assistant chief."

"What else do you know about me?"

"I know about your boy."

"Goddamn!" Sidney Blackpool said, shocked to see how much he was sweating from the swell time he was having with all the free drinks and the promise of a golf vacation.

"While we were talking about my boy your lieutenant said you'd lost your boy too, in a surfing accident."

"My lieutenant's got a big mouth."

"It's another omen! It's more than that. Helping me might help you. Father to father. My justice might in some small way . . ."

"You already said you don't want justice. Look, Mister Watson, my kid's been dead fourteen months. I'm nearly past the crazies. I don't need this father to father bullshit."

"If I could buy the right kind of help I would. For the first time in years I need something desperately and it's not for sale. I feel totally helpless. It's an awful thing for a man like me to be helpless. Listen, you've got your twenty years in, right?"

"Twenty-one."

"You could retire from police work if you could afford it, but you can't live on the pension, right? You probably have an ex-wife to pay?"

"No, the bitch did me a good turn. She remarried a few years ago."

"Other kids?"

"A daughter seventeen. Lives with her mother."

"I'm just winging it, Sid. You see, I don't know much about you, only what I need to. So I figure you'd probably love to leave the street garbage but you can't live on the pension without working, right? Do you know Deputy Chief Phil Jenks?"

"He retired a few years back. I knew of him."

"He's head of security for Watson Industries. He's also a security adviser to three cellular-mobile-phone companies I'm associated with in San Francisco and San Diego and Denver. I pay him ninety thousand a year."

"That's very nice for him."

"I was getting ready to raise his salary to an even hundred when he had a serious heart attack last month. Seems like we'll have to replace him. We're looking for a younger man this time. A retired law officer, of course. We prefer a single man who doesn't mind traveling to some pretty nice cities."

"I don't know a goddamn thing about computer hardware, Mister Watson."

"You know about thieves, don't you? A thief's a thief. What else's to know? Sid, if you bring me what I need from the desert, you'll have all the qualifications I could *ever* want. With Phil Jenks I signed a play or pay deal, as they say in my wife's business. If he didn't like the job, he could quit and I had to pay a year's salary. Call Phil Jenks. I'll give you his number. Ask him how he liked the job. He's a golfer too. We've got corporate memberships in country clubs in San Diego, San Francisco and Denver. We've got season's tickets to Lakers games and . . ."

"Yeah, yeah, I get it," Sidney Blackpool said. "And right now I got a Kareem Abdul Jabbar migraine."

"Call me tomorrow, Sid," Victor Watson said, opening the door for the detective. "Remember, if nothing ever comes of it you still got yourself a nice golf vacation in Palm Springs, all expenses paid. And I mean *all.*"

"Nothing could ever come a something like this," the detective said.

"Omens, Sid." Victor Watson's voice was as hollow as his eyes under the track lights. "Maybe we're linked, you and me. Because we understand it."

"It?"

"The ancient inherited shame of fathers and sons. *Now* we understand it. I got to have a payoff, Sid. Some kind of payoff for all . . . this . . . fucking . . . *rage.*"

"I'll call you either way."

"Call me," Victor Watson said, closing the door to the salon while the detective wove his way through the vases and urns and pots, vaguely realizing that all this designer crockery was probably worth ten times more than the play or pay deal he was just offered. Which made him feel like he had a mouse waterskiing in his stomach. He hoped he could find a men's room pronto.

Chapter 3

THE MUSIC MAN

"Give us your tired, your poor, your huddled masses," Chief Paco Pedroza once said to a gathering of all the heads of law enforcement in the Coachella Valley. "We'll take some a the third-round draft picks you can't use but don't give us your whodunits! I got one detective, and far as crime labs go, the only labs around Mineral Springs *cause* crime. I mean the speed labs operated by the outlaw bikers. So if your whodunits leech on into Mineral Springs, just be ready to handle them without too much help from my nine-person work force."

Paco Pedroza never had any trouble with whodunits from Palm Springs or anywhere else until the disappearance of Jack Watson back in 1983. Victor Watson's residence was in the old Las Palmas section of Palm Springs, not far from homes formerly owned by Hollywood legends. Now the desert's best addresses are moving down the valley, but in the old days Las Palmas was the center of a posh bedroom community. The homes are large and old, concealed by walls and nearly impenetrable oleander. Most of the streets circle mazelike, and many a new cop in town has gotten lost chasing wily local kids around the Las Palmas neighborhoods.

The residents of Las Palmas, particularly the older residents, seldom go shopping. Groceries and other essentials are brought in by delivery vans. In fact, after Jack Watson's disappearance, a delivery boy with a burglary record was questioned for three hours at the Palm Springs Police Department.

On the second day of Jack Watson's disappearance, even before the victim's terrified parents flew into the Palm Springs airport from Los Angeles by private jet, the police had given the Las Palmas residence a pretty good going over. In the beginning they thought the young man might've been kidnapped from his bedroom while sleeping. The bed was unmade, the burglar alarm was not set and a sliding door in the guest bedroom wasn't entirely closed.

Victor Watson's home was so well alarmed that he even had a dozen point-to-point infrareds on the outside. They cost $1,000 a pair and were mounted high up on the fence that enclosed the property. They were designed to detect climbers, but they were not wired into recording channels like the inside alarm. The outside infrared system would ring only at the residence, alerting the Watsons or neighbors or passing patrol cars. The reason they could not transmit by radio wave or telephone is that there were too many false alarms. Birds, animals, a falling leaf could trigger the system.

The infrared had a transmitter and receiver on one end of an invisible beam that traveled a straight line, hitting a mirror and bouncing back, striking the receiver precisely. It was remotely possible that someone with a great deal of training and practice could interrupt the beam with another mirror if it could be so finely and instantly adjusted that the beam came back precisely to the receiver. James Bond could do it, they decided, but probably no thug in Palm Springs.

There were lots of false trails taken by the police and F.B.I. during those first days, while Victor Watson hovered over the scene, cordless phone in hand, experiencing for the first time the impotence of the crime victim. He received the telephone call at 6:00 P.M. of the second day. It was from a woman who said that Jack Watson was being held "close by in the desert" and to await instructions. Of course "close by" in open desert could mean anywhere within five hundred square miles. Victor Watson thought he heard the sound of air brakes in the background and cars whizzing by at high speed. It was the only clue except that an elderly neighbor had seen a red pickup truck turn around in the Watson driveway the day before. It may have meant nothing, but it was all they had.

A telephone call from Palm Springs P.D. to Mineral Springs P.D. was made at 7:00 P.M.

when Chief Paco Pedroza was home mopping up five thousand calories and neither of his sergeants was in the station. Unfortunately for Paco, the cop who was in the station that night was Officer Oscar Albert Jones, a twenty-four-year-old former surfer who'd worked a year for the Laguna Beach P.D. and a year for the Palm Springs P.D. before he felt it was wise to move on. While still with the Palm Springs police, O. A. Jones spent most of his time in Whitewater dove country blazing away with his 9mm automatic at doves and jackrabbits who were perfectly safe in that O. A. Jones couldn't have hit them with a shotgun. Still, he'd shoot up a box of reloads nearly every night. Once he'd gotten so carried away he shot up every silver-tipped hollow point he had and was caught bulletless by a sergeant, after which O. A. Jones became known as Outta Ammo Jones.

On the night that encouraged O. A. Jones to resign from Palm Springs P.D. and get picked up on waivers by Mineral Springs, he was patrolling Indian Avenue and happened to spot a drunk staggering across the street against the red light. O. A. Jones followed the drunk, who wore shorts and a tank top and was shuffling north on the sidewalk.

When O. A. Jones got abreast of the guy, he saw that it wasn't a drunk at all. It was Hiram Murphy, eldest son of Moms Murphy, boss of a clan that, Gypsy-style, traveled all over the desert valley pulling pigeon drops on the many retirees, stealing their life savings in confidence scams and using the money to buy speed to slam in their arms. In fact, the narcs had found fresh tracks on the arms of Moms' youngest son, Rudolph. He was nineteen but had the mind of a six-year-old, and his brothers shot him up not with crank but heroin since it kept him quieter. That was the kind of family Moms Murphy shepherded, so O. A. Jones was delighted to see Moms' oldest boy, Hiram, in a state of stagger from an overload of crystal and bar whiskey.

Hiram had been in a gay bar trying to expand the family business to include fruit-rolling. Except that he was so ugly he couldn't score. He had eyes and ears like a bat and he smelled like a ruptured appendix.

"Hello, cretin," O. A. Jones said, rolling up beside Hiram Murphy in his patrol car. "You're too loaded to walk. Let's ride."

Hiram Murphy was as surly and mean as usual, but he was also a coward. He wouldn't pick a fight with anybody, let alone a strapping young cop like O. A. Jones, unless he had at least one brother lying in wait with a claw hammer. He mumbled a few "pricks" and "motherfuckers" under his breath, but got in the backseat of the police car, his hands cuffed behind him.

While driving to the station, the blond cop gave Hiram Murphy a "screen test" which Hiram didn't like at all. The former surfer

43

whispered something that Hiram didn't hear, and when Hiram said, "What's that?," the young cop turned in profile as he drove and whispered it in a slightly louder voice. But it was still unintelligible to the cranked-out thug.

"Speak up, goddamnit," Hiram Murphy said, feeling very grumpy about going to jail without his mama.

It was dark enough now to turn on headlights, and O. A. Jones switched his on, turned toward Hiram Murphy in the backseat and said it *again.*

This time, Hiram Murphy got *very* testy. He leaned forward and said, "Speak up, asshole! What's a matter with you anyways?"

And then: WHANG! Hiram Murphy's face was flattened against the heavy steel-mesh screen as O. A. Jones stood on his brakes going into four-wheel lock.

After Hiram Murphy stopped cussing and yelling, O. A. Jones said, "I was just *trying* to tell you that a poodle ran out in front of us. I had to hit my brakes to save the poor little thing! I'm soooory." Hiram Murphy had his screen test.

They were only three blocks from the station when a sheriff's unit went into pursuit on Highway 111 and announced that he had been *fired* on. Within ten seconds O. A. Jones' pink ears were leaking adrenaline and he was roaring toward the pursuit car, which was having trouble keeping up with a stolen

1983 BMW sedan.

Thirty minutes after dark, twelve other police units from Palm Springs, CHP, Riverside sheriffs, Indio P.D. and even Mineral Springs P.D. had joined the chase on Interstate 10, first toward Indio and then back, as the pursued car kept doing sliding U-turns, wheeling off and on the freeway.

The BMW, it turned out, contained a pretty good catch. It was the stopwatch bandit, so called because during the robbery of four valley banks, he checked his watch before and after vaulting the tellers' counters and was long gone before the cops could respond to a silent alarm. On this night, the stopwatcher had been on his way home from robbing a bank in Indian Wells when a sheriff's car tried to stop him for being a bit late on a traffic light. The chase was on.

The stopwatcher was careening down Monterey Avenue in Palm Desert when O. A. Jones, listening to the radio pursuit, intercepted him coming the other way. The young cop played chicken with the approaching headlights, veering at the last second, but was a little late. With Hiram Murphy screaming in his ear, O. A. Jones got clipped on the right front by the speeding BMW and was spun in a terrifying 360, crunching against a forty-foot telephone pole, which bent the police car in half. The rocketing BMW went airborne, crashing against a date palm and throwing the stopwatcher into the street alongside a handcuffed and very dead

Hiram Murphy, who was himself blown from the backseat of the police car at the second of impact.

O. A. Jones remained belted in the front seat with only a bloody nose and a mild concussion, realizing foggily that he was in trouble. That was the best he could manage with his head feeling mushy and his brain slogging around in there, but within minutes, while a dozen sirens converged on the crash site, O. A. Jones was understanding that by going into that suicidal pursuit with a prisoner helplessly handcuffed in the backseat, he could be charged with manslaughter. He could see quite clearly in the headlight beams that Hiram Murphy looked like a speed bump in the asphalt.

O. A. Jones began pulling himself out of his totaled patrol unit, trying desperately to put together a "Gee, Sarge!" story that was *remotely* plausible, when a CHP officer came running into the headlight beam and said, "You okay?"

"For the moment," O. A. Jones mumbled, hoping that he would get put in the cops' tank at the county jail, because a twenty-four-year-old former surfer, who was also a former *cop*, would be Sadie Thompson'd in the regular tank within three minutes.

Then the Chip said, "You didn't have to handcuff that pukus delicti. He's deader'n gramma's clit. So's the other one!"

O. A. Jones was trying to make sense of *that* when two more units skidded to a stop. More

46

were coming, the sirens whooping from three directions.

The second cop on the scene, a sheriff's deputy, said, "Damn, I thought there was only one in the BMW! The second one musta been hiding in the backseat. May as well take your cuffs off him, he's deader'n John De Lorean's MasterCard."

And so they did. They gave the handcuffs to O. A. Jones who was starting to be able to add two digits, and who wisely kept his mouth shut.

The newspapers announced the death of the stopwatch bandits, *both* of them, one of whom was a member of a Gypsy-like pack of desert confidence men who screamed to no end that their kin, Hiram, was only a crank dealer and a burglar and a pursepick, but had never robbed a bank in his life. But pretty soon Moms Murphy had second thoughts. Maybe her boy Hiram wasn't the slimy little fuck they'd always thought. He led a secret life! Hiram was wheelman for the famous stopwatch bandit! Moms Murphy was actually kind of proud.

But a Palm Springs sergeant who checked the crashed cars felt some confusion. How did the blood, which O. A. Jones said was *his,* get on the *back* window of the patrol car? There were some strange questions about that smashup.

He took a sly look at O. A. Jones and said, "I'd like to retrieve the black box from *this* crash and see what *really* happened."

And since his sergeant didn't like O. A.

Jones any better than his lieutenant who didn't like him at all, O. A. Jones said, "Gee, Sarge! You know, Chief Pedroza at Mineral Springs is looking for an experienced man. I been thinking about going up there and talking to him. Maybe tonight?"

"You can wait till tomorrow," the sergeant said. "He should be glad to hire the cop who brought down the stopwatch bandit. *And* his crime partner."

So O. A. Jones decided to trade his Palm Springs tan for Mineral Springs blue. He met Sergeant Harry Bright who convinced Paco that O. A. Jones was a "good lad" and deserved to stay in law enforcement. And O. A. Jones happened to be on duty when the call came in to the Mineral Springs police station concerning the ransom demand for Jack Watson.

The Mineral Springs P.D. had been notified in the first place only because Victor Watson thought, in addition to the whine of speeding cars in the background, he might've heard the blast of air brakes. The F.B.I. concluded that the call might have come from a truck stop or diner. All jurisdictions were being given that information with instructions not to go near a likely truck stop, but to give the F.B.I. and Palm Springs P.D. its whereabouts if they had one in their area.

That was all it took for O. A. Jones, who was anxious to make an impression on his new boss, Paco Pedroza. He vaulted the counter at the police station like the late stopwatch bandit and jumped in his patrol car, scorching off toward the truck stop on the highway to Twentynine Palms. He discovered belatedly that he was driving the out-of-service patrol car with the bum radio.

O. A. Jones spent the rest of the night blowing up dust clouds on every road or trail within ten miles of the truck stop, almost getting his rear wheels sand-locked on two occasions. The desert night, being quite cool even during a hot season, would have provided him with a decently comfortable trek to the highway, except that O. A. Jones waited until his graveyard shift was just about ended and the dawning fireball was visible over the mountains before he managed to lock his patrol unit into three feet of the softest desert powder. After which he turned his ankle trying to dig out.

There were soon *two* searches going on in the desert. One for the son of Victor Watson, one for Officer O. A. Jones of the Mineral Springs Police Department.

The F.B.I. agent riding shotgun with the sheriff's chopper pilot was enjoying some very spectacular scenery late that afternoon. The pilot was a hotdog Vietnam vet called "Sky-pork" by the street people but preferring the nom de guerre of "Pigasus." They had already refueled and had flown to the Salton Sea, a lake 228 feet below sea level, occupying the site of a prehistoric lake whose waterline was etched in white travertine along the granite hillside.

They then powered north over the Painted Canyon and northwest toward Thousand Palms. They flew back into Palm Springs and up the sheer rock face over Andreas Falls where Frank Capra filmed part of *Lost Horizon*, and into local canyons on the theory that the kidnappers were being truthful about being "close by." Pigasus soared west to the Palm Springs tram, showing off for the tourists on the tram car, then veered north toward the Little San Bernardino Mountains with their canyons and hiding places and desert accessible only to four-wheel-drive vehicles.

The air show was mostly cosmetic for the benefit of Victor Watson, and because Pigasus enjoyed scaring the living shit out of the F.B.I. agent who was turning green from the mini-aerobatics. There were *lots* of red pickup trucks in a valley this large and even more that *appeared* to be red from the sky, and lots of others that were not quite red but could appear to be so when seen at ground level by an overheated seventy-eight-year-old Las Palmas gentleman with trifocals.

In the desert you don't get very much mileage from your fuel. When you're walking, that is. You can get about ten good miles out of your body *if* you fill your body tank with a gallon of water. You get lots less if you're wearing a navy-blue police uniform and Sam Browne, lugging a 9mm pistol and a hideout gun in a leg holster. Especially if you have a severely sprained ankle and don't know diddly about the desert in the first place.

When O. A. Jones got so hot and tired he was about to drop, he plopped down prone and breathed through his mouth on the desert floor, which was about 25 degrees hotter than it would be one *foot* off the ground. When he could gather up the strength to continue, O. A. Jones ignored the many desert birds that would give a rat like Beavertail Bigelow a clue to water holes. He knew nothing of quail flying *toward* water in the late afternoon, and had never noticed all the times he shot at doves that they also flock toward water holes in the late afternoon and evening. He didn't know of indicator plants — sycamore, willow, cattail, cottonwood — where he might dig. He staggered right past a limestone cave that contained a large pool of cool clean water. He made a painful detour because he was scared of encountering a mountain lion, though one hadn't been seen in those parts for thirty years.

O. A. Jones was having some very troubling thoughts: If only summer hadn't come so early this year. If only he'd stayed in Laguna Beach where he grew up. If only he hadn't got all hyped about the kidnapping of the rich guy's kid. If only he hadn't taken that trail off into the canyon because he thought he saw a campfire. If only everything would speed up so he wasn't seeing birds fly in slow motion. If only his arms and legs weren't tingly. If only he weren't turning bluer than his uniform.

Then O. A. Jones heard it: the music. And he thought, This is it! Fucking harps and angels! Then he heard it *again*. It was a banjo! Somebody was playing the banjo and singing!

O. A. Jones lurched to a stop and listened. He didn't know how confusing sound can be out there as it bounces off canyon walls and ricochets like a rifle shot, especially if your body temperature is up four degrees and climbing. O. A. Jones heard what sounded like a car engine starting up. O. A. Jones started hobbling in slow motion on his swollen ankle. The wrong way.

Meanwhile, Victor Watson, with an F.B.I. agent monitoring, had received his *second* telephone call from the woman, who this time was calling from a place that offered no sound clues. She instructed Victor Watson to obtain $250,000 in tens and twenties and pack it inside a large suitcase. He was told to drive his white Mercedes on a circuitous route that made no sense whatever to the Palm Springs police who were playing second banana to the feds. He was to head out Whitewater Canyon, then to double back on Highway 10, then up Route 62 toward Devil's Garden, then back toward North

Palm Springs. It was apparent that if the kidnappers were watching the drop car they'd need an aircraft to do it, and the only aircraft in the skies that day were commercial flights out of Palm Springs and choppers belonging to law-enforcement agencies. Victor Watson was ordered to call home at precise twenty-minute intervals, which was impossible given the desolate stretches up toward Little San Bernardino Mountains and back again.

After a *third* call the kidnappers stopped dicking around. Mrs. Watson received it while her husband was gone. She was ordered by the woman to tell Victor Watson when he called to drive out Highway 10 to the Thousand Palms turnoff, then to proceed north to the oasis by Dillon Road.

As it turned out, the kidnappers weren't kidnappers at all. They were a pair of drifters named Abner and Maybelle Sneed, who usually made their living growing pot in Oregon but had migrated south after the law started applying so much heat to the Oregon plantationers. They had stopped in Palm Springs for a three-day holiday, heard on the news about the disappearance of Jack Watson, and gone to the library to look through a copy of the "Gold Book," Palm Springs' *Who's Who*. Then they'd stopped at the pharmacy nearest to the Watson residence, and while Maybelle Sneed kept the pharmacist busy, Abner grabbed the Rolodex from behind the register and found customer

Victor Watson's phone number. It was all done in about 120 seconds by people with 75 I.Q.'s, this after Victor Watson had spent more than $15,000 for intruder alarms and sophisticated protection.

The only surprising move made that day by the would-be extortionists was that Abner rented a motorcycle and was lying in wait near Pushawalla Palms for the Watson Mercedes to pass north. The plan was to scan the skies for cops, and if it looked okay, to whip on out the highway, overtaking Victor Watson and holding up a sign that said: "Toss out the money and you will be told where your boy is."

Abner and Maybelle were very fine pot farmers, diligent and fair to customers. They took pride in their product and refined it carefully, putting it up like grandma's peaches, with jars, rubber gaskets and labels. But they were not kidnappers and were lousy extortionists. Abner scanned the skies for aircraft with a pair of brand-new binoculars, but never even thought about a radio transmitter in the Mercedes that was signaling the feds hovering far beyond his line of sight.

Just after Abner roared up on the Honda and made contact with the Mercedes, a signal from Victor Watson brought Pigasus driving in. Moments after Victor Watson threw the suitcase from the car window, the F.B.I. agent had Abner, the failed extortionist, in his scope sight.

Meanwhile, Maybelle was waiting at a date bar on Dillon Road. It was one of those roadside shacks that sell Coachella Valley dates and date candy and date milk shakes. Maybelle was on her third date milk shake when she spotted Abner roaring up on the Honda, all dust and teeth and giggles, the suitcase balanced across the handlebars. While Maybelle fired up the family sedan, Abner scooted west to the side trail and ditched the rented Honda behind a tamarisk tree where he tried to open the locked suitcase.

"Abner, git in the fuckin car!" Maybelle hollered with her squeaky little voice. "We'll open er later!"

But Abner couldn't wait to see what $250,000 looked like and he started cussing at Maybelle as though it were her fault that the bag was locked.

"We gotta git!" Maybelle squeaked, jumping out of the car and running toward the tamarisk tree where Abner was banging on the suitcase like the gorilla in the Samsonite luggage commercial.

Maybelle was first to sight the helicopter in the distance. She pointed and screamed and when the spotter knew they'd blown their cover, Pigasus closed in on Abner and Maybelle. Abner was like a monkey with his closed fist in a jar trap. He just couldn't let go even after they jumped in the car. He was still fussing with the suitcase lock when Maybelle pulled a bogus carbine from the backseat and aimed it at the bubble of the chopper.

"To scare them off," she later said.

While Maybelle was speeding northwest on Dillon Road, Abner took a peek out the window at the trailing chopper. A muzzle flash was the last thing he ever saw.

Abner didn't die right away and Maybelle didn't die at all even though she had a bullet in her leg and another lodged near her collarbone when the chase ended.

It was a typical police chase. Before it was over, six different law-enforcement agencies were in on it, which is very common. Everybody did sliding U-turns, which is very common. Shots were fired by several units, which is very common. This one nearly turned into an intramural fire fight with cops shooting each other during the thirty-five-minute high-speed chase, and this too is fairly common.

It was a semispectacular chase, as desert chases go. In open country they often last a very long time. It was fortunate for O. A. Jones that this one lasted all the way to a remote canyon not far from Mineral Springs where he had decided to hole up and rest because he thought he was hearing banjos and car engines and singing voices in the middle of nowhere.

By the end, there was fear and pandemonium and adrenaline leaking everywhere. When Maybelle did her last sliding U-ee and crashed near a canyon road leading to O. A. Jones, the result was exactly the same as it always is in high-speed pursuits. The first thirteen cops to jump out of their cars, or point guns out the car windows, yelled thirteen conflicting orders to the suspects.

All of the conflicting orders had one thing in common: they all ended with the word "motherfuckers."

While all the yelling and motherfucking and gun waving was going on, a car skidded in driven by Chief Paco Pedroza. He jumped out and ran toward the lead cops hiding behind the first chase unit with handguns and shotguns pointed toward the steaming wreck.

The loudest uniformed cop outyelled everyone. He bellowed: "You motherfucking sonofabitch cocksucker, put your hands out the window or we'll blow your fucking face off!"

And Paco Pedroza with his badge pinned to his aloha shirt ran up yelling, "Everybody shut up! I'm in charge!"

But the big loud cop was operating in another zone. His eyes were bulging and his face was raw meat and his shotgun was shaking, and he bellowed: "You motherfucker sonofabitch cocksucker, put your hands out the window or we'll blow your face off!"

So Paco screamed: "SHUT UP! I'LL DO THE TALKING!" which got everybody's attention.

Then Paco, finally in command, turned his own face toward the suspects' car and his eyes were bulging and his face was raw meat and Paco yelled: "You motherfucker sonofabitch cocksucker, put your hands out the window or we'll blow your face off!"

Maybelle complied, but Abner was lapsing into a coma from which he would not recover.

It was over. And then, since nobody wants to admit that he was doing some very dangerous shooting, especially in case some bullets landed where they shouldn't, all the chase cars started to find reasons to leave the scene almost as fast as they came in. This is also very common at the scene of high-speed chases. It's like lifting a rug in a wino hotel: they scatter like cockroaches.

No one ever found out for sure who put all the slugs in Maybelle and Abner. Not that it mattered. Everyone agreed they deserved getting ventilated, and the cops only wished they could've dipped their ammo in cyanide since Maybelle didn't croak.

Before the chopper pilot turned back toward Palm Springs police station where Victor Watson was now waiting with the F.B.I., he spotted what looked like a large animal scrambling up a hillside. It was a strange animal, white on top and dark on the hindquarters. Pigasus soared in a little closer and saw that the white on top was the sunburned flesh of O. A. Jones who had foolishly removed his shirt in his delirium.

They picked him up on the side of a little ridge. On the other side of the ridge was a trail leading into the canyon. Off the trail, down in the canyon where it had plunged sixty feet, was a burned Rolls-Royce containing the remains of Jack Watson.

The first cop into the canyon almost gagged when he saw the charred corpse, which had been dined on by turkey vultures and coyotes. The coyotes had almost destroyed the skull with their gnawing. If they had, a bullet hole would have been impossible for the pathologists to locate. The case might have been classified as a car accident and closed.

Paco Pedroza was absolutely ready to fire his surfer cop for driving out there in the first place, except that O. A. Jones provided the only possible clue to the murder. After the F.B.I. pulled out of the case, Palm Springs P.D. was left with a whodunit homicide, and all they had was O. A. Jones who convinced everybody that he was not delirious when he heard the guy playing the banjo and singing, followed by the sound of a vehicle racing away. It was theorized that the killer of Jack Watson had returned to the burned car two days after the murder. Perhaps to retrieve something. Officer O. A. Jones had heard a music man.

O. A. Jones persuaded a local reporter to write a story calling him "the key to the riddle." The reporter also dubbed him a "courageous officer" who took it upon himself to scour the desert canyons for the missing Palm Springs lad.

Paco Pedroza would still have liked to send his freaking hero back to fighting kelp in Laguna Beach on his potato-chip surfboard. Only he couldn't because the Mineral Springs City Council was giving O. A. Jones a citation for extraordinary police service.

Chapter 4

PRESIDENT McKINLEY

Otto Stringer looked like the winning ticket in a state lottery. He was waiting on his front porch with two suitcases and a set of golf clubs. He saluted his neighbors like Ronald Reagan at the door of Air Force One. He was wearing a brand-new pink polyester golf shirt that matched his plump cheeks, an acrylic sleeveless sweater with a pink-and-green argyle pattern, and a green Ben Hogan golf cap. He'd considered investing in plus fours but figured a guy should maybe break a hundred one time before blowing into Palm Springs all gussied up like a quarter-ton Byron Nelson.

When he got Sidney Blackpool's phone call about the Palm Springs holiday he couldn't believe it. He couldn't believe *any* of the good things that had happened to him since he'd gotten out of a crazy narc job and into a crazy homicide job at Hollywood dicks where at least he felt safe. During his last months at narcotics he'd been getting a whole bunch of obvious messages from The Man Himself. Otto wasn't a very religious person — a lapsed agnostic, he called himself — who reverted to his early

Presbyterian ways only in dangerous situations. The hints he figured The Big Boss was giving him weren't those "for your eyes only" messages he used to fear Jimmy Carter would *think* he got while sitting by the nuke hot line. No, these were plain enough for everyone to see. And they were *ominous*.

For example, there was the time near the end when he let himself get talked into going in on a coke buy with an undercover snitch, and why a sixteen-year cop nearly forty years old didn't know better was in itself a mystery and a portent. The snitch was one of those hepatitis hypes who bragged to every cop who busted him that he worked for the F.B.I. or the Drug Enforcement Agency. Otto Stringer told him that as far as he was concerned anybody who'd pal around with feds was about as welcome as a crotch full of herpes since the DEA was always trying to steal the city narcs' credit when they weren't stealing their informants.

After they understood each other, the snitch talked Otto into going in with him on the coke buy so Otto could bear the brunt of the later court testimony. The snitch convinced Otto's lieutenant that none of the other narcs in the squad looked *less* like a cop in that Otto was built like something you slam-dunk at the sports arena.

Problems popped up the second they walked into the motel room where the buy was to go down with "a very nice Hawaiian dude." The biggest problem was that there was no snort. Nor any other drugs. Nor any Hawaiian dude, nice or otherwise. It was a straight rip-off. They were met by three Samoans, the smallest of whom couldn't have squeezed into a phone booth and who had a one-track mind.

The Samoans patted them down for weapons but missed the body wire buried under Otto's tummy fat. But the transmitter had gone bad. The wire was not sending the action to the narc who sat on the bug in the panel truck just beyond the motel parking lot. The questions were very simple and to the point.

"Where's da money, bro?" a Samoan asked.

"I wanna talk to Sammy," the snitch said. "Where's Sammy?"

SMACK. "Where's da money, bro?"

"So this ain't no business deal!" the snitch bellowed for the benefit of the bug monitor. "This is a straight rip, huh?"

SMACK. "Where's da money, bro?"

"I shoulda knew this was a rip," the terrified junkie screamed for the wire. "A fuckin rip!"

SMACK. "Where's da money, bro?"

"Look, I can git the bread for ya!" the snitch shrieked. "Jist lemme take ya to it! Jist open the door and let's . . ."

SMACK. "You tell me," said the Samoan with the one-track mind. "I go get it."

By now, Otto Stringer, unarmed and helpless, was holding paws with the second Samoan. The third had him by the back of the neck with a longshoreman's hook that turned out to be his hand.

The blood from the snitch's mouth and nose was spattering the wall and Otto figured that the action was not being transmitted by the wire so he decided to take matters in hand and make an announcement. He said: "This's gone far enough! I'm a police officer! I order you to get away from that man and open the door!"

SMACK. Otto's skull bounced off the wall, leaving a crack in the plasterboard.

"Okay, then, I *ain't* a cop," said Otto.

SMACK. It didn't seem to matter either way to the Samoans.

"No more bullshit, bro. Where's da money?" the first Samoan said to Otto Stringer.

Just then the wire inside Otto's pants started to function. The cop monitoring the bug gave an emergency signal, but by the time six narcs smashed down the motel door, Otto had been spreadeagled across the kitchen table by all three Samoans who were only hitting him with open hands. Which had only dislodged one tooth and loosened two others and given him eyes by Picasso. They were taking turns. Before Otto passed out he thought of the ice-cream store. Pick a number! Next? Who's next?

Of course the rescuers played catch-up for Otto, in that all the Samoans "resisted hand-cuffing" and had to have buckets of water poured on them so they could wake up and resist some more. But it was small consolation to Otto Stringer. The thumping he got from the Samoans put him off duty for five days. And it wasn't even the last straw.

That occurred on "federal Friday," which was what the cops call Friday afternoon when the federal building looks like it received a bomb scare. All the civil servants and bureaucrats get an early start on the weekend rush-hour traffic, especially after getting their paychecks.

That afternoon the narcs were waiting at L.A. International Airport for a Colombian coke connection, and because of a sudden starburst of romantic passion, Otto Stringer and several other cops almost lost their lives.

Officer Heidi was a narc. She was a sleek beautiful leggy athletic ninety-pounder, and, bitch or not, she was the most aggressive that Otto had ever seen. No one had ever known a Doberman as strong as Heidi. In fact, on one narcotics raid she had grabbed the handle of a locked dresser drawer and pulled the entire piece of furniture across the room. Heidi was very good at her job and she knew it. She would never miss an ounce of flake or crystal or pot when she was sniffing luggage, and she was in fine fettle that day at the airport. Heidi went at the Colombian's luggage with a will. Her handler was so proud. The other narcs were so proud. Officer Desmond was so *aroused*.

Desmond was a bomb dog. He had never

seen Heidi before. He had never seen any narcotics dog. Desmond wasn't sleek or beautiful or athletic. Desmond was a seedy half-bloodhound with a bad case of dandruff, halitosis, and eyes like Walter Mondale. Desmond, like Otto Stringer, was a law-enforcement burnout.

The L.A. cops were working a routine bomb check that afternoon. Some overzealous security cop had a hunch about a goofy-looking student who'd just asked the employee at the ticket counter some odd questions about luggage. Desmond was called in to do a little sniffing to satisfy the airport people who were still overwrought from a recent bomb scare involving a terrorist. Desmond was sitting there in the customs office doing his thing, which was dozing by the air conditioning, when Heidi came prancing in looking *good*. Looking for *action*.

Heidi was so stoked by her job that she cried in anticipation, she whimpered with impatience, she uttered little growls of ecstasy when she made a hit on a bag of dope. Desmond watched Heidi's heaving chest, her swelling hocks, the rippling of her neck as her black coat glistened in the light, and his bloodshot Mondale eyes popped round as Orphan Annie's.

His handler said later that he never guessed old Desmond was getting funny feelings in his tummy. His handler too was busy admiring Heidi, the way she'd rip into each piece of luggage and try to tear it to pieces before they could pull her away and seize the dope. But for certain, saliva was seeping over Desmond's floppy lips onto the floor. And the handler got the picture after he noticed what was hanging down all pink and shiny below Desmond's belly. Old Desmond had sprouted a woody!

Of course, bomb dogs are supposed to be the opposite of dope dogs. Bomb dogs are supposed to be docile, *very* docile. They're supposed to sniff the explosives and then calmly saunter away and sit right down, content to let the bomb experts do their thing.

It was on Heidi's fourth hit that it happened. Maybe Desmond just heard one too many of those incredibly sexy little growls, nobody knew for sure. Desmond went madly shockingly passionately bonkers. While the loony student was repeating his "who me that's not *my* suitcase why are you treating me like this?" routine, Desmond let out a terrible howl.

They later realized it was his statement to Heidi: "You like real clangers? I'll show you a pair that gong like Big Ben!"

Desmond hit that suspicious suitcase like the Raiders blitz a quarterback.

The student didn't *have* to confess. They never had to advise him of his constitutional rights. The student shrieked, "NOOOOOOOOO!" and dropped like he was head-shot. So did Otto Stringer. So did all the narcs. So did the airport

67

security cops, U.S. Customs officers, Desmond's handler, and everybody else with an I.Q. higher than Desmond's. Everybody except Heidi who stopped her work and started admiring old Desmond, thinking he was looking pretty damn hot tossing that suitcase all over the room like that.

The contents as it turned out could have leveled that corner of the building. It didn't. And Desmond the hound was *through* checking luggage at the airport. And so was Otto Stringer, who said, "Thank you, but I already know about the power of pussy so I didn't have to see Desmond go ga-ga over Heidi. And I don't think I need any more scenes with jungle guys that oughtta be back home in coconut-shell jockstraps knocking down palm trees instead of cops. So I think I'll just go ahead and accept that transfer to Hollywood dicks. Scratch one dope cop."

Sidney Blackpool pulled up in Otto Stringer's driveway at 10:00 A.M. as promised. He was driving his Toyota Celica and wasn't nearly as sartorially splendid as Otto. Sidney Blackpool wore a navy-blue cotton golf shirt and tan cotton pants and loafers.

"You look devastating," he said to Otto, "but any more luggage and we rent a U-haul. We're loaded to the gunwales."

"I'd like to remind you we're going to Palm Springs, dah-ling!" Otto said, trying to cram his clubs into the backseat of the Toyota. "You got to arrive looking three under par. You really oughtta gussy up a bit, Sidney. I don't wanna be embarrassed."

"I bet a hundred baby argyles died in agony for that sweater," Sidney Blackpool said. "Wanna drive?"

"I'm too stoked," Otto said. "I didn't sleep three hours last night. Whaddaya think our hotel room's gonna be like? Room my ass. Suite! Sooooo-weeeeet!"

Sidney Blackpool headed toward the Hollywood Freeway and they were on their way. As they cruised past the downtown interchange, Otto glanced toward the police building at Parker Center, got a shudder thinking of the tour at narcotics just ended, and found it impossible to straighten out the holiday grin. He was starting to believe that he might just survive to collect his pension now that he was ensconced at Hollywood Station and teamed up with Black Sid whom he'd known twelve years ago when they both worked patrol at Newton Street. He just wished Sid wasn't so gloomy all the time.

"Wait'll the Dragon Lady hears about this," Otto said dreamily.

"That your ex? When'd you see her last?"

"I never see her *or* her little dragonettes. I never got a kind word from either a those adolescent brats the whole two years we were married. My *ex*-ex had three cubs and they

69

all were mean."

"A policeman's lot is not so hot," said Sidney Blackpool.

"Maybe in Palm Springs I'll meet a new ex-wife," Otto said. "A nice one. A rich one. Both a my exs only closed their eyes during sex cause they hated to see me have a good time. Most fun I ever got in bed was when they *moved*, which happened twice, once on each honeymoon. They put me into bankruptcy. My creditors finally said they'd clear my debts for ten cents on the dollar and I said, are you crazy? Who has *that* kind a money! If they could see me now!"

"Maybe we better turn around and visit your old squad room downtown," Sidney Blackpool said. "You could use a dozen downers. Save a little rocket fuel for reentry, will ya? Our vacation might turn out to be a drag."

"Never happen!" Otto said. "I already heard about our hotel, and this guy Watson, you *know* who his old lady is. He does *nothing* on the cheap. He wants results."

"Not gonna be any results, Otto."

"Yeah, but we can make it look good. When we're not on the links, that is. Hey, remember that putter I was gonna buy last time we played Griffith Park? I shoulda bought it. I bet they jack up the prices in Palm Springs. Think maybe we should stop on the way and buy some golf balls?"

"Great golfers like us only need one each."

"You know, Sidney, maybe we can *both* find a rich broad in Palm Springs. I mean, how many chances like this we ever gonna get? Living in a hotel suite, just signing our names for drinks and meals and . . ."

"One wife was enough for me," Sidney Blackpool said. "More than enough."

"Yeah, but you shouldn't marry good-looking broads. I bet your ex is a looker."

"A looker. Yeah, she is."

"I want an ugly one next time," Otto said. "They're more appreciative. And it's okay if she's old. Shit, *I'm* old."

"Younger than me."

"Yeah, but I'm facing the big one, Sidney. Number four-oh. In two freaking weeks I'll be *middle-aged!*"

"Forty isn't middle-aged. Not exactly."

"Do you know Paul McCartney is exactly your age? Ain't that amazing. Seems like a year ago the Beatles were kids, don't it? I can't get my head off my fortieth. I'm taking it real hard. Thank God for this vacation, take my mind off middle age. First thing goes is your memory."

"That's the second thing."

"I know, I know! Think *that* doesn't scare me?"

"Settle, Otto," Sidney Blackpool said. "Don't jettison your parachute. The vacation may bum out."

"Black Sid," Otto said, shaking his head.

"You don't just see the glass half empty, you don't even see the glass. Must get a parched throat being you. By the way, I saw a piece in the *Times* the other morning about anhedonia. Ever heard of it?"

"Can't say I have."

"Well, I think you got anhedonia. It affects maybe one out of a hundred. It means you can't have fun. No kind of fun. Just like you on a golf course. You look like Torquemada's got the hot pliers on your nuts instead a just enjoying the game."

"Nobody *enjoys* golf," Sidney Blackpool said. "And what makes you think it's a *game?*"

"Anyway, people with anhedonia never get turned on by anything. They just go through the motions."

"Like me."

"They don't know if it's congenital or not. People just go around, don't give a shit. I thought a old Black Sid with the blank stare."

"Maybe it's not always congenital," Sidney Blackpool said, and Otto Stringer's rosy jowls flushed, and Sidney Blackpool knew that Otto had suddenly thought about Tommy Blackpool although they'd never discussed his boy.

Otto suddenly changed the subject saying, "Wish I hadn't buffaloed-up like this. If I was still in uniform, I'd need the jaws of life to remove my Sam Browne. Think I'd look funny in golf knickers?"

"No funnier'n Pavarotti or Tip O'Neill,"

Sidney Blackpool said, turning the radio to an easy-listening station and adjusting the volume just enough to give Otto some competition.

"You're thin *and* you still got hair. It ain't fair, middle age."

"You got several hundred left," Sidney Blackpool said. "We'll get you a toup in Palm Springs."

"Marry a rich broad, I could afford a weave."

Sidney Blackpool had been teamed with Otto Stringer for only two months and liked him fine except he figured he might have to buy a pair of earmuffs from a TWA mechanic in order to cope.

"Did you get . . . philosophical about turning forty, Sidney?" Otto asked.

"No," Sidney Blackpool said. He was still forty years old when he last saw Tommy. Sidney Blackpool stopped fearing middle age after that. In fact, he feared nothing.

"I'm getting that way," Otto mused. "I think I'm old enough to settle down with a nice ugly rich broad. Wonder if Yoko Ono goes to Palm Springs. I got this fantasy I'd like to skizzle old Yoko in a strawberry field. Tribute to the Beatles, sort of."

"That's very philosophical, all right," Sidney Blackpool said, kicking the Toyota into fifth and getting a bit less cynical about the vacation. Maybe he could straighten out the duck hook that was wrecking his tee shots lately.

The hotel was as good as the town had to offer. In the lobby was a tiled fountain with blue and red lights under the water. There was lots of rattan and wicker, and white ceiling fans. The hotel had a baby grand in the bar and ersatz Mexican arches over the balcony and Formica cocktail tables and more hanging ferns than Hawaii. In short, it was just ugly enough to make Otto Stringer say it was absolutely mah-velous.

While they registered and were waiting for a bellman, Otto ran to a wicker throne chair, put on his sunglasses and said, "Quick! Who am I?"

"I dunno," Sidney Blackpool said. "Who *are* you?"

"Reverend Jim Jones, dummy!"

"He shot himself," Sidney Blackpool said.

"Don't be morbid, Sidney," said Otto.

It was a friendly hotel like most in the desert, and like most it looked as though it was designed in the 1950s, a lousy decade for architecture, but for most desert rats the last decade that was ever worth a damn. This desert attitude was reflected in many ways. When all the tourists went home to Chicago and Canada and Beverly Hills, the desert residents settled back into the Eisenhower era. Though only two hours from L.A. it was definitely *not* a town for nouvelle pizza topped with Dijon mustard and truffles.

A man at the registration desk said, "Oh,

Mister Blackpool and Mister Stringer? I have a package for you."

He disappeared for a moment and came back with a manila envelope that was sealed and taped shut. He handed it to Otto who grinned and winked at Sidney Blackpool. It had to be the money. Victor Watson's secretary had promised that all hotel expenses and golf arrangements were being taken care of by her and that some "expense money" would be awaiting them in the hotel safe.

There was the usual Palm Springs mix in the lobby. Conventioneers from Iowa wearing sport jackets that looked battery operated, a William Morris junior agent in for the weekend with his Indiana Jones leather jacket and a copy of *Rolling Stone,* and several ex-leg breakers from Las Vegas with cigars and diamonds and not a button nose in the bunch. There were also two hookers working the early shift who were pretending to be interested in going for a swim but were flying around the conventioneers like turkey vultures.

While they were following the bellman up one of two swooping stairways, Otto said, "I used to hear that Palm Springs is where rich Jews go to die."

"Yeah, if they can't stand Cubans and Haitians."

"I could die here," Otto said.

"Doesn't matter where you die," Sidney Blackpool said. "It's *when* that matters. And sometimes that doesn't matter."

"*Try* not to be morbid, Sidney," Otto said. "Hey, I think I just saw Farrah Fawcett in the lobby!"

Their suite, which was composed of two bedrooms and two baths, thrilled Otto who tipped the bellman a five in a fit of extravagance. There was an ice bucket waiting, a bottle of pretty good California wine, and a fruit basket, compliments of the manager.

Sidney Blackpool was testing his king-size bed when Otto came running in through the connecting door, his rosy cheeks gone white.

"What's the matter, too much luxury for your little heart to bear?" Sidney Blackpool asked.

"Sidney!" Otto cried. "Whaddaya think Watson's giving us for expenses? I mean for a *week's* expenses?"

"Five hundred?" Sidney Blackpool shrugged. "I mean, food and drink here at the hotel're comp'd so . . ."

Otto turned the manila envelope upside down and they fell out on the bed. Twenty of them: five-hundred-dollar bills.

"I didn't even know whose picture was on one!" Otto whispered. "Hello President McKinley!"

"He said we might have to pay for some information, but . . ."

"We can't keep it, Sidney."

"Why can't we?"

"Ten thou? I don't have my goddamn pension secured yet! Four years to go, baby."

"We're not being *bribed,* for chrissake."

"Okay, we gotta make a ledger and keep track a every dollar. If we get any leads and pay snitches we gotta keep track."

"Are you crazy? We came here to play golf. The investigation's bullshit!"

"I know, I know! We gotta give him back at least nine grand. Damn, I got Hershey squirts in my shorts!"

"I'm impressed by the money, Otto. I mean *really* impressed. I never had ten grand at one time but . . ."

"Okay, okay, but you got a lock on your pension. I don't. Let's give him back eight grand. Two we can justify for a week's expenses. Buying drinks for cops, and buying snitch information, and like that."

"Let's just think about it," Sidney Blackpool said. "What's ten K to a guy like Watson? In his office he had more than that invested in a freaking desk that looked like a piece a rotten liver."

"Okay, okay, we give back six grand," Otto said. "I can live with that."

"Let's run down to the bar and get a drink," Sidney Blackpool said. "I need a Johnnie Walker."

"Run down to the bar?" Otto cried incredulously. "Call room service! We don't have to run anywheres. Shit, I don't see how we could spend ten grand if we tried. Maybe five. I wonder how much a massage costs in a place like this. I wonder how much you should tip for a massage? I wonder if we could spend that even if we was to *try*. Maybe seven. Maybe we could justify keeping seven. If we *tried*. Wait a minute! Didn't somebody *shoot* poor old fucking McKinley?"

Chapter 5

THE BELIEVER

He'd been called Wingnut since grammar school. The reason was obvious: his ears. Willard Bates looked like a wingnut all right, or like a VW bug with the doors open. For thirteen months he was a cop in Orange County and had nothing but grief, and thought about giving up police work altogether.

Big problems for Wingnut Bates started there in Orange County two weeks after he finished police training. One afternoon he was driving his patrol car by Disneyland with his training officer riding shotgun. His partner, Ned Grogan, happened to be eyeballing a little cupcake in the crosswalk who was dressed in shorts and a "Kiss" T-shirt for her day in the magic kingdom when suddenly she almost *got* kissed by a Lincoln with New York plates. It failed to brake for pedestrians and blew by at forty miles an hour.

Wingnut punched it on the amber light and sailed through a six-lane intersection after the New York Lincoln. His partner tightened his seat belt and said, "Easy, kid. This is only a traffic ticket."

Wingnut managed to catch the car since the driver was weaving from lane number one to number two and back again even though there were no cars directly in front of him.

"A deuce," Ned Grogan griped. "I don't wanna book a deuce right now. I wanna go get a hot pastrami."

He was a deuce all right, so drunk he didn't see the gumball lights behind and didn't hear Wingnut toot his horn for a pullover. Wingnut had to blast the siren in the drunk's ear before the Lincoln made a lurching stop against the curb.

Wingnut had never booked a drunk driver up to then. He was anxious to give his first field sobriety test and was trying to remember all the instructions without checking his notebook. But Ned Grogan preempted his act.

"Over there," Ned Grogan said to the middle-aged tourist who staggered out of the Lincoln. "On the sidewalk before you get killed by *another* drunk."

"Marvin Waterhouse," the drunk said, trying to shake hands with Ned Grogan. "Hope I wasn't speeding, Officer. Get a little confused on these California highways. Not like back home."

"May I see your license, please?" Wingnut asked, and Marvin Waterhouse looked at the young cop's freckled nose and said, "You a *real* cop, sonny?"

"Just give him the license, Marvin," Ned

Grogan sighed. "Let's get on with it."

"Sure, sure," Marvin Waterhouse said, making Ned Grogan step back from the blast of 80-proof bourbon. "Was I speeding? I'm very sorry."

As Wingnut was about to get into the drunk test, Ned Grogan said, "Look, Marvin, you know and we know you're too drunk to drive *or* walk."

"I don't think I'm . . ."

"Don't jive me, Marvin, I'm about to give you a break."

"Yes, *sir*." Marvin Waterhouse was no fool. "Whatever you say, Officer."

"Where's your hotel?"

"I'm at the Disneyland," Marvin Waterhouse said.

"Okay, now there's a taxi stand across the street. I want you to lock up your car and get in a cab and go back to the hotel and go to bed. Will you promise me you'll do that, Marvin?"

"Yes, sir!" Marvin Waterhouse said. "Right this second."

Wingnut was disappointed, but it wasn't the first time he'd lost an arrest when Ned Grogan wanted a pastrami or an enchilada or something. Wingnut figured his partner'd eat a stray dog.

As Marvin Waterhouse was starting to stagger into the crosswalk, Wingnut grabbed his elbow and said, "I better help you."

Ned Grogan stayed on the far side of the

81

crowded intersection and watched across six lanes of Disneyland traffic as Wingnut Bates, looking like a gun-toting Boy Scout, steered the New York tourist toward the taxi stand.

And then Marvin Waterhouse made a mistake that lots of easterners make when they come out west for the first time. He reached in his pocket, pulled out a $20 bill and tucked it inside Wingnut's Sam Browne belt.

It happened so fast that Marvin Waterhouse was half inside the cab when Wingnut looked at the money. The street was packed with cars and pedestrians, but nobody noticed Marvin's gesture of New York gratitude. Except that Wingnut Bates felt a thousand eyes. The guy thought he was a grafter! He'd just been fucking *bribed!*

"We don't do things like this!" Wingnut Bates cried, leaping toward the cab. "You can't . . ."

It was too late. The door was slammed by Marvin Waterhouse and the cabbie drove off.

"HE BRIBED ME!" Wingnut screamed across the traffic noise to Ned Grogan who was trying to figure out if his rookie partner had gone crackers in the heat.

"What?" Ned Grogan yelled.

"I BEEN BRIBED!" Wingnut Bates screamed, running after the taxi, which had crossed the intersection but was stopped by traffic trying to get into the Disneyland parking lot.

"Wingnut, come back here!" Ned Grogan hollered, but Wingnut was hotfooting across the intersection trying to remember the penal-code section for bribing a public officer. He nearly caused two collisions as cars mashed on their brakes to avoid killing a uniformed cop.

Ned Grogan was caught on the wrong side of the six-lane intersection with the light timed to accommodate the Disneyland flow. The cop jumped into the patrol unit planning to spin a U-ee and shoot through the traffic, except that the second he pulled out into the lane his patrol unit was clipped by a tourist from Duluth, giving him a whiplash that put him off duty for a week. Ned Grogan managed to drag himself out of the wrecked patrol unit and saw to his horror that a huge crowd had gathered a block north and he could guess why. He picked up the radio and asked for help.

When Wingnut caught the taxi, the driver was startled. Marvin Waterhouse was very startled.

Wingnut came puffing up and jerked open the door. "We don't do this!" he panted. "If I thought you had criminal intent I'd *book* you!"

"What's wrong with you, kid?" Marvin Waterhouse was astonished. "Take it! I want you to buy a drink after work!"

"I'm not taking your money, mister," Wingnut cried.

"Well, I don't want it. Give it to a cop charity!" Marvin Waterhouse said stubbornly.

"*You* take it!"

"I ain't taking it!" Marvin Waterhouse said.

Wingnut tried to shove the crumpled twenty into Marvin Waterhouse's shirt pocket, but the drunk, on his own turf more or less, got belligerent. "Keep your hands off me!" he bellowed. "I ain't taking nothing."

By the time the first police car arrived at the scene, Marvin Waterhouse and Wingnut Bates were rolling around in the gutter in an all-out donnybrook. A crowd of about sixty people was watching, among them a couple of tanked-up ironworkers who didn't like seeing a young cop beating on some middle-aged guy with tattoos. The hard hats started mouthing off and one thing led to another.

When it was over, Marvin Waterhouse *and* the two ironworkers went to jail for battery on a police officer. The miserable taxi driver lost a day's pay sitting at the police station dictating statements. Wingnut Bates' patrol car had to be towed to the garage and Ned Grogan had to be towed to the hospital for X rays and a neck brace.

The last thing Ned Grogan said as he was being hauled away by paramedics was "Tell Wingnut it was a real honor to witness such a display of law-enforcement integrity. I'm *so* proud. And tell the little jug-eared fuck, he better be ready to *draw* soon as I'm on my feet cause when I see him he's gonna have about as much chance as a Bonwit Teller in Bangladesh."

The incident with Marvin Waterhouse made the vice sergeant notice Wingnut Bates. He noticed that Wingnut looked as coplike as Alfalfa in *The Little Rascals*. Therefore he'd make an excellent undercover operator during the height of the tourist season when they were getting complaints of hugger-mugger whores rolling the out-of-towners, a bad thing in a town that boasted Disneyland.

When he asked Wingnut Bates if he'd like a temporary vice assignment the rookie jumped at it, especially since Ned Grogan would be coming back to duty soon and Wingnut was feeling as secure as a U-2 flight over Kamchatka, or the U.S. Football League.

Wingnut thought he was going to like being a vice cop, but they started playing tricks on him right away as vice cops are wont to do. For his first assignment he was told by a pair of older cops that he was going to operate a notorious call girl who posed as an outcall masseuse. She advertised in underground newspapers in a classified ad that said: "If you want me, call the number in this ad and tell me what you want and how much it means to you. Be *specific*, darling."

The reason for the admonition to be *specific* was that the girl didn't want any calls from vice cops, and like all hookers she was better acquainted with case law on entrapment than most Orange County lawyers. Any cop who phoned got a recorded message repeating the admonition and asking for a call-back number. The hooker would only then make the call and discuss the transaction. She did most of her business with male tourists so they didn't mind leaving the telephone numbers of hotel rooms.

Wingnut was told that they wanted the hooker to become acquainted with his telephone voice so there would be no problem when he showed up later at the rendezvous. He was told by the other cops that he was to get on the telephone and read a carefully worded script.

After reading the vice cops' message, Wingnut Bates said, "But isn't that entrapment, saying stuff like this to a hooker?"

"Noooo problem," the vice cops told him. "The laws on entrapment are constantly changing. Just say *exactly* what's in the script."

So, while Wingnut rehearsed his lines in the squad room until all three vice cops agreed that he had it *just* right, one of them dialed the hooker's number. Only it wasn't the hooker's number. It was Wingnut's home number. The vice cop waited until Wingnut's new bride answered and then said, "Just a second," into the phone. Only it *wasn't* Wingnut's new bride. It was her mother, Eunice, who didn't think much of her Penny marrying a cop when she'd had an offer from a Costa Mesa dentist with some prospects in life.

When Eunice said, "Who *is* this?," the phone was handed to Wingnut Bates, who delivered his lines. He said, "Hello, lover-buns. Yes, I got your message and yes, I want you to sit on my nose and yes, fifty bucks is ooo-kay! Just talking to you I got me a woody bigger'n a thirty-eight-ounce Louisville slugger!"

And then Wingnut Bates heard his mother-in-law scream, "Willard! Willard! Have you gone *crazy?*"

That was the kind of thing that happened to new vice cops. Once he was operating a complaint about wienie waggers inside a movie house adjoining a dirty bookstore that was disturbingly close to Disneyland. The cinema was showing *Doing Debbie Dirty*, which starred a surprisingly hot-looking porn star with a supporting cast of thirty-seven guys. They put Wingnut down in the front row with instructions to come running toward the back of the theater if they gave a signal. A signal meant they'd caught some guy milking the anaconda. They also told him they hoped he'd worn a jockstrap because it would be very unprofessional if he were to grow a woody watching Debbie being done dirty.

Five minutes later, one of the vice cops posing as a customer stormed huffily out to the lobby and told the manager, "That little guy in the front row with the gremlin ears, he's low-crawling people's crotches! He's a pervert! I want my money back!"

And then another vice cop posing as a customer stalked out saying indignantly, "I goddamn near broke my ankle slipping on the floor down in front! There's a little jerk-off down there going splooey all over the place! You could hydroplane on all the sapazzola in this freak show! I want my money back!"

And so forth.

While the vice cops went outside to giggle, the theater manager, who was sick and tired of dummy floggers chasing off legitimate customers, grabbed Wingnut by the scruff of the neck and dragged him right out of his seat, which resulted in a reflexive swing by Wingnut and a retaliatory punch by the theater manager, and pretty soon there was a screaming wrestling match that had all the customers pouring out of the cinema in panic.

By the time the other cops realized that another prank had backfired, and came running back into the theater, the fight had spilled over next door into the X-rated bookstore where the theater manager was doing a rain dance from having taken a swing and smacked the wall. He was jumping up and down with a busted hand, yelling and screaming, and Wingnut was sprawled between the dildos and the transvestite pinups thinking that vice wasn't going to be much better than patrol.

His Orange County police career ended not because of any backfired pranks but on a legitimate whore operation at a high-rise hotel where he almost got shot. On this operation, Wingnut was supposed to be a young insurance adjuster who was in town to assess the damage that a winter storm had done to a piece of waterfront property in Seal Beach. That was the cover story if he was lucky enough to meet a suspected hooker who'd been working a certain hotel bar for several weeks.

Wingnut was under strict instructions not to make any overt move with the hooker until midnight, which was the earliest that the cover team could finish a surveillance they were doing across town. He was just supposed to mosey around the bar and engage the girl in conversation if he was lucky enough to make contact, and then to stall until the cover team arrived. He was to give them a prearranged signal if she made an offer of prostitution. Then they'd move in, hook her up and haul her off to the slam.

That was the plan. Except that Wingnut had three margaritas before he saw the petite young lollipop stroll in and sit at the bar two stools away. She wasn't any older than Wingnut. She sort of reminded him of Debbie of the aborted movie review. Wingnut was feeling sorry for her but he'd already worked vice long enough to have regretted feeling sorry for hookers. He had once let one go pee during a vice raid, and when they broke down the locked bathroom door they found only the curtains blowing through an open window. That, after she'd already asked six other cops if she could go to the john and been refused, earning dipshit-of-the-month award for Wingnut.

So Wingnut, fried on tequila and salt, made friends with the girl. Her name was Sally, and she wouldn't go far enough with her "offer" to satisfy the state penal-code requirements. She asked Wingnut if they could go to his room to continue his conversation.

"Let's wait awhile," Wingnut said. "What's your hurry?"

"Ain't you in a hurry?" Sally smiled slyly. "Ain't I something you wanna *hurry* for?"

"Yeah, sure," Wingnut said. "But we haven't talked . . . *business* yet."

"Let's do that in your room," she said.

"It might not be agreeable, the terms I mean."

"It'll be agreeable," she said.

"Gimme a hint," Wingnut said, and now *he* was trying to be sly except that she was starting to look fuzzy. That was a *lot* of cactus juice for the young cop.

"Let's go on up and I'll talk more when we're alone in the elevator," she said.

"Let's have another drink," Wingnut said.

"Listen, honey, you're awful cute," Sally said, "but I ain't got all night. If you're not interested I'm gonna have to move on down the road."

"Wait a minute!" Wingnut said, seeing his arrest slipping away. "Okay, we'll talk on the elevator." What the hell. He couldn't have much trouble from such a frail little girl.

The hotel was very quiet at that time of night. There was a nice-looking fellow already standing at the elevator when they strolled up arm in arm like honeymooners. The young man was wearing a cardigan, pants with cuffs, and penny loafers, so it never occurred to Wingnut that he could be a hooker's main man. They were all supposed to be bad-looking spades with silk shirts and earrings and alligator boots.

Wingnut wished the elevator was empty. He had to have the offer quick because there *was* no hotel room. "Which floor you want?" Wingnut said to the young man in the cardigan, hoping he'd get off on a lower floor, giving Wingnut some time with the hooker.

"All the way up," the young fellow smiled, and when Wingnut pushed the button the young fellow said, "All the way up."

"I *pushed* the top floor," Wingnut said testily.

"I mean your *hands*," the young man said, producing a chrome-plated .32-caliber revolver. "Put them *all* the way up."

They took him out on the tenth floor. They were efficient and very fast. While the hooker held the elevator doors open, her partner pushed Wingnut against the wall and had his wallet, wristwatch and flash money within thirty seconds. Then the partner found Wingnut's handcuffs in the young cop's back pocket.

"Are you a cop?" the hooker gasped.

"Yeah, I'm vice," Wingnut said. "You're under arrest."

"You're dead," the young man said.

"You're not under arrest," said Wingnut.

"Get back in the elevator," the young man commanded, but Wingnut said, "Hey, tell you what! You let *me* go and I'll let *you* go!"

"I ain't as stupid as you," the young guy said, handcuffing both Wingnut's wrists to the handrail in the elevator.

"Please don't do that," Wingnut said, as the elevator descended. "Just go ahead and run. I'll give you a head start."

"You already did," the young guy said, before he and the whore got out, waved bye-bye and pushed the button that sent Wingnut to the penthouse.

The handcuff chain allowed him to reach the elevator panel all right. Wingnut mashed the emergency button with his freckled little nose, and when the hotel employees found him and called the police station for a spare handcuff key, Wingnut Bates decided that Orange County was full of hard luck.

He had a feeling he might still like a career in law enforcement, but maybe in a less populated, quieter sort of place. He heard they were looking for cops at a small department near Palm Springs. Wingnut met Sergeant Harry Bright who interviewed him and said that he had potential and seemed to be a good lad.

Ironically, it was yet another prank at the Mineral Springs police station that was to lead to a tiny break in the Jack Watson murder case.

There has never been a squad of cops anywhere that didn't have to endure at least one prankster. Since Mineral Springs had nine cops, they were lucky to have only one. His name was Frank Zamelli and they called him Prankster Frank. He'd been a cop for eight years in the Bay area, and in some other life he was the guy who ran around the throne room in size seventeen pointed bootees slapping the duchess in the ass with a pig's bladder. He was thirty-two years old, tall and wiry, and more lizard-eyed than Geraldine Ferraro's old man. The other cops wished vaudeville would be resurrected so maybe he'd give up police work.

For one thing, he was bonkers over mace canisters. Prankster Frank'd mace anything. In the winter he'd mace the patrol cars, just inside the grill where the vent hoses are. Then when they'd turn on the heater on a cold night they'd be crying like their dog died before they realized what happened. He'd also mace their radio mikes. They didn't know it until they picked it up to talk and their eyes started watering from the gas residue. Or he'd mace a helmet before a big inspection. That was a gas, all right. Standing there at attention with a helmet down over the nose and the eyes on fire. Prankster Frank Zamelli made lots of death wishes surface.

A variation on the mace was the bag-and-poopsicle routine where he'd scoop up a pile of warm dog crap with a bag and popsicle stick, and stash it up under the dashboard of a patrol car if the cops were dumb enough to leave it unlocked when he was within five miles. He just *loved* to hide out somewhere and watch two befuddled cops leap out of their car and sniff around each other like cocker spaniels after checking shoe bottoms.

Even civilian employees weren't safe when Frank was in a prankster frenzy. There was a very buxom married secretary at his old station who was secretly dating the captain, and who spurned all Frank's advances.

It was rumored that she was hosed down by the captain every time her old man flew down to L.A. on business, but she affected chastity and carried herself like Princess Di. Finally, when an overheated Prankster Frank wouldn't take yes for an answer after he asked if she'd like him to *stop* asking her for dates, she said, "Listen, maybe you don't appreciate subtlety. Let's put it this way: I'll date you when Jeane Kirkpatrick becomes a Playboy bunny."

Then Frank was ordered by his sergeant to stop "pestering" the boss's secretary. The word came from the captain himself who referred to Frank as "the wop cop." The ethnic slur did it. They got on Prankster Frank's list. But he couldn't very well mace the waspy bitch or the captain. What he *could* do was wait until she

94

went home one night and attack the photo cube she displayed on her desk. It was full of pictures of her preppy nineteen-year-old daughter who was vying for Miss California and whom she treated like a nun with the holy stigmata. Prankster Frank slipped a picture of his own into the side of the cube that faced toward the squad room where several passing detectives later did a take and said, "Who's *that?*"

"My daughter!" the secretary answered proudly until the third detective asked the same question. It gave her pause because they all knew very well whose pictures were in the cube. Then she turned it around and screamed.

Prankster Frank had inserted a shot he found in *Hustler* magazine, a beaver shot, a *yawning* beaver shot. In color.

When she ran into the captain's office to demand the head of Prankster Frank, her boss and not-so-secret lover tried to calm her down by pointing out that she had no proof it was the dirty dago and it might be better to make no more of it for the moment. Until she pointed to the trophy table behind him and a portrait of his wife, Rosey, and their son, Buster, who was posing cheek to cheek with his doting mother on his tenth birthday. Except that the face in the picture no longer belonged to Buster. The captain's snotty little kid now had the kisser of a local junkie with a Zulu hairdo. Buster looked like Rupert the Hype who looked like Leon Spinks after Larry Holmes beat the living shit out of him making him uglier than ever.

The thing that finished off Prankster Frank was a reign of terror at the county jail that was almost traced to him. It started when a drunk described him to his face in twenty-seven words ending with "guinea prick." The drunk also started screaming about suing for false arrest and police brutality until Prankster Frank got a headache from all the motor-mouthing. He was going on vacation soon and didn't want any court subpoenas, so instead of giving his own name at the county slammer as arresting officer, he impulsively listed his name as Officer U. F. Puck along with a bogus serial number.

The reign of terror was launched. For the next couple of weeks Prankster Frank disposed of seven slime-mouths by booking them drunk at the county jail, arrested by U. F. Puck. Prankster Frank then told a few other cops how easy it was to dispose of smart-mouth pukes who were "almost" drunk enough to book legitimately. Pretty soon there were lots of borderline drunks with very bad attitudes being booked by Officer U. F. Puck.

Then the jig was up. Especially since Officer Puck never showed up for trial and was described by outraged defendants as a tall white man, a short black man, a fat Mexican.

One defendant was absolutely certain that Officer Puck was Chinese-American and he ought to know, he said, because *he* was Chinese and they spoke the same dialect.

There was a big internal investigation over this one, which involved three police agencies. Prankster Frank Zamelli was ordered to take a polygraph exam but said he was insulted that his word as an officer and gentleman was being challenged, and he was sick of the damp climate in the Bay area, which was making his knee joints ache, and he was going south around Palm Springs where he was told people lived longer than goat herders in Abkhazia.

Six months later, Prankster Frank was working for Chief Paco Pedroza after Sergeant Harry Bright found Frank to be a good lad who *might* need extra supervision. Paco actually came to appreciate Frank's tricky ways as long as they got results. For instance, one day the county sheriff's deputies were trying to serve a search warrant on a Mineral Springs crank dealer, and they asked Paco if any of his cops knew the dealer's M.O. They wanted to get in the house *fast* with their search warrant before the crystal got flushed and other evidence got destroyed.

"Noooooo problem," said Prankster Frank, who knew that the crystal chemist had a restored 1959 Mustang he loved more than ether. Thirty minutes later, the scruffiest-looking dope cop from the sheriff's squad was being "arrested" by Officer Zamelli who, in full uniform, was dragging the undercover cop down the street with his hands cuffed behind him, yelling loud enough to wake the neighborhood, most of whom were asleep by ten o'clock.

Prankster Frank made lots of noise when he stomped up on the porch of the two-story frame house with his "suspect" by the arm. He leaned on the bell until he heard a voice from the upstairs window say, "Yeah, whaddaya want?"

"It's the police!" Prankster Frank yelled. "Somebody in this house own a Mustang?"

"What about it?" the man's voice asked with some alarm.

"I caught this guy lifting the car radio. I think he busted in with a tire iron. The paint's all scratched and the window's busted and . . ."

The crank dealer slid down the banister. Prankster Frank heard two bumps and in ten seconds the "chemist" in his bare feet and bathrobe threw open the door yelling, "My Mustang? This fuckface tore up my vintage Mustang?"

While the crank dealer was being restrained from attacking the "prisoner," all the deputies swooped in. The chemist found himself changing places with the little fuckface and soon sat bellowing in the same handcuffs while the dope cops strolled leisurely through the methamphetamine smorgasbord, scooping up drugs in both hands.

Paco Pedroza admired resourceful cops like Prankster Frank, but then, Frank never played tricks on his chief. Nor on the sergeants. First of all, he liked Sergeant Harry Bright too much, and second, he was scared shitless of Sergeant Coy Brickman who was not really mean but *looked* mean. Prankster Frank didn't like guys who stared at you like they hadn't blinked since 1969. He only played pranks on the other eight members of the Mineral Springs police force. One of his favorite victims was of course Wingnut Bates.

Wingnut was a bit heavier now and had matured during the two years he'd been in Mineral Springs. He liked almost everything here better than Orange County. Of course, he didn't like the summers when the temperature shot up past 120 degrees Fahrenheit. And he didn't like the *animals*.

Prankster Frank caught a raccoon on a prowler call after the little masked burglar had torn a hole in the roof of a house and gotten inside. He surreptitiously dumped the animal in Wingnut's patrol car, which pissed off the raccoon *real* bad. The raccoon *ate* Wingnut's uniform jacket. Wingnut endured it.

But there was an animal he could not endure: a snake. Rattlers, sidewinders, gopher snakes, it didn't matter. He was scared of all snakes. He was even scared of *pictures* of snakes. When he'd get a snake call, there'd be no air between himself and the citizen, Wingnut being the one behind. Learning that, Prankster Frank went out and bought himself a four-foot rubber snake and rigged an elaborate booby trap in Wingnut's locker. When Wingnut opened the locker after coming in from swing shift one Sunday night, the snake fell on his shoulder, sending poor Wingnut screaming out of the locker room, down the stairs and out the door of the station, scaring the crap out of the graveyard relief who figured Wingnut had found a bomb.

Wingnut Bates was still trembling when he arrived at the Eleven Ninety-nine Club that night. Though not an aggressive or violent young fellow, Wingnut Bates was looking for Prankster Frank Zamelli who was home in bed dreaming up his next one.

It had taken about thirty minutes after the Mineral Springs Police Department was formed for an entrepreneur to buy out Cactus Mike's Bar and Grill and have himself a hot little cop saloon. J. Edgar Gomez, a retired highway patrolman, named his bar the Eleven Ninety-nine Club after the radio code used by most California lawmen to announce that a cop needs emergency help. To "decorate" the saloon, the ex-Chippie selected several icons. One, framed in gold leaf and illuminated with a painting light, was an eight-by-ten glossy of Clint Eastwood holding a .44 magnum beside his face. Another was of General George S. Patton hefting one of his automatics with the ivory grips. And on the only wall large enough to accommodate "art" he commissioned one of the drove of local alcoholics to paint a mural designed by J. Edgar Gomez himself. It was a miniature of Michael Jackson with his hair on fire, and Prince in his *Purple Rain* costume. Michael Jackson's hair was being extinguished by amber rain supplied from above by a life-sized study of John Wayne in cowboy regalia pissing on the androgyny of today.

The ex-Chip tossed in a few obligatory wall mottoes for good measure. One said: "Unemployment is degrading. Give Mr. Ellis back his job" — which referred to the name used by the Canadian public hangmen who had gone into forced retirement when that nation placed a moratorium on the death penalty.

A second motto said: "Support the eternal flame. Flick your Bic for Jan Holstrom" — which reminded bar patrons of the pledge drive that enabled the Eleven Ninety-nine Club to send a gift of 154 Bic lighters to Soledad Prison for the use of Jan Holstrom, the inmate who had set fire to Charles Manson, almost killing him.

There were other notices hastily tacked up from time to time depending on the season. One sign over the bar said: "No trash sports allowed." This one pointed to the latest craze for midget tossing. One of the bar's best customers was a midget named Oleg Gridley who not only condoned being tossed from one end of the bar room to the other but actually encouraged it because some of the girls would invariably get into the tossing frenzy and he could cop a feel here and there.

The women's rest room said: "Female mammals only." In short, you needed hip boots to wade through the testosterone overflow, making the Eleven Ninety-nine Club a fairly typical cop's watering hole.

Seated at the bar were about twelve cops from all over the valley, two groupies from No-Blood Alley who were starting to look twenty years younger at that time of night, and a trucker who was trying in vain to argue with J. Edgar Gomez that his latest Moral Majority wall motto had things in common with babies and bath water and should possibly be rewritten. It said: "Women wanting an abortion should be summarily executed. We're pro life."

Involved in the debate was O. A. Jones, who was still being closely monitored by Paco Pedroza who had not found grounds to fire him. There was the stopwatch bandit. There was the discovery of the Jack Watson death car. Everything he did was questionable, but somehow he was becoming a local legend.

Paco Pedroza said there hadn't been such potential disaster in a desert since Mussolini took Ethiopia. Paco worried about having troops like Prankster Frank and Outta Ammo Jones and Choo Choo Chester, but at least they kept him from getting bored.

Choo Choo Chester Conklin was one of the last patrol cops hired by Paco Pedroza, and the only black man. Chester had been with the

Coachella Police Department for five years and might have stayed a lot longer except that he was accused of sending special delivery parcels to 1600 Pennsylvania Avenue, Washington, D.C.

They didn't actually *prove* that Chester was the one sending parcels to the White House, but a railroad stakeout team caught him wrestling with a sleeping ragpicker's body on the bed of a freight car. Chester claimed that he was trying to pull the wino *out* of the boxcar to take him to jail even though it was well known that town cops didn't go around cleaning up for the Southern Pacific.

He really had a hard time of it when the railroad cops found an envelope tied around the ragpicker's neck addressed to then White House Counsel Edwin Meese. The letter said, "I am truly needy. There really is hunger in America. Keep me and I will vote Republican."

Also involved in the barroom debate was Beavertail Bigelow, who had been permitted in the saloon by J. Edgar Gomez only after swearing he hadn't voted for the Democrats on November sixth as he'd been threatening to do. J. Edgar Gomez, like most ex-cops and cops in general, was a right-wing Republican as a result of street cynicism run rampant. He wanted the Eleven Ninety-nine Club to deliver 100 percent to Ronald Reagan and his party.

Beavertail was almost up to his Beefeater limit for this twenty-four-hour period and he was getting surly and ready to pick a fight. He started to badmouth the victorious Reagan-Bush ticket until J. Edgar Gomez, who was behind the bar rolling a cigar in his mouth and trying to doze standing up, opened one blood-shot eye and gave him a glare that said, "You're only in here on a pass."

Beavertail was halfway boiled, but he got the message. "Okay, then," he said. "They're *all* wimps and bitches and pussies and geezers!"

It was okay to put down Reagan and Bush *if* you included Mondale and Ferraro in the same breath. Then Beavertail looked across the bar at the only black guy in the place, Choo Choo Chester, and said, "I suppose you voted for Reagan. After all, you sent Edwin Meese all those . . ."

"Don't *start* that shit!" J. Edgar Gomez warned, his eyebrows all spiky. "That rumor's dead and we're sick of it! Now drink your gin and don't cause no trouble tonight!"

So the old desert rat and the young black cop just drank their drinks and pretended to ignore each other, but everyone figured that Beavertail wasn't through with Choo Choo Chester who was one up on him for *maybe* being the guy who sent Beavertail on that bus ride to nowhere.

Choo Choo Chester then started picking an argument with J. Edgar Gomez about the jukebox. The young cops were always beefing with the saloonkeeper about his choice of records.

"I don't see why we can't have one freakin song that was written in this century!" Choo Choo Chester moaned. "I'm *sick* a Harry Babbitt and Snooky Lanson. I'm sick a Frank Sinatra singin 'Set em up, Joe'."

"Maybe you kids ain't even *capable* a understanding songs like 'Bewitched, Bothered and Bewildered,' " the saloonkeeper sighed. "What's gonna be the memory a your youth? 'Wake Me Up Before You Go-Go'?"

"We gotta play somethin new," Choo Choo Chester persisted. "Shit, I might as well be a telephone operator, goin through life with a fuckin headset glued to my ears!"

It was true. Four out of the twelve cops in the saloon were wearing headphones with their ghetto blasters sitting beside them.

"What's wrong with Van Halen or Duran Duran?" O. A. Jones argued.

"No hard rockers," J. Edgar Gomez said.

"Okay then, Elton John. Shit, he's an *old* guy."

"No soft rockers," J. Edgar Gomez said.

"How about The Police then?" Choo Choo Chester asked. "How can a guy like you, who gave thirty years to the law, object to a rock band called The Police?"

"Don't try to be cute," J. Edgar Gomez said.

"Damn, Edgar, at least get *one* Hall and Oates side! They're mellow!"

"They're scumbag rockers," said J. Edgar Gomez.

"I suppose even the Beatles ain't old enough yet?"

"They started this shit," J. Edgar Gomez said. "Shoulda depth-charged their fucking yellow submarine."

And so forth. It was virtually hopeless, but the young cops protested every night. It was pops of the thirties, forties and fifties, and a little country. J. Edgar Gomez allowed Willie Nelson because the saloonkeeper figured that Willie was into the hippie-cowboy trash because he couldn't handle middle age. J. Edgar could understand mid-life eccentricities all right. Yet he allowed Willie Nelson's music only after the singer recorded *Stardust* and did almost as good a job as Hoagy Carmichael himself.

"What's wrong with you?" O. A. Jones said to Wingnut Bates when the jug-eared young cop came shuddering into the bar and threw his ten-dollar bill on the bar with a trembling hand.

"N-n-nothin," said Wingnut Bates. "Except I'm gonna kill Frank Zamelli."

"Oh yeah, when?"

"Tomorrow. *Tonight* if he comes in."

"Yeah? Well, it's been pretty dull around here."

"I'm gonna kill him. G-g-g-g-gimme a *double* margarita, Edgar."

"What'd Prankster Frank do this time?"

O. A. Jones asked Wingnut as he eyed a sagging mid-lifer from No-Blood Alley who'd look like a $6,000 facelift by 1:00 A.M.

"A sn-sn-snake!" Wingnut cried.

"He put a *snake* in your car?"

"My l-l-l-locker," Wingnut said.

"That's going too far," O. A. Jones said. "Even for Prankster Frank. Was it a king snake? Don't tell me it was a rattler! I wouldn't believe that!"

"R-r-r-rubber," Wingnut Bates said, grabbing the margarita in both hands and gulping half of it down.

"Oooooooh, rubber! Well, that ain't *too* bad, Wingnut. That ain't so bad."

"I b-b-believe I'm gonna kill him," Wingnut said. "Jesus, I'm st-st-stuttering!"

"You sure are. Finish your drink, maybe you'll calm down."

"I believe!" Wingnut cried. "I believe I'm g-g-gonna . . ."

"What's that?" O. A. Jones cried out.

"Keep it down!" J. Edgar growled. "Only freaking rest I get around here is when I doze standing up. Like a freaking parakeet."

"I believe!" O. A. Jones said, running over to the jukebox, which was playing *Green Eyes* by Helen O'Connell. "I believe! Hey, Edgar, ain't that a song from *your* time? Ain't that one you used to have on this box?"

"What?"

" 'I Believe'! How's it go?"

107

Without removing his cigar or opening his eyes, J. Edgar Gomez sang, " 'I believe for every drop of rain that falls, a flower groooooows!' "

"Yeah, that's it!" O. A. Jones said.

" 'I believe that somewhere in the darkest night, a candle gloooows.' "

"Okay, enough!" O. A. Jones said. "That's it! Wingnut, that's it!"

"What's it?"

"The song I thought I heard the killer singing in the desert when I found that Watson kid fried in his car!"

"You said it was 'Pretend.' "

" 'Pretend you're happy when you're bluuuuuuue,' " J. Edgar Gomez suddenly sang. "I just *loved* Nat King Cole."

"I thought it was 'Pretend,' " said O. A. Jones, "but the song never did sound right when the Palm Springs dicks played it for me. I mean, I thought I heard the guy singing something about pretending. Now I think it was 'I Believe.' Yeah! I think that's it!"

"That ain't nothing like 'Pretend,' " J. Edgar Gomez said, finally opening his eyes. "You been drinking too much vodka. I told you whiskey's better for your head."

"I know it was *something* about 'believe,' " O. A. Jones said, wrinkling his brow.

"I *can't* believe this is so important," J. Edgar Gomez said. "And I wish you'd keep your voice quieter. Beavertail's nodding off.

Might get by without a fight tonight."

" 'I Believe,' " O. A. Jones said. "Tomorrow I'm calling the Palm Springs dicks. I'm the only lead to the killer!"

"That don't seem like much of a clue to me," J. Edgar Gomez said, closing his eyes again.

"I'm calling them tomorrow," O. A. Jones said.

"I'm killing Prankster Frank Zamelli tomorrow," Wingnut Bates said.

Chapter 6

FLOATING COFFINS

"Don't look for mercy from that son of a bitch," Otto Stringer said, referring to their captain. "He's the Cotton Mather of the cop world."

"I don't think we'll need mercy, Otto," Sidney Blackpool said. "Nobody's ever gonna know about the ten grand, and even if they do, it's expense money. No strings attached."

"The amount, Sidney. *That's* the string. In fact it's a rope. In fact it's a *noose* if our department ever hears about it."

"Nobody's gonna hear. Relax. Finish your tequila and tomato juice. How can you drink that stuff?"

"Like this," Otto Stringer said, stretched out at poolside on a lounge chair at dusk.

He guzzled the tall one and waved to a waitress with a gardenia in her hair who swayed over to poolside in a persimmon muumuu, Palm Springs being big on Hawaii and exotica in general.

"Another?" she smiled, making Otto deeply regret the big four-oh and sexual extinction.

"That was de-voon, dahling," Otto said,

"but I think I'll try another kind."

"That's the fourth other kind you've had," Sidney Blackpool said. "Mixing is tricky."

"Not to worry," Otto said. "Let's see, I never been much on martinis so I think I'll try a martini. How about a vodka martooni, my dear."

"Twist or olive?"

"Both. And a cocktail onion. Make it two cocktail onions."

"Vodka martini," she said, writing on her pad. "With a dinner salad."

As the cocktail waitress hip-swayed toward the bar, Otto sighed and put his hands behind his head and stopped sucking in his belly. He was wearing brand-new white doubleknits and white loafers with yet another acrylic golf sweater, this one pink and maroon, over a maroon shirt.

Sidney Blackpool was wearing the same pants as earlier, but had switched to a green golf shirt and white V-necked sweater for the evening. Palm Springs is very casual and they'd been told that only a few restaurants in the entire desert required a jacket. Nobody demanded neckties except dining rooms in the country clubs, but they'd brought coats and ties in case.

"Was it hot enough for you today, dah-ling?" Otto asked, watching a pair of thirtyish women stroll out by the pool, look toward the two detectives, and go back inside without apparent interest.

"Yeah, I guess it was hot enough," his partner shrugged.

"That's half a the conversation. Now, where we eating tonight?"

"I dunno. Should I worry about it?"

"That's the other half a the conversation."

"What conversation?"

"The Palm Springs conversation," Otto said. "I listened to a bunch a people by the pool today. That's the only thing they say. Hot enough today and where we eating tonight. That's it."

"Exciting."

"That's all people got to worry about around here," Otto said. "They don't even move enough to keep their watches wound."

"Rich people, Otto. Not people like you and me."

"We're rich, Sidney," Otto reminded him.

"This week only."

"You got *that* right," Otto said, which next to Tom Selleck aloha shirts and moustaches was this year's cop mannerism. The phrase "You got *that* right."

"That waitress is all time," Otto said. "She's the kind tries to lick you with her eyes."

"I thought you said you were looking for ugly broads."

"To marry. A rich ugly broad to marry. Not to spend a vacation with. That's what I like about Yoko Ono. She looks like the leading lady in Kabuki theater and they're all men. I'd marry her in a minute."

"Let's sign for the drinks and go to dinner," Sidney Blackpool said.

"Signing for drinks." Otto grinned. "Let *me* sign. I wanna write in a big tip for that little heartbreaker. She'll remember Otto Stringer before this week's out."

"I hope ten grand's gonna be enough," his partner said, as they strolled inside.

The dining room was like the rest of the hotel, but there was less wicker and rattan, and the floral patterns weren't out of control. The maître d' dressed formally and the waiters wore standard desert chic: white dress shirt, black bow tie, no coat.

The menu required two hands to lift. In fact, Otto Stringer, hidden behind it, said, "Sidney, I could take this thing out by the pool tomorrow, shove two poles under it and have enough shade for me, a golf cart, and Liz Taylor."

"She's not your size anymore," Sidney Blackpool said, trying to decide whether to order things he couldn't spell or keep it a cop's night out. That is, steak or prime rib.

"I'm glad they translate the French," Otto said. "I hate restaurants where the menu's all in French or Italian."

"How often do you eat at restaurants where the menu's in any language but English, Spanish and Chinese?"

"Sidney, I'm a man a the world! Let's get a

113

wine steward."

Just then the dining-room captain came to the table and said, "Have you gentlemen decided yet?"

"I'll have grease," Otto said. "I usually eat grease."

Otto didn't end up with grease, but he did get a lot of unfamiliar and very rich continental cuisine. He started out with champagne and escargots, and red caviar because they didn't have the good stuff. He went on to veal with a champagne cream sauce you could lose a fork in. He had a side of fettucine Alfredo because, like Mount San Jacinto, it was *there*. He finished up with half a pound of marzipan and a flambé crepe because he wanted something they set on fire.

Sidney Blackpool, realizing that he was way past his limit of Johnnie Walker Black, had only one glass of champagne, veal piccata with lemon and capers, a Bibb lettuce salad and no dessert.

Otto was halfway through the crepe, saying, "Sidney, you gotta relax and let yourself go," when he started to hiccup.

"Damn," he said.

"Let's order you some bitters and lime. It works for me," Sidney Blackpool said.

"These hiccups feel funny," Otto said, his upper lip beading with sweat. "I think I'll run to the john and . . ."

He barely made it. Otto upchucked for ten

minutes. When he returned, he was pale and shaky.

"You're a little green around the gills," his partner observed.

"I just lost a hundred bucks worth a fancy groceries!" Otto moaned.

"Well, it was your first time, Otto. You'll do better tomorrow. Your tummy's a rookie on *this* beat."

"Ooooh, I'm sick," Otto said. "And now I'm hungry!"

"Let's go to sleep," Sidney Blackpool said.

"But I wanted to see the *night* life."

"Let's get a good night's rest. Tomorrow you can order breakfast in bed. You'll be a new man."

"Tomorrow I'm sticking to grease," Otto said.

"I'll have room service bring you a plate a grease first thing in the morning," his partner promised.

A deluge. There had never been so much rain in the desert. Sidney Blackpool watched a terrifying flash flood swell like a tidal wave on the very crest of Mount San Jacinto, then cascade down on the hotel. Men and women were screaming. It was awful, and though his own life was in jeopardy, he had to stand and face the next wall of water because he could see it riding the crest: a coffin. The lead-lined coffin rode like a fiberglass surfboard. Sidney

Blackpool was weeping with the other doomed hotel guests, but not for his imminent death. He wept because he knew the coffin bore the half-drowned body of Tommy Blackpool who, wearing a red-and-black wet suit, clung like Ishmael as the coffin suddenly began cartwheeling away, down the Coachella Valley.

"Tommmmmmmy!" he sobbed, and then he was awake. It was dawn. He hadn't awakened at the dreaded drinker's hour as he deserved, having put away so much Johnnie Walker Black. The bed was soaked as always after a recurring dream about Tommy Blackpool.

In the dream, Tommy would often be clinging to his coffin, or sometimes to his surfboard, which had been torn from his ankle strap by the huge wave in Santa Monica that drowned him.

Sometimes Sidney Blackpool would dream simply that Tommy was getting soaked to the skin lying in that coffin in the cold ground. This, during rainstorms. Sidney Blackpool hated rainstorms now and had begun to wish that he'd had Tommy cremated. His ex-wife had suggested it, but deferred when he insisted on burial in the ground. Like many lapsed Catholics he could not entirely escape the tenets drilled into him in grammar school. Even though the modern Church no longer cherished mystery and ritual and burial in the ground. The dead with bones intact to await the Redeemer? He never really knew why they used

116

to demand it, but he had buried Tommy in the ground. And now he regretted it every time it rained. He used to read weather forecasts even before the headlines in the days when he was going mad.

In all his years as a cop — even during the Watts Riot when he was trapped inside a burning warehouse believing he'd be burned alive — he'd never awakened in what they call a cold sweat. Dreams of fire had never tormented him. It was these dreams of water, and Tommy so cold. The detective was shivering as he plodded toward the shower, feeling very old, hoping he could stem the headache starting at the base of his skull.

Cold sweat. A parent who dreamed of something as *outrageous,* as *unnatural* as his eighteen-year-old child lying in the ground, *that's* who coined that one. He showered, shaved, dressed, took three aspirin and went downstairs hoping the hotel coffee shop opened early.

Otto Stringer had breakfast served in his bedroom as promised. It was a typical Palm Springs November day. "The kind you expect" as the radio disc jockey said. About 78 degrees with humidity around 19 percent, making it comfortable and invigorating. Otto finished four eggs, two orders of bacon, toast, jam and coffee. He showered, shaved, put on a baby-blue golf shirt with a navy sweater tied around his neck, and realized they hadn't decided where to play.

They had the names of three head pros who would arrange games for them at some of America's most famous country clubs. Victor Watson's secretary had assured Sidney Blackpool that even if all the courses were not yet ready for the official opening of the 1984–85 desert season, she could make arrangements for them at just about any club that was. When Otto arrived at the coffee shop, his partner had a copy of *Palm Springs Life* on the counter beside him, along with the file containing the police reports dealing with the murder of Jack Watson.

"Which one's most fun to read?" Otto asked, nodding to one of the desert's thousand daytime waitresses who have a tough time making it during the short tourist season, and who all walk like their feet hurt.

"Morning," she said, pouring Otto's coffee. "Hot enough for you today?"

"Sure is," Otto said.

"That's half a the day's conversation," Sidney Blackpool said to Otto.

"Where we eating tonight?" Otto asked, thus completing the other half.

"You wanna play golf today or make our show for Watson?"

"I was thinking, Sidney, maybe we oughtta get the business over with in case he calls and wants a report."

"I don't think he'll call," Sidney Blackpool said. "He must know unconsciously that this is a fantasy. He's just . . . just a screwed-up father who can't deal with the loss of his son. Maybe lots a guys in his shoes if they had his money'd do strange things to try to find some . . ."

"Justice."

"I was gonna say peace. He told me he knows there's no justice."

"I feel sorry for the guy, Sidney. Let's work on his case today. We got all week to play golf. Wanna drop by Palm Springs P.D.?"

"I was thinking about going by Watson's house," Sidney Blackpool said. "After all these months I don't suppose Palm Springs P.D. knows anything we don't already know. The houseboy's supposed to be there."

"How long's he been with the family?"

"Only two years."

"Let's pin it on him."

"Maybe we could get in nine holes this afternoon," Sidney Blackpool said.

The Las Palmas residence of Victor Watson was a disappointment to both cops. They were expecting a Beverly Hills mansion rather than a sprawling one-story home without real style that couldn't even be seen behind the jungle of oleander. In Beverly Hills the residents claimed they wanted privacy but made sure that the ogling masses could at least see upper windows and gabled roofs over the vine-covered walls and through the wrought iron.

Victor Watson's home was 1950-ish, flat-roofed, spread around a large oval pool with a small grove of orange trees at the rear. The property was about an acre and a half in size. The drive-in gate was locked and they rang the buzzer but got no answer.

"The houseboy might be out to the store or something," said Otto.

"Might be back in that grove," Sidney Blackpool said, climbing up on the gate to take a peek.

"I got my new pants on, Sidney, and I'm too old to climb."

"It's only an electric gate. Just lean on it with the whole two-sixty."

"Probably set off an alarm," Otto said, leaning his weight onto the gate and pushing against the jointed arm, which creaked and gave. The gate clanged shut after they were both inside.

"Cost the ten grand he gave us just to repair our damage," Otto said.

"Can't waste too much time, Otto. We gotta play golf."

Both men went to the driveway on the side of the house and Otto yelled, "Helooooo!," but there was no sound from the grove except for desert birds chattering in the trees.

Sidney Blackpool peeked in the garage and saw the Watson Mercedes. Otto rang the front doorbell and could hear music inside.

"Let's go around to the pool," Otto said. "Maybe he was working on his tan and fell asleep."

The pool was impressive because of its size. There was a separate spa, large enough to accommodate the kind of orgy Otto dreamed of joining this week.

"Whaddaya think, Sidney?" he winked toward the spa. "All this privacy. Bet they could throw some parties."

"What the hell's that?"

By a chaise lounge in the shade of the patio roof was a coffee cup spilled. Sidney Blackpool touched the coffee, which was cold. On the patio stones near the overturned cup was an unmistakable smear of blood. It looked very fresh.

"Let's get in that house pronto," he said.

It wasn't difficult. The French doors leading to the patio were unlocked and the detectives entered carefully, looking at each other as they both realized they were ready for a golf vacation, not a homicide investigation. They were unarmed.

"Anybody home?" Otto yelled, half expecting an intruder wet with gore to come slashing out of a closet.

The home bore the touches of Mrs. Victor Watson. There was the same dizzy designer mix that Sidney Blackpool had seen in Watson's outer office: Grecian urns, broken remnants of

Roman antiquities in bas relief, pre-Columbian artifacts, eighteenth-century English landscapes, and three "conversation areas" that were overwhelmed by massive sofas, settees and loveseats, which were supposed to say, "We are desert casual in this house," but which to Sidney Blackpool said, "I am without subtlety but do I *ever* have megabucks."

The radio's music was coming not from the main bedrooms down the hall by the entertainment area but from the other side of the house, just off the kitchen. Otto picked up a vase, hefted it like a club, shrugged at Sidney Blackpool and put it back down. Both detectives were a little tense as they crept past a huge kitchen containing commercial gas ranges and ovens, freezers and refrigerators, all in stainless steel, which would've satisfied the needs of any restaurant chef in Palm Springs. There was an old chopping block in the center of the kitchen, showing a patina of fifty years. On the chopping block was a fourteen-inch butcher knife, stained by blood.

Now Otto Stringer wished he'd kept the vase, and started looking for a *real* club. They crept a little more quietly toward the sound of the radio. It was turned to one of the Palm Springs stations, which, like the rest of this valley, refused to march with Time past the era of Dwight Eisenhower.

The song on the radio was "Wheel of Fortune" by Kay Starr. They could hear the sound of a shower running. Kay Starr finished her song and the programmed music segued into "Long As You Got Your Health," by Ozzie Nelson.

Otto tried to break the rising tension by whispering, "I didn't know he sang."

"Who?"

"Ozzie Nelson. I thought he was just Ricky's old man on television."

Sidney Blackpool stuck out his foot and nudged the bedroom door open. The music and shower got louder. They tiptoed toward the bathroom and could see that the shower curtain was drawn but there was no one standing behind it. Then they saw the outline of a human figure crumpled in the bathtub.

Sidney Blackpool leaped forward and jerked the shower curtain back.

A hairless man screamed, "Yeeeee!," dropping his toenail clipper and leaping to his feet. He was jockey size. His reflexes didn't make him throw up his hands in defense. His hands flew over his genitals. He stood with his hip toward the detectives, his knee raised, covering his crotch. "Who *are* you?" he cried.

"Sergeant Blackpool and Detective Stringer," Sidney Blackpool said. "We were told you'd be expecting us. There was blood on the patio. And a butcher knife. We thought . . ."

"Oh, God!" the little man cried, wrapping himself with the shower curtain.

"We'll let you get dressed," Sidney Blackpool

123

said, and both detectives retreated to the living room.

"Poor little guy," Otto said. "Coulda swallowed his tongue."

"Make him a little more security conscious," said Sidney Blackpool, wondering if the well-stocked bar in the living room contained Johnnie Walker Black. Then he looked at his watch and saw that it wasn't 10:00 A.M., and thought that the Johnnie Walker impulse was very bad, vacation or not.

A few minutes later the houseboy came padding in barefoot. He wore a peppermint-green kimono with enormous sleeves and a silk-screen flying crane on the back. He was about sixty years old and now wore a strawberry-blond toupee slightly askew.

"Golly you scared me!" he said, extending a hand palm down to Sidney Blackpool.

After shaking hands with both detectives, he smiled and said, "My gosh! When that shower curtain came swishing back I expected to see Anthony Perkins standing there in drag! I was *so* disappointed! Would you like coffee or a drink or something?"

"No, thanks, Mister Penrod," Sidney Blackpool said. "Sorry to meet you this way."

"It's okay," the little man said. "And *please* call me Harlan. Everyone does. I can see how you'd get suspicious, being cops and all. Pardon me, policemen, I mean."

"Cops is fine," Sidney Blackpool said.

"Really? On *Dragnet* Jack Webb always said you didn't like to be called cops."

"Jack Webb wasn't a cop," Sidney Blackpool said.

"Well, sit for goodness' sake," said Harlan Penrod. "I must look a fright." And after touching his toupee he realized he did. "Oh gosh," he said, trying to tug it into place subtly. "I was just clipping my nails when you pulled the curtain back. The blood? Well, I was reading the *L.A. Times* and cutting a peach and oh, I just get so mad reading about Rose Bird and her California Supreme Court. We keep voting for the death penalty and they keep fixing it so these killers stay alive. I was so mad at Rose Bird I sliced my finger instead of the peach!"

"We just stopped by to acquaint ourselves with the house and ask a few questions." Sidney Blackpool glanced at Otto who knew what he was thinking, If we can think of *what* question to ask in a seventeen-month-old homicide.

"We wouldn't have to put up with Rose Bird if that so-called governor Jerry Brown hadn't appointed her," Harlan Penrod said. "Did you see the portrait of him they hung in the state capitol? I mean, did the artist *ever* capture that repressed reclusive paranoid? In another life Jerry Brown was Emily Dickinson. I only wish we could get rid of Rose Bird and the rest of Jerry Brown's supreme court. I think just like a cop. I'm all for death!"

"We're awful sorry to disturb you like this, but . . ."

"Oh, you're not disturbing me. Do you know how *lonely* it gets here? Mister and Mrs. Watson never come anymore since Jack died. Gosh, unless they let some friends use the place for a weekend I don't see anybody. Do you know how lonesome it gets in a house like this all by yourself?"

"Are you allowed to have friends come over?" Otto asked, his arms on the back of the sofa as he admired all the museum pieces that Sidney Blackpool hated.

"Golly yes. Mister and Mrs. Watson are very nice to work for. And of course the property keeps me busy enough. I'm not that young anymore." Harlan Penrod took a sneaky little tug on his toup when he said that, but still wasn't satisfied that it was centered. "This is a good job, believe me. I'm not complaining. I just miss having people here to take care of and cook for. Hey! When Mister Watson called, he said that you two gentlemen might be here for a week. Would you like me to cook a dinner for you?"

"Well, I don't think so," Sidney Blackpool said. "We have our hotel and . . ."

"Oh, it's no trouble! I'd just love to. My training was originally as a chef, you know. What do you like? I could fix you anything. I have carte blanche at Jurgensen's Market. You could invite your wives. Did you bring them along?"

"We're not married," Otto said. "Both divorced."

"Really!" Harlan Penrod cried. "Oh, you *must* come to dinner!"

"Well, maybe later in the week," Sidney Blackpool said. "Now about the murder."

"Are you going to solve it? I mean, do you have some new clues?"

"Not really," Otto said. "We're just gonna go over the old clues. Except there ain't any."

"I know," Harlan Penrod nodded, wrapping his kimono modestly around his bony knees. "I was wondering why two detectives came clear from Hollywood. I know you got lots of cases to work on there."

"We got cases by the gross, by the pound, by the case," Otto said. "We're sort a doing a favor for Mister Watson. Just taking another look."

"Jack was such a beautiful boy," Harlan Penrod said. "He was so sensitive, so intelligent, so . . . *kind*, you know? He was at the age where kids can be fresh and know-it-all, last year of college and all that. But not Jack. He was basically such a *sweet* person."

"To you?" Otto asked.

"Golly yes," Harlan Penrod said. "He was so . . . comfortable to be around. He liked people and was concerned about them. I think he cared about me, I really do. Like a family member, not just an employee."

"The police report says you were out of town the night he disappeared," Otto said, going through the motions of a homicide follow-up.

"Yes, to L.A. I've hated myself for not being here. You have no idea how many times I've thought of it."

"Why'd you go to L.A.?"

"Well, I never admitted it to the Palm Springs detectives, but after all this time I guess it doesn't make any difference. I had to testify in a criminal trial and I didn't want Mister Watson to know. It was soooooo lurid."

"A criminal trial?" Otto cocked an eyebrow at Sidney Blackpool. "Were you involved in a crime?"

"Gosh no! I was sort of a witness. Oh, it was awful!" Harlan Penrod jumped up and took several little steps over to the bar where he poured himself some orange juice from a pitcher. "Care for some juice? Fresh-squeezed."

"No, thanks," Otto said, while Sidney Blackpool shook his head and spied the bottle on the bar shelf — Johnnie Walker Black.

"Well," Harlan Penrod said, returning to the sofa and crossing his legs after making sure the kimono didn't flop open. "I actually left Hollywood and came to live in the desert *because* of that terrible business. You see, I used to work for one of the sound studios on Santa Monica where people with no talent whatsoever go to cut records. Oh, it was so sad. All these young boys and girls with hopes and dreams.

Little rock bands with some awful song they wrote. Hopes and dreams. I was so depressed all the time."

Sidney Blackpool looked at his watch and Otto said, "We, uh, have an appointment in a little while."

"Do you?" Harlan Penrod was crestfallen. "Anyway, one day in the studio when they were doing a sound mix, my boss who was oh so nelly got in a terrible row with his boyfriend, this person named Godfrey Parker, a bitch if there ever was one. They were almost slapping each other's face when I went home. And the next day they found my boss. Oh, it was unspeakable!"

"What happened?" Otto was getting caught up in Harlan Penrod's narrative.

"It was a typical queen murder," Harlan said. "I remember one in my apartment building. A closet queen cut his lover to *pieces*. When the cops came they found all these trash bags in the apartment. 'He's in this one,' a cop would yell. 'He's in this one too,' another cop would holler. Oh, it was *awful*. The best part of him was found in an alligator bag!"

"But back to the sound studio," Otto said, pouring himself some orange juice after all.

"Yes, well, the police came the next morning after the janitor called and they found my boss lying dead right there in the studio. With a studio microphone . . . oh, this is awful . . . sticking two feet out of his rectum!"

"That's pretty gruesome, all right," Otto said.

"And Godfrey had turned up the volume full blast! He was a fiend! And those cops that came that morning, do you know what they said?"

"Can't imagine," said Sidney Blackpool.

"The first one said, 'Well, I know who the deceased must be.' And then he named that T.V. reporter on Channel Seven? You know, the one that's always doing exposés on the L.A.P.D. And the policeman said, 'The suspect's one of *us*. Some cop finally did what we've *all* been threatening to do.' Well, they had to cut the mike pole out of him with a bolt cutter!"

"That's what Reagan felt like doing when he made the joke about bombing the Russians," Sidney Blackpool said. "But getting back to Jack Watson. We have some new information that he may've driven to Hollywood the day he disappeared. He bought a tire at a Rolls-Royce dealership. Would you have any idea why he might've gone to Hollywood?"

"Hollywood? No! I'm shocked! He came to the desert that weekend because he was tired from final exams at college. His fiancée was coming. We have a Rolls dealer here in Palm Springs. Why would he go clear to Hollywood for a tire?"

"He wouldn't," Otto said. "He must've had another reason for going."

"I have no idea why he'd drive two hours when he was here to rest. And I can't imagine why he'd take the Rolls."

"Why do you say that?" asked Sidney Blackpool.

"He hated the Rolls. So pretentious, he always said. Wouldn't even ride in it. He had his own car, a Porsche Nine-eleven his mom bought him. If he was going into town for something urgent he'd drive that Porsche."

"You sure about that?" Otto asked.

"Without a doubt. He never told his folks how he hated that Rolls but he told me lots of times. That's why he never flew here when he'd come on weekends. He didn't want to be stuck driving a Rolls-Royce. He always drove down to the desert so he'd have his own car to run around in."

"Did he come here often? To rest, I mean?" Sidney Blackpool asked.

"Oh, maybe twice a month during the school year. For two or three days at a time."

"In the police report his dad said that Jack seldom came here alone."

"Actually, Jack came here more than they knew," Harlan Penrod said. "His mom and dad're very busy people and he usually told them he was staying at the fraternity house, but he'd come here. I never mentioned it because right after he died I didn't want to say anything more than I had to."

"Why's that?" Otto asked.

"I'd only been working for the Watsons about six months at that time, and I heard Mister Watson describe Jack to the police. Such a bright, decent, hardworking student, he said, and yes, Jack was all that, but . . ."

"What?"

"Jack frequently came to Palm Springs to spend weekends, but never when his folks were here, and he never wanted them to know. He told me not to let on."

"Did you ever ask him why?"

"He said his dad treated him like a kid and might snoop around."

"Snoop around?"

"Sergeant, he was a gorgeous kid twenty-two years old! When he went out at night I imagine he ended up at a disco. I mean, he had a fiancée, sure, but lots of pretty college girls come in from San Diego and L.A. You know how it is to be twenty-two."

Sidney Blackpool looked at Otto and said, "Anything else?"

"Did *you* ever think he was kidnapped from the house?" Otto asked.

"Really, no," Harlan said, and his eyes had started to fill from talking about Jack Watson. "I mean, I know how dark it is in this neighborhood at night and how close we are to a ghetto, but everyone has all sorts of burglar alarms. And people are so careful. The old rich people, they'd rather have too much darkness than streetlights that might disturb their sleep.

They don't even want police helicopters. Everyone's in bed at nine o'clock."

"Rather curse the darkness, eh?" Sidney Blackpool said, standing up. "Do those infrareds still work, the ones on top of those walls?"

"I think so."

"Do you always turn them on?"

"Oh, yes. I arm the burglar alarms inside and out before I go to bed, and whenever I'm out. Sometimes, though, it gets so lonely I'd almost welcome a burglar. If he wasn't *mean*."

"Careful, Harlan," Otto said. "Sometimes strange bedfellows make *strange* bedfellows."

Chapter 7

THE WEAPON

Officer Barney Wilson would've had an uneventful career in the Coachella Valley if he hadn't gotten caught up in the labor movement. His career somewhat paralleled Ronald Reagan's. That is, he was just a spear carrier until he made a speech on behalf of a colleague who was running for president of the police union. But Barney Wilson never would've made that speech nor *any* speech were it not for a desert physician who, during a routine annual physical, called the twenty-nine-year-old cop into his office and gave him the good news first. No, he didn't have the clap as he'd feared. He could keep the same girlfriend and he wouldn't have to make any confessions to his wife. The bad news was that he'd only have the girlfriend for two years. Ditto for the wife.

Barney Wilson stared dumbstruck at the doctor who looked mildly cranky, as though he had to take a no-pay emergency and couldn't lay it off to the county.

"You've got red blood cells in your urine. Acute glomerulonephritis. Two years *maybe*," the doctor said, checking the wall clock because he had a Wednesday afternoon golf date.

During the next three weeks a Coachella Valley legend was born. Barney Wilson stood up for a buddy and addressed the entire police department during a very controversial police strike. And after consuming twenty-two cans of beer in a three-hour period he said that the chief of police was a pompous asshole with all the humility of Fidel Castro, Muammar Qaddafi and Barbra Streisand. He said to the delight of the sign-carrying cops that they ought to sabotage the chief's hemorrhoid-alleviating whoopee cushion with gelignite, and load his cigarettes with PCP.

And since a dying man knows few limits, Officer Wilson delighted the mob of recalcitrant cops by calling the chief a plastic man who probably used Armor-all in his bathtub. At the end of the rousing speech, while all the local newshounds were snapping pictures like mad, Officer Wilson said that the chief ran his department like a banana republic, and with eyes overflowing at the thought of his imminent demise, he finished to a thunderous ovation by saying to the chief whose lieutenants recorded *every* word: "Give us liberty or give us death!"

From that day forward Officer Barney Wilson became known all over the Coachella Valley as Nathan Hale Wilson, and was nominated as president of the police union.

Then, to satisfy his grieving family, he went to his mom's hematologist for a second opinion.

The blood doctor asked if he'd had the flu prior to the examination when he'd gotten the Bad News. Receiving an affirmative answer, the new croaker asked if he'd taken up jogging at about the time he had the first exam, and when Nathan Hale Wilson said, yes indeedy and how long do you think I got? the physician said, "Fifty years if you take care of yourself. Lots less when the chief of police discovers you're *not* a dying man."

That afternoon, with the assurance that he *was* going to need a job for a very long time, Nathan Hale Wilson found himself driving up to Mineral Springs to see if Paco Pedroza could use a cop with a short-lived career in the American labor movement.

"I might give you a chance," Paco Pedroza warned Nathan Hale Wilson that day. "But I don't need no César Chavez around here."

"I'm through with organized labor, Chief," Nathan Hale Wilson promised. "I was just off my nut for a while because a that croaker I'm gonna sue."

"That's good," Paco said, "cause you know that golf course down in Indian Wells? The one owned by the Teamsters Union? I heard that Jimmy Hoffa lives there. *Under* the sixteenth fairway."

"I'm through with labor unions," Nathan Hale Wilson promised. "I won't even watch a movie with Charlton Heston or Ed Asner in it."

136

"He seems like a good honest lad," said Sergeant Harry Bright, the chief's confidant.

"Okay, I'll take a chance on you," Paco Pedroza told him. "I'll give you to my F.B.I. man to break you in."

"F.B.I. man?"

"Full-blooded Indian. Maynard Rivas. Probably find him in the Eleven Ninety-nine Club later today. Just look for flowered wallpaper. That'll be him. He likes loud shirts."

"Big guy, huh?"

"*Lots* a room for tattoos," Paco nodded.

Maynard Rivas grew up on the Morongo Reservation. All the Morongos had in this world was some arid desert land and a bingo parlor large enough to house the Spruce Goose.

Maynard spent his life wishing he were an Agua Caliente Indian, that band of Mission Indians who own big chunks of downtown Palm Springs. Every other square mile is theirs and the tenants pay rent that has gone through the roof in modern times. One local Indian, it was rumored, received $20,000 every ninety days. Another, it was said, got that much every *month*.

The Palm Springs Indians are the richest per capita in America and are no longer under the care of the Department of the Interior, which was accused of "commingling" the Indians' trust fund. (It was awhile before the Indians were informed that "commingling" is called "stealing" in their language.) The Indians don't pay income tax on their trust, only on their investments. Some are sophisticated and take advantage of tribal scholarships. Some would just as soon sit under a tamarisk tree forever. Some are hypes and angel-dusters.

So when tourists ask the locals, "Where do the Indians live?," the locals answer, "Wherever they want. They got the bucks."

If only the Morongos and Agua Calientes had swapped land eighty years ago Maynard would be driving a Ferrari while *they*'d be pulling into gas stations for two bucks' worth of gas saying, "I keep it light for racing." And they'd be listening to a bunch of maniac housewives from Banning screaming "Bingo!" in their nightmares.

Maynard Rivas had always wanted to get away from the Morongo Reservation and especially the bingo parlor. It was a few miles from two life-sized statues of dinosaurs, an enormous fruit stand, and a few thousand wind turbines. Other than looking at the big lizards and windmills, there just wasn't much to do but get drunk. He had moved to L.A. County a few years earlier and hired on as a cop.

Many of the Morongos were large, but Maynard was a jumbo Indian. A four-inch service revolver looked like a derringer in his hand.

During his rookie year he won a citation for heroism for saving the life of a phantom who'd been driving the police nuts. The phantom was one of those "radio announcers" that just pop up from time to time at police agencies everywhere. The kind that sneak into police cars if the cops leave them unlocked and unattended for five minutes and pick up the mike to talk dirty to the communications operators. This particular phantom radio announcer would just say, "Cocksucker." That's all. When asked to repeat his message, he sometimes would. Or sometimes he'd just say, "That is all." Or "Over and out." Or "Ten-four." Or some such radio gibberish.

It was Maynard Rivas who caught the phantom announcer when he was sneaking into a sergeant's car while the sergeant was having a jelly roll at Winchell's. The radio announcer had hair like Harpo Marx and looked twice as dumb. The big Indian chased him into an office building and up the stairway where the phantom climbed out on the fire escape and attracted a crowd, several of them cops who yelled, "We'll catch you!" But not being *that* dumb, he didn't jump.

Maynard Rivas talked a construction foreman into putting him in the bucket of a crane and he was lifted up to the fire escape. Maynard confused the phantom by saying, "You don't wanna breathe my air no more? You want me outta your face? Okay, bye-bye."

And while the phantom radio announcer contemplated that suicide meant no more days of whispering "cocksucker" into police radio mikes, Maynard Rivas made a daring leap from the crane onto the fire escape, snatching the phantom under his arm like a football. But he wasn't a hero for long.

What ended the big Indian's police career in Los Angeles County was a South American fish. In fact, several of them who had no business being in America in the first place.

Maynard was providing backup to some narcs on a raid on a million-dollar house in the foothills. As it turned out, the raid netted them only two Peruvian dope dealers and an Eastern European student who was there to buy some flake. They found a very small amount of cocaine on the student who happened to be the kid of a Bulgarian diplomat. The old man had diplomatic immunity and later argued that his kids did also.

It was a very disappointing raid and six of the cops left quickly. Two uniformed cops, one of them Maynard Rivas, ended up with the three prisoners while the plainclothes narcs searched the guesthouse out back.

The smallest Peruvian looked at one uniformed cop and then at Maynard Rivas and said, "Señor, may I speak to you privately?"

Maynard Rivas, who was about three times as big as the Peruvian, wasn't too worried about tricks, especially since all three suspects were handcuffed.

"Keep an eye on them," he said to his

partner, taking the Peruvian into the foyer.

"If joo weel take my handcuffs off, I weel locate the cocaine," the Peruvian said.

"Oh, yeah? I look like I just walked out of a teepee, huh? You wanna tell us where the coke is, do it with the cuffs *on*. In fact, tell the narcs. I'm just here to baby-sit anyways."

"They slapped my face. I weel not tell them nothing. I weel tell joo or I weel tell nobody."

"So tell me."

"Please, señor, my wreests! I am een much pain. Joo have searched me. I am a leetle man. Joo are a giant."

Maynard waffled for a moment, but decided if this squirt could take Maynard Rivas, he *should* go back to the reservation and spend his life screaming "B ten" and "O seventy-five."

"You and me're gonna hold hands while you show me," Maynard said, removing the cuffs and letting the Peruvian rub some circulation back.

"Thank joo berry much, señor," the Peruvian said. "Please come weeth me, and I weel geev joo what joo weesh."

It was a fish tank. But what a fish tank. It dominated the living room: a hundred-gallon, lighted, filtered aquarium housing twenty fish. They were funny-looking black fish and they had very big teeth.

"Een there," the man whispered as his crime partner cried, "*¡Silencio, cabrón!*," and tried to jump up from the couch but was jerked back by Maynard's partner.

"In there?" Maynard Rivas pointed.

"There!" the Peruvian nodded.

There was a clear plastic bag at the bottom of the tank. The cocaine was camouflaged by the white material on the tank bottom. It looked like a three-pound bag, at least.

Maynard Rivas started rolling up his sleeve, hoping to surprise the narcs who would be back in the main house in a few minutes.

"They are piranha, señor," the Peruvian said calmly.

"Piranha!" his partner said, and he left the prisoners momentarily to step over to the huge aquarium, which was mounted at eye level on a massive credenza.

There was a tool box containing plumbing equipment beside the tank. The cops were amazed at the voracious fish swimming in frantic loops, examining the faces outside the tank with dumb savage eyes.

"Piranha!" Maynard Rivas said.

"Piranha!" his partner said.

"Monkey wrench!" the Peruvian said.

He snatched it from the tool box: a monkey wrench. He used the Jimmy Connors two-handed, off-the-feet service return. On the glass.

And then people were screaming and jumping and yelling.

"Killer fish! Killer fish!"

"Look out! Look *out!*"

"Watch joo feets! Joo *feets!*"

The piranhas were all over the floor and all over the huge Indian cop who was skating all over the floor, and the little Peruvian had himself a big .45 caliber automatic, which had been hanging on the back of the credenza, and he started for the back door.

Maynard Rivas grabbed the other Peruvian in a choke hold and put his own gun to the guy's head, saying, "Drop your gun or I'll shoot!"

Maynard realized how stupid *that* was when the little Peruvian shrugged as if to say, "Then I get to keep *both* shares."

Greed got the doper. He stopped long enough to pick up the plastic bag when he should have run straight outside. He was coldcocked from behind by a sneaky narc, and he flopped on the floor beside the killer fish.

An official protest was made from the Bulgarian ambassador to the United States Secretary of State, deploring the fascist behavior of Officer Maynard Rivas who got reprimanded for improper police tactics. Maynard decided that if a Native American could be attacked and nearly killed by Peruvian dopers and nearly eaten by Brazilian fish and called a fascist by a Commie Pope-shooter, he was going back to the Coachella Valley where life was a whole lot less complicated.

But he knew he had a choice of pulling numbered balls from a wire cage or finding a local police force that wanted a good old home-boy redskin. He ended up in the office of Chief Paco Pedroza who along with Sergeant Harry Bright listened to Maynard's life story. Paco finally said, "Can you track people in the desert and stuff like that? Real Indian stuff?"

"Chief Pedroza," Maynard said patiently, "I can do street police work good as anybody, but if you need an injun in braids and moccasins, you better call Marlon Brando for a referral."

"Well, you seem like a fine strong lad. I imagine you'd be a good worker," Sergeant Harry Bright said.

"I'll give you a go, Maynard," Paco said. "But I wonder, could you sometimes help my wife on Thursday nights? See, she runs the bingo game at Saint Martha's Church."

Maynard Rivas and Nathan Hale Wilson were doing some plain old ordinary Mineral Springs police work on the morning that Sidney Blackpool and Otto Stringer visited the Palm Springs residence of Victor Watson.

Maynard took a radio call and asked for a backup when he realized the address of a disturbance was the home of Clyde and Bernice Suggs who, whenever they got drunk for breakfast, slugged it out by lunchtime for sure.

This particular fight was pretty much like the last except for the weapons involved. As usual, Clyde got sick and tired of Bernice's rolling her mean little woodpecker eyes just because he put a little *too* much into a turkey trot he did with a seventy-five-year-old pepper-pot at the Moose Lodge seniors' dance. He told her that if she didn't quit clicking her dentures he was going to dump his bowl of All-Bran right on her head. One thing led to another and she took the old James Cagney role and shoved a grapefruit in *his* face. He threw the All-Bran. At first, both were careful not to spill the jug of Sweet Lucy on the kitchen table, but things got totally out of hand when he claimed that she was a lousy lay and had been for the forty-eight years they'd been together. That *really* started the yelling and screaming, and pretty quick they were both tossing everything that wasn't too heavy, and the neighbors put in the call that had become a weekly experience for the Mineral Springs P.D.

When Maynard Rivas and Nathan Hale Wilson arrived, the domestic violence was still in a semi-explosive state though both combatants were now wheezing and blowing and too exhausted to do more than slap at each other with wimpy blows. She was bigger and he was two years older so it wasn't a mismatch. In fact, Clyde was in pretty bad shape because his tracheostomy tube nearly jumped out of his throat every time she popped him a good one.

The little guy was still trying gamely to give as good as he got, and his dirty white undershirt was dripping sweat when Maynard Rivas slipped into the living room and lifted him off his feet, while Nathan Hale Wilson carried Bernice over by her rocker where their tomcat, Jasper, sat inspecting his ass, not even remotely concerned by all this human drama.

"Break it up, Clyde!" Maynard Rivas commanded.

"Lemme go, you big asshole!" Clyde said. "This is *my* house!" Because of the tracheostomy he sounded like a cross between Wolfman Jack and the demon from *The Exorcist*.

"Not till you stop fighting," Maynard said.

"I'll sue you!" Clyde croaked.

"Injuns got immunity," Maynard lied.

"The only good Indian is a . . ."

"Yeah, yeah, I saw all the cowboy movies," Maynard said. "Now relax and quit squirming!"

"Make her promise first! She'll blind-side me, the sneaky bitch!"

"Promise you won't hit him, Bernice," Nathan Hale Wilson ordered the old woman.

"I ain't promising nothing!" Bernice Suggs said, still kicking. "Let him fight like a man!"

It was no use telling them they were going to jail. They knew very well that the cops wouldn't risk the bad press Mineral Springs would get if they booked these miserable old geezers. Even though every cop in town would dearly love to toss them in the slam. They'd *all* been spit at, cursed, and reviled by Clyde and Bernice Suggs.

"Okay, you'll go to the station and sit in the holding tank till you promise to behave!"

Maynard said, heading for the door with Clyde tucked under his arm.

"Wait a minute, you big prick!" Clyde croaked. "Lemme go! I won't fight no more!"

Maynard reluctantly released Clyde who hobbled stoop-shouldered over to the rocker where he punched at the tomcat who hissed but gave up the chair. Clyde sat for a spell, fussing with his trachea tube, trying to get sufficient air to make one of his long croaky speeches about the mentality of cops, especially big Indian cops and scrawny paleface cops that're probably dumber than big Indians.

Nathan Hale Wilson made the mistake of letting Bernice go just because she stopped fighting. The old woman mumbled a few cuss words and looked as though she was going to surrender, but while the two cops were giving the tipplers their standard warning about not tolerating this disgusting behavior anymore, Bernice grabbed something from the sideboard where it rested next to the Mineral Springs penny saver.

Just as Clyde was getting ready to deliver his monologue about police mentality, Bernice swung. Clyde caught the leading edge smack behind the skull and his upper plate shot through the air, bouncing off the ample belly of Maynard Rivas. Then the fight was *really* on. Bernice jumped on Clyde and jerked the trachea tube out of his throat and wouldn't let go even when the big Indian pounced on her and Nathan Hale Wilson grabbed at her crooked fingers.

"Uuuuuuuhhhhh!" Clyde croaked, while Bernice clamped onto that tube and with her one remaining eyetooth glinting wolfishly said, "Now let's you and *me* do the turkey trot, you old son of a bitch!"

Since Bernice was a touch arthritic and not as tough as she used to be, Nathan Hale Wilson got the tube out of her claws while all four wrestled on the floor.

"Let go the tube!" Maynard yelled. "He can't breathe!"

"I'll stuff it with cat shit!" Bernice screamed back at him until Maynard gave her such a shove she did a backward whoop-de-doo and bumped her head on the coffee table, out of action temporarily.

Twenty minutes later the two cops, uniforms dusty and torn, were at the police station with Clyde and Bernice Suggs *and* the weapon.

"I can't book these people!" Paco Pedroza whispered after Clyde and Bernice were cooling their heels in the holding tank. "They're nearly eighty years old!"

"That's an ADW," Nathan Hale Wilson said. "A felony. I'm sick a these old fuckers, Chief."

"A ukulele ain't exactly a deadly weapon," Paco said.

"No, but jerking out his trachea tube is a pretty goddamn aggravated assault, you ask me!"

148

"Oh, so you wanna book Bernice and let Clyde go home, huh? He's more acceptable?"

"He's as acceptable as a lesion on my dick," Nathan Hale Wilson said, with the conviction of a man who's had a few. "But at least one a them oughtta get something outta this."

"If they both apologize will you be satisfied?" Paco argued. "And if they promise *never* to do it again? Jesus, can you imagine the picture in the newspaper if we take these two down to the Indio Hilton and lock them up?"

"Okay, okay," Nathan Hale Wilson said finally. "But don't make us drive em back home. That's degrading!"

"The walk'll do em good," Paco said. "Let em out five minutes apart. Okay with you, Maynard?"

"Okay," the Indian said. "Which one gets the weapon?"

"Lemme see that," Paco said. "Funny-looking ukulele. One, two, three . . . this one's got *eight* strings. Never saw a uke with eight strings." Then he strummed it a few times. "Wish I could play music."

Clyde Suggs made an announcement from the holding cell: "This is the Foreign Legion for misfit cops, but Paco Pedroza sure ain't no Beau Geste!"

"See, that's part a the problem here," Paco said to Maynard. "Clyde's read a couple books in his time and thinks he married beneath him."

149

Five minutes later, when Maynard Rivas was leading Clyde to the door, Paco was sitting with his feet up on his desk singing his heart out. " 'Ain't she sweet!' " he sang, strumming away discordantly.

Maynard interrupted him. "Uh, Chief, time to give Clyde back the deadly weapon."

"Oh, yeah," Paco said. "Here you go, Clyde. Nice uke."

"I bought it to serenade Bernice," the old man croaked. "Now I'd like to stick it in her . . ."

"Okay, *enough* violence!" Paco warned.

The old man was still mighty pissed off as he trudged down the Mineral Springs main drag. He started toward the back door of the Eleven Ninety-nine Club but stopped when he thought about all the goddamn cops that hung around there. He cut through the eucalyptus trees toward the Mirage Saloon.

"I'll have a beer," Clyde said, when he hobbled up to the bar. "A pitcher. Will you take this for a pitcher a beer? Make it *two* pitchers."

"A uke?" Ruben the bartender said. "Where'd you get it?"

"Paid fifteen bucks for it from Beavertail Bigelow," Clyde said. "You can have it for two pitchers."

"Okay," the bartender said. "Looks like it's in pretty good shape except for this dent."

"That's from my skull," Clyde croaked. "I

was gonna serenade Bernice with it. Now she can just watch *Love Boat* and go suck her tooth."

Chapter 8

REQUIEM

The detectives couldn't get away from Harlan Penrod until they'd had a complete tour of the Watson property, which meant a dissertation on Coachella cacti and desert flora in general. And while Otto Stringer was learning about how such spiny plants could produce such lovely blossoms, Sidney Blackpool was satisfying himself that, just as the Palm Springs detectives had concluded in their reports, nobody who wasn't played by Sean Connery or Roger Moore could defeat the infrared on the top of the fence with the old mirror trick. And if the system was armed, nobody could have silently forced open the electric gate as he and Otto had done. Harlan Penrod was adamant that Jack Watson was as careful as he about setting the inside and outside alarm systems before retiring for the night. That didn't mean that he wasn't snatched from the house, but if he was, it probably wasn't by an unknown intruder.

Instead of going to Palm Springs P.D., they went back to the hotel. Otto wanted to "take" brunch.

"Is this going to be part a your life now, Otto? Taking brunch?" Sidney Blackpool asked, as they left his car with the valet-parking boy.

"I'm hungry from all the good police work, Sidney," Otto said. "I think we should go to Palm Springs P.D. tomorrow. Maybe we oughtta play a few holes today after brunch."

"I don't think I'm ready to eat. I'll go up to the room and give the P.D. a call."

"You're getting too skinny, Sidney," Otto said. "Come and join me."

"I'll have dessert later," Sidney Blackpool said, leaving his partner in the hotel lobby.

When Sidney Blackpool got to their suite, he found a bottle of Dom Pérignon champagne and a card saying: "Hit em long and straight. Victor Watson."

He lit a cigarette and flopped down on the bed, trying not to think of Victor Watson. He hadn't felt sorry for anyone except himself in a long time. He didn't want to start feeling sorry for some guy who probably owned his own jet and didn't bother to play golf in places Sidney Blackpool dreamed about because Watson probably enjoyed himself even more in other places. But then the detective had to admit that the man he'd met in the Century City office wasn't enjoying himself anywhere. That was an incomplete human being looking for missing pieces.

He realized that the radio was on. The housekeeper had made the beds and tidied up the suite but let the radio play. It was a Palm

Springs station with music that wasn't so easy to find on the Los Angeles scene. Marlene Dietrich was singing "La Vie en Rose" and "Lili Marlene." Sidney Blackpool's parents and his older brothers listened to music like that when he was a boy. There was something about the desert. You *did* feel that time had regressed thirty years or more. There was something in the air, and not just the dry heat. Those mountains surrounding? Like *Lost Horizon* with Ronald Colman clawing his way toward the hidden valley, toward peace and longevity. But you didn't live forever in Palm Springs either, as Jack Watson discovered.

Then his heart missed a regular beat, and another, and he felt an emptiness in his chest and swelling in his throat that made it hard to swallow. He had an indescribable longing? For what? He used to think the dreams came because he kept family pictures beside the bed, but after he put them away he still dreamed. That was something else that Victor Watson had probably learned: you're afraid to be reminded and afraid *not* to be reminded.

Victor Watson probably learned that the first weeks after his son's death were nothing compared to what would come. The shock and horror and grief is impossible to accommodate those first weeks, as you gradually come to grasp what *forever* means. There is nonsense which your mind seizes upon. Should Tommy be put in the ground or cremated? As though a decision to keep Tommy's fingernails and teeth and bones intact was a meaningful one.

Yet all that was nothing like the despair that peaked eight months after Tommy was gone. When, for the first time in forty-one years of life, Sidney Blackpool had to confront this *outrage*, a son preceding his father to the grave. This *perversion* of the natural order.

He came close to the end at a police department retirement party in Chinatown. He heard a morose retired cop crying in his whiskey because he no longer had camaraderie and purpose. The cop said he couldn't enjoy things any longer and talked about looking for pieces of himself. Sidney Blackpool could've told him a thing or two about that, about being *incomplete*.

But he listened and started to despise the cop. He despised him so much he found himself starting to cry. The first time ever in a public place. Of course, he had also been drinking that night. He rushed outside to the parking lot and looked not up to the smog-shrouded sky but at the lights of downtown Los Angeles.

He thought of that maudlin cop, and he cried out: "Why are *you* alive then? Why *you* and not Tommy?"

Then he saw another cop stagger out of the party heading for a car he shouldn't have been driving, and he scared the man by yelling: "Why *you*? Why *you*, you son of a bitch? And why *me*?"

Then Sidney Blackpool for the first time *did*

look up (childhood training perhaps) and he shouted, "Okay, that's enough. I've had enough now. That's it. I've had *enough!*"

He knew he was *very* close then. He used to sit alone in the night, cold sober sometimes, and indulge dangerous fantasies. The setting of all fantasies preceded the day in 1983 when Tommy died. He could somehow stop the event from happening, in the fantasies.

And sometimes he indulged in daydreams set in the present. He'd receive an urgent call from his ex-wife saying, "Sid! Sid! It's a miracle! Tommy's alive! It wasn't *his* body they pulled from the surf! It was a mistake and Tommy's been in Mexico all this time and . . ."

It was so absurd and pathetic and shameful that he was never able to indulge that one to the end. He didn't will it, but the fantasy came. After the night in Chinatown he knew that if he let this continue he would die. He read that it most often happened on a Monday, on the fifth day of the month, and in the spring. He decided that since something had ruthlessly reversed the natural order of things in his life, he would perversely defy statistical probability. He came very very close one Saturday night in September, the twenty-second day of the month. Only thinking of his daughter, Barb, at the last moment saved him from smoking it.

Sidney Blackpool sat up in the hotel bed, cursed himself, *hated* himself, and dialed the Palm Springs P.D. asking for the homicide investigator named on the reports.

"Finney's not here," the telephone voice said. "This is Lieutenant Sanders. Can I help you?"

"Sid Blackpool, Lieutenant. I think your boss was told we were coming?"

"Oh, yeah, sorry about Finney. His mother's real sick and he took off yesterday for Minnesota."

"When's he coming back?"

"Depends on her."

"Can anybody else talk about the Watson case?"

"I guess I can. You have copies of the reports, I understand. Not too much to add."

"The reports said you checked out all the radio stations in the desert about that singing voice."

"Finney even checked stations in L.A., Vegas and San Diego in case it was some high-powered radio heard by the Mineral Springs cop. Nobody played 'Pretend' at that time of day. And no singer ever recorded 'Pretend' with only a banjo behind him, far as we know. So Jones either heard a live voice or a tape. He was damn near into heat stroke so we can't be sure."

"If it was a live voice it's kinda bizarre."

"Kinda morbid. If it was live it means the guy that killed the kid came back and sang a little requiem over the corpse."

"Are you sure the car was actually torched? I mean, it *did* crash down a canyon."

"No, we're not positive. The gas tank was ruptured by the crash. That car could a caught fire on its own. In fact, if it wasn't for that thirty-eight hollow-point slug in the skull, we had nothing but a fatal traffic accident. The kid drove off a dark canyon trail where he never shoulda been without a four-wheel-drive vehicle. His car caught fire and he died a crispy critter. Period."

"Too bad there wasn't a gun found at the scene," Sidney Blackpool said. "You coulda maybe figured it to be a suicide where the car rolled off the hill after the kid shot himself."

"No gun," the lieutenant said. "And a very bad angle for a right-handed suicide."

"About how many people live in those canyons?"

"No people. About sixty dirtbag methamphetamine dealers. No *Homo sapiens* allowed in Solitaire Canyon. They cook up speed in those shacks, but it's almost impossible to get probable cause to bust them. Even if you have a warrant, they can see you coming for two miles and bury the evidence in holes they dig. Lots a those bikers are Vietnam vets. They're a chapter of the Cobras motorcycle gang."

"Any chance he drove up there because he *wanted* to?"

"Not much chance," the lieutenant said. "He seldom drove the Rolls. In fact, I was surprised to get the call from Watson saying the kid drove the Rolls to Hollywood. He wasn't a speed user. And not that it was productive, but we *did* question every crank dealer and desert rat living around that particular canyon. All negative. We have this crime-stoppers program where citizens donate reward money. Better known on the streets as dial-a-snitch or burn-a-buddy. And after Victor Watson offered a fifty-thousand-dollar reward I think lots a cranked-out bikers'd roll over on each other if they knew *anything*. We got nothing. All we know is Watson's car went over the canyon and caught fire. He was pinned in the wreckage. Turns out he was shot in the head before he got cooked, lucky for him."

"Of course no chance to dust for prints in a burned wreck."

"We got a very diligent fingerprint man. Name is Hoffman. He dusts everything. He even dusted the dust. Once he dusted an assault victim's tits, which bought him a three-day suspension. We call him Dustin Hoffman. He got nothing."

"And then a freak came back a few days after the murder and sang 'Pretend.' "

"That's about it. The singer mighta been some prospector or nature lover. Or even a speed head who was just out for a stroll in the canyons after shooting his arms full a crystal. Officer Jones mighta just heard an innocent bystander."

"Could be," Sidney Blackpool said.

"But we doubt it."

"Why's that?"

"In those canyons there's no such thing. Everybody that lives there's a *not* so innocent bystander. The Mineral Springs cop probably heard the killer all right."

"Returning to sing a requiem?"

"Maybe to look for something he lost."

Sidney Blackpool gave the Palm Springs lieutenant his telephone number and said goodbye, took two aspirins, rinsed his face and lit a cigarette. He was entering the dining room where Otto was still working on his brunch when the bell captain came in.

"Mister Blackpool?"

"Yeah."

"The front desk just took a call for you from the Palm Springs police."

"I just hung up." Sidney Blackpool shrugged to Otto who was leering at a huge wedge of coconut-cream pie.

"Have a bite first," Otto said.

"Lemme go see what it is."

While Sidney Blackpool was gone, Otto not only ate the pie but asked the waiter if he thought a piña colada would be too rich as an after-brunch drink. When his partner returned, Otto was leaning back in the chair, his belly pressing the table, sucking a tall coconut and vodka special with a little parasol stuck in a wedge of orange.

"This is the life, Sidney," he said with three rapid-fire belches.

160

"Guess what?" Sidney Blackpool said. "That was the Palm Springs lieutenant. They got a call earlier this morning that he just learned about. The Mineral Springs cop who found the body called to say he's decided the song the suspect sang wasn't 'Pretend.' It was 'I Believe.' "

"Not sure I know that one."

"You'd know it if you heard it. A Frankie Laine hit. You're old enough."

"Thank you very much, Sidney. You're so kind to remind me."

"Anyway, whaddaya think a that? The very day we get on the case, they receive the first piece a new information they've gotten in over a year."

"Sidney, it can't make any possible difference what the lunatic was singing. *If* in fact that *was* the killer returning to the scene a the crime like in Agatha Christie."

"I know, but it's the coincidence of it. It seems like *more* than a coincidence. We come here and something happens. After all this time."

"What's *more* than a coincidence mean?" Otto asked, looking sorry that he'd had the piña colada.

And then Sidney Blackpool thought of the tortured face of Victor Watson, an old man's hollow face under those track lights. "I don't know," he said. "Maybe an omen."

Instead of playing nine holes they were off to Mineral Springs to talk to Officer O. A. Jones about his musical revelation.

"Jesus, how we gonna find out if every radio station in two hundred miles didn't play 'I Believe' on that day last year?" Otto asked. "We *gotta* get in some golf. All I'm doing is eating and drinking!"

" 'I Believe' with a banjo? I think someone was there that day. Maybe Jones heard a live voice."

"All we gotta find is a banjo man with a taste for old songs. Let's see, Steve Martin plays one, I think. Maybe Roy Clark or Glenn Campbell? Jesus."

"Shaggy clouds and shaggy trees," Sidney Blackpool said. "It's got a threatening look sometimes, this desert."

"Know what I noticed, Sidney? It changes. I mean, it never looks the same one minute to the next."

"The cloud shadow," Sidney Blackpool said, looking up from under his sunglasses as he drove. "It throws shadow and light and color everywhere. And the colors change. This is a strange place. I don't know if I like it or not."

"I'm gonna love it," Otto said. "If we ever get on the freaking golf links. I ain't hit a ball in over a month."

"Three weeks," his partner reminded. "At Griffith Park. I bet these courses won't look like Griffith Park."

"You mean no tank tops? No beer cans or tattooed arms? No sound of thongs slapping the feet when your playing partner steps outta his Ford pickup? Hey, what's that?" Otto pointed three miles off in the distance toward the base of the mountains.

"That's where six thousand souls survive in this desert because a the golf and tennis and piña colada we just left," said Sidney Blackpool. "That's Mineral Springs."

"Kinda windy around here," Otto said, watching a dozen whirlwinds dancing across the desert in the shimmering rising heat. "Bad place to die out in those lonely canyons."

"Doesn't much matter where," Sidney Blackpool said, lighting a cigarette, looking at the shacks that dotted the trails high in the hills. "Have to be *real* important to drive up there at night."

"I'd have to be *forced* to make the drive."

"Possibly," Sidney Blackpool said.

When they arrived, Chief Paco Pedroza had a case of heartburn from yelling at Wingnut Bates and Prankster Frank. He had forbidden any more threats to shoot Prankster Frank on sight, explaining that he needed every cop he had. And he prohibited snakes — real, rubber or photographic — from being brought into the station. In that spirit, Paco even removed the picture of the sidewinder on the sign that said "We don't give a shit how they do it in L.A."

After sending his cops back to work he was dozing with his feet up when the Hollywood detectives announced themselves to Anemic Annie, the pale, birdlike civilian at the front desk.

"In here, fellas," Paco said. "Siddown. Want some coffee?"

"No, thanks, Chief," Sidney Blackpool said, as the three men shook hands. "He's Stringer. I'm Blackpool."

"Call me Paco. I used to work Hollywood. You mightta heard?"

"We did," Otto said. "We were both at Newton Street at that time."

"Pinkford was captain then," Paco said. "He still on the department?"

"Yep," Otto nodded, "and will be till Ronald Reagan goes gray."

"Pinkford never wanted much outta life," Paco said. "Just enough glue to stick his face on Mount Rushmore. I woulda walked a beat in Sri Lanka to get away from him. Anyways, I'm glad to see you boys're wearing your golf rags. Most L.A. cops come out this way in suits and neckties even if it's a hundred and twenty degrees."

"Actually, Chief, this is sort of a vacation," Sidney Blackpool said.

"Paco."

"Paco. We're just here for some golf. Our boss said we might do a little follow-up since Victor Watson recently learned that his kid visited Hollywood on the day he disappeared from Palm Springs. Apparently the kid made a quick trip into town and back to the desert."

"Mean anything?" Paco asked.

"Not yet," Otto said. "Reason we came to your department is to talk to Officer O. A. Jones. He called Palm Springs P.D. today with some new information about the song he heard the suspect singing."

"O. A. Jones," Paco grunted. "That little fucker's gonna get me indicted some day. Does a job all right, but everything he does looks like it mighta happened a little different than he says. In fact, no desert's seen so much single-handed swashbuckling since Lawrence of Arabia. I don't know if you can rely on everything that surfer says."

"Surfer?" Sidney Blackpool said. "Where would he surf out here?"

"Ex-surfer," Paco said. "Used to be with Laguna Beach P.D. and then Palm Springs P.D. I took a chance on him and so far he ain't got in any traffic accidents where there might be one body too many. But that's another story. He's on duty today. Want Annie to call him for ya?"

"If you would," Otto said.

The three men walked from the chief's office into the main room of the police station. "Want a tour?" Paco asked.

"Sure," Otto said.

"Okay, turn around," said Paco. "There,

that's it. You got the tour. Except there's a john down the hall and ten wall lockers upstairs and a holding tank for two prisoners, long as they're little or awful friendly. The adjoining door goes to another room which is City Hall so we gotta keep our arrestees quiet till we get them down to the county jail."

"How do you keep them quiet?" Otto asked.

"Shoot the fuckers with a tranquilizer dart," Paco said. "What would *you* do with the animals we got around here?"

Anemic Annie tried without success to get O. A. Jones on the radio.

"He's probly got his ghetto blaster going full on," Paco said. "Why dontcha go on over to the Eleven Ninety-nine across the street. Get a cold one. I'll send O. A. Jones to ya in exactly forty-five minutes."

"*Exactly* forty-five minutes?"

"That's when his shift ends and he'll suddenly be all through with whatever sleuthing he's doing. He likes to get to the Eleven Ninety-nine before the first wave a secretaries and manicurists arrive from their jobs in Palm Springs. Among his many other faults he's got a permanent erection."

"So much for hitting the links," Otto sighed.

"By the way," Paco said, "when I got word where you boys're staying I figured things've changed at L.A.P.D. since I worked there. When we'd go out a town on a case they'd put us up at the Nighty Nite Motel with enough expense money for two hamburgers and a soda pop."

The detectives were saved from Paco's curiosity when the door swung open and Sergeant Coy Brickman entered. He was a tall man, taller than Sidney Blackpool, with furrowed cheeks and a mean-looking build. He was slightly older than Sidney Blackpool but looked lots older. His auburn hair was parted on the side and was receding. He stared at the two detectives without blinking and without speaking.

"Coy, this's Blackpool and Stringer," Paco said. "My sergeant, Coy Brickman."

They shook hands, and still without having blinked his eyes, Coy Brickman said, "Welcome to Mineral Springs. Hear you're gonna crack the Watson murder case."

"Not in my lifetime," Otto said. "We're just doing a semi-official follow-up to keep our boss happy."

"New leads?" Coy Brickman asked.

"Just bullshit," Otto said. "Some crap about the Watson kid visiting Hollywood the day he disappeared from the Palm Springs house. It's nothing."

"Well, anything we can do," Coy Brickman said.

"You the only field supervisor?" Sidney Blackpool asked.

"I got one other sergeant," Paco said. "Harry Bright. He was one good cop. Gonna have trouble replacing him."

"Was?"

"Harry had a stroke several months ago," Paco said. "Then a heart attack. He won't be coming back. Maybe not to this world even. Just lays in the hospital like petrified wood."

"He's holding his own," Coy Brickman said.

"Anyway, go get yourselves a cold one," Paco said. "I'll send O. A. Jones over soon as he blows in from his latest crime-crushing adventure."

J. Edgar Gomez was washing dishes behind the bar of the Eleven Ninety-nine Club when he saw the two strangers stop in their tracks to gape at the mural of John Wayne pissing on the miniature of Michael Jackson and Prince.

"I shoulda put Boy George between those two gender benders," J. Edgar Gomez said. "Maybe I'll do that one a these days when my artist is sober."

"Couple a beers," Sidney Blackpool said, checking his watch and seeing that it was still too early for Johnnie Walker Black.

"Kind you want?"

"Drafts," said Otto, thinking that if they were back in Palm Springs he'd order a beautiful exotic drink to put him in a holiday mood. It was depressing being in a cop saloon.

There were ten men and one woman sitting at the bar or at wooden tables scattered around the little dance floor. One look and the detectives knew they were all cops except for a desert rat in a brand-new cowboy hat who was sitting alone next to the jukebox glaring at everybody who stepped up to drop a quarter in. Beavertail Bigelow was not in a party mood that afternoon.

Six of the cops were from other desert police agencies. Representing Mineral Springs were Choo Choo Chester Conklin, Wingnut Bates and Nathan Hale Wilson, who was pretty well bagged for so early in the day.

The cops were moaning about what working in the desert was doing to them.

"Chapped lips. Jock rot to the knees," Wingnut moaned. "Sometimes I think I never shoulda left Orange County."

"How about what this freaking desert air does to your hair and fingernails?" Nathan Hale Wilson griped. "I can't keep them trimmed, they grow so fast. I was here a month and I looked like Howard Hughes!"

"You should work Indian territory," an off-duty Palm Springs cop complained. "I got a drunk call on two Agua Calientes yesterday and there's me all by myself and I got these two Indian brothers fighting each other cause they didn't have nobody else to fight, and they're so big they look like dueling refrigerators, and one throws a punch from the vicinity of Arizona and knocks the other one clear over my car. And I'm standing there thinking, he's a three-hundred-pounder. He thinks he's Crazy Horse. He's into a total uprising at this moment. He's got two broken beer bottles in his mitts. And he's *rich!*"

"Yeah, well you should see Cat City now," said a Cathedral City cop who was almost as drunk. "Sodom and Gomorrah East is what it is. AIDS and palimony is what it's all about."

J. Edgar Gomez eyed the two strangers and said, "What department you guys work?"

"L.A.P.D.," Otto answered, wincing. The beer was so cold he put the glass down and grabbed his skull.

"Drink it slow," J. Edgar Gomez said. "Keep our beer icy. Come outta the heat and drink too fast it's like a buck knife stuck in your skull. Here." He gave Otto a glass of warm water. "Sip it."

"Wow!" Otto said after the pain subsided. "That is *cold* beer."

"Customers like it that way. How come you guys're way out here?"

"We're in Palm Springs on vacation," Sidney Blackpool said. "Have to talk to O. A. Jones. Know him?"

"Sure," the saloonkeeper said, scratching his belly, which was covered by an apron and a wet T-shirt. "He'll be in pretty soon."

The door banged open just then and three policemen from Palm Springs P.D. swaggered in. J. Edgar Gomez shook his head and said, "Young cops these days, nobody can open a door without knocking holes in your plaster."

"Fred Astaire?" Sidney Blackpool said, pointing toward the jukebox. "I haven't heard Fred Astaire, or even a jukebox, in I don't know how long."

" 'Putting on the Ritz,' " J. Edgar Gomez grinned. "Far as I'm concerned, the world is divided between two groups a people: those that think Fred Astaire's 'Putting on the Ritz' is the greatest side ever cut, and scumbags that don't."

"My name's Stringer," Otto said, shaking hands with the saloonkeeper. "This is Sidney Blackpool."

"J. Edgar Gomez," the saloonkeeper said, and then added, "Oh, shit!"

They followed his eye line and saw that J. Edgar was looking about three feet above the floor at a midget in a tennis hat and tennis whites and a desert tan darker than any unemployed actor's.

"Oleg Gridley," the saloonkeeper said. Then he glared at the cops at the other end of the bar and pointed at the "No trash sports" sign over the bar, causing Otto and Sidney Blackpool to shrug at each other.

Oleg Gridley looked around the gloomy barroom, spotted the lone busty woman at the far end of the bar and hopped on the stool next to her by chinning up with both hands. He sat at eye level with her tits.

"Hi, Portia," the suntanned midget leered.

"I knew this day was going too good," she said, tipping up her glass of beer, looking like she'd had lots of them.

"Portia Cassidy," the saloonkeeper whispered to the detectives. "Not much of a face, but the best body in Mineral Springs. Everybody wants her, especially Oleg. We call them Bitch Cassidy and the Sunstroke Kid."

Just then Bitch Cassidy said to the midget, "No, Oleg. It's just that I don't like perverts. Even *big* perverts."

Then after the midget whispered in her ear again, she said, "Oleg, I wouldn't care it was big as King Kong's. Size don't impress me and I do not *want* a chiffon body wrap and a whipped-cream rubdown!"

"I'd be good to you, Portia," the passionate midget murmured. "I'm slow but thorough."

"Yeah, like a tarantula. I ain't interested. And I *don't* wanna do those filthy midget things, and if you don't leave me alone I'm calling a cop!"

"Maybe the things only *sound* filthy to nonmidgets," J. Edgar Gomez offered.

"I don't understand you anymore!" Oleg said testily. "J. Edgar, gimme a double bourbon on the rocks. And give the *lady* another beer."

"It's a living soap opera," J. Edgar Gomez said to the detectives, as he poured the midget's whiskey. "I'm starting to wonder how it's gonna come out."

And then they began to arrive. First a pair of hairdressers from the ladies' spa at the biggest downtown Palm Springs hotel. Then five tellers from a Palm Desert bank. Then four waitresses from a Rancho Mirage country club. Then the day-shift boys from eight police agencies, and by 5:30 in the afternoon the saloon was packed with drinkers, dancers, lechers, drunks, midgets and desert rats. Sidney Blackpool wondered how in hell they were going to find Officer O. A. Jones even if he did show up, and he should have arrived by now.

The conversations raged around them as the saloon got hotter and smokier. Both detectives switched to hard booze in self-defense. The only difference from any cop saloon in L.A. was that the talk was often weather-oriented.

"It's *so* hot in summer," Prankster Frank said to a new desert cop, "that I've started thinking in Celsius. It *sounds* cooler that way."

It was not *essentially* different in that most conversations were about women.

"*Look* at her!" Nathan Hale Wilson said of Portia Cassidy who was dancing with a Palm Springs detective and trying to avoid the "accidental" touches of Oleg Gridley every time he waddled to the jukebox. "She's the Lucretia Borgia of this valley but she could suck the Goodyear blimp through a garden hose."

"I got two planned parenthoods and one drunken mistake!" a drunken Maynard Rivas suddenly whined to a tipsy waitress from an Indian Wells country club who couldn't care less.

After the dance, Portia Cassidy tried to move

down the bar, hoping Oleg Gridley would get trampled if he tried to make open-field moves among three layers of legs. But the midget was relentless.

The detectives heard him whisper, "I gotta go to the little boys' room, Portia. I'll be right back and we'll talk."

"I can't wait," Bitch Cassidy sighed. "Like I can't wait for an acid rainstorm or world war three."

Oleg Gridley did not go to the little boys' room. The little boys' room was too *big* for Oleg Gridley. When the toilet stall was occupied, Oleg Gridley was out of luck because he couldn't possibly reach the urinal. Oleg grumbled and stormed out the back door to pee on the eucalyptus, which formed windbreakers to keep the Eleven Ninety-nine Club from doing business in Indio, minus its foundation. He saw Ruben, the bartender from the Mirage Saloon, walking by and singing "Pennies from Heaven" at the top of his lungs as he strummed on a stringed instrument he couldn't play at all. Suddenly he thought of Portia Cassidy getting stolen away and he ran back inside.

A lachrymose Maynard Rivas on Bitch Cassidy's left said to Nathan Hale Wilson, "It ain't that my wife's fifty pounds overweight. It's just that she's got inverted nipples. They look funny. I'm *so* unhappy!"

By now, J. Edgar Gomez was really hustling. His nighttime waitresses had arrived and one was washing glasses behind the bar while the other served Edgar's "chili" from a huge pot simmering in the kitchen.

"Goddamn, this chili's greasy!" Choo Choo Chester yelled. "Can I just have the grease mainlined straight into my arm, J. Edgar? Sure would save my stomach."

"You don't like it, don't buy it," J. Edgar Gomez muttered, puffing on a cigar as he poured a line of seven drinks with a phenomenal memory for the orders being screamed out by patrons over the din.

"Hey, Edgar," Wingnut yelled, "you got a wine list?"

"You want the wine from K mart or the stuff from Gemco?" the saloonkeeper hollered back.

"K mart."

"Three ninety-nine a bottle!" the saloon-keeper bellowed.

"Got any cheaper?"

"Gemco's three fifty."

"I'll take it. What color is it?"

"Off-white I think, with little dark freckles."

"Make it *two* bottles!" the young cop yelled, happy for a bargain.

"Jesus Christ!" Prankster Frank cried. "A spider just did a Greg Louganis in my chili!"

"That's a dirty lie!" J. Edgar Gomez said, but someone had turned up the jukebox and Ethel Merman was screaming about show business louder than any live voice in the saloon.

"Knock that off or I'll eighty-six ya!" J. Edgar Gomez suddenly warned Prankster Frank, Nathan Hale Wilson and the Palm Springs fingerprinter, Dustin Hoffman, who were all holding up cocktail napkins with scores of "9.9, 9.8, and 9.8" written in lipstick at the diving spider who was swimming for his life.

Just as Otto was about to suggest that O. A. Jones wasn't going to make it, a young cop with fluffy blond hair tapped him on the shoulder and said, "Sergeant Blackpool?"

"I'm Stringer," Otto said. "He's Blackpool."

"I'm O. A. Jones," the kid said.

Sidney Blackpool stared at him. He *did* look like a surfer.

"Sorry I'm so late," he said. "Sergeant Brickman sent me out to Solitaire Canyon, out to where I found the Watson car. Told me to go over the area one more time to see if there was anything we missed. He said since you guys from Hollywood were coming we oughtta take one last look."

"For what?"

"That's what I asked. For what? He said he'd just like me to go over the area one last time for anything that didn't belong. He was out there with me for a while, and when he went to the station he told me to give it a try for an hour."

"Funny he didn't mention it," Sidney Blackpool said to Otto. "He never said you were gonna be late because you were out there."

"Sometimes us small-town boys don't like to look like we're intimidated by you big-city guys." O. A. Jones grinned. "He probably didn't wanna say that we'd be *real* embarrassed if you lucked onto something the wind uncovered after all these months."

"Let's go somewhere we can talk," Sidney Blackpool said. "Got your drink?"

The young cop hoisted a beer bottle and they gave up their bar seats to the delight of Oleg Gridley. The midget darted around the legs of two women and crawled up on the vacant stool before Portia Cassidy could escape.

"You hold that beer bottle like an Olympic torch!" Oleg said passionately.

"E.T., go home," she said.

When the detectives finally found a semi-quiet corner in the saloon, Sidney Blackpool said, "Tell us about your call to Palm Springs P.D. today. We're checking out a possible Hollywood connection to the death of Jack Watson."

"Okay," O. A. Jones said. "I was in here last night with a couple a guys and one a them said something about 'I believe.' Not even sure now what he was talking about. He just said 'I believe.' And it clicked something in my head."

"What's that?" Otto asked.

"Well, when I was lost out there in the desert and heard that guy singing and playing the banjo, I really couldn't say at first what the song was. It seemed like something with 'pretend' in it. The Palm Springs detectives played this old record for me. Nat King Cole. I'd never heard him before."

"You never *heard* Nat Cole?" said Otto.

"I mighta, I'm not sure," the young cop said.

Otto rolled his eyes and felt old. As old as murder.

"Now you've changed your mind?"

"Well, it's bothered me a lot for several months. See, I started tuning in these hokey Palm Springs stations to listen for old songs. I started doubting that it was 'Pretend.' The voice was . . . well, I tried to tell them. It was like a thin quivery voice. Like you'd hear in old movies about the nineteen-thirties or something."

"You were uncertain if it was a live voice or a radio voice or a taped voice?"

"I still can't say for sure. Like, I can't even say if it was a car engine or a truck engine or a bike engine. I was in real bad shape that day in the desert."

"Okay, about last night," Otto said. "Have you ever heard the song 'I Believe'?"

"Today," the cop nodded. "I went to a record store in Palm Springs and found it. Frankie Laine. I bought it and played it. He's pretty good."

"And?"

"And . . . well, I *think* it's the song but not the voice. At least it was something about believing. Somebody 'believes.' Something like that. I don't know why I ever thought it was 'Pretend.' It's very mixed up in my mind. Well, that's it. I guess it won't help but I wanted the dicks in Palm Springs to know. Now they know. Now you know."

"It's good you're so diligent," Sidney Blackpool said. "Can we buy you a drink?"

"Like to, but I got this girl over there by the dance floor. She promised me a dance."

"Got it," Sidney Blackpool nodded. "You still surf?"

"Heard I was a surfer, huh?" The young cop grinned. "I must be famous. The Desert Surfer they call me."

"Ever surf the Wedge at Newport?"

"Yeah! How'd you know about the Wedge?"

"I used to watch surfers at one time."

"Maybe I shoulda *stayed* in Laguna." O. A. Jones shrugged. "Well, I'll call you if anything jells in my head about the music. Know what? I'm starting to like old songs. Hanging around here and all, and listening for that *kind* a voice I heard." Then he added, "An *old* kind a voice, you know?"

"An old man's voice?"

"No, I don't mean that. An old *style* a voice. I'll listen to the Palm Springs stations and try to get you a singer's name who had that kind a style. If I do I'll tell Chief Pedroza and he can give you a ring."

"Take care, son," Sidney Blackpool said.

As they were leaving the Eleven Ninety-nine Club for the boozy ride back to their hotel suite, they heard Bitch Cassidy tell Oleg Gridley that she'd like to stuff him in her microwave, causing the lovesick midget to cry out desperately: "Why do you do this to me, Portia? Why do you treat me like I butt-fucked Bambi?"

Chapter 9

THE *BISMARCK*

"Another fun-filled evening in the desert resort," Otto moaned during the ride back from Mineral Springs. "This is about as much fun as a month in Gdansk."

"That sergeant, that Coy Brickman's a strange guy, isn't he?"

"Strange, yeah. I don't like guys that only blink their eyes every other Tuesday. He looks as warm as the ace of spades. Goddamn, this desert's *black* at night!"

"But look at the stars. Baskets of them. When was the last time you saw that in L.A.?"

"When those Samoan stevedores played Ping-Pong with my head. Let's go to the hotel and meet some *women*. That broad in the Eleven Ninety-nine scared me to death. She had veins on her veins. She looked like the monster that ate Akron. She even had pimples on her teeth. And she was talking to the midget about AIDS! Do you know they're gonna put in a resort hotel for AIDS victims in Palm Springs?"

"That's a *last* resort," Sidney Blackpool said. "I'd like to stop by the Watson house one more time. I got a question about Jack Watson's

Porsche and I can't find the answer in the Palm Springs police report."

"After hearing about AIDS, we gotta go see Harlan Penrod? Keerist, I don't even wanna *think* about AIDS. Straight people can get it too, ya know. I used to worry about crabs when I'd meet a broad in a gin mill. The thought a AIDS makes the hair on my crabs stand on end! But if we *gotta* see him I'd rather do it tonight and get it over with. So what about the Porsche?"

"The Watson kid's Porsche was at the house when they found him missing."

"Of course."

"Did you peek in that garage? Big house, small garage. There were three rooms of old furniture and a dune buggy and Oriental rugs and their new Mercedes in there."

"So?"

"So, after they parked the Rolls in the garage, there'd be no room for a Porsche."

"So?"

"That driveway turns. If you park a Porsche or anything else in the driveway, you'd have to back it up and get it out a the way to get at the Rolls."

"So?"

"So nothing, except if there was a kidnapper, did he move the Porsche out? If so, where'd he put it? Or was it maybe parked in the street by Jack Watson that night?"

"Since there's no mention in the reports I

imagine it was parked in the street by the Watson kid before he went to bed."

"Remember what Harlan Penrod said about the Las Palmas area? About how dark it is?"

"Yeah."

"I heard a couple a Palm Springs cops in the bar saying that when local folks hear a splash in the swimming pool at night, it's either a raccoon, or a cop falling in chasing a prowler."

"What's that got to do with the Porsche?"

"Would you park a Porsche Nine-eleven on a street *that* dark and secluded?"

"Not if I wanted to keep the car stereo. Not to mention what it's attached to."

"That's what I wanna talk to Harlan Penrod about. The more I think about it, I wonder if Jack Watson drove the Rolls out to Mineral Springs of his own free will."

"And if he did, what would that prove?"

"Not a thing, maybe."

"Has ten grand made you this diligent?"

"We'll have plenty a time for golf, Otto," Sidney Blackpool said.

"Wake me when we get there." Otto scooted down in the seat and adjusted the radio volume. "Rolls-Royces, Porsches, how do I know what rich people do with their wheels? I just wish I could buy a Camaro Z-twenty-eight like a twenty-two-year-old cop. Trouble with working homicide is these whodunits. Least when I worked narcotics we usually knew *who*dunit, it was just how do we catch him *with* it. Whodunits make me sleepy."

While Otto dozed during the ride back to Palm Springs under a glittering desert sky, Sidney Blackpool thought of how ten thousand dollars did *not* make him so diligent. But one hundred thousand dollars a year, and a clean job with Watson Industries with all privileges and perks attached thereto, *that* made him more diligent than he thought he could still be. He didn't believe there was a chance of an outsider clearing this homicide, but if he went through the motions with sufficient zeal Watson might be impressed.

Victor Watson would need a new director of security whether or not he ever learned who killed his boy. So what if the detective came back from Palm Springs with little more than a golfer's tan? After twenty-one years of blowing bureaucratic smoke as a Los Angeles civil servant he ought to be able to compile a report to make a neurotic millionaire think that he'd made a run at it. Watson was no fool, but overwhelming grief softens up the brain's left hemisphere, oh yes, it does.

Suddenly he noticed that Hildegarde was singing, " 'I'll always be near you, wherever you are. Each night in every prayer . . .' "

That lets me out, Sidney Blackpool thought. He used to pray as a reflex action. Those millions of little incantations they drill into you in Catholic grammar schools. A prayer for every occasion. He stopped that long before he lost

Tommy, but he still went to mass in those days just to have something to do together with his children. He wondered if that ritual made them closer or drove them farther apart during those last few years when Tommy and Barb lived with their mother and Sidney Blackpool got them only on weekends. Of course adolescents want to be in their own homes, in their own neighborhoods, with *their* friends and not with their old man on weekends.

What was it Watson said about the bad times? You only remember the *bad* times. Sidney Blackpool had a thousand bad times to remember after the boy started cutting classes and doing pot and hash and ludes with the other surfers. Like the time he went to the beach in Santa Monica on a winter day and caught Tommy riding four-foot swells, so loaded he'd left his new wet suit on the beach and didn't even know he was blue from the cold. That one had ended with Tommy shoving his father and running off while a bunch of beach bums threw beer cans and forced the detective to retreat to his car. Tommy was missing for ten days.

Why does a father of a dead son think only of those times? The night dreams were never like that. The night dreams were sometimes wonderful, so wonderful he would awake sobbing into a damp pillow. Too many of those wonderful dreams could kill a man, he was convinced.

The recurring dream hardly varied at all. His former wife, Lorie, and his daughter, Barb, would be playing Scrabble on the floor of the living room, and Tommy, at age twelve, would be watching a football game on television in the den, showing his special sort of chuckling grin whenever the U.S.C. band struck up their "Conquest" theme after scoring a touchdown.

In the dream Sidney Blackpool would take his wife aside privately and make her promise not to tell the secret. The secret was that they had re-created Tommy at the most wonderful time, before the rebellion and the misery of adolescence and drugs. The dream was strange in that it was understood that somehow they had *willed* him back to them, but the dream was unclear as to whether he was alive as far as anyone else was concerned, or even if Barb was aware.

The dream was so incredibly joyous he never wanted it to end, but of course it always did and he was powerless to change the ending. The dream was over when his wife would say, "Sid, we can enjoy him forever now. But you *mustn't* tell him he's going to die when he's eighteen. You mustn't tell him!"

It was so contradictory and irrational that it made perfect sense to Sidney Blackpool. And in the dream he'd always say to her, "Oh, no! I'll never tell him that. Because he loves me. And . . . and now he forgives me. My boy *forgives* me!"

186

And then he would wake up sobbing and smothering in the pillow. It was always the same and he dealt with it the same. He would take four aspirins and half a tumbler of Johnnie Walker, which would be hard to hold with both trembling hands.

" 'Just close your eyes . . . and I'll be there,' " Hildegarde sang. " 'If you call I'll hear you, no matter how far. Just close your eyes and I'll be theeeere.' "

"Damn! Goddamn!" Sidney Blackpool said.

"What happened?" Otto bolted upright.

"We, uh, almost hit a . . . jackrabbit," Sidney Blackpool said.

"This *is* one dark neighborhood," Otto said, as his partner parked in front of the huge wall of oleander and cut the engine.

And while the detectives were locking the doors of Sidney Blackpool's Toyota, a tipsy Harlan Penrod was mad as hell because a British telephone operator was trying to explain that it was too early in London to be connecting him with anyone at Buckingham Palace.

"Well, aren't they up with the baby?" he demanded. "What kind of parents are they?"

"I'm very sorry, madam," the operator said, making Harlan drop his voice an octave or two.

"I'm not a madam, nor do I live in a place where madams reside," he said.

"I beg your pardon, sir," the operator said. "Will that be all then?"

"I'll call later," Harlan warned. And then he

added, "Do you by chance know if Vera Lynn is listed in the London directory?"

"Lynn? How is it spelled?"

"Vera Lynn! Vera Lynn!" Harlan cried. "She's only the greatest singer England ever produced! She's a personal friend of the Queen Mother, for crying out loud! How old are you, anyway?"

"Would you care to speak to my superior, sir?" the operator asked.

"Oh, what's the use!" Harlan said, draining his martini. "If you don't know who Vera Lynn is, England's finished. You might as well tell me Margaret Thatcher's gonna mud-wrestle in Soho."

"Will that be all, sir?"

"Yes, good night, or good morning, as the case may be."

Harlan hung up and mixed himself another Bombay bomber.

He was surprised to hear the gate buzzer. Probably that bitch, Freddie. He said he'd never see Freddie again but . . . Harlan went to the intercom and pushed the button.

"Yes, may I *help* you?" he said sweetly.

"It's Blackpool and Stringer," Sidney Blackpool said. "Can we talk for a few minutes?"

"Can we talk? Can we talk?" Harlan cried, sounding like Joan Rivers. "Just walk in the gate when you hear the buzzer, gentlemen."

Harlan Penrod was framed dramatically in the doorway when the detectives approached the house through the cactus garden. He was wearing a white *guayabera* shirt, a blue-silk ascot, white slacks and white deck shoes.

"Sorry to bother you," Sidney Blackpool said as Harlan stepped back and welcomed them with a flourish and his palm-down handshake.

"Not at all," Harlan said. "I was just calling London and the fools frustrated me no end."

"London, huh," Otto said. "England?"

"Oh, yes. I often call England. I've tried several times to get a message to Vera Lynn. They're very nice, the people at Buckingham Palace who take the messages. I forgot how early it is there. It's tomorrow actually. I should call later. I've called President Nixon in Peking. I called President Ford in Korea and, let's see, I also called President Reagan in Peking. I wish he'd go to Moscow. I'd love to call him there."

"And they talk to you?"

"Would you like a drink?" Harlan asked. "No, they don't talk to me, but do you know how impressed the aides are to get overseas calls from Palm Springs? I've talked to Secret Service men lots and lots of times. They've always taken my messages for the presidents. I never called President Carter. I don't like Democrats in general. Is either of you a Democrat? I apologize if you are."

"Cops're all Republicans," Otto said. "Capital-punishment buffs. Pro death, remember?"

"Can't I get you a drink? I'm *so* glad you dropped by!"

189

"Mister Penrod," Sidney Blackpool began.

"Harlan."

"Harlan."

"How do you like Palm Springs so far?" Harlan interrupted. "Bet you haven't seen any movie stars, but they're here, I promise you. James Caan, Sonny Bono, George Peppard, Mitzi Gaynor, the Gabors. They all live fairly close to here. Gosh, we used to have Elvis Presley and Red Skelton and William Holden, and right close by, the chairperson of the board."

"Who's that?" Otto asked.

"Liberace. And of course everyone knows about old ski nose and blue eyes. We've named streets after them."

Otto's stomach growled fiercely and Harlan said, "That reminds me, Rin Tin Tin visited Palm Springs in the old days. Are you hungry?"

"So hungry I can't think," Otto said. "I just tried to eat a bowl a chili but there was a pair a spiders doing synchronized swimming in it."

"Let me fix you some sandwiches and we'll have a nice talk."

"Tell you what, Harlan," said Sidney Blackpool impulsively, "this is turning into an all-work no-play vacation. How about coming to our hotel? We'll have a meal in the dining room and send you home in a taxi afterward."

"Oh, what a wonderful idea!" Harlan cried, fussing with his ascot and putting the martini on a cocktail table next to a love seat. "All

190

work and no play makes . . . ."

"For a bent putter," Otto said. "Tomorrow we play golf, Sidney."

"Just let me freshen up," Harlan said. "I'll be with you in a jiff!"

"It'll turn into a vacation tomorrow," Sidney Blackpool said.

After Harlan was gone, Otto said, "He's probably in there putting sheep cells on his skin or giving himself an egg-white facial. You know, I could be back in L.A. watching the news. This is about as exciting as seeing the greengrocer cleaning his pomegranates seed by fucking seed."

"We'll play golf tomorrow," Sidney Blackpool promised.

"Let us make haste, gentlemen!" Harlan Penrod whisked into the room, resplendent in a red ascot.

After setting the alarm and locking the front door they were off.

The hotel was bustling by ten o'clock when they were seated in the dining room.

"A light supper, gentlemen?" the captain asked, handing the wine list to Otto Stringer.

"A complete dinner," Otto said. After the three had placed their cocktail order, he said, "Sidney, if you didn't feed me tonight, you'd wake up in the morning and find a dead jackrabbit in my bed. I was getting *wild*."

"Really?" Harlan batted his eyes in delight,

191

causing Otto to roll his in exasperation.

"We wanted to talk to you about Jack Watson's car," Sidney Blackpool said.

"Sure," said Harlan. "By the way, Barry Manilow lives here, and of course Gene Autry, and . . ."

"Where was the car parked when Jack disappeared? The Porsche, I mean?"

"Let's see, the police found it parked and locked in front."

"Outside the gates? In the street?"

"Yes. Do you see that man over there? The guy in the tacky silk suit with the big cigar and flashy diamonds?"

"What about him?"

"He bought a nightclub in town. Claims to be an East Indian prince. Sure. He just *reeks* of olive oil and goat cheese. A Syrian from Vegas. Lives in Tuscany Canyon with ten huge watchdogs that eat third-world gardeners. I heard they found a skeleton in his yard with nothing left but a few tacos hanging from a rib cage."

"Some mixed appetizers," Otto said to the waiter. "And I want rare prime rib, the King Henry the Eighth cut or whatever you call it here. And a bottle of, let's see, number twenty-seven looks like a vintage French red."

"That's French white, sir," the waiter said.

"Aw, screw it. You pick it. Make sure it's at least fifty bucks a bottle."

"Very good," the waiter said.

Sidney Blackpool ordered a Cobb salad and Harlan had a bowl of leek soup and a veal chop.

"I've been trying to lose a few pounds," he said to Otto.

"You're in pretty good shape for your *age*," Otto said, and Harlan looked as though he could slap Otto's face.

"Harlan, did Jack Watson *ever* park his car in the street at night?" Sidney Blackpool asked.

"Once in a while."

"Really? A car worth forty grand on those dark streets? Must have a few auto thefts around there."

"A Porsche Nine-eleven's worth more than that," Harlan said. "And this *is* a transient town. He didn't do it very often."

"How often?"

"Maybe only a few times. When he came home very late."

"What's very late?"

"When it wasn't dark anymore."

"He came home at dawn? Where would he go all night? This isn't a late town."

"This is an early town," Harlan said, draining the Bombay martini and smiling demurely when Otto signaled for another round. "Maybe two hundred and fifty thousand people come to this valley in season, but in the summer it's a very small town with a small-town mentality. Have you listened to the commercials on radio and T.V.? I heard a girl today announce the bill at

193

the multiple cinema. "In TheATER One, she says, is *I'm a douche*. I thought it was a porn flick till I realized the poor thing was trying to say *Amadeus*. Oh, I miss the big city sometimes, but I'd never go back to L.A. When Mister Watson asked me if I'd accept the wages he offered, I countered by dropping on my knees. You can keep Hollywood."

"About the car," Sidney Blackpool said, as the second round of drinks arrived.

"Cheers, dears!" Harlan cried, lifting his martini.

"He'd come home at dawn sometimes? Where would he spend the night?"

"Sergeant, he was a gorgeous young rich boy. He could spend the night anywhere he wanted. I'm sure he loved his fiancée but he was young."

"How long had he been engaged to his girlfriend?"

"Not long. Three, four months, I think. Her family and his were very good friends, but I'm sure he loved her. He wouldn't do *everything* his father wished."

"Okay, so sometimes he came home at dawn or close to it, and he wouldn't bother to pull in and block the driveway with the Porsche. He'd park outside and come in through the walk-in gate, right?"

"Right."

"Well, if his car was parked in front of the house and locked, were the keys to his Porsche found on his body?"

"No. As I recall, his keys were in his bedroom where he always kept them."

"Okay, Harlan, then it's very unlikely that he was forced to drive the Rolls from the house, or forced to leave the house in any fashion. An intruder wouldn't pull the Porsche out of the garage, park it in front, lock it up and return the keys to Jack's bedroom, now would he?"

"I guess not," Harlan said.

"Didn't you think the same thing on the day Jack was discovered missing? I mean, didn't you tell the F.B.I. and the Palm Springs police that it was likely that Jack parked in front that night so he could drive the Rolls out later? And wouldn't that just about rule *out* any notion that he was snatched from the house?"

"I was so confused back then! Mister Watson just sort of took over from everybody. Do you know how forceful a man he is? He was running around with one of those cordless phones his company makes, and, I don't know, it was like the red-phone syndrome: *Get me Washington!* He told the F.B.I. men right in front of me that his boy was kidnapped out of the house and I still can't say he *wasn't*. Like I said, Jack hated to drive the Rolls-Royce."

"Is it that Victor Watson wouldn't even consider the possibility that his son might drive the Rolls up to a canyon in Mineral Springs of his own volition?"

"Maybe that's it. And I still don't know that he would. What would Jack be doing in a place like that?"

"What's your opinion?"

"Gosh, I don't know what to think." Harlan dabbed his eyes with a dinner napkin. "He was like my son, that boy. He and his dad argued sometimes, and he'd talk to me about it later. I think he hated it, being dependent on his dad all the time. He used to call him *da-da*, but not to his face. And he used to say things to me like 'Well, guess I'll go ask Daddy Warbucks for my allowance.' My impression is that when he finished his education he was never again going to take money from his father."

The waiter arrived with samples of mozzarella marinara, coquilles St. Jacques and lox with capers. Sidney Blackpool tried the mozzarella, Harlan tasted the scallops, Otto ate what was left.

They had three bottles of wine during the meal and Otto insisted on champagne and cherries jubilee for dessert because, as Otto put it, "Who ever heard of eating cherries jubilee without champagne?"

Harlan was bagged by then, but still regaling them with Palm Springs lore. "And Steve McQueen lived up on Southridge by William Holden and Bob Hope. And Truman Capote lived in Las Palmas, and Kirk Douglas, and there're *so* many more!"

By now, Otto was nearly as bombed as Harlan who was weaving in his chair. The dining room maître d' kept looking at them and at his wristwatch. Two other tables were occupied by quieter drunks who looked like they might be leaving soon.

"Tell me, Harlan, how'd you get to know so much about this town?" Otto asked.

"Small-town gossip. You just hang around the bars and pretty soon you know everything. In Palm Springs there's only a population of thirty thousand who own homes and pay taxes and lots of them're rich people who aren't around much. You should see these bars. They're nothing like Hollywood." Reconsidering that, he said, "Well, they're *something* like Hollywood. We have lots of wanna-be cowboys driving around in Datsun pickups looking very butch but just reeking of Pierre Cardin. Do you know this is the only place where you can go into a bar that's frequented by the cowboy and hard-hat set along with wetbacks from Sonora? And they get along okay. When it's one hundred and twenty degrees outside I think people start to tolerate each other. It's us against the desert. But we also have our slums. Only town in the valley without a slum is Rancho Mirage. Do you know how many celebrities live in the country clubs in Rancho Mirage?"

"I'm getting sleepy," Otto said. "My lips're getting numb."

"Where do you suppose Jack Watson would go on his nights out, Harlan?" Sidney Blackpool asked.

"We have half a dozen discos in town now. Lots of airline stews and girls from Newport Beach come in for the weekends. Jack'd probably go to a disco. I never saw him dance but I know he'd be good. He'd never be out there on the street at two A.M. suffering from disco heartbreak, I can tell you. Jack could have *any* girl he wanted. You know why I say that?"

"Why?" Sidney Blackpool asked, while Otto tried to catch the eye of the cocktail waitress who was still working the busy cocktail lounge as well as serving the drunks left in the dining room.

"There're other kids with curly black hair and eyes like Paul Newman, but he had more."

Something troubled Sidney Blackpool suddenly. He felt a shadow, then a shiver. He wasn't sober enough to put it all together just now.

"Jack had a quality that very few twenty-two-year-olds can match. Jack was nice. He was a *nice* human being. Yes, I think he dearly wanted to be independent of his father someday. He was special."

"I hear that young people hang around Palm Springs all hours a the night," Sidney Blackpool said. "Did Jack do that?"

"Do you know who hang around? Teens and marines from Twentynine Palms. These macho boys who spend all day learning how to drop napalm on rice paddies and kill with their bare

198

hands come to Palm Springs for the weekend. No hair, no money, in their jacked-up Camaros with rebel flags on them, and a can of Skoal in their back pocket. They've got nothing to do but get in fights. Do you think Jack would be roaming the streets with those people?"

"How much did he drink?"

"Like any college kid."

"Did he do drugs?"

"I'm sure he smoked a number once in a while. I don't think he did coke, but I have to tell you it *is* the most abused substance in Palm Springs. I see waiters and waitresses running in and out of the rest room all night, stuffing it up their noses at a hundred and twenty dollars a gram."

Just then the cocktail waitress came by with the check for Otto. He leered at her cleavage, signed the check and wrote on a cocktail napkin: "Please help me escape! I am being held hostage by terminally boring people! I am a wealthy man!"

She giggled and thanked Otto for writing in a 30 percent tip, after which she sashayed back to the cocktail lounge.

"It's hard to believe I'm almost old enough to be her daddy," Otto sighed. "I may not survive this birthday."

"Well, I guess it's time to go to bed," Sidney Blackpool said.

"So soon?" Harlan said. "I could talk for hours."

"I want you to call me here if you think of anything else about the Watson case," Sidney Blackpool said. "Try to remember if he ever talked about any girl he may've met here. Did he ever bring a local friend to the house?"

"Not while I worked for the family."

"I guess that's it then. We'll see . . ." Suddenly it clicked, the reference to Paul Newman's blue eyes. Newman had a son with whom he no doubt had a turbulent relationship. He'd lost that son. Paul Newman knew what Victor Watson and Sidney Blackpool knew, about fathers and sons.

"Something wrong?" Harlan asked.

"I just thought of a guy . . . It's nothing. Now I'm gonna put you in a cab."

"Gosh, I wish we didn't have to go so early. I was just . . . oh, my Lord!"

"What is it?"

"Look at that!"

Three men had walked into the dining room and were having a short conversation with the maître d' whose grin registered about $200 on the gratuity scale as he led them to a table in the corner.

The man in the lead could've been thirty years old or sixty. His hair was done in a henna perm, and his transparent flesh was stretched so tight across his cheeks and mouth that he could barely smile. He had Jean Harlow eyebrows, and dressed like Oscar Wilde complete with carnation. He was followed closely by two handsome young Japanese in matching double-breasted red blazers, white pants and red loafers without socks.

"Do you know who *that* is?" Harlan whispered. "My Lord, ever since Betty Ford got her face-lift *everybody's* coming to Palm Springs for a cut and stitch. Look at that job! I mean, last time I saw him he could pack his rainbow undies in his eye bags. I mean, you talk about eyes by Louis Vuitton!"

"Who is he?" Otto was getting interested.

"And those little pals, calls them his aides-de-camp. Sure. I know a massage-parlor duo when I see one. Some day he'll be giving palimony to those little harbor bombers."

"Who *is* he?" Otto wanted to know.

"That man," Harlan said, "is the last of a famous German family who kept Hitler's war machine going. In his father's factories slaves were hanged from the rafters when their output wasn't sufficient. In nineteen thirty-nine his family was as powerful as the Rothschilds. Now he spends his life in a bikini with a tan line that touches."

"He looks like a Vincent Price movie," Otto said.

"Palm Springs is a larger version of Harry's Bar," Harlan declared proudly. "You can watch the whole world pass by. Gentlemen, he is living proof of a design in the universe. From the battleship *Bismarck* to the good ship

Lollipop in a single generation. That's the way a dynasty ends — not with a bang, but a giggle."

Chapter 10

THE WALL

Once again, Sidney Blackpool slept right through the drinker's hour and knew he didn't deserve it after what they'd consumed at the marathon dinner. He decided it must be the desert air. It was miraculous to escape the drinker's dreadlies, the hours when reality and fantasy were harder than usual to sort out. The adjoining bedroom door was closed but he could hear Otto snoring. He had a shower and shave and decided to take a drive to see what the desert looked like at dawn.

He brought his tourist map and headed away from the big mountain. In fifteen minutes he found himself circling the desert's only private golf course, which surrounds the home of Walter Annenberg, publishing mogul, friend of presidents, and former ambassador to Great Britain. In a valley that boasted more golf courses per square mile than any other place on earth, he thought it appropriate that at least one local millionaire had a backyard large enough to accommodate his own.

Then he saw something so startling that he had to pull over on Bob Hope Drive, careful to keep his wheels on the asphalt and off the powdery sand. He got out of the car and ran to the top of a dune. At 6:30 A.M. on this splendid November day, the desert was putting on a show for him. Behind him were the Shadow Mountains whose low peaks of pink and copper and purple were shattered by cloud shadow. There was an amazing slash of color over the Santa Rosas, as though a heavenly house painter had dipped a wide brush in fire and painted a stroke across a silver canvas. The sweep of fire had a beginning and end, and all the bristle streaks. But what astonished him even more was that the sun was rising behind the Santa Rosa Mountains at the same time that the full moon, pale and translucent, was setting behind Mount San Jacinto.

At precisely 6:32 A.M., the rising sun rested for several seconds on the Santa Rosas and the setting moon did the same on San Jacinto Peak. Sunrise and moonset on the mountaintops within the span of his outstretched arms. There he stood on the dune, shoes buried in white powder, among patches of verbena and sand drops, which would blanket this desert in the spring.

He held the sunrise and moonset as long as he could between his hands, though the rising fireball was blinding in the crystal air. Time stopped for an instant. Then the moon was gone and the sun was soaring over the peaks and he realized how he must look out there in the desert to the working stiffs driving by on Bob Hope Drive to Palm Springs.

Still, he couldn't leave just yet. He took off his shoes and socks and walked barefoot through the dunes, the cool sand sucking at his ankles. He sat on a large dune and thought of how, by tomorrow, this hill of sand might vanish in the wind. But it might reappear ten yards away. Or ten miles away. Maybe it didn't really vanish at all. And then he thought that he was getting a bit too close to the self-help nonsense that had never worked for him after Tommy died.

Victor Watson said he'd tried God and Zen and they didn't work any better than psychotherapy which didn't work at all. When the sand dune vanished, that sand dune would never return. Maybe they'd use it for cement. He snuffed out his cigarette and put the butt in his pocket. The desert could burn anything clean given time, but he wouldn't leave his trash in this beautiful place, not today. Not after the sun and moon and light show that the desert had given him free of charge.

While Sidney Blackpool was standing ankle deep in sand looking like a desert crucifixion, Otto Stringer was having his breakfast in bed and finding it hard to concentrate on the *Today Show* movie reviewer who looked and sounded dumber than usual. The reason he was having so much trouble concentrating was that he was feeling disturbed that they had not played golf

205

and were working harder than the police task force at the recent Olympic games. Otto finished his coffee and decided to bypass the croissants. He picked up the telephone and dialed Hollywood information. Three minutes later he was talking with a Rolls-Royce dealer.

"This is Detective Stringer, L.A.P.D.," he said. "I'm calling about Mister Victor Watson's homicide investigation. I believe you're a friend of Mister Watson's?"

"He's an old client," the car dealer said. "And yes, we're friends."

"We're having some problems with this case," Otto said. "Mister Watson said you informed him that his car showed up in your store on the day his son was murdered."

"Yes, that's right. My service manager, he uh, he identified a picture of Jack that Victor . . . that Mister Victor Watson showed him."

"I wanna talk to that service manager."

"He, uh, he's . . . I don't think he's available. He may be off today. I'll have to check and call you back."

"Listen," Otto said, "this is a very serious investigation. There's been lots and lots a man-hours expended and lots and lots a blind-alley chases. I wanna know something, and be absolutely sure when you answer me. Could you be . . . mistaken? That is, could your service manager *be mistaken?*"

"Uh, how do you mean that?"

"What if it was some *other* Rolls that came in that day? What if some *other* young guy was driving? Is it possible he's confused? It would be a serious matter if a police investigation was geared around a . . . *mistake*. Someone could even get in trouble."

There were several seconds of silence and then the car dealer said, "Well, anything's possible."

"I know anything's possible. Is it maybe more than possible that your service manager is mistaken?"

"It's . . . at least very possible," the car dealer said shakily. "I would . . . I'd have to talk with him."

"Thanks very much," Otto said. "If we have any more questions, we'll call you."

"Do you think you'll have more questions?" The car dealer sounded ill.

"I doubt it," the detective said.

When Sidney Blackpool came back to the suite, Otto was all gussied up in his best golf outfit, the one with the pink argyle sweater. He was in the sitting room reading the newspaper.

"Thought you might still be asleep," Sidney Blackpool said. "I went for a ride. Stayed longer than I thought."

"We playing golf today, Sidney? Or we gonna set up roadblocks and start searching cars for the murder gun?"

"What's wrong?"

"You see, partner, I'm just an old narc and a brand-new dead-body dick, but even old narcs can figure things out after a while."

"What're you talking about?"

"I been wondering why you didn't wanna go to that Rolls-Royce dealer to verify the hot new clue about the Watson kid driving the Rolls to Hollywood. But I just figured, well, Black Sid's the homicide cop. Me, I'm just the new kid on the block, so I didn't say anything. But I got to thinking."

"Thinking what?"

"Thinking that you're working this case like it's the Lindbergh baby snatching, not a no-clues homicide where we're supposedly just going through the motions."

"So what've you decided?"

"I decided to call the Rolls dealer who's a pal of Victor Watson. I could get more sincerity from a wedding chapel in Las Vegas."

"And?"

"And he's about as reliable as a *Pravda* editorial. Watson cooked this thing up with his pal just to get L.A.P.D. drawn into a Palm Springs case. Am I right?"

"I didn't call the car dealer. You did."

"Look, Sidney, I'm not a Mensa, but I'm not real dumb."

"You're not a bit dumb, Otto."

"You figured all along that Watson set it up to bring us in. You *wanted* to be brought in."

"Let's say you're right."

208

"Hey, I don't care if you did it because you wanted a Palm Springs holiday. I don't care if you figured he'd lay some expense money on us. Maybe you even knew it'd be ten grand. I don't know what-all's behind it, but I think if I'm riding shotgun, I got a right to know if I'm gonna get waylaid by hostiles."

Sidney Blackpool lit a cigarette and straddled his chair and looked away. Then he said, "Okay, Otto, you're right. I *did* figure from the git-go that Watson cooked up the Hollywood connection, but I went along. And not just for a fun-filled week in Palm Springs."

"So far, we ain't having much fun. We're working."

Sidney Blackpool took a big hit on the cigarette and blew a cloud through his nose, saying, "I didn't know he'd give us ten thousand, but that's not what's making me take a run at this case. Watson offered me a job *if* I could impress him."

"What job?"

"Security director for Watson Industries. Hundred grand a year. Travel. Country-club privileges. Perks. I won't be super rich but I can *live* rich."

"Every cop's hope and dream," Otto whistled. "How to turn twenty years of shit into sunshine."

"It's the first thing I've been a little stoked about in a long time, Otto. It's something to . . . go for."

"Go for? I'd kill for it. You shoulda told me."

"Sorry, partner."

"So now I know, let's forget the golf. I'll work all week if that's the payoff for you. I can always play golf in Griffith Park."

Sidney Blackpool grinned and said, "Thanks, but guess what?"

"What?"

"We're gonna hit the links today."

"All right!" Otto said. "Which course?"

"You pick it. We got three to choose from."

"Eeny meeny miny Tamarisk! Let's go play Tamarisk Country Club."

"Kay by me," Sidney Blackpool said. "Hey, guess what I saw out in the desert?"

"What?"

"A bird I saw in the desert magazine. A butcher-bird they call it. It impales mice and lizards on thorns and barbed wire, then eats them. Beautiful songbird. Teal-colored back. Gray cap, black mask, wings silver gray like a Mercedes. With white pinstriping. A gorgeous *deadly* little songbird. Reminded me a my ex-wife."

"Sidney, puh-leese!" Otto said. "You *promised* not to get so morbid!"

The clubhouse at Tamarisk was brand-new but the golf course was old. Along with Thunderbird Country Club, it was the oldest posh club in the desert. The detectives weren't certain what

210

to do, but started lugging their own clubs until a kid saw them and took their golf bags, directing them to the locker room where they changed shoes.

The new clubhouse was perfect for the desert: lots of glass and space, decorated in desert pastels. There was a membership roster on the wall inside the lobby. Otto saw Gregory Peck's name and began getting panicky. He half expected to run into Yoko Ono.

Although he'd played an occasional game of golf over the years, Otto had never really gotten interested in the game until he started working with Sidney Blackpool, a pretty good golfer. In their months together, Sidney Blackpool had managed to get them some play at a few of the second-line private clubs in Los Angeles County, which were goat tracks compared to the manicured perfection of the desert country clubs.

"Oh, my God, Sidney!" Otto said when they were standing with the club pro looking at the eighteenth green. "I never seen anything like this. It's . . . It's . . . I used to date a girl with a pussy like that!"

"Green?" said the club pro.

"Velvet," Otto said. "It looks like velvet around that pin. And look at the fairways, not a blemish. Do you use Clearasil on them, or what?"

"Have fun, fellas," the pro said. "You'll make a threesome with Mister Rosenkrantz.

He's on the first tee warming up."

"Thanks much," Sidney Blackpool said, needing to take Otto's elbow to get him away from the eighteenth green. The boy already had their clubs loaded on an electric golf cart and was wiping down their woods.

"Do we tip the kid or what?" Otto whispered.

"After we're through," Sidney Blackpool said.

"Do we pay green fees or what? Is ten grand *enough* for green fees?"

"Relax. Victor Watson took care a everything," Sidney Blackpool said. "Imagine what it'd be like working for a guy like him."

"Imagine what it'd be like living in a place like *this*, Sidney. I *gotta* find me a rich woman in this town!"

The man waiting on the first tee was about sixty-five years old and fatter than Otto Stringer, but stood only about five feet six. He wore a floppy golf cap that came to the top of his ears and plastic-rimmed glasses that kept slipping down his nose. He smoked a cigar that was bigger than a twelve-ounce sap.

"You must be Mister Guildenstern," Otto said, sticking out his hand.

"I'm the other one," the man said. "Rosenkrantz with a *K*. Glad to know you boys."

"He's Sidney Blackpool and I'm Otto Stringer. Thanks for letting us play."

"Glad to do a favor for friends a Victor Watson," he said. "Call me Archie. What's your handicap?"

"He's about a twelve," Otto said. "Me, I'm a beginner. Thirty handicap oughtta do it."

"Last guy told me that beat me like a whorehouse rug," Archie Rosenkrantz said. "So I give you fifteen strokes. Sidney, you give me three. How about we play for twenty bucks four ways. Front, back, automatic press on the back and totals."

"Sounds okay," Sidney Blackpool said. "You go ahead and show us the way, Archie."

While Archie Rosenkrantz was getting himself ready on the first tee, Otto felt the panic bubbling. He whispered to his partner, "Did you trade President McKinley for a whole *bunch* a Andrew Jacksons? We never played for more than two bucks at Griffith Park!"

"We got money, don't worry," his partner whispered back.

Just then, a mixed foursome drove up in two custom golf carts and parked at the tee. One golf cart was Chinese red, built to resemble a baby Rolls-Royce. The man driving was older than George Burns. The girl in Ultrasuede was younger than Brooke Shields. Otto felt eight eyes on him. Disapproving eyes, he figured. He was sure they knew he was a Griffith Park hacker.

Then Otto heard a sound that reminded him of the Samoan's hand colliding with his skull. Fat old guy, my ass! The freaking ball rocketed out there 220 yards. Dead *straight*.

"Can we just pay you now and get it over with?" Sidney Blackpool asked, as he stepped up and stuck a tee in the ground.

"Lucky shot," Archie said, puffing on the Havana.

Otto kept glancing behind him at the clubhouse. He just knew there must be fifty people looking out through the tinted glass. He held his breath for twenty seconds and blew it out. He flexed his fists, forearms and biceps, then relaxed them. When he'd whiff at Griffith Park to the delight of some plumber, it was no big deal. But in *this* place?

Sidney Blackpool smacked it as hard as Archie Rosenkrantz, and being younger and more limber, he got an extra fifteen yards out of it. The ball faded but settled on the right side of the fairway.

"You ain't so bad yourself, kid," Archie said, chewing the cigar to bits. "I ain't gonna get fat on you boys, I can see."

Otto was starting to feel all wrong. His lime-green doubleknits suddenly bit at his crotch. His argyle sweater chafed his armpits. His golf shoes seemed to be rubbing blisters on his ankles though he hadn't walked twenty feet. Even his goddamn Ben Hogan cap was too tight. He was a wreck.

Otto took a practice swing and sent a thirteen-inch slab of Tamarisk flying twenty yards. He ran off the tee and retrieved the chunk of turf while Archie Rosenkrantz puffed on the Havana and said, "There's an eighty-year-old member here wears a toup looks just like that divot, cept his is orange. Don't be scared, kid. Just kick back and L.T.F.F."

"What's L.T.F.F.?" Otto asked, feeling his jaws going tight.

"Let the fucker fly," Archie said.

But suddenly Otto's golf gremlin showed up! His fear gremlin looked like Renfield, that giggling little fly eater in the old movie who leads you to your room in the west tower and tells you to ignore that flapping outside the window because it's just some old drag queen from Bucharest and if you give him a peek at your bare bum and some warm milk with a Tollhouse cookie he'll flutter on home. Sure.

"Let the fucker fly," said Otto bravely.

"Heh heh heh," said Renfield, crunching on a blood-bloated horsefly as big as a pistachio.

Otto let the fucker fly all right.

"That wouldn't be bad distance," Archie said, "if that was the ball instead a the club."

"I can't understand it!" Otto cried, looking over his shoulder at the mixed foursome who were getting a real bang out of the gifted athlete on the first tee.

Sidney Blackpool trotted out to retrieve the graphite driver and Archie said, "Tell you what, son, let's call off the bets. This frigging game's got enough stress built in. Let's just go out and have some fun, enjoy the day, have a laugh or two and a drink later."

"Okay by me," Sidney Blackpool said, handing Otto his driver.

Otto told himself it'd be easy now. The pressure was off. Except that the women in the mixed foursome were whispering, and Otto's ears were the color of the pink argyles on his tummy. Still, he forced himself to move that club low and slow. He took it back slower than Don January ever thought of doing. He was feeling loose and dreamy. He was sooo slow. He was sooo relaxed he just might fall asleep. Except that just as he got that club past horizontal, Renfield said, "There's nothing to fear but fear itself. Heh heh hee heeeee!" Otto knew that hovering rodent outside the window *only* had the face of Bela fucking Lugosi!

Otto gave it a Reggie Jackson fast-ball swing. With the same result. He whiffed that baby so bad he torqued like a licorice twist and found his head looking straight behind him like a cockatoo. Right at the two women in the mixed foursome who were beaming like two stews on Aloha Airlines: "Welcome to paradise, stranger!"

"So I lied," Renfield shrugged, his teeth full of flies.

Archie Rosenkrantz almost lost his cigar. "Did I hear a growl?" he cried. "Lon Chaney needed a full moon to lunge like that!"

"Let's forget the first tee," Sidney Blackpool suggested. "Otto'll settle down after we get out on the fairway."

"Palm Springs ain't heard a bigger swish since Liberace came to town," Archie said. "Okay, let's move along. My varicose veins're break dancing."

The first hole was a five par, 483 yarder, which shouldn't have caused too many problems. Otto was allowed to place his ball 200 yards out, near the drives hit by his playing partners.

"Now, Otto," Archie said. "There ain't nobody watching you so just step up there and look around at the mountains and smell the flowers and think how lucky you are that God gave you this happy day. Just say this to yourself: Aw, fuck it! And if I can't fuck it, I'll cover it with chocolate like old Mary See!"

So Otto stepped up and addressed the ball, letting his arms and forearms and wrists and hands and hips and legs go limp, and thought, "Fuck it or cover it with chocolate." And he let er fly and heard a dull thunk.

"Where is it?" Otto asked, shielding his eyes from the sun. "Did it come down yet?"

"Worm burner," Sidney Blackpool said.

"Bug fucker," Archie Rosenkrantz said. "Not *real* bad though. You got maybe thirty yards."

Archie laid into his shot with a three wood, and his short backswing put it out there nearly 200 yards, leaving him a pitch to the green.

Sidney Blackpool hit his three wood farther but drew it too much and faced a tricky wedge shot.

Otto incinerated a battalion of worms and ravished a bunch of bugs before finishing the first hole. In fact, when he landed in the trap on the right side he had his worst moment. Sidney Blackpool and Archie Rosenkrantz both dumped their third shots into the trap on the left, making it three on the beach and everyone moaning.

Archie blasted his out nicely and it landed twenty-five feet past the pin while Otto stared at his own sand shot and felt his sphincter tighten.

"Nice out," Otto said enviously.

Sidney Blackpool took a bit too much sand but got away with it and his ball landed on the green and took a good roll thirty feet short of the flag. Otto felt his sphincter get tighter.

"Nice out," Otto said enviously.

Then it was his turn. Otto lowered that wedge until it just brushed the sand two inches behind that ball and tried to ignore Renfield's demented cackle.

Otto made a solemn vow that he was going to let his entire body relax no matter what happened to the sand shot. And he succeeded. He let his entire body go utterly limp and loose. He was sooo slow. He was sooo loose that he farted.

"Nice out," Archie Rosenkrantz said enviously.

All in all it wasn't a bad day. Otto started to get better after checking in with a slick seven on the four-par third hole.

After five holes Archie said, "You got a full house, Otto: three nines and a pair a sevens."

On the four-par number six Otto actually sank his second putt for a bogey five. "Fever!" Otto cried. "Gimme a fever!"

"Five for Otto!" Archie said, writing his score on the steering-wheel card holder. "Now you're cooking, kiddo. You finally stopped looking like Gary Gilmore with a target pinned to his shirt."

"I got a five," Sidney Blackpool said.

"No blood," Archie said. "We tied on that one."

"Otto, let's give you the honors."

Otto Stringer was so stoked from his bogey that he let it fly, but got under the ball. It was a 200-yard tee shot. Straight up.

"Where'd it go? Where'd it go?" Otto wanted to know.

"Fair catch," Archie Rosenkrantz said. "No run back on that one."

By the time they reached the sixteenth hole, Otto had transferred his clubs onto the golf cart driven by Archie Rosenkrantz. Archie had told them that he was the father of two psychiatrists and Otto figured he might be able to help his golf swing.

"See, Archie," Otto said while they waited for a twosome who were lost in the eucalyptus trees. "It's like I got no muscle memory. My golfing muscles're forty years old and they already got Alzheimer's disease."

"It's the muscle in your head's the problem, Otto," Archie said, lighting a fresh Havana since the old one looked like spinach. "The toughest six inches in golf is between your ears, right? You take it too serious. I wanna see you loosey goosey up there on the eighteenth tee."

"It could be my basal ganglia," Otto offered. "That's what allows you to ride a bike or swing a golf club without thinking."

"L.T.F.F., Otto."

The eighteenth was a beauty, 522 yards looking right at the new clubhouse, which was framed by San Jacinto Peak. The fairway was lined by trees: pepper, palm, pine, willow, olive and rows of eucalyptus. There was flowing oleander on the right, which made Otto tense. He didn't want to fade into the bushes.

"I slice into that stuff I may as well eat some and die," Otto said to Archie.

"Now you ain't gonna slice, Otto," Archie said soothingly. "Straight back and through and easy."

"And look at all that eucalyptus!" Otto said. "Enough to feed every koala in Australia."

"Now stop those negative thoughts, Otto," Archie said, while Sidney Blackpool sat with his feet up on the empty seat in his golf cart, looking at a smear of sunlight on the side of the mountain.

"I sure wanna finish strong," Otto said. "But what if I duck hook like I did on number three?

Sometimes I lose my banana slice and find a duck hook. I might duck hook right into that house on the left."

Then Otto looked curiously at the fenced property beside the fairway. It was totally enclosed, with security lights all the way around. There was a sign on one gate that said: "Never mind the dog. Beware of the owner." There was an American flag flying to indicate that the owner was in residence.

Otto made the mistake of asking who lived there, after which his golf swing was doomed.

Sidney Blackpool was startled when Otto ran to his golf cart and shook him by the shoulder.

"Sidney!" Otto cried. "Do you know who lives over there? Him! Him!"

"Whom? Whom?"

"The Boss!"

"Bruce Springsteen?"

"The boss of bosses!"

"Don Corleone?"

"The chairman of the board!"

"Armand Hammer or Lee Iacocca?"

"Don't be stupid. Ol blue eyes himself!"

"Yeah?" Even Sidney Blackpool looked a bit impressed. "I thought his house might be a little more grand."

"Whaddaya want? The guy's from Hoboken."

"Well, he's not gonna ask us in," Sidney Blackpool said. "So let's tee er up and get to the nineteenth where we can all kick our golf anxiety."

Archie Rosenkrantz, who was studying Otto's now bulging eyeballs, whispered sadly, "Otto's gonna kick anxiety about when Hugh Hefner kicks silk pajamas."

Otto turned toward the house three times even before he stuck a tee in the ground. He could almost hear a voice singing, " 'Strangers in the niiiight!' "

"There ain't nobody watching you!" Archie said nervously.

"Ol blue eyes don't scare me!" Otto said courageously.

"Scoobie doobie doo, you putz!" Renfield said merrily.

Otto Stringer jerked the Top-Flite dead left. It caromed off Sidney Blackpool's golf cart and ricocheted back into the shin of Archie Rosenkrantz who couldn't duck as fast as the younger men.

"Oh, my God!" Otto wailed. "I'm as useless as Ronald Reagan's right ear!"

Archie Rosenkrantz limped it off for a moment before saying, "Tell you what, Otto. Let's go to the bar and shmooz. I ain't never been much for blood sports."

After they changed shoes, Otto headed back to the lobby to check the membership roster for celebrities. When he found Archie and Sidney Blackpool in the bar, he said, "Does Gregory Peck come here?"

"Naw," Archie said. "He might've when the

club was new. No more."

"Saw the chairman's name," Otto said.

"He don't play golf," said Archie. "Maybe eats in the dining room once in a while. I think he got mad cause someone told him not to bring Spiro Agnew around no more."

"So who else you got here?" Otto asked.

"Lots a people whose names begin with R-O-S-E-N and G-O-L-D," Archie said. "Let's get you a drink."

They put away the first cocktail before the bartender had time to ring up the check for Archie to sign. "Hey, kid," he said to the bartender, "only one ice cube. Whaddaya think this is, a club for the *goyim?* You wanna work Thunderbird or Eldorado maybe?"

The bartender grinned and dumped two ice cubes, pouring more bourbon.

"Less ice than this scuttled the *Titanic*," said Archie.

"This a Jewish club?" Otto asked.

"Whaddaya think, kid?" said Archie. "Do I look like Henry Cabot Lodge? This club was built by Jews when they wouldn't let em in Thunderbird. I heard they even turned down Jack Benny. Nowadays they might keep a few Jews but they ain't allowed to drop kippers on the greens and they gotta tie building blocks to their foreskins till they stretch. Gotta drop their drawers before they even get on the driving range, I hear."

"I thought if you just had enough dough,

223

you were like the big monkey, go anywhere you want."

"You got a lot to learn, kid. Where do you guys belong anyway?"

"Well, we don't actually belong to a club exactly."

"We're cops from L.A.P.D.," Sidney Blackpool said.

"Yeah?" Archie said. "I played a few games with two a your deputy chiefs one time. Over at Hillcrest."

"Is it nice as this?"

"Sure. Gimme your business card," Archie said. "I'll have you over some time."

"No movie stars around here, huh?" Otto was checking out the people coming from lunch.

"Maybe see Lucille Ball. Her husband's a good golfer."

"They live here?" Otto asked.

"Naw, they live in Thunderbird."

"Why doesn't he belong to Thunderbird?"

"He's a Jew. He lives there, but he's a member a *this* club."

"Look here, Archie," Otto said, "we play in Griffith Park with a bunch a cops. Among em there's two Mexicans, a brother, and a Jew. Now, you tell me if we all win the California lottery we can't join a fancy country club together?"

"People say they wanna be with their own kind, kiddo," Archie said.

"But they're cops. They *are* my kind!" said Otto.

"You little *mensch*," Archie said. "If you could figure out a golf swing that quick you'd be the best fat golfer since Billy Casper."

Otto was truly amazed. "A few million bucks can't get a leg over the wall if you're not the same *kind?*"

"Easier to get a leg over the Berlin Wall," Archie Rosenkrantz said. "Heading west. How about another drink, kiddo? With one ice cube."

Chapter 11

GARGOYLES

By the time they were on their way back to the hotel Otto felt like he needed a piña colada and a soak in the spa and maybe a nap before contemplating the recent disaster.

"Sure was a beautiful place," Sidney Blackpool said, trying to make conversation.

"I don't wanna talk about golf."

"Otto, it was you that said I take golf too . . ."

"I don't wanna talk about it."

"It's only a game, Otto."

"Like firewalking's a game. Or playing chicken with Andrei Gromyko. Like a game of twenty questions in an Iranian jail."

"At least we met somebody."

"I like Archie fine. The people treated us nice. The country club's beautiful. Now pull over to the curb and park."

"What for?"

"I wanna toss my sticks down the sewer."

"So you were a slight failure at golf."

"Like Charlie Manson was a slight failure at parole."

"Wait till we get back and have a couple

drinks. You'll feel different."

"I feel like a brain tumor. They should stick me in a jar for study by future generations."

"Maybe you should get a massage."

"What's the use. I probably couldn't even hit the massage table with my ass."

"Have it on the floor. Call a masseuse up to the suite."

"*That* don't sound like too bad an idea," Otto had to admit.

When they got back to the suite the message light on the phone was blinking, so Sidney Blackpool called the operator. The message was from Harlan Penrod.

"Probably wants another date tonight," Otto said. "He's more ready for adoption than Oliver Twist."

Harlan Penrod answered by saying, "Hel-looooo. The Watson residence. May I help you?"

"This is Sidney Blackpool, Harlan."

"My favorite sergeant since Gary Cooper!" Harlan twittered. "Do I have some news for you!"

"What is it?"

"I rummaged through all of Jack's things and found something stuck in a textbook with school papers and other junk. I don't imagine the police saw it."

"What was it?"

"A picture of Jack and a girl."

"So?"

"The background's a swimming pool here in Palm Springs! I recognize it because I used to have a friend who stayed there when he was in town. The reason I know that stupid pool is because one night we got in a fight and he tossed me in and I banged my head on the handrail that's in the picture. I lost all my clothes and a new pair of shoes and a wristwatch."

"Is that all? I mean, a picture of Jack in a hotel pool with a girl?"

"Well, isn't that something?"

"Yeah, it's worth a look."

"Maybe she was some girl from college, maybe not. At least we can check it out."

"Okay, Harlan. You gonna be home this evening?"

"You bet!" Harlan cried. "Do I dress casual or do we try to fit in with the hotel guests? Lots of Vegas hotel workers use that place. Shall I go more for the dated disco king, or trash Vegas flash?"

"Use your own judgment," Sidney Blackpool said. "We'll be by in a couple a hours."

When he hung up, Sidney Blackpool said to Otto, "Can you put off the massage for a while? Harlan's got a picture of Jack Watson and a girl. I think he wants to sign on as our secret agent."

"Haven't I had enough tragedy for one day?" Otto groaned, flopping down on the sofa. "I feel like the paddock at Santa Anita — all tromped on and covered with shit."

"Harlan's one of our only links to Jack Watson. We can't afford to make him mad at us."

"Do you think the guy with the deerstalker at Two twenty-one B Baker Street woulda stayed in business if he had to humor the Harlan Penrods of this world? I don't know, maybe I'll *never* be a corpse cop. I *know* I'll never be a golfer."

"You're on your way to being both, my boy. Take a little rest. I'll send for some drinks."

Harlan Penrod was already waiting when at 6:30 P.M. they pulled up in front of the Watson home.

"Sam Spade Junior," Otto said.

Harlan wasn't dressed like Sam Spade but he did have a Burberry trenchcoat over his shoulder and it wasn't raining. Otto didn't comment, but rolled his eyes at Sidney Blackpool who, like Otto, was still dressed as a resort golfer.

"Here it is!" Harlan hopped into the backseat of the Toyota with a small flashlight, which he shone on the photo.

"I see you came prepared," Otto said. "Hope you're carrying a piece. We weren't expecting that much trouble on this case and we left our iron in L.A."

"She's a beautiful girl," Harlan said. "Just Jack's type. His fiancée's a blonde like that. Tall like him and leggy."

229

"About all we can do is drop by the hotel and see if anybody at the registration desk might recognize her. Or maybe the cocktail girls who work around the pool."

"Boys," Harlan said. "That hotel uses pool boys and waiters."

"Maybe it'll turn out she was with the other kid," Sidney Blackpool said, pointing at a second young man.

In the photo, Jack Watson had a girl around the waist and was about to dunk her under. A blond, broad-shouldered young man had her by the feet and was almost out of frame. All three were laughing into the camera.

"Fine-looking boy, all right," Sidney Blackpool said.

"A very foxy young lady," Otto said.

"Lucky girl," Harlan remarked. "*Two* beautiful boys."

"Well, it's all we got to start with," Sidney Blackpool said, as he drove the Toyota toward Palm Canyon Drive.

"They didn't start with much in *The Maltese Falcon*," Harlan remarked.

"I told you, Sidney," Otto muttered, while Harlan's eyes glistened like desert stars.

The hotel wasn't exactly as upmarket as they would've expected. But then, they figured the girl in the photo could just as easily have been an airline stew or a teacher from Orange County or a tourist from Alberta whom Jack Watson met in some night spot.

There were two pairs of men sitting in the lobby enjoying a cocktail before dinner, and another pair of men breezed through on their way to the dining room. A man and a woman were checking in and had the front desk occupied, so the detectives and Harlan Penrod strolled out by the swimming pool. Another pair of men sat with their feet in the water and sipped mai tais, chatting with the waiter who was dressed in a white shirt and black pants with a red bow tie and red cummerbund. There were a man and woman watching a candlelit game of backgammon being played by yet another pair of men at a poolside cocktail table.

"Harlan," Sidney Blackpool said. "Is this a gay hotel?"

"Of course not."

"Is it a *mixed* hotel?"

"You might say that," Harlan nodded.

"Did you think it odd that Jack was at a *mixed* hotel?" Otto asked.

"Of course not. There's often a price break at mixed places. Maybe she's some secretary from Culver City who couldn't afford a more upscale hotel."

"Okay, let's check with the front desk," Sidney Blackpool said.

They showed the picture to everyone working in the lobby and pool area: front desk, bellmen, waiters. Nobody had ever seen the laughing blond girl in the photo, even though it was clearly the hotel pool in which she frolicked. Nor did anyone recognize Jack Watson or the other lad. Harlan Penrod was looking dejected, figuring they were about to take him home, when the valet-parking boy in a blue golf shirt, white shorts and white tennis shoes came running in from the parking lot.

"I'd like to show you a picture of a girl," Harlan said, and Otto smirked at Sidney Blackpool in that Harlan was now directing the investigation.

"That's our pool," the kid said.

"The girl was probably a guest," Harlan said. "Ever see her?"

"No," the kid said, "but I know the guy."

"You know the guy?"

"He worked here."

"Jack Watson worked here?" Otto pointed at the photo.

"Not the guy with black hair," the boy said. "The other guy. The blond guy holding the girl's feet. His name's Terry something. He was a parking attendant for a week maybe. Worked nights when I was on days."

Five minutes later, the detectives and Harlan Penrod were in the hotel office with the night manager who was digging through employee files, saying, "Well, we shouldn't have too much trouble, Sergeant. Hotel employees in this town have to have police identification cards. We send our people to the police when we hire them and they get their pictures and

232

fingerprints taken. Everyone who might have access to rooms, that is: maids, bellmen, even valet parkers."

"Our first *real* lead!" Harlan said, looking as though he'd just found the elusive bird from Malta.

The young man's name was Terry Kinsale. He'd given an address in Cathedral City and a local telephone number. He listed his permanent address as Phoenix, Arizona, with a Phoenix telephone number in case of emergency. A sister, Joan Kinsale, was the person to contact.

The detectives and Harlan Penrod took down the information, thanked the night manager and headed back to the front where the parking boy had the Toyota waiting.

Sidney Blackpool said, "You did good," and tipped the kid twenty bucks. They were off to the address given by Terry Kinsale.

"I don't know about that address," Harlan said. "Highway One eleven isn't a residential zone. Unless maybe it's a motel, or he lives upstairs of a store or something."

It was neither. It was a bar. A gay bar close by two other gay bars.

"Maybe the name's bogus," Otto said.

"He wouldn't a been able to keep the job if he had a rap sheet," Sidney Blackpool said. "Palm Springs P.D. mugged and printed him."

"Hey, how about letting me go in alone?" Harlan suggested. "I can show the picture to the bartender and customers. Nobody's gonna get hicky about me."

"*Hinky* is the word they always use on the cop shows," Otto said.

"Yeah, nobody's gonna get hinky about me. They'll tell me if they know Terry."

"Here's a twenty for some drinks," Sidney Blackpool said. "We'll be waiting across the street at the other bar."

"Don't get caught cruising!" Harlan said with a naughty smile.

"Hurry up for crying out loud, Harlan!" said Otto. "I'm getting hungry."

After the houseboy was gone, Otto said, "We really going in *that* saloon?"

"You wanna wait at the gas station?"

"One drink I'll catch AIDS, my luck," Otto said. "And my lip'll rot off like a leper on Molokai."

"It's not that kind a disease, Otto," Sidney Blackpool said as they parked on Highway 111.

The saloon was empty except for a pair of middle-aged men sitting at the far end of the bar bickering about something. The bartender looked about as swishy as Rocky Marciano. His face was a pink-and-white mass of old lumpy tissue.

"Jesus," Otto whispered after he took their drink order. "Know what I saw shining there on the top of his face? Eyes. He's got two of them back in there somewhere."

"Lemme have all the quarters and dimes you

can spare," Sidney Blackpool said to the bartender, putting a twenty on the bar. "I gotta make a long-distance call."

"Whadda we doing, Sidney, calling Buckingham Palace? This turned into the search for Vera Lynn?"

"I may as well call Terry Kinsale's sister in Phoenix while Harlan's doing his sleuthing. I'll use the phone booth next door at the gas station."

"You leaving me here alone?"

"Say hello to Mister Goodbar if he drops by."

"Hurry back, will ya?" Otto said, inspecting the lip of his bucket glass before sipping the booze.

"Is Terry all right? Was it an accident?" Joan Kinsale asked, after Sidney Blackpool identified himself.

"I'm sure he's okay. We're trying to find him," the detective said. "We're working on the murder of Jack Watson and thought you or Terry might be able to help us."

She waited several beats and then the young woman said, "Who?"

"Jack Watson."

"Watson?" she said. "Was that his last name? You mean Terry's friend Jack? The good-looking guy with black curly hair?"

"The one with you in the hotel swimming pool," Sidney Blackpool said. "We have a snapshot of the three a you. It *was* you, wasn't it?"

"He's dead?" Joan Kinsale said. "When?"

"A year ago June. He was found shot to death in his car."

"Terry never mentioned it! But I've only heard from him a few times since then. I met Jack when I went to visit Terry for a few days."

"Did you ever date Jack?"

"No, he was Terry's friend."

"Is Terry gay?" the detective asked abruptly.

"Well, I don't think so. Not really," the young woman answered. "He was a little . . . *confused* about himself."

"Where is he now?"

"La Jolla. At least he was last time he wrote. Hoping to work at a hotel, he said. No real mailing address. He's a bit immature, but a really good kid. Everyone likes him."

"He ever been in trouble with the law?"

"Never that I know of."

"He use drugs?"

"Not that I know of. I mean, maybe he smokes a little grass like everybody else."

"When did he leave Palm Springs?"

"I don't know," she said. "Over a year ago, I guess."

"If he calls or writes I'd like to talk to him," Sidney Blackpool said. "I'm going to give you my office number. They can reach me."

Meanwhile, Otto Stringer finished his second

236

drink and was trying to avoid eye contact with a Harlan Penrod lookalike, this one with his own hair, who sat at Otto's end of the bar nursing a virgin margarita while an Anthony Newley oldie played on the Palm Springs radio station.

He managed to look directly into Otto's eyes as he sang it with Tony: " 'This is the moment! My destiny calls me!' "

Otto's eyes slid back in his skull and he ordered another double, AIDS or not, just as Harlan came bubbling into the saloon.

"I'm onto something!" he whispered breathlessly to Otto.

"So's he," Otto said, pointing to the lip-syncher. "Angel dust maybe. So how's the life of a secret agent?"

"Terry Kinsale's been away and now he's back in town! He was in the bar Saturday night!"

In a few minutes Sidney Blackpool returned and began comparing notes with Harlan while Otto's admirer gave up and started singing to a bogus cowboy in dirty jeans who ordered two beers the moment he sat down.

"We'll check with Palm Springs P.D. tomorrow and see if Terry Kinsale's trying to register for hotel work. Meantime, let's keep it very quiet, Harlan. He left Palm Springs about the time Jack was killed so this could turn into something."

"I think I might die of excitement!" Harlan

cried. "But I'll keep it on the q.t. Where're we going now?"

"Otto and I have to go back to Mineral Springs."

"We do?" Otto said.

"Good. I've never been up there!" Harlan said.

"Uh, Harlan, how about you hanging around the gay bars tonight? Ask around about Terry. You might come up with something."

"I'll bet," Otto muttered.

"You might even come up with *Terry*," Sidney Blackpool said. "Here, this should be enough." He handed the houseboy four twenty-dollar bills. "You can cab it home afterward."

"Okay," Harlan said, "but let me know tomorrow what we're working. I would've dressed a little less butch if I knew we were coming out here."

"Call you tomorrow," Sidney Blackpool said, as they left Harlan to finish his drink at the bar.

"So why're we going to Mineral Springs again tonight?" Otto wanted to know as they drove away.

"So we can look at it at night. I mean really look at it."

"A little town like that? What's to look at?"

"I wanna see the road Jack Watson took for his last ride. I wanna see how it looks at night."

"Why?"

"I don't know why."

"Then why do it?"

"We might get an idea."

"About what?"

"I don't know. I don't know any other way to work a whodunit homicide. It's the way I was trained."

"You know, Sidney, I don't think I'll ever make a good corpse cop. Maybe you oughtta bounce me over to the robbery detail or something."

"You'll be a corpse cop and a twelve handicapper before I'm finished with you, Otto."

" 'This is the moment!' " Otto suddenly sang. " 'My destiny calls me!' "

"That's the spirit, kiddo," Sidney Blackpool said, à la Archie Rosenkrantz. "Golf's a mystery but murder isn't. You look at a whodunit the way you look at the desert. This desert changes from one minute to the next. Same with a whodunit. But you gotta be able to *see* it."

"Hope I don't get the spider in my chili tonight," Otto said. "Looks like we're *dining* at the Eleven Ninety-nine Club."

Twenty million years ago the Coachella Valley was created by fault action, and today the huge San Andreas Fault runs along the mountains on the north side of the valley. Mount San Jacinto and the Santa Rosas, which partly shelter this valley, are much younger than the neighboring San Bernardino Mountains, less rounded, more dramatic and impressive to the human eye. The bottom of the Salton Sea is 273 feet below sea level, only a few feet higher than Death Valley. In the daylight this desert valley seems lifeless and inhospitable. But the desert at night is quite another story.

The Santa Rosas are home for 650 bighorns. There are birds as huge as the turkey vulture soaring over open country. There is the great horned owl glowering forever like the boss ayatollah, and there's the spotted skunk, which can fire its scent while doing a handstand like an Olympian. There is an occasional lion sighted in this country and packs of coyotes everywhere. There are diamondbacks more than six feet in length.

And there are smaller, more secret night prowlers, the kit fox for one, no larger than a house cat. And kangaroo rats, as cute as chipmunks, with large white tails used for balance as they hop. There are leaf-nosed bats flitting like shadows on the desert floor in the moonlight. There are black widows, scorpions, cockroaches as big as locusts, and 340 species of birds. The desert at night is not at all lifeless. But it can be inhospitable, especially to detectives from Hollywood.

Sidney Blackpool drove as far as was comfortable into Solitaire Canyon on the main asphalt road. Then he took a flashlight from the glove box and led Otto on foot toward the smaller canyon where the Watson car was found.

"You didn't happen to stick an off-duty gun under the seat a your car when we left L.A., did you, Sidney?" Otto asked hopefully.

"Didn't think we'd be up against too much physical danger on the links," Sidney Blackpool said.

"This freaking place's spooky," Otto said. "Listen to the wind howl. When it really blows I bet it could turtle the *Queen Mary*."

"It sounds like surf crashing against the rocks," Sidney Blackpool said. Then he switched off his flashlight and gazed up the canyon toward the lights in the shacks and cottages occupied by outlaw bikers.

Smoke trees clawed wispily at the wind. On the rocky slope a tree of vertical whips cracked out from the hillside. It was twelve feet tall and the branches floated and wavered in the moaning wind as though it were underwater. All around them were twisted tormented shapes of desert plants and trees, gargoyle shadows. And there were banshee laughs and screams of nocturnal creatures killing and being killed on this perfect November night. Neither detective knew for sure if the demented sounds were made by animals or by those who lived on the road above in the shacks where the lamps flickered in utter darkness.

"Listen!" Sidney Blackpool said.

Under a desert willow that would soon

have flowers of rose and lavender, they heard the melody of a burrowing owl living in an abandoned coyote den: COO-COO-COOOOOOO.

Then as Sidney Blackpool stepped closer in the darkness, the owl felt threatened and cried "KAK KAK KAK!"

Sidney Blackpool stepped yet closer and the owl imitated the buzz of an angry diamondback.

And two city boys turned tail, hotfooting it toward the road.

"Kee-rist!" Otto cried.

"Was that what I thought it was?"

"What the hell you *think* it was?"

"Well, I was reading in the tourist guide that desert creatures can imitate rattlesnakes. It could've been a desert impressionist."

"A hog's ass could be kosher, but I don't think so! And I don't wanna catch his act again, even if it was Rich Little! Now let's get *out* of this freaking place before we get gobbled by buzzards or something."

Then they heard it coming: a motorcycle. A Harley came thundering down the dirt road from the shacks at a speed that seemed impossible at night. The driver was obviously very sure of himself or didn't give a damn.

Instead of going out the main road, he turned the bike back into the canyon, back by a stand of strange shaggy trees. He stopped the bike and got off. He stood for a moment and peered around in the light from the Harley's headlight.

"I got a feeling," Sidney Blackpool said quietly.

"You got a feeling what?" Otto whispered.

"That he's looking in the very spot where the Watson car was found. I bet it was down in those trees."

"My neck hair's doing the boogaloo and the freak-a-deek," Otto whispered. "Let's make a run for the car."

"Let's duck behind the rocks and watch him."

"He might catch us and think we're cops!"

"We *are* cops, Otto."

"I'm losing my fucking mind! I mean he might think we're local dope cops. He might shoot first and apologize later after he finds out we're only harmless homicide dicks from Hollywood . . . who don't even have a nine iron to defend themselves with!"

The biker gave up looking and got back on the Harley, digging it into the sand, which made him get off and rock it out. He was a very big man, that much was certain even at a distance.

"Too late to run now," Otto breathed. "Here he comes."

The Harley growled toward them at a much slower pace. Then the driver spotted the Toyota far down the road and made straight for it. Both detectives peered over the rocks as he passed, but he punched it and kicked up a dust cloud. They could see his silhouette stop beside the Toyota as he peeked inside for a moment. Then he was off and heading toward the main highway and Mineral Springs.

As they were walking back toward the car, Otto said, "Sidney, I really want you to get the job with Watson and all, but maybe I don't want it as much as you want me to want it. I mean, when that biker was jamming by I was maybe two inches from a spiny plant shaped like something that hangs over the top of a French church. One more foot sideways and I'd have more harpoons in me than Moby Dick. Are you listening to me, Sidney? I'm forty years old. I should be an awning salesman in Van Nuys. Now I need some maxi pads. I can't take this kind a fun no more. Are you listening to me, Sidney?"

Sidney Blackpool shone the flashlight back down the dirt road toward the stand of shaggy trees. "Otto," he said, "if you were driving a big car out here at night and you wanted to get to that row a shacks up on the canyon wall, you could easily get confused. The road that goes off left toward the houses crosses the other road. Did you notice how it crossed back there where we heard the owl?"

"You ain't been listening to me," Otto said.

"So it'd be easy to get on the wrong one and keep climbing and not realize you were going the wrong way till maybe the condition of the dirt road gave you a hint. And then it'd be very hard to get a big Rolls-Royce turned around on that trail."

"So?"

"I was wondering. The Palm Springs lieutenant said at first they thought it was an accident. I can see why."

"Listen, Sidney. We already discovered that the Watson kid was probably A.C.-D.C. Now're you saying this is a gay version of Chappaquiddick? If so, you got two problems: he was alone when he went over the canyon and he was shot through the head."

"I was wondering if the killer shot him and drove him up here maybe trying to go to one a those shacks. And then got himself turned around and . . . no, that doesn't work. I forgot the kid was belted in the driver's seat. Goddamnit, nothing works! It doesn't make sense no matter how you figure it."

"It makes sense only one way, the way it's been figured all along. The kid was shot. He was driven up here by the killer or killers. He was strapped behind the wheel, but I don't know why. The car was torched and pushed over the canyon into all that desert shrubbery and it wasn't found for a couple days. Period."

"But there're so many better places to dump a car with a body in it. Less risky than dealing with a big Rolls up there on that skinny dirt road. I just can't work it out to have it make sense."

"Let's go over to the Eleven Ninety-nine and eat some grease," Otto said. "Couple drinks it won't matter so much to ya."

Sidney Blackpool stared up at the canyon wall and listened to the chirp and chatter of desert birds and insects and the yapping of a young coyote loping along a ridge, and beneath it all was the relentless moaning of the wind. He said, "Murder should make sense on *some* level even if the killer's nuts."

"There's not a cause for every effect," Otto said. "Life's a crap game."

"Partner," said Sidney Blackpool, "you have to *make believe* there's a cause and effect at work or you'll never solve a whodunit."

"Sidney, I realize an old corpse cop like you has instincts about dead bodies. Just like the buzzards and coyotes and scavengers around these parts. But if you don't get me fed soon, I'll be the *second* cadaver they pull outta Solitaire Canyon."

"Let's go get some grease," Sidney Blackpool said.

At about the time that Sidney Blackpool and Otto Stringer were in the desert getting faked out of their loafers by a foxy owl, Prankster Frank Zamelli was patrolling the outskirts of Mineral Springs so bored he could spit. He was teamed up with Maynard Rivas but couldn't get the big Indian cop to go along with anything.

"I'm depressed, Maynard," he said. "What say we drive by the exterminator's store, steal the big statue of the Terminix bug and sneak it into the Mineral Water Hotel. Then we could call the maid and say, 'Come quick! We got a big roach in our room!' "

"Paco said no more pranks. You're starting to wear him down a little bit."

"But I'm depressed!" Prankster Frank griped as the Indian cruised the main drag watching Beavertail Bigelow staggering against the red light, heading for the Eleven Ninety-nine.

"Good thing Beavertail don't drive no more," Maynard Rivas said.

Just then O. A. Jones came blasting by on his way to the station after having booked a drunk driver down at the county slam in Indio. He was trying to get to the Eleven Ninety-nine before the first gaggle of manicurists went home to dinner.

"There he goes," the Indian said, "taking his end-of-shift O. A. Jones Memorial Roller Coaster Ride. Only thing can stop that guy is a high curb."

"I'm depressed," Prankster Frank said again. "You wouldn't wanna *borrow* J. Edgar's catamaran, would ya? We could raise the sails and haul it to the hotel swimming pool. Then we could call J. Edgar and . . ."

"The possum gag was enough for one night," Maynard Rivas said. "We'll be lucky we don't get beefed over that one."

"It was worth it," Prankster Frank said.

He was referring to a call earlier in the evening at No-Blood Alley where one of the old dolls was in a tizzy because an opossum had gotten into her mobile home. Upon spotting the animal she immediately went flying out the door but her cat didn't make it. When the cops got there the terrible yowling of the cat and hissing of the opossum had died to a dreadful silence.

"Officers," the old dame wept. "Millie's inside. The possum probably killed her!"

"Who's Millie?" Prankster Frank asked.

"My cat!"

Prankster Frank and Maynard Rivas drew their sticks knowing that an opossum can have a nasty temper when riled. Both had worked the desert long enough not to be fooled by any possum-playing either. The little bastards would lie there belly up with tongue lolling and eyes staring as unblinking as Sergeant Coy Brickman's, and the second you got close they'd come up like a furry knuckleball. Both cops had their clubs cocked and ready.

Prankster Frank crept into the bedroom of the mobile home and heard the soft mewing behind the bed. He'd never heard of an opossum killing a cat but you never knew. The mewing got rhythmic and louder. He crept in after waving Maynard Rivas to stand still. He peeked behind the bed and caught them in the flashlight beam. It was the same as many other sneaks and peeks in his police career, exactly the same.

The opossum had that spotted tabby pressed

against the wall and was humping for all he was worth. In fact, Prankster Frank hadn't seen such a hosing since Johnny Holmes stopped doing porn flicks. He switched off the light, turned and walked back outside with Maynard Rivas.

"Just leave the door open and wait a while," he told the distraught old dame. "He'll be through in a few minutes. Of course they might want a cigarette after."

When the cop told her what was going on in her bedroom, she got mad and said she didn't like the way he was making light of a tragedy, and she was calling Paco Pedroza about his unprofessional demeanor first thing in the morning.

Afterward, Maynard Rivas asked Prankster Frank if he *had* to make the crack about the cigarette.

"Maynard, when you get a chance for a line you gotta deliver the line," said Prankster Frank.

"If you're Johnny Carson," the big Indian said. "I don't want another lecture from Paco. He already said he didn't appreciate you getting Choo Choo Chester to do his Stevie Wonder smile-and-head-roll when he was jerkin off that rubber dildo in the locker room."

"I thought it was a panic," Prankster Frank said. "Old Chester going 'Ain't it wooooonder-ful' while he's loping that old rubber donkey!"

"Yeah, but you shouldn't a sent Anemic

Annie in there on a phony errand. Poor old broad."

"I'm soooorry," Prankster Frank said. "Hey, tell you what! Let's drive by Shaky Jim's just one time! Just one lightweight prank and I'll call it a night and go to sleep or something."

"Okay," Maynard Rivas sighed, pressing the accelerator and heading for the outskirts of Mineral Springs.

There were a few houses scattered in the path of the wind funnel, houses unprotected by eucalyptus. The residents, who got in there for very low rent, usually called it a wrap after one winter of living in the gales. Not so Shaky Jim. He wanted to be out of town but he was afraid of the crank dealers in the canyons. He settled for the wind, but he always had nightmares of being blown, like Dorothy and Toto, clear into another county.

Shaky Jim had lots of fears. He feared that if he got arrested one more time for dealing pot, the cops might contact the welfare people and try to cut off his monthly checks. Knowing this, Prankster Frank liked to cruise down the highway and suddenly whip into Shaky Jim's driveway. He'd jump on the brakes so hard he'd go into a locked skid, and start yelling and slamming all four doors of the police car like it was the biggest dope raid since the French Connection. After which, Shaky Jim would invariably run to his stash and flush it all — maybe $500 worth of grass, which was

all he could afford to deal at one time —
thereby clogging his pipes. The local Roto-
Rooter man just loved Prankster Frank who
had brought him lots of business since joining
the Mineral Springs P.D.

Prankster Frank and Maynard Rivas were out
there on the highway terrorizing Shaky Jim
when Sidney Blackpool and Otto Stringer came
driving by. The detectives looked curiously at
the Mineral Springs patrol car, which did a
wheelie in the driveway of a lonely house, after
which two uniformed cops started slamming
car doors and yelling commands in different
voices and languages.

"Hands up!" Prankster Frank yelled.

"*Más arriba!*" Maynard hollered.

"*Dung lai!*" Frank bellowed, calling on his
memories of Vietnam.

And so forth. They yelled nonsense and any
gibberish that came to mind and then jumped
back in the car ready to do a U-ee and scorch
back toward Mineral Springs, except that Sidney
Blackpool got out of his Toyota and waved
them down.

"We're on a hot call!" Prankster Frank said,
figuring a lost tourist needed directions. "We
gotta go!"

"We're Blackpool and Stringer from
L.A.P.D." The detective showed them his
badge.

"Oh, yeah," Prankster Frank said, and

Maynard cut the engine. "You were in the Eleven Ninety-nine the other night. Heard all about you."

As he was satisfying the curiosity of the detectives as to what the hell the performance they'd witnessed was all about, Shaky Jim came shaking out of the house in his undershirt and bare feet with his hands high in the air, hands all green from processing pot.

He was younger than Harlan Penrod but not by much. He was smoking a cigarette, or rather, one dangled from his trembling lips.

"I can't take it no more!" he cried. "I'm moving away. I can't take it no more!"

" 'Shoot if you must this old gray head!' " Prankster Frank said. "He gets real dramatic sometimes."

"I quit! I had enough!" Shaky Jim cried. "I'm moving to Sun City. You can just go wreck Billy Hightower's business. You ain't gonna have me to kick around no more."

Shaky Jim stood like that in the beam of the headlights while the detectives looked on in amazement.

"I think maybe you guys went a little too far," Otto said. "He's quoting Richard Nixon."

"Who's Billy Hightower?" Sidney Blackpool asked.

"A biker lives up in Solitaire Canyon. President of the local chapter of an outlaw motorcycle gang that does nothing but cook methamphetamine and ride their choppers and

252

hogs all over the desert."

"Why don't ya never bust Billy Hightower?" Shaky Jim wailed. "He deals more in a week than I made all year. You let the spook slide just cause he was one a you!"

"What's he babbling about?" Otto asked.

"Billy Hightower's an ex-cop," Maynard Rivas explained. "San Bernardino sheriffs, I think. He was fired for knocking his captain into a punch bowl or something at some kind a cop party. He's a Nam vet like most a the bikers in the gang. A crank dealer. I never heard a any those lowlifes having the class to deal real big. Crystal's their thing. A lowlife drug."

"Yes, he does!" Shaky Jim said, approaching the patrol car with his arms still in the air. "Billy Hightower deals big to kids from down Palm Springs. You never bust Billy cause he's one a your own!"

"Go back to bed, Jim," Prankster Frank said. "You're spoiling my prank with all this hollering."

While Shaky Jim trembled back toward the house, Sidney Blackpool looked up the canyon to the lights twinkling by the dirt roads on the plateau. "Think he's smoking it or what? I mean, about Hightower dealing to Palm Springs kids?"

"I never heard it," Maynard Rivas said. "But you never know about Billy. He's got a little more class than the rednecks he runs with."

"A brother running with redneck bikers?" Otto said. "An ex-cop to boot?"

"That's why they like him," Prankster Frank said. "He knows police work. Also, he can beat the living shit outta any two of them at once. He's got more redneck admirers than any spade this side a Charlie Pride."

"He ever come into town?" Sidney Blackpool asked.

"Every night just about," Maynard Rivas said. "Remember the other night at the Eleven Ninety-nine? That dude sporting his colors?"

"Colors?"

"His bike jacket with the Cobras logo on the back. That big mean-looking motherfucker in the corner was Billy Hightower."

"He drinks in a cop bar?"

"Guess he still likes to pretend," Maynard Rivas said. "Maybe he's snooping. Anyway, he behaves himself and don't bother nobody and nobody bothers him. Course none of us ever sit with him or talk with him or anything. Except Sergeant Harry Bright. He used to always buy Billy a drink. Harry Bright'd see some good in a sidewinder if it had him by the nuts. Harry Bright had a stroke. Ain't around no more."

"So we heard," Sidney Blackpool said. "Back in Solitaire Canyon over to the right there's a bunch a shaggy trees. Just past the fork in the road, I mean. Was the Watson car found there?"

"Those're tamarisk trees," Maynard Rivas said. "Big ol dirty things. They shoot em on sight down the other end a the valley. Yeah, that's where they found the car all right."

"We saw a biker out there tonight nosing around," Otto Stringer said.

"Could be he was dumping a load a drug garbage," Maynard Rivas said. "There's always a lot of syringes laying around below those shacks and I don't think there's a diabetic up there."

"Awful dark in the desert at night," Prankster Frank warned. "I knew a local cop shot his own car to death chasing a burglar. That's almost suicide, I guess."

"We gotta go now," Maynard Rivas said. "Better stay out a the desert at night or that Toyota's gonna have more dimples than Kirk Douglas."

Chapter 12

THE OUTLAW

There were two women employed by the Mineral Springs Police Department, but only one was a sworn law officer. Ruth Kosko, the department's sole detective, was known of course as Ruth the Sleuth. The other woman was Paco's secretary, record clerk and radio operator, Annie Paskewicz, called Anemic Annie from the days when she worked for the crime lab in San Diego, drawing blood from arrestees suspected of being under the influence of drugs.

There seemed to be someone like Anemic Annie in crime labs and county morgues everywhere. She was pallid in winter and summer, not albino white but close, and she'd formerly spent her days drawing and analyzing blood while seeming to have none of her own. Anemic Annie always wore sensible shoes that made clunky footsteps like Boris Karloff, and she was yet another law-enforcement burnout, biding her time for a pension. It was because of her ravaged nerves that she'd left her job in San Diego and come to Mineral Springs. She'd gotten so nervous in mid-life that she couldn't make a clean hit anymore.

Once when they brought in a junkie for a blood sample, Annie broke the Guinness world record for misses with a syringe. She made twenty-six straight attempts to hit a vein without success. The horsed-out junkie started yelling and screaming about Annie poking more holes than the Three Musketeers, and the narcs who'd arrested the hype decided that Annie's antics would be deemed cruel and unusual punishment so they had to let the guy go.

People started spreading rumors that poor Annie carried her syringe at port arms. They claimed she had pulled out bone marrow during that world-record performance. Cops said that she *had* to work nights, and never ate garlic, and slept in a box of dirt with a lid. People warned if you owned her favorite flavor, type AB, not to get your neck too close or you'd be sporting the world's biggest hickey.

Finally she got sick of it and telephoned a cop she used to know in San Diego who was working as a sergeant at a little police department in the Coachella Valley. An interview was arranged during which Sergeant Harry Bright said, "Paco, you'll never find a harder-working woman than Annie here."

Anemic Annie gave up orchids in San Diego for a cactus garden in Mineral Springs, and found that if she wore a big straw hat and long skirts, her pale skin did okay in the dry heat. She was generally much happier than when she was bloodletting down south.

On the evening that Sidney Blackpool and Otto Stringer were getting the crap scared out of them in the desert, Anemic Annie and Ruth the Sleuth were commiserating at the Mirage Saloon, neither wanting to drink at the Eleven Ninety-nine Club because of all the chauvinist pigs that hung around there. But both knew if they wanted to score with some young hunking cop they had little choice in Mineral Springs other than to boogie over there in the shank of the night.

Ruth the Sleuth was in a snit because she'd worked Mineral Springs for over two years and despite all her sleuthing hadn't solved a single whodunit homicide. Of course there hadn't *been* a whodunit homicide in Mineral Springs during the two years, but Ruth couldn't hold her bourbon and wouldn't be mollified.

She said to Anemic Annie, "I bet I could've done something by now with the Watson case. They found the body in our town and Palm Springs P.D. never even asked me to come in on the investigation. And now two dicks from Hollywood show up and they don't ask me either!"

"I wish Gerry Ferraro had got elected," Anemic Annie griped. "*Then* they'd treat us different, the bastards."

They both knew that they'd better leave *that* kind of talk outside if they eventually sauntered over to the Eleven Ninety-nine to search for a big hunk.

Ruth the Sleuth was a burly young woman, and thus had some appeal to the midget Oleg Gridley who was sitting morosely at the end of the bar, his chin just above bar level where he cried in his beer over Bitch Cassidy, but despaired of winning her heart.

"Harry Bright was the only human being in this sexist organization," Ruth the Sleuth griped. "Probably replace poor old Harry with another Prankster Frank or something."

"I'd like to stick a needle in Prankster Frank's frigging arm and suck him dry," Anemic Annie said to her fourth Tom Collins, making Ruth the Sleuth wonder if the vampire rumors had some substance.

"I'd like to stick Portia Cassidy's little pink rose with anything that'd make her *love* me!" Oleg Gridley cried boozily from his end of the bar.

"You got awful big ears for a teeny guy," Ruth said. "Whadda we gotta do for some privacy around here?"

"You think men treat you bad?" Oleg wailed, nearly drunk enough for a crying jag. "That's cause they're bigger'n you. Everybody's bigger'n *me*. Your left tit's bigger'n my ass!"

"You oughtta clean up your act, Oleg," Ruth advised, as boozy as the midget. "You get drunk'n you always start talking like a disgusting scum-sucking little creep. That's why Portia Cassidy hates your disgusting little guts."

"I just don't understand the female sex,"

Oleg moaned. "I do everything for women and I can't get love!"

"So get rid of your collection of revolting sex aids you're always bragging about," said Anemic Annie.

"I'd do *almost* anything," said Oleg Gridley. "I wouldn't give up my genuine oak chastity belt with the glory hole drilled in it. That's an *antique!*"

"Lemme think about your problem," Ruth the Sleuth said, tapping on the glass with her pencil. Then she looked behind the bar, made a sleuthlike note or two, and grinned at the midget.

"Elementary, my dear Oleg," she said. "I can help you score with Portia Cassidy."

"You can, Ruth?" the midget cried. "Oh, I'd be so happy! I'd do anything for you! I'd even put you in the Wamsutta wonderland of my little trundle bed! I'd show you my blow-up donkey with the life-size . . ."

"Knock that shit *off*, Oleg!" Ruth barked. "That's your problem, you rotten little slime bucket!"

"Okay, okay, I'm sorry. So what can you do for me?"

"Well," Ruth said, "you got only one thing going for you, far as I can see."

"What's that? My auto-parts store? I made fifty grand last year."

"Okay, you got *two* things going for you. You're rich and you're pretty cute-looking."

"I am?"

"Yeah, you're pretty frigging cute," Anemic Annie also had to admit, and now she was slurring as badly as Ruth the Sleuth.

"Gee, Annie, I only do the deed of darkness with real *big* girls," Oleg apologized. "But what's a little fellatio among friends. Can you put your feet behind your ears?"

"Here's my plan, you maggot-mouth," Ruth interrupted, looking behind the bar at the eight-string ukulele that Ruben the bartender had propped up by the cash register. "That uke gives me an idea."

"What's the idea, Ruth?" Oleg cried. "Stop teasing me!"

"We're gonna change your act. What kinda clothes you got at home? Annie, you can help. We're gonna need to borrow a hairpiece from Edna's Salon before she closes. We're gonna make Oleg into somebody Portia can't resist."

"We are?" the midget squealed in delight.

And though she could never have guessed it, Ruth the Sleuth had taken a significant step toward her consuming ambition of solving a whodunit homicide.

By the time Sidney Blackpool and Otto Stringer got to the Eleven Ninety-nine Club, the walls were starting to vibrate. It sounded like someone was lobbing mortars from the top of the mesa and they were landing short, thumping steadily.

"Must be payday," Otto observed. "Maybe

we'll get lucky and J. Edgar won't have no chili left."

When they got inside, Wingnut Bates was standing at the bar hoisting his third margarita, complaining about a citizen who was threatening to sue him.

"She said she's suing me and the city for eighty million dollars!" Wingnut wailed. "I shot her dog in the *foot* is all. Just as he came to the end of his chain which I didn't see. All I saw was teeth that don't let go till you cut the head off!"

"I know that broad," Nathan Hale Wilson commiserated. "She's one a those loonies from the Animal Liberation Front. Brought a stray inta the station and says, 'What'll you do with this poor little thing, Officer!' 'Grind it up and feed it to the other dogs,' I says. She threatened to sue *me*, for chrissake!"

"That's what police work's come to," J. Edgar Gomez observed. "Every time a cop cranks on the cuffs too tight some guy shows up in court with a surgical collar, a body cast, and F. Lee Bailey."

"We don't get paid enough to put up with lawsuits on top a everything else," Maynard Rivas groused. "If I was the right brand a Indian I'd walk away from this shit in a minute. If I was an Agua Caliente I'd drive a Ferrari instead of a five-year-old Ford pickup with a transmission whinier than John McEnroe."

"I hate poor-mouthing! Gimme your phone

number so I can call in a pledge!" yelled Beavertail Bigelow from his seat by the jukebox, causing all the cops to glare at the desert rat for his heartless ways.

"Least police work's steady and gives you a regular paycheck," O. A. Jones said, pissing off everybody for looking on the bright side. "I know a cop in Orange County quit to become a movie star and doesn't make five hundred bucks a year. He'll spend his old age broke and senile, yodeling his heart out like Johnny Weissmuller in the actors' rest home."

"You hear about Selma Mobley, that bubble-assed female cop in Palm Springs?" Nathan Hale Wilson asked. "She's marrying her lieutenant."

"I just love cop weddings," Prankster Frank observed. "They're about as safe as a San Francisco bathhouse."

"Oughtta give them his-and-hers saps for those special family disputes," said O. A. Jones.

"Well, they're both cops," Pigasus, the sheriff's chopper pilot, noted. "They oughtta understand each other."

"Like Snoopy and Cujo're both dogs," said Dustin Hoffman, the fingerprint man. "He's Snoopy, the poor fucker."

Sidney Blackpool looked around the bar and at first the only black man he saw was Choo Choo Chester. He was making a serious move on a masseuse from a hotel in Rancho Mirage, but she wasn't treating his complaints about his wife with too much sympathy.

"So how'd you meet your wife?" the girl asked.

"I bought a couple dances with her," Chester whined. "It was *all* a mistake!"

"You gonna dump her or what?"

"I can't," Chester moaned. "She's expecting a kid in three months!"

"Really, honey?" the masseuse said. "Is it *yours?*"

Hoping he might have a chance to steal the masseuse right out from under Chester, Prankster Frank sidled up on her left side and whispered, "Baby, you got a body any eighteen-year-old would want."

"Yeah," said the sulky masseuse. "So send me an eighteen-year-old and maybe I'll loan it to him."

"You're about as exciting as a wet dream," Prankster Frank sneered, moving back down the bar to greener pastures.

"Don't plan to end up in my diary, funnel-face," said the masseuse.

J. Edgar Gomez tried to avert a brawl by yelling, "Who wants another round? I'm extending happy hour fifteen minutes!" It brought a chorus of cheers and hoorahs. When people started getting surly, J. Edgar knew to ease them into the next stage.

Sidney Blackpool started searching for another black face, one that rested on a much bigger body. Then he saw him, away from the cops, on the side of the saloon occupied by civilians. He was two tables from Beavertail Bigelow. He was alone. It was the president of the local chapter of Cobras, Billy Hightower.

Sidney Blackpool and Otto Stringer both ordered a drink and a bowl of J. Edgar's infamous chili, and this time there was nothing still alive in the bowl. They could have had a table alone near the John Wayne mural, but walked to the side of the saloon where Billy Hightower sat nursing a double vodka, silently watching the revelry.

"Can we join you?" Sidney Blackpool asked.

Billy Hightower studied both men, and then looked toward the table on the other side of the room, then back at the detectives.

"I'm Blackpool. He's Stringer. We're dicks from Hollywood Division, L.A.P.D."

That was enough to make Billy Hightower curious, so he nodded at the empty chairs and they sat. Otto started spooning through the chili for dead bodies.

"Buy you a drink?" Sidney Blackpool asked.

"I got a drink," said Billy Hightower.

"We're working on the Watson homicide," Sidney Blackpool said, sipping at his Scotch. "The Palm Springs kid they found in the Rolls?"

"Little off your beat, ain't it?" Billy Hightower said, toying with the double shot of vodka. Up close he looked like a real boozer and Sidney Blackpool had to resist a policeman's urge to glance at the biker's enormous forearms for meth tracks.

"We have some information that the Watson kid might've been in Hollywood the day he was killed," Sidney Blackpool said. "That's how we got involved."

Billy Hightower looked from one man to the other, then at Otto's brown gruel. "It ain't Hollywood, but it ain't bad," he said. "Microscopic animals can't live in it."

"Hollywood ain't Hollywood, neither," Otto shrugged, and he tried a spoonful. It *wasn't* bad!

"Hear you used to be on the job," Sidney Blackpool said. "San Bernardino County sheriffs, was it?"

"Uh-huh," Billy Hightower said.

"Hear you were in Vietnam," Sidney Blackpool said.

"Served my country and served my county," Billy Hightower said. "They gonna do a cop benefit for me or what?"

"We asked around about you cause we got a little something on the Watson case. Maybe."

Billy Hightower watched Sidney Blackpool's hand reaching into his pocket, the way a cop watches hand movements, the way a crank-dealing outlaw biker would surely watch sudden hand movements. His muscles tightened and relaxed when he realized there could be no threat.

"Just on the remote chance that this kid might've come up to the canyons to score some drugs," Sidney Blackpool said, pushing the picture across to Billy Hightower.

The biker picked up the photo and held it toward the dim light from a shaded wall sconce. Then he lit a match and examined the snapshot more closely. Then for the first time he smiled, displaying large broken teeth.

"So, my tip might work out after all?" he said.

"Your tip?" Otto said, chewing up a mouthful of chili beans.

"Yeah, this is the guy I called in about."

"The Watson kid?" Sidney Blackpool said, pointing at the picture.

"No, *his* picture was in the papers. The other kid. *This* kid." He pointed a thick scarred forefinger at Terry Kinsale.

"I'm not following," Sidney Blackpool said.

"You musta got this picture from Palm Springs P.D., right?"

"No," Sidney Blackpool said. "This is a lead we're developing independent of Palm Springs P.D."

"Guddamnit!" Billy Hightower whispered. "What *is* this shit? I gave up this dude three days after they found the body. Soon's I read about the old man posting a fifty-thousand-dollar reward! If this kid's the one that smoked Watson, that reward's *mine*, guddamnit!"

Sidney Blackpool felt his heart jump. Even

Otto Stringer paused with the spoon halfway to his mouth.

"You help us and if this kid's our man, you'll be in line for Watson's reward," Sidney Blackpool said.

"I want your word on that, man," Billy Hightower said.

"You got it. I'll put it in writing if you want."

"Was that your Toyota out in the canyon tonight?" the biker asked.

"Yeah."

"Gimme thirty minutes and then drive back to that spot," Billy Hightower said. "I'll send someone to meet you and drive you up the hill to my house. We'll talk on my turf, not yours."

"Okay," Sidney Blackpool said.

"That money's mine," Billy Hightower said. "You unnerstand what I'm sayin?"

When he stood, the biker was even bigger than he seemed. He crossed the saloon with six boot-crashing steps and was out the door before Otto had his last bite swallowed.

"We gotta go back out there," Sidney Blackpool said to his partner who nodded unhappily but didn't comment.

They hadn't noticed when Anemic Annie and Ruth the Sleuth entered the bar and selected a 1950's tune on the jukebox, one that J. Edgar Gomez tolerated because it was old enough. The record started spinning just as Ruth's husky voice boomed over the din, amplified by a police bullhorn that scared the hell out of everybody.

"Ladies, gentlemen and others!" Ruth announced on the bullhorn. "The Eleven Ninety-nine Club is proud to present the one and only — Elfis himselfis!"

When the first beats of Elvis Presley singing "You ain't nothin' but a hound dog" crashed out of the jukebox, Anemic Annie threw open the front door and Oleg Gridley waddled in.

He was wearing a white satin shirt with collars bigger than his head, a remnant from his disco days. He was wearing the tightest pants he could find from when he still weighed seventy-five pounds and hadn't ballooned up to eighty-three. He had on a drum majorette's sequined boots that Annie had borrowed from the daughter of a hairdresser at Edna's Salon, and on his head was a black pompadour wig with sideburns drawn in black mascara over half his face.

He carried what looked like a midget-sized eight-string guitar but was actually a ukulele borrowed from Ruben, the bartender at the Mirage Saloon.

" 'You ain't nothin' but a hound dog,' " Elvis sang while Elfis himselfis lip-synched the words, driving the crowd mad with delight.

Oleg Gridley had all the moves. He did a bump. He did a grind. He'd turned his back to the raucous crowd and shook his booty. He was, to Portia Cassidy, adorable.

"This, ladies and gentlemen," Ruth bellowed over the horn, "is show business!"

Bitch Cassidy jumped off the bar stool and wildly applauded her relentless suitor.

Toward the end of his number, Oleg Gridley parted the crowd and waddled right up to Bitch Cassidy showing her the best miniature Elvis impression the Coachella Valley was ever likely to see.

He lip-synched, " 'You ain't never caught a rabbit and you ain't no friend of miiiine!' "

And Portia Cassidy nearly swooned right on top of the midget. Ruth the Sleuth was so proud.

The detectives had to sit through one more lip-synched Elvis classic. Oleg stood on a bar stool and "sang" "Love Me Tender" to Bitch Cassidy who was drunk enough to get all teary-eyed, resigning herself to a midget in her bed.

Only Beavertail Bigelow, drunk and surly as usual, didn't get a bang out of Oleg's performance. In fact, he looked downright mad. He staggered out of his chair while the crowd was screaming "Encore!" and demanding a curtain call. He strode right up to the midget and accused him of larceny: "That's Clyde Suggs' uke! Where'd you get that uke, you little thug?"

"Get away from me less you want it in your hat!" Oleg warned. "They don't serve Beefeater highballs in the intensive-care unit!"

"He stole this uke from Clyde Suggs," Beavertail announced to the crowd, who lost interest since Beavertail was obviously in his fight-picking mode, and in these parts that was as predictable as big wind.

"I found this uke out in Solitaire Canyon," Beavertail Bigelow accused. "I sold this uke to Clyde Suggs."

Of course, by now nobody in the saloon was even listening to all this bullshit. Everyone had returned to drinking, dancing, griping, lechering. Except for Officer O. A. Jones, who gave up trying to seduce a Palm Desert bankteller and approached the surly desert rat.

"Where in Solitaire Canyon did you find it, Beavertail?" O. A. Jones asked.

"By the road that goes up the hill. Past the fork."

"Can I see that, Oleg?" O. A. Jones asked the angry midget who said, "Sure. I don't know what this rat's talking about. We borrowed it from Ruben over at the Mirage Saloon. Ruth and Annie were with me."

"Then *he* stole it from Clyde Suggs," Beavertail said, looking for justice somewhere in this miserable fucking world.

"Why don't you go back to your table, Beavertail," O. A. Jones said. "I'll take over this big larceny investigation."

"Probably let that rich pygmy bribe you outta doing your duty," Beavertail complained, but did as he was told.

"Be right back," O. A. Jones said to Oleg Gridley, who was now snuggled up to Portia

Cassidy, basking in all the attention, wondering how he could drink the freebies that were being bought by his admiring public.

"See, you don't have to be an evil disgusting pervert when you put your mind to it," Portia Cassidy cooed to the now popular midget. "You can be awful sweet and nice."

"Portia," Oleg said somberly. "I *do* have a confession to make. I got a real ugly dingus. One night last year Maxine Farble slammed the window on it when I was sneaking outta her bedroom cause her old man came home early. And the biggest woody I ever get might look to you like a belly button."

"Size and beauty ain't important," said Bitch Cassidy, nuzzling up to the brand-new celebrity, Elfis himselfis. "I don't care if you gotta jerk off with tweezers."

Sidney Blackpool was about to tell Otto Stringer that they could get started for the canyon when he looked up and saw the surfer cop holding a ukulele.

"This might be the *banjo*," O. A. Jones said.

It took ten minutes to trace enough of the Mineral Springs ukulele odyssey to get an idea that this could indeed be the stringed instrument heard by O. A. Jones one day last year when he discovered the burned corpse of Jack Watson.

"It *sounded* like a banjo," the young cop explained.

"It's a strange-looking uke," Sidney Blackpool said. "Wish I knew something about ukes. Eight strings. What would a regular uke have?"

"Four, I think," Otto said.

"Maybe it's got nothing to do with the case," O. A. Jones said. "Maybe somebody just lost a uke sometime, back there in the canyon."

"It's at least worth checking out," Sidney Blackpool said.

It was a finely made old instrument. There was a maker's tag on the head of the ukulele that read C.F. MARTIN & CO., NAZARETH, PA. Sidney Blackpool recorded that information in his notebook.

"Tell you what," he said to O. A. Jones. "Let's keep an evidence chain intact in case this amounts to something. You hold onto this uke personally. Tell the bartender at the Mirage Saloon you're going to borrow it for a couple days."

"I better call Palm Springs detectives tomorrow," O. A. Jones said.

"Don't do that . . . *yet*," Sidney Blackpool said, and this caused Otto to do a take. "The detective that worked on the case's outta town. Don't tell *anyone* about this. I'll make a few calls and if it seems promising I'll notify Palm Springs. We can book it down there as evidence if and when the time comes. Okay?"

"Okay." O. A. Jones shrugged, strumming the uke a few times. "Maybe I oughtta try this out on that sexy little bankteller who keeps shining me on. It worked for Oleg."

"I'll contact you in a couple days about the uke," Sidney Blackpool said. "Remember, don't talk about it to *anyone*."

"By the way," the surfer cop said, "I heard an old-time singer on the Palm Springs station that sounds like the voice I heard that day. Guy named Rudy Vallee."

Suddenly, Maynard Rivas who had been almost into a crying jag because so many scum buckets were suing cops these days, came very close to his first Indian war whoop. "There's a cricket in my chili!" he screamed at J. Edgar Gomez.

"That's a dirty lie!" the saloonkeeper yelled back, up to his elbows in slimy water at the bar sink. "There ain't no crickets in my freaking chili!"

"It's got a big ugly mouth, a wimpy body, and hops around like a speed freak!" cried the outraged Indian. "It's either a cricket or Mick Jagger!"

"Lies! Lies!" J. Edgar Gomez hollered.

"My whole life's nothin *but* crickets in my chili! Well, I had enough! I'm hirin me a ruthless Jew tomorra morning. I'm gonna *own* this fuckin joint!" the Indian promised.

They were halfway out the highway toward Solitaire Canyon before Otto spoke. "I don't like this, Sidney."

"I'm not fond a driving out here myself, but . . ."

"I don't like the way we're going about this."

"Whaddaya mean?"

"This is a Palm Springs homicide all the way. If that uke has anything to do with it, *they* should be told. I don't like withholding evidence. It makes me real nervous."

"We're not withholding evidence. This might not even *be* evidence."

"That's not for us to determine. It's for *them* to determine. It's their case."

"Damn it, Otto, their detective isn't even in town now. We can check it out. No harm done."

"We could also keep them informed a what we're doing, yet we haven't set foot in their police station."

"We will if and when the time comes, Otto."

"This is what the feds used to do to us all the time," Otto said. "They'd keep us in the dark and try to steal the glory."

"I'm not doing it for glory, Otto."

"I know, Sidney," Otto said, looking out the window at the desert landscape sailing by in the headlight wash. "You're doing it for money."

"For the *job*. I want that *job*."

"I'll play along," Otto said, "but if this case starts developing any further, I wanna go down to Palm Springs P.D. and tell them everything we've learned. I don't have my pension in the bag yet. I wanna protect *my* job."

"Fair enough, Otto," Sidney Blackpool said.

"I wouldn't do it any other way."

The asphalt road seemed darker, if that was possible. The moon looked smaller but there were more stars glittering. The moaning wind sometimes shrieked. They drove farther down the asphalt road and saw a large shape on a dirt road to the right. A van was parked in the darkness with its lights out. The van flashed its lights on and off when the detectives got close.

"Must be our ride," Sidney Blackpool said.

"This is about as safe as the Khyber Pass," Otto said. "Or a Mexican wedding."

Sidney Blackpool turned onto the dirt road just past the fork, parked, and locked the Toyota. Otto took the flashlight from the glove box and they waited for the four-wheel-drive van to pull out from the trail where it waited. The van moved forward slowly with the high beam blinding the detectives. Satisfied, the driver dimmed the lights, pulled up to the two men, leaned across and unlocked the door.

"One a you jump in the back," she said.

The driver was a young woman in her late twenties. Her hair could make a home for three chipmunks and a kangaroo rat. She wore a dirty tank top and a biker's jacket with the Cobra colors across the back. She looked like a girl who could be working at any lunch counter in the Coachella Valley, and may have been, before being "adopted" by outlaw bikers. She

276

was a pretty girl in a life where they grow old before they grow up, if they ever do.

"My name's Gina," she said. "I'll take you guys to Billy's."

Gina didn't talk during the five-minute ride up the hill. Not until the asphalt was gone and they were on a gravel road that forked left. They passed six houses on the way, every one with a noisy watchdog. The gravel road veered close to the edge of the canyon. There was a small stucco house perched too near the brink, especially for flash-flood country.

"That's where Billy lives," she said.

"You live with Billy?" Otto asked.

"I live over yonder, the other side a the canyon," she said. "Me'n my old man."

"He a Cobra?"

"Everybody's a Cobra. Everybody in *my* life," she said.

"Who does Billy live with?" Sidney Blackpool asked.

"Whoever's around," Gina said, carefully watching the gravel road, which was partially washed away where it looped into a turnabout in front of Billy Hightower's hillside lair.

Billy Hightower opened the door when the van parked in front, nearly obliterating the backlight with his bulk. He'd removed his Cobra jacket and it was plain that his massive body was going to fat. But he still cut a very impressive figure.

Sidney Blackpool led, and Otto followed

behind Gina. Billy Hightower showed his fractured teeth when the detectives entered the little house.

"This ain't Hollywood neither," he grinned, "but it's all mine and paid for. Wanna drink? I got vodka and beer."

"I'll take a beer," Sidney Blackpool said.

"Me too," said Otto.

The detectives sat on a velveteen sofa that no doubt had had a color at one time. There were grease smudges everywhere. Outlaw bikers had left their tracks where they walked, sat, lay. The carpet was uniformly stained by engine grease.

Another thing stained by engine grease was the dirty yellow tank top worn by the girl. The cotton was stretched tight by her big arrogant breasts. She helped Billy get the beer and examined the two detectives in a curious friendly way.

Then she said, "Billy, I'm a mess. Mind if I take a shower? Ours ain't been workin for a week now and Shamu won't fix it."

"Help yourself, babe," Billy Hightower said, and seemed amused when Gina stripped off the tank top in front of the men.

"Way you can tell a biker momma is her tits're dirty," Gina said to the detectives. "From hangin against a guy's back all day. Just look at my shirt!"

Of course she knew that the detectives weren't looking at her shirt, which she pretended to be inspecting. They were looking at her breasts, especially the right one, which was decorated by a tattoo of a bearded biker on a Harley. Her right nipple was the bike's headlight.

"You might get a fifty-grand endorsement from Harley Davidson if they got to see *that*," Otto said.

The girl smiled saucily and winked.

"Speaking a fifty grand . . ." Billy Hightower began, then turned to the girl. "Go take a shower, momma. We gotta talk bidness."

When they could hear the shower running, Billy Hightower chuckled and said, "She's real proud a that tattoo. Jist gotta show everybody."

"Her old man gonna mind her in your shower?" Otto asked, sipping the beer.

"We ain't possessive out here," Billy Hightower said. "We left all that back where we came from. Here we share and share alike."

"After you left police work . . ." Sidney Blackpool began, but was interrupted by the biker.

"After they *fired* me."

"After they fired you, what made you come out here?"

"I jist drifted with the wind."

"But why a motorcycle club?"

"Because they *wanted* me," said Billy Hightower.

"And you ended up president a your chapter."

"Ain't that some success story," Billy High-

279

tower said, draining his beer and thumping into the tiny kitchen to get another. When he returned he said, "They ain't so bad, these redneck motherfuckers. Jist like most a the guys I was in Nam with. I showed em how to act with cops when they get in a stop and frisk. I taught em a few things about probable cause, and search and seizure. And also, I beat the fuck outta their baddest dudes till they came to love me. Everybody needs a daddy."

"What about the rumor a you dealing to Palm Springs kids, Billy?" Sidney Blackpool asked.

"I wish it was true," said Billy Hightower. "Only thing gets dealt outta these canyons is crystal, and it stays local. I ain't sayin nothin everybody don't already know. Nearly every shack up here's a speed lab. Ain't nobody gonna get rich manufacturin crank but it ain't too bad a life."

"How much is crystal going for out here?" Otto asked.

"Bout sixty-five hunnerd for half a pound a meth plus half a pound a cut. Trouble is, all these jackoff Cobras get hooked behind this shit. Better'n junk, they say. You don't zombie out for three hours, they say. You kin change the engine on your bike, you kin paint the kitchen, you kin bone your old lady twice. But they never get *that* job finished when they're cranked out."

"You ever shoot speed?" Otto asked.

"Not like these rednecks around here. All these crankers'll tell you they toot it. Bullshit. They *mainline* it. I think they oughtta make it legal, though. You wanna reduce taxes? This'd be better'n a state lottery. We buy the makins under the table from legit pharmaceutical houses. When I was a cop I wish I knew what I know now. I coulda retired to Acapulco."

"Good profit margin?" Otto was still a narc at heart.

"Damn right. Red phosphorus is legal to buy and hydriodic acid too. An idiot could brew it. Then somebody's always makin it easier for us. The Germans came up with ephedrine, their biggest chemical discovery since Zyklon B. Almost wiped out the Jews with that one. They're gonna git the rednecks with this one. You use ephedrine and one hydrogen atom and you get meth real easy."

"Where the hell do you buy a hydrogen atom?" Otto wondered.

"Anyways, I'd rather deal snort," Billy Hightower said. "You get thirty percent more a gram, and a nicer clientele. But it's jist too hard for guys like us to get it at a price. So you heard there's Palm Springs youngsters bein dealt to by Billy Hightower? I ain't never dealt to juveniles. And that brings me to the subject a this meeting, genlemen. That young dude in the picture you showed me."

"His name's Terry Kinsale," Otto said.

"I don't know no names a people that buy

crystal, but I don't forget faces. I saw that kid twice, once in a bar down in Cathedral City, once up on this hill the night the Watson kid disappeared. And I reported that fact to the police. So it's *me* that should get a reward if he's the one that iced Jack Watson."

"How'd you meet him?" Sidney Blackpool asked.

"I went with one a my guys on a run one night. Delivered an ounce a crystal to some sissies at this gay bar on Highway One eleven. This kid was one a the guys that took delivery."

"Did he pay you the money?"

"Naw, his sugar daddy did."

"Who was the sugar daddy?"

"Jist some faggot. My man knew him so it was okay. Some local sissy with lots a green and a thing for pretty young boys like this guy Terry. Terry said he'd like to do business with us from time to time. Said he liked to mix speed with other stuff. His funeral, I figgered."

"Then you saw him on the night a the murder?"

"There was a little *too* much bidness goin on at the time to suit me. Too many a those Cat City dudes comin up here to score. I told my people it had to stop, that we'd go down there to do the transactions. But we got this one Cobra, he does real good for hisself down there in the gay bars. Good-lookin dude all covered with leather and flyin his colors, he thrills the shit outta all the sissies and they buy him lots a drinks. That night he wanted an ounce a crank from my stash, but I wouldn't give it up. He said he had a customer waitin down where the asphalt road runs out. I didn't like the sound a the whole thing so I walked down there with a shotgun to check it out. It was this guy Terry and another dude."

"Not Watson?" Otto asked.

"Naw, a jarhead from Twennynine Palms. A freckle-nose skinhead marine shakin in his twenny-dollar shoes. I recognized Terry from the other time."

"Did you sell them the crank?"

"I told em to get the fuck outta here and don't ever come up in my hills again or I'd feed their ass to my dog."

"Whaddaya think he was doing with the marine?" Otto asked.

"Whadda *you* think?" Billy Hightower said. "He was scorin some crank to get the kid loaded so he could fuck him. What else you do with a nineteen-year-old marine?"

"So after you read about them finding the Watson car down on the other side a the canyon, what'd you think?" Sidney Blackpool asked.

"I worried it was one a my guys that shot him. Man, we don't need that kind a heat up here. I'm tryin to get these rednecks organized into some legit bidnesses. Look at the Hell's Angels. They're makin toy runs for the poor every Christmas. Pretty soon there's gonna be

Hell's Angels teddy bears and Hell's Angels Cabbage Patchers. We can learn from them, I tell my people. Then I fronted them off about the Watson kid. I interrogated em one by one. And I scared the fuck outta the ones that scare easy. I got nothin. Nothin at all. I know none a my people shot the kid. So I think, okay, how about the sissy and the marine? Terry was up on the hill that night. But I also think, well, maybe he's got nothin to do with it. Maybe some righteous kidnapper snatched the Watson kid and somethin went wrong and they shot him and jist picked our canyon because it was on their way home to Vegas. So I don't worry about it for a few days."

"Then what?"

"Then Watson comes on T.V. and offers a fifty-grand reward. Then I say, fuck it, Terry's a long shot, but for fifty grand you take a long shot. That's when I made the call."

"You called Palm Springs P.D.?"

"I don't know em so I don't trust em. I called somebody I trust and told him about Terry, and his car, and the gay bar where I met him."

"What kind a car was it?" Otto asked.

"A Porsche Nine-eleven," Billy Hightower said. "Black on black. I figured it belonged to one a Terry's sugar daddies."

Sidney Blackpool looked at Otto who'd been a cop long enough to play it like aces wired. He sipped his beer and said calmly, "Who was the cop you trusted? Who'd you tell all this to?"

"Only one cop I *do* trust. Harry Bright over at Mineral Springs P.D. Now I'm trustin *you* guys cause it's my on'y chance for the reward."

"Why'd you trust Harry Bright?" Otto asked.

Billy Hightower smiled and said, "You ever met Harry Bright you wouldn't ask. If I worked for a guy like that when I was on the job I'd still be *on* the job. He's a cop's cop and he's a good guy. To this day he's the only cop ever walked over and sat down and bought me a drink in the Eleven Ninety-nine Club. Till you guys did it tonight. They all think I'm some kind a killer-freak dope fiend or somethin. I met Harry when I first joined the Cobras. He even tried to get me on Mineral Springs P.D. when it was first formed, but you don't get hired after you put a police captain in jaw wires and plastic surgery. Whether the motherfucker deserved it or not. I spent lots a time with Harry Bright the last six years. Lots a drinks, good cop stories and laughs. Jist him and me."

"Where? At the Eleven Ninety-nine?"

"I wouldn't do that to Harry," Billy Hightower said, shaking his head. "I wouldn't want the others to see him bein too friendly with a guy like me. He had his career. He was too close to a pension to get it fucked up. When Harry'd wanna sit with me in the saloon I'd make some excuse and leave. Jist to protect him from any trouble. I'd visit with

Harry right here."

"In this house?"

"Right in this house. Some nights when the graveyard shift needed a sergeant, or one a their guys was sick and Harry had to cover, he'd come up here and talk to me. Park his unit down the road and stroll right on in, in full uniform. One night, I had a guy here almost had a heart attack seein Harry walkin up the road with his five-cell flashlight. We'd sit'n drink, Harry and me. He always drank way too much. I worried more about his job than he did. Sometimes he'd get so tanked he'd sleep in his patrol unit right down where you met Gina."

"How old a man's Harry Bright?" Sidney Blackpool asked.

"I happen to know cause he's eligible for retirement this Christmas. They're on the state pension. Two percent a year and go out at fifty years. Harry'll be fifty years old in December. Poor Harry. He ain't gonna know it when he *does* get that pension."

"When'd he have his stroke?" Otto asked.

"Last March, I think it was," Billy Hightower said. "I went to see him twice in the hospital. I even cleaned up and wore a suit so I wouldn't panic the little candy stripers. I couldn't stand to see him like that. Harry was a big ol corn-beef daddy cop. Like the daddy you always wanted instead a the motherfucker you ended up with. Harry was everybody's old man on

286

that police force. Paco's the boss but Harry's the daddy and Paco listens to him. And now I wanna know somethin from *you*."

"Anything we can tell you," Sidney Blackpool said.

"Where'd you get that kid's picture?"

"From Victor Watson's house. The houseboy found it and gave it to us in the hopes it might be a lead we could develop."

"You mean to tell me, in all the reports and follow-ups, there ain't *no* mention a me or my tip on that kid Terry?"

"Well there *might* be," Sidney Blackpool lied. "We haven't seen everything. Maybe the Palm Springs homicide dicks just put that in a separate file we haven't seen. You know how dicks carry notes hanging outta every pocket."

"Yeah, well, I can't believe Harry Bright wouldn't a told them about it. He was too good a cop to ignore a tip like that. So I want you to run this down and get back to me about it. If that kid's involved in this I got a *right* to the bread."

"Okay," Sidney Blackpool said. "Too bad we can't talk to Harry Bright."

"Nobody's ever gonna talk to Harry again," the biker said. "Last time I saw him he looked real bad and I heard he's deteriorated since then. Jist stares straight ahead. Don't even respond with blinks they tell me. I can't stand to see Harry Bright like that."

"Who knows him best?" Sidney Blackpool

asked. "I mean, besides his family?"

"Harry ain't got no family," Billy Hightower said. "Lives alone in a little mobile home over the other side a Mineral Springs. Always invited me to visit him, but I wouldn't do that. I wouldn't want him to be seen with me. Told him I'd come for supper the first week after he had a lock on his pension. Then I wouldn't give a shit what people said to the mayor or the district attorney. He lived all alone. Divorced."

"Who knows him best?" Otto asked.

"That's easy," said Billy Hightower. "The other sergeant. Coy Brickman knows Harry best. He used to work with Harry at San Diego P.D. years ago. He's Harry's best friend, far as I know."

"One other thing," Sidney Blackpool said. "Earlier tonight we saw you drive your bike down toward the tamarisk trees where they found the Watson car. Why'd you do that?"

"The other day I saw that young cop O. A. Jones nosin around the canyon. I got curious if there was somethin new after all this time. Then today before it got dark, I was comin in from the post office and I saw *another* cop back there goin over the place. It looked like Coy Brickman, and I think, what *is* this shit? Then tonight I see *your* Toyota back there. I already heard all about you from the other night at the Eleven Ninety-nine."

"You don't miss much, Billy." Sidney

Blackpool grinned.

"Mineral Springs *ain't* much, man. We reduced the size a our world considerably."

Suddenly they heard footsteps on the gravel outside and Billy Hightower held a thick finger up to his lips. He tensed, and then smiled and said, "Come on in, Shamu, you clumsy motherfucker, before somebody shoots you down like a coyote."

The door opened and a man entered who was just a little shorter than Billy Hightower. He weighed less than a tractor. He wore a Greek sailor's cap over black hair that could scour every griddle in the House of Pancakes. A gray-streaked black beard exploded from a grimy face studded with blackheads. He wore the inevitable boots and filthy denim. His belt buckle was turquoise and silver, about the size of a turkey platter. He wore turquoise and silver Indian rings on six fingers so scarred and battered they looked like chunks of jagged coral. And he was drunk. *Mean* drunk with a wired look as though he'd been mixing booze and crank.

"Where's Gina?" he said, glaring at the two detectives.

"Takin a shower," Billy Hightower said.

"In here, baby!" Gina yelled from the bathroom. "I washed my hair! I'll be right out!"

"What the fuck these porkers doin? Gina told me you sent her to bring em up here!"

"They ain't dope cops," Billy Hightower said. "They're workin on that murder where the Rolls was dumped in the canyon."

"Cops is cops," Shamu said, and he lurched sideways when he tried to lean on the doorjamb. "They all smell the same."

"Gina!" Billy Hightower yelled. "Come on out here and get Shamu home to bed. He ain't in a good mood tonight. How bout a beer, brother?"

"You got no right to bring em up here," Shamu said, and now he was glaring at Billy Hightower, his lip sullen and drooping.

"I use my own judgment," Billy Hightower said, his voice as soft and cool as a prison yard. "I'm the president."

"You're a smart-mouth fuckin nigger that's jist gettin too big for your boots is what you are," Shamu said. "Where's my woman?"

"She ain't your woman, brother," Billy Hightower said. "She's *her* woman. She can do what she wants on this hill. With anybody she wants to do it with. Remember the rules."

"GINA!" Shamu bellowed, as Otto waited for the windows to shatter.

Otto was one unhappy Hollywood detective a long way from home. Shamu looked like one of those Cossacks who only drank champagne so they could eat the glass.

The girl came out fully clothed, drying hair that now looked sandy instead of mousy brown.

"Get your ass home, you cunt!" the boozy

giant said. "I din't tell you to come over here'n jump outta your clothes."

"I'm comin Shamu, just lemme get . . ."

He hit her so hard with his open palm that her body jerked sideways and knocked over a table lamp before thudding to the floor beside the sofa. She lay there weeping.

"You jist insulted me," Billy Hightower said, standing up very slowly. "You jist used violence in my house on one a my guests. You broke the *rules*."

The bearded behemoth looked as though he wasn't mad anymore. He started to giggle, as though he was suddenly in a wonderful mood. He lowered his head and charged. The crash of bodies sent nearly six hundred combined pounds of outlaw flesh hurtling into the tiny kitchen, collapsing the table like a shoe box.

Both detectives leaped up and started to come to Billy Hightower's aid, but in the hug of Shamu, and writhing in pain, he yelled, "STAY OUTTA THIS!"

Then the two bikers, grunting like grizzlies, staggered back into the living room where Shamu braced against the wall and got Billy Hightower in a very good choke hold.

"Jist . . . jist . . . like . . . like the *cops* do it!" he grinned, as he applied the forearm and bicep to Billy Hightower's throat, pinching the carotid artery.

Sidney Blackpool was making a move to use a kitchen chair on Shamu's skull when Billy

Hightower took three short strangling breaths, puffed his cheeks, dropped his chin and clamped down on Shamu's hairy forearm with those huge broken teeth.

It took perhaps three seconds, but then Shamu began howling. He leaped away from Billy Hightower as if the Cobra leader was on fire. Billy Hightower, with Shamu's blood dripping down his chin, fell back against the wall wheezing and holding his throat.

"MY ARM. LOOK AT MY FUCKIN ARM!" the bearded biker roared.

There was a flap of skin and muscle hanging loose, and Otto Stringer thought he could see a tendon wriggling like a nightcrawler. Shamu was still staring in shock and pain at his ravaged arm when Billy Hightower drove his fist straight in like a saber thrust. He hit Shamu in the solar plexus and the giant crashed back against the wall blowing like an elephant. Then Billy Hightower did it again. The same shot in the same spot and Shamu's head shuddered and his teeth cracked shut like a trap and he genuflected. Then Billy Hightower stepped back and affected a grin with black blood-flecked lips and said, "Don't . . . don't never try to choke out a . . . a hard-core street cop!" Then he added, "I gotta . . . gotta mark you for this. Sorry, my man."

He took a step and kicked the giant in the side of the face with his boot. Shamu hit the floor like an anvil. Sounding like one lung had collapsed and the other was going.

"Shamu!" Gina cried, running to the fallen giant. "Baby, baby!"

"You guys better go now," Billy Hightower said. "I kin handle this."

There wasn't anything to say so they didn't try. Sidney Blackpool and Otto righted some of the overturned furniture as Shamu rolled over on his stomach. Attempting to kneel. Attempting to breathe.

"I kin do that," Billy Hightower said when Otto plugged in the lamp and put it back on the table.

The bearded biker was now braying in pain and sobbing, "Gina! Gina! I hurt!"

"I know, baby!" she said. "I know." Then she said, "Billy, help me get Shamu outside."

Billy Hightower grabbed Shamu around the belt, saying, "Okay. It's okay. I got ya. You're okay."

"I'm sorry, Billy," Shamu blubbered.

"I know," Billy Hightower nodded. "We jist gonna forgit all about it tomorra."

That was the last the detectives saw of them, the troglodyte and the tattooed girl, hobbling down the road to their shack where the shower didn't work but wasn't needed very often.

The detectives were standing in the darkness when Billy Hightower said, "Kin you walk back to your car? I ain't feelin too good."

"You oughtta go to a doctor," Otto said.

The outlaw biker shuffled bent and wounded

toward the door. He turned and watched the detectives walking down the gravel road. It obviously hurt to speak but he said, "I . . . I didn't *mind* talkin to you guys tonight. Maybe some time we could . . ." Then he thought it over and shook his head and started to shut the door. But at the last second, just before it closed, he said, "This ain't a bad life. These people, they *want* me."

Chapter 13

OMENS

Sidney Blackpool chain smoked all the way back to the hotel. Otto had to open the window to breathe, shivering in the night air that blew through the canyons.

"Making any sense yet, Sidney?" Otto finally asked.

"I dunno. Sometimes part of it does, then it doesn't."

"A dope dispute? Naw, we ain't talking big dopers. How about a straight rip-off by the Cobras? They set up the gay boys in the bar, bring them up to the canyon with a promise of low-priced crank and waylay them."

"Why two cars then? Why was Jack Watson in the Rolls and Terry and the marine in the Porsche?"

"Yeah, and why wouldn't Terry step up and tell his story right away if he saw somebody kill his pal? Especially after the reward was posted."

"Maybe he was already outta town by then. Anyway, Billy Hightower says he's sure his people didn't do it. Billy *does* seem to have effective interrogation methods."

"And what's Harry Bright got to do with it? And why's Coy Brickman nosing around out there now that we're stirring things up?"

"There's always the possibility that Terry planned the kidnap and ransom of his pal Jack with the help of Bright or Brickman," Sidney Blackpool said.

"Should call this place *Urinal* Springs, you ask me," Otto said. "The whole place stinks, far as I'm concerned. It's like the city of Gorki, closed to foreigners. And we're foreigners, baby."

"First thing tomorrow let's work on the uke. We'll call the manufacturer. See what they can tell us. I wonder how many music stores there are in this valley? Not many, probably."

"It's hard to imagine Harry Bright involved in a murder, ain't it?" Otto said.

"You never even *met* Harry Bright."

"You're right. This place is making me goofy. It ain't real hard to think a Coy Brickman icing somebody down. Those eyes a his, probably the freaking buzzards got eyes like he's got."

"We gotta get this connection between Harry Bright and Coy Brickman. Maybe it started back in San Diego P.D."

"What?"

"Whatever might make one a them or both a them kill Jack Watson."

"We're getting real close to where I say we call Palm Springs P.D. and cut them in on this, Sidney. We coulda *bought* it tonight, if that

296

creature from the black lagoon turned on *us* instead a Billy Hightower."

"Another day, Otto. Let's see how it develops after *one* more day."

"One more day," Otto sighed. "Wonder if it's too late for room service. I think I got me a live one after all. Something in my stomach just did a two and a half forward somersault, with a full twist."

Sidney Blackpool wasn't able to sleep. A double shot of Johnnie Walker Black didn't help a bit. He could hear Otto snoring in the other bedroom.

He tried the technique taught by the police department to reduce stress. He concentrated on his toes, feet and ankles, gradually working up until his shoulders and neck and jaws began to relent. Sometimes he imagined himself in a meadow or in a solitary cottage in an isolated valley. Tonight he thought of lying on a blanket under a tamarisk tree, the shaggy branches wafting like an ostrich fan as his body contour settled into the warm sand. He slept soundly until just before daybreak when he had a dream.

It was a joyous dream, a triumph, a *wonder*. Of course, the dream took place before Tommy died. In the dream, Sidney Blackpool was alone, ankle deep in cool sand, atop the tallest dune in the desert. Though it wasn't particularly hot in the desert he was pouring sweat from every pore. It was morning and yet there was no sun anywhere on the horizon. The moon was translucent white, and directly overhead. There were a few clouds scudding in the wind. It was a Mineral Springs kind of moaning wind and he was being sandblasted so badly he thought his flesh might tear, but he dug his feet deeper into the sand until it gripped his ankles like concrete. He believed that nothing could blow him off the dune.

He could hear the savage ocean surf crashing against the Santa Rosas on the far side, and some of it even lapped over the top of Mount San Jacinto and splashed down toward the tram car.

Suddenly the moon was *not* overhead. His heart nearly stopped because he thought he'd missed his chance! Then he saw that it was hovering over the mountain peak.

Sidney Blackpool extended his arms, his body a cross buried in the sand. The sun appeared over the Santa Rosas, a fireball powering upward. When the sun was precisely atop the peak of Mount San Jacinto, he started screaming.

It wasn't a scream of pain or rage or terror, it was a scream of absolute triumph and joy. He was holding them at bay, the sun and moon. The sun could not rise, the moon could not set. Sidney Blackpool held them powerless with his outstretched arms and his scream of triumph. Time could not advance. He was making time stand still.

Now there could be no waves crashing, no floating coffin. He would spend eternity alone in the desert screaming with his lungs and his heart. He would never see Tommy Blackpool again, but Tommy would *live*. This was his destiny.

No man had ever known such joy. His happiness was so great that he awoke weeping. He tried to muffle his sobs with the pillow so Otto wouldn't hear him.

Because of the three-hour time difference between California and Pennsylvania, Sidney Blackpool was finished talking with a man at the Martin Guitar Company long before Otto came shuffling into the sitting room in his underwear, scratching his balls.

"I bet I could get rid a this blubber if I only slept thirty minutes a night like you," Otto said to his partner who was showered, shaved and dressed, with a legal pad full of notes in front of him.

"Morning, bright eyes," Sidney Blackpool said to Otto. "Here's what I found out from the guitar company. It's a very rare ukulele, called a Taro Patch. Probably made between 1915 and 1920. The old Hawaiians loved its sweet sound. Liked to play it while they watched the taro grow."

"I need some breakfast," Otto said. "I can't figure out whose tongue I got in my mouth."

"This kind of ukulele wouldn't be found in

a regular music store. It'd be the kind of antique to end up in a pawnshop. The good news is there're only six pawnshops in this whole valley."

"The bad news is it might not've been bought in this valley," Otto said.

"That's a possibility," Sidney Blackpool agreed. "But look on the up side. Don't be so morbid."

While Otto ordered a titanic breakfast from room service, Sidney Blackpool took notes and smoked and waited anxiously for the hour when a pawnshop would open. It made him think of the dream for an instant, the yearning to manipulate Time. He got one of those shivers in his heart and swelling in the throat, but he pushed it away. He started calling before nine o'clock but pawnshop proprietors in the desert valley are in no hurry. Otto was finishing breakfast before Sidney Blackpool started making contact.

It was on his fourth call that he reached a man who said, "Yes, I know what a Taro Patch uke is. I played one nearly fifty years ago on Catalina Island. It's a wonderful instrument."

"I'm Sergeant Blackpool, Los Angeles Police Department. We're investigating a crime involving a Taro Patch uke. Have you ever had one in your shop? Anytime in the last few years, if you can remember?"

"Matter a fact I had one maybe two years ago," the pawnbroker said. "Shoulda kept it, but you can't keep everything. Wished I'd a kept it though. Never gonna see another."

"Would you have your records from two years ago?" Sidney Blackpool raised a fist at Otto. "I have to know about it for an important police investigation."

"Can I call you back? I can't remember who brought it in. Some trucker from Blythe, I think. It ain't my fault if it was stolen. I always take identification and comply with the law."

"Don't worry," Sidney Blackpool said. "I'm really only interested in finding out who bought it. We found it and wanna return it to its owner."

"Well, that I can tell you soon as I look up his name. He was in uniform, I know that. A policeman. From maybe Indio P.D."

"How about Mineral Springs P.D.?" Sidney Blackpool asked.

"Could a been," the pawnbroker said.

"Wonder if his name was Harry Bright?"

"That don't sound familiar," the pawnbroker said. "Lemme look it up and call you right back."

"I'll wait," Sidney Blackpool said.

"I better get my ass in the shower," Otto said. "We ain't playing golf today."

He hadn't finished toweling off from the shower when he heard Sidney Blackpool say into the phone, "Yes. Yes. Okay. Thanks very much. Yes, we'll see that he gets it back. Thanks very much."

Otto stepped out of the bathroom saying, "Well?"

"Coy Brickman," Sidney Blackpool said. "He bought the uke just over two years ago. That means he owned it long before the Watson murder."

"I *really* don't like this, Sidney," Otto said. "He's a policeman. We shouldn't be playing this lone hand, not on *this* case."

"We haven't got a damn thing yet, Otto. Just pieces. We'll call Palm Springs P.D. tomorrow morning one way or the other."

"And we'll do it before I even have my breakfast," Otto Stringer said, looking his partner dead in the eye. "I *mean* it, Sidney!"

By 10:00 A.M. they were yet again on their way to Mineral Springs, causing Otto to say, "Why don't we just get a room next door to the Eleven Ninety-nine? We could save Victor Watson a whole lotta hotel expenses, not to mention all this wear and tear on your car."

"We gotta be careful talking to Paco Pedroza," Sidney Blackpool said. "In fact, maybe we *shouldn't* talk to him."

"We gotta level with somebody," Otto said. "Unless you think even the chief's involved in this nutty case."

"I don't know who might be involved. First rule of homicide investigation . . ."

"I know, I know. *Everybody's* a suspect," Otto said. "Even an old lady in an iron lung."

302

"And that reminds me," Sidney Blackpool said. "I'm not ruling out Harry Bright. I wanna see him with my own eyes. Maybe he's made a startling recovery."

"Corpse cops," Otto said, shaking his head. "I wonder when you're gonna add *me* to the suspect list."

"You're right about having to trust *somebody*," Sidney Blackpool said. "Let's find that young cop, O. A. Jones. Somehow I trust that surfer."

They didn't want anyone in the police department to know they were in town so they parked off the main drag half a block from the station house. They had to wait only twenty minutes before O. A. Jones came cruising by, drinking a soda pop and listening to the ghetto blaster in his patrol car. Sidney Blackpool tooted and waved the young cop over.

"Follow me," he said and made a right turn and another, before pulling to the curb.

O. A. Jones drove up behind and got out. "What's up, Sarge?" he asked, approaching on Sidney Blackpool's side.

"If I asked you for your help and requested you not to tell a living soul, would you do it?"

"I'm a policeman. Why not?"

"What if it was concerning *another* policeman? Would it make a difference?"

"You mean on *my* department?"

"Yeah."

"Does Chief Pedroza know about it, whatever it is?"

"No."

"Why're you telling me then, and not the chief?"

"Because you already know a piece of it and nobody else does."

"About the uke?"

"Yeah. And also because I trust you in general."

The young cop chewed on that one for a moment and said, "Chief Pedroza gave me a job when I wasn't welcome in Palm Springs anymore. I don't wanna get him mad at me."

"I promise that in a couple a days I'll talk to the chief one way or the other. I just want you to keep this confidence. For a couple a days."

The young cop hesitated but said, "Okay."

"Good. Now all we really want you to do is tell us about Sergeant Brickman and Sergeant Bright. That's all. You see, that uke belonged to Sergeant Brickman. He bought it from a pawnshop two years ago."

"Wow!" the young cop whispered. "You don't think he . . . that ain't possible!"

"Probably not. But tell us what you know about them. Start with Sergeant Brickman."

"Well, he used to be on San Diego P.D. So was Sergeant Bright. Harry Bright was the one recommended Coy Brickman to the chief long before I came. In fact, Sergeant Bright recommended everybody. Chief Pedroza won't hire anyone without Harry Bright's okay." Then the young cop scratched his neck nervously and said, "Sarge, Coy Brickman couldn't kidnap and kill somebody! He's a little quiet and standoffish, but he's a good sergeant. And Sergeant Bright? Harry Bright's like . . ."

"Everyone's daddy," Otto said.

"Yeah, that's right. He couldn't be involved in any kind a crime, let alone kidnap. Let alone *murder!*"

"I get the feeling most people on your department were in trouble or unhappy somewhere else before coming to Mineral Springs," Otto said.

"We all worked other departments, that's true," O. A. Jones said, leaning in the window now, looking furtively up and down the street.

"Did Sergeant Bright and Sergeant Brickman get in trouble in San Diego?"

"Not that I know of," O. A. Jones said. "Sergeant Brickman once told me he got a low placement on the sergeant's list because some deputy chief hated him. He figured he'd spend his whole career as a patrolman so he called Harry Bright who was already here. And he made the move. Far as Sergeant Bright, well, he mighta got in trouble drinking down there, I don't know. He was way over forty years old when Chief Pedroza hired him, so our city musta waived the age requirement to get an experienced sergeant from a big city. Harry Bright's been a heavy drinker for a long time, I think."

"He's a drunk, you mean," Otto said.

"Well, you know how it is in police work. There's a guy or two at every station. Whiskey face, whiskey voice, whiskey eyes, but they always show up to work on time. Always have a shoeshine and a pressed uniform. Always do a job. That was Sergeant Bright." The kid wrinkled his brow, saying, "I don't like this at all, Sarge. Harry Bright's the best supervisor I ever met."

"We've heard sometimes he'd get drunk on the graveyard shift," Otto said. "Maybe sleep it off parked on a trail over in Solitaire Canyon. He wasn't a saint, for chrissake."

"Look, son," Sidney Blackpool said. "We're not Internal Affairs headhunters trying to nail a cop for boozing on the job. We're investigating a *homicide*. We need a feel for these two sergeants. You're not being asked to be a snitch."

"*Everybody* hits the hole over in Solitaire Canyon," O. A. Jones said. "That's where the cops around here catch a few z's on a quiet graveyard shift. You know what it's like trying to stay awake in a town like this when there ain't a call for six hours? Far as him being drunk on graveyard, sure, I seen him looking awful bad at eight o'clock in the morning just before he went home. But he was always *there* if you called him. Harry Bright'd never let you down."

"Know where they live?" Sidney Blackpool asked, "Bright and Brickman?"

"Here in town," O. A. Jones said. "Harry Bright lives in the last mobile home on Jackrabbit Road. A residential cul-de-sac with about eight little mobile homes on it. There's no one there now that he's had his stroke. We check it a couple times every night to make sure the place is secure."

"Who has a key?"

"Sergeant Brickman waters the plants and such. He's keeping the place up till Harry Bright gets well, but from what I hear he ain't never gonna get well."

"Where's Sergeant Brickman live?" Otto asked.

"Smoke Tree Lane. First house on your left off of Rattlesnake Road. Two-story wood frame, with blue shutters. Lives with his wife and two daughters."

"Are they best friends?" Otto asked. "Bright and Brickman?"

"I'll tell you how good," O. A. Jones said. "When Sergeant Brickman's oldest girl had a kidney disease and was on dialysis, Sergeant Bright went into the hospital and tried to give up one of his kidneys for a transplant. We heard about it from the doctor who gives us our annual physicals. Everybody got a big laugh over that one. The croakers looked at Harry and explained how he wasn't quite a suitable donor. For one thing, Harry looked like he *needed* a couple organs. Like a new liver and maybe a heart, they told him. Turns out they were right about the heart. I don't think the liver's failed yet but it probably will. Anyway, that's the kind a man he is. I'm telling you, Sarge, you're following a false trail here. If that uke's the music box I heard, there *has* to be an explanation."

"Does Coy Brickman sing?" Sidney Blackpool asked. "Or play a stringed instrument? Or Harry Bright, maybe?"

"I don't know," O. A. Jones said. "Not around the station anyway. Maybe in the shower."

"By the way," Sidney Blackpool said. "You said Sergeant Brickman takes care of Harry Bright's mobile home. Where's Harry Bright's relatives?"

"His ex-wife lives in one a the country clubs down in Rancho Mirage. Married to a rich guy. Chief Pedroza told me Harry had one kid, but the kid was killed. Bought it in that San Diego jet crash several years ago. A boy."

Sidney Blackpool didn't hear another word. His mind was racing but it had nothing to do with whatever O. A. Jones was saying. He was trying to ward off a panic attack.

"I said, is that all, Sarge? Can I go now? I better get back on the air."

"What is it, Sidney?" Otto said. "You look like you just got a mouthful a J. Edgar's chili."

"It's uh . . . it's . . . I just had an idea.

308

Nothing. It's uh, nothing."

"Well, if that's it, then," O. A. Jones said. "Lemme know how this goes. It's bothering me a lot. I feel a little sick to my stomach."

"Sure, uh . . . sure," Sidney Blackpool said, feeling the sweat beading on his forehead and lip and armpits. "Yeah . . . uh, *wait*. One more thing . . ." He was stalling, trying to pull himself together. The cold fire was leaving his temples and neck. The panic was now just a chunk of lead in the pit of his stomach.

"What's wrong, Sidney?" Otto was starting to look alarmed.

"It's a . . . an idea. An . . . uh, elusive thought. You know how that happens sometimes."

"Happens to me sometimes," O. A. Jones said. *"Déjà vu."*

"Something like that," Sidney Blackpool said, wiping his upper lip. "One more thing comes to me now. Where's Harry Bright being treated?"

"He was in a regular hospital for a long time," O. A. Jones said. "Now he's in a nursing home, a semi-hospital kind a place. Down near Indio. I drove Sergeant Brickman down there one night when we were the only two on graveyard. He visited Sergeant Bright for maybe ten minutes. I waited in the unit listening for calls. That was maybe three months ago. It's called Desert Star Nursing Home, on Highway One eleven this side a the Indio city limit."

"Has anyone actually seen Harry Bright lately?" Sidney Blackpool asked. "Besides Sergeant Brickman?"

"I don't think so. He's the representative of our department. Chief Pedroza said it's too depressing. Harry just laying there like that, wasting away."

"Okay, son, you can go now," Sidney Blackpool said. "Stay in touch."

"Did you think a what gave you the feeling?"

"What?"

"That *déjà vu* feeling. Did the thought come to you?"

"It will," Sidney Blackpool said. "Be seeing you."

Otto had to settle for two Big Macs, fries, and a milk shake. And he had to eat them on the run. Sidney Blackpool was determined to see Harry Bright with his own eyes. Neither man spoke, Otto because he was trying to eat the hamburgers while his partner pushed the Toyota seventy miles an hour down the desert highways, and Sidney Blackpool because he hadn't quite recovered from the shock of hearing that Harry Bright had lost a son.

Sidney Blackpool knew he'd have to deal with it soon. He wanted to hold off until later when he could afford to let the fear and despair run rampant. Three A.M. would be the perfect time for such an exercise. He could even make it doubly frightening by drinking lots of booze.

But he'd have to deal with it tonight: Victor Watson, Sidney Blackpool and now Harry Bright! All victims of the most outrageous of nature's reversals. Wanderers looking for pieces of themselves. It couldn't be just a perverse bit of chance. An omen, Victor Watson had said. But detectives don't believe in omens, not detectives like Black Sid. He hadn't believed in omens even when he still believed in *something*.

It looked more like a motel than a nursing home or hospital. It was a one-story complex of flat-roofed buildings scattered around two acres. The sign in front was neon lit. But it was tidy and probably as acceptable as a middle-income nursing home ever gets. Which is to say it looked like the kind of place that would precipitate a self-inflicted gunshot wound should Sidney Blackpool ever find himself so helplessly in need.

The detective was pulling into the nursing-home parking lot when he saw it: a Mineral Springs patrol car.

"Goddamn!" He cranked the wheel to the left and punched the accelerator.

"Coy Brickman?" Otto said.

"Must be."

Sidney Blackpool parallel-parked the Toyota half a block down the street, hidden from view by a Salvation Army truck. Both detectives got out, walked toward the far side of the nursing

311

home's parking lot, stood behind a smoke tree and watched.

There were a few people coming and going in the parking lot. They saw two elderly women in wheelchairs being taken for an outing by Latino orderlies. Then they saw a blue Mercedes 450 SL pull into the lot and park beside the patrol car. A slender suntanned blonde got out. She wore a blue, yellow and gray graphic-silk chemise with blue pumps.

She was the kind who made it tough for a policeman to guess her age. Designer clothes, winter tans, hundred-dollar haircuts and tints, Mercedeses, face-lifts. Sidney Blackpool always supposed that such women were ten years older than they looked: the Alfred Hitchcock lady. She leaned against the Mercedes and smoked. She didn't walk toward the door of the nursing home.

The detectives watched her because she didn't fit. There weren't any other visitors driving a Mercedes to this seedy nursing home. They watched for fifteen minutes. Then the door opened and Coy Brickman, in uniform, emerged from the building. The woman walked up to him and they shook hands.

"I'd give the rest a the ten grand to hear this little conversation," Sidney Blackpool said.

"I'd give a couple bucks myself," said Otto.

When Coy Brickman turned as though he were about to say good-bye, the blonde shrugged her shoulders and extended her hand again to

Coy Brickman who took it for a second. Then he turned and got into the patrol unit.

"Damn!" Sidney Blackpool said. "Can you make out her license number, Otto?"

"You kidding? My eyes're forty years old."

"Come on, Brickman, get your ass *out* of that parking lot!" Sidney Blackpool muttered.

But the woman in the Mercedes drove out first and turned back on the highway toward Palm Springs. The detectives jumped in the Toyota and Sidney Blackpool started the engine and watched through the rearview mirror.

"Come on, come on!" he said.

Finally Coy Brickman drove out, turned left on the highway and cruised in the same direction as the Mercedes.

"We gotta risk it, you wanna get her number," Otto said.

Sidney Blackpool nodded. The blonde wouldn't be the type to spot a tail, but Coy Brickman might. And she was already a quarter of a mile ahead of them. Sidney Blackpool was hanging back in the number-two lane behind a pickup truck when they got a break. Coy Brickman turned the patrol car right on Cook Street in Indian Wells, heading toward Highway 10 and Mineral Springs.

Sidney Blackpool stepped on it, blowing through a red light when there was no cross traffic coming, and caught her three signals later.

"Hope you got this Toyota well insured," Otto said.

They got close enough for Otto to jot down her license number, then they backed off and followed the car through Indian Wells, Palm Desert, and into Rancho Mirage where she turned right.

The detectives quickly found themselves looking at a guarded kiosk and a funny-looking Indian totem bird and a sign that said THUNDERBIRD COUNTRY CLUB.

"It's on our list!" Otto said. "Tamarisk, Thunderbird, Mission Hills. Let's see, what the hell was the name a the member at Thunderbird we were supposed to ask for? Shit. I left all the notes in the room."

"Think, Otto," Sidney Blackpool said.

"Let's see. Penbroke? No. Pennypacker? No. Pennington! That's it. Pennington at Thunderbird!"

"Good boy!" Sidney Blackpool said.

The detective pulled up to the gate and Sidney Blackpool said, "We're Blackpool and Stringer. Mister Pennington's arranged for a game of golf for us. I believe he left our names with the club pro."

It took the security office a couple of minutes to make the call, then he said, "Drive right in, gentlemen. The doorman can direct you."

"Jesus Christ, Sidney!" Otto Stringer cried as they were driving toward the clubhouse.

"What is it?"

"A former president of the United States

314

lives here! What if we have to play a game to make our investigation look kosher? What if *I'm* playing golf with a freaking ex-president of the whole freaking United States?"

Chapter 14

CHARADE

Otto Stringer was directed by the doorman to the pro shop where he introduced himself and got a starting time for a game he knew might not be played. Sidney Blackpool headed straight for the bar, looking for a telephone so he could run the license number to get a name and address that he hoped would belong to a Thunderbird member. Of course, they both believed that the blonde had to be the former Mrs. Harry Bright.

The clubhouse was not as stylish as the one at Tamarisk. It was done in rugged flagstone and featured lots of Indian art, the staple of desert designers, along with a mix of Chinese artifacts. It had the comfortable look of a clubhouse that had been there awhile, to which the pictures in the lobby attested.

There were photos of Bob Hope who is at least an honorary member of nearly every club in the desert, along with those of the other man who shares that distinction, former president Gerald Ford. Sidney Blackpool recognized one of Thunderbird's first members, the late Hoagy Carmichael, and Bing Crosby.

He found a pay phone and ran the license number through his office at Hollywood detectives. It was registered to Herbert T. Decker with a Rancho Mirage address, which Sidney Blackpool figured to be a street right here at Thunderbird Country Club.

He walked into the luncheon room looking for the blonde. A fiftyish waitress said, "Help you, sir?"

"No, thanks," he said. "I'm a first-time guest. Just moseying."

"Have a look around," she said, as friendly as they'd been at Tamarisk. She was clearing the luncheon tables.

"Have you seen Mrs. Decker?" he asked. "I believe that's her name. A very attractive blond lady."

"Yes, that'd be Mrs. Decker. No, I haven't seen her today, sir. Have you checked the Copper Room? There was a private party in there today."

Sidney Blackpool strolled back into the foyer and through the main dining room, which wasn't in use during the day. He noticed some people in a mirrored room off to the left. He got closer and saw where it got its name. All of the service was copper, or appeared to be: platters, plates, goblets, knives, forks. Then he saw her.

She was talking to a dowager in a wool crepe jacket studded with rhinestones, worn over ballooning tuxedo trouser pants. The older

317

woman was overdressed for this time of day but would be ready for action six hours later. The blonde was obviously apoligizing for missing whatever had been going on there. She shook hands with several people, kissing the cheek of one woman and two men before she left. Instead of going back toward the foyer, she turned and walked out onto the patio beside the pool. It was a contemporary U-shaped pool with a small bandstand behind it. Sidney Blackpool could imagine parties and luaus on this patio. He might attend parties in places like this as an executive for Watson Industries.

He stood behind the blonde, who hadn't seen him, and said, "Must taste like a mouthful of pennies in there."

She turned and he said, "All that copper."

She smiled politely and he liked that a lot. She had great teeth, but then, money could also buy plenty of porcelain.

She looked as though she was about to leave so he bit the bullet and said, "Ma'am, just a second, please. I think I know you. Really, I'm *sure* I know you. Have you ever lived in San Diego?"

That stopped her. She looked troubled by it, but she said, "A long time ago."

"My gosh, I *do* know you," Sidney Blackpool said. "I used to be with San Diego P.D."

He had it right. Her expression changed from a hint of anxiety to resignation. Up close he believed her to be about forty, give or take a few years for cosmetic surgery, which he couldn't really detect. She was a cool elegant Alfred Hitchcock blonde all right.

"You must've worked with Harry," she said. "Harry Bright."

"Of course!" Sidney Blackpool said. "You're Mrs. Bright! I met you at a party, let's see, where was Harry working then? God, must've been ten years ago."

"Southern substation," she said. "Must've been *twelve* years ago, at least. We've been divorced that long."

"Oh, I'm sorry, Mrs . . ."

"Decker," she said. "Patricia Decker."

And then, because he trusted absolutely no one even remotely connected with Coy Brickman or Harry Bright, he said, "My name's Sam Benton. Can I buy you a drink? It's great to see someone from the old days. Pardon me, the recent past. You're not old enough to've been around in the old days."

"I really should be running along, Mister Benton."

"Listen, lemme level with you," he said. "I only left police work a year ago. I'm director of security for an aviation plant in the San Fernando Valley and I'm here for a golf outing with my boss. And . . . well, I'm a little intimidated. This is pretty tall cotton for a guy that used to work the streets around Southern substation. How about *one* drink? Gosh, you look the same except you're even more . . ."

319

"Sure, sure," she said. "You still *sound* like a policeman. Okay, the bar's this way."

"I already found it," he said. "I wasn't a cop twenty-one years for nothing."

"Twenty-one years," she said. "You don't look that old."

"We are *really* gonna get along," he grinned.

Sidney Blackpool spotted Otto outside the foyer looking for him and he said, "Mrs. Decker, could you order me a Johnnie Walker Black Label, please? I just have to tell a friend where I am."

He caught Otto as he was about to head back to the pro shop.

"Otto!" he said. "I've met her. She *is* Harry Bright's ex-wife! I told her my name's Sam Benton in case it comes up. I don't want her telling Coy Brickman she met the Hollywood dicks on the Watson case."

"Whaddaya want me to do?"

"Play golf."

"What?"

"Play a round. Tell the pro that your partner got detained. If this washes out I'll grab a cart and meet you out on the course. Or maybe at the turn."

"Play *without* you?"

"You've played without me before."

"Not in a place like this! What if I get another stress attack like over at Tamarisk? What if they put me in a foursome with an ex-president and Betty Grable, for chrissake?"

320

"She's dead."

"Well, who's the one that was married to Phil Harris? I see he's a member here."

"Alice Faye."

"Yeah, what if they put me with Alice Faye?"

"Go play golf, Otto," Sidney Blackpool said.

When he returned to the bar she was well along with her martini. It looked like vodka. That was very good for Sidney Blackpool. She liked to drink. The problem would be in controlling his own bad habit while encouraging hers.

"Sorry," he said, placing a twenty-dollar bill on the bar.

"Put your money away," she said. "I sign for the drinks around here."

"But I invited *you*."

"To the bad old days," she said.

"To our alma mater," he said, clicking glasses. "Southern substation."

"I should tell you, I haven't seen Harry in years."

"What's he doing now?"

"He lives here in the Coachella Valley. He was with another police force here. Mineral Springs."

"Was?"

"He had a stroke last spring. And then a heart attack. He's . . . they tell me he's very bad. It was a long time ago when we parted."

"Well, what're you doing now besides playing golf?" He touched her left hand, which was several shades lighter than the other suntanned hand. Her hands said she was in her forties, even if her face didn't.

"Still a cop, I see," she smiled. "We play quite a bit of golf."

"And how do you shoot?"

"Awful."

"I'll bet. Not with that athlete's body."

He was delighted to see that she was down to one more sip, and that it *was* a double vodka martini. The mere smell of gin nauseated him, and straight vodka drinkers were the biggest lushes of all. To keep *her* going, he told himself, as he drained his Johnnie Walker. Not because *I've* got a drinking problem. Oh no.

"Please let me buy us another one," he said.

"I've told you your money doesn't work here," she said, nodding to the barman. They were the only two at the small bar.

The luncheon room was nearly cleared by now, and there were just a few people passing the foyer. The barman poured her a double. Sidney Blackpool imagined that country-club bartenders had to know their members.

"Whadda you do when you're not playing golf?" he asked.

"Nothing much. A little tennis, but my legs aren't what they used to be."

"Well," he said in obvious disagreement.

She didn't mind. She knew what kind of legs she had. "Sometimes we play *Oklahoma* gin — from the stage play not the state. What I like is when we have fourteen ladies and play two against one. It's a rotating game we call 'kill your sister.' You can lose a thousand a day." Then she gave a lopsided grin and said, "Came a long way from Southern substation, haven't I?"

He liked that sardonic, weary, lopsided smile. It looked very familiar.

"What's your husband do?"

"Oil leases. He spends a lot of time in Texas and Oklahoma. Sometimes in the Middle East. We summer in Lake Tahoe or Maui." Then she realized how *that* one sounded to a guy just out of police work, and she grinned in apology. "What can I say?"

"Thanks, I guess," said Sidney Blackpool. "You're a lucky girl. All you can say is thanks."

"Sure, thanks," she said.

And then he thought about it. He thought about her son, Harry Bright's son. He said, "Do you have children?"

"No. No children."

He despised himself for an instant, but he said, "That's funny. I could've sworn Harry had . . ."

"Our son was killed. Long after we were divorced." She really took a hit at the vodka, but smiled wearily. "It's okay. Not all San Diego policemen knew about our boy. He was on PSA Flight 182. He was nineteen years old in his first year at Cal."

"I'm truly sorry, Mrs. Decker. Really I . . ."

"Lots of other people's children died that day too." Then she drained the glass and said, "Well, I think I should be . . ."

"I'm feeling real bad for prying. I'd do almost anything if you'd have just one more," he said. "Please . . . Patricia."

"They call me Trish," she said, and then she looked sadly at her glass and at the bartender.

The bartender poured them *both* doubles this time, knowing a heavy hitter when he saw one.

"This is a drinking man's club," she said. "This and Eldorado."

"We played Tamarisk the other day," he said.

"That's not a drinking club. This is a drinking club and a gambling club." Then she looked at him with her sad eyes and there were a lot of things he didn't want to ask this woman. But there was something he did want to ask. Even if it never helped to solve the murder of Jack Watson.

"Trish, would you have dinner with me tonight? I'm lonely here in the desert."

She didn't waste time with the third martini. "How long'll you be here?" she asked.

"Till the end of the week."

"Are you married?"

"No."

"I believe you. You don't look married."

"Please. How about it?"

"And what should I tell Herb?" she asked, looking at her wavering reflection in the martini.

"My husband."

"You . . . you could invite him along," he said. "I'd be happy to have both of you."

She laughed at that one, and looked up from her drink. "Would you now, Sam?" she asked huskily. "From one old cop to another, would you *really* like him to come along?"

"If it's the only way I could see you," he said earnestly, and his thigh was brushing hers. It had been a long time since Sidney Blackpool had courted any woman except for an occasional cop groupie whose name he wouldn't remember three days later. And who would just as easily forget his.

"I don't run around to desert restaurants when my husband's out of town. Doesn't look appropriate. But I hate dining alone. How would you like to be my guest tonight? Right here at the club. Say about seven?" She glanced at her Cartier Panthère wristwatch.

"I'll be here," he said.

"Sorry, but you'll have to wear a jacket and tie."

"I'll manage," he said.

"Now I've got to take my afternoon nap," Trish Decker said, standing a bit unsteadily. "That's something else I do as regularly as golf and cards."

Otto was in the men's locker room watching a dozen men at two rows of felt-covered tables playing something they called Bel-Air gin. He was fascinated, until he found out that the stakes had gotten as high as fifteen cents a point. Otto did some fast computing and realized from the figures written beside one player that the man had lost at least twelve hundred dollars that afternoon.

There was a poker game going in another room to the right of the gin room and the small bar was getting lots of afternoon action. And this, Otto realized, was just an ordinary weekday before the season was in full swing. Otto decided he wasn't quite ready for this even with his pocket full of President McKinleys. He walked outside where his bag was propped beside a golf cart. He took his putter and bought a dozen golf balls from the pro shop before heading toward the practice green.

By the time Sidney Blackpool found him, he was having a fine time with a woman he'd met on the practice green. She was at least twenty-five years older than Otto, and even rounder. She wore a golf skirt and blouse in Easter egg colors, and a yellow floppy hat. Her hair was a ginger shade, but it was definitely time to get to the beauty shop for a retouch. She wore oversized hexagon eyeglasses with persimmon rims.

They were in a putting contest, tapping twenty footers at three designated cups. Sidney Blackpool could see they had some sort of bet going.

"Okay, Fiona," Otto was saying when Sidney

Blackpool found them. "This is my chance to get even. Don't stand too close to me or my little heart will make bunny bumps and I'll miss!"

"Oh, Otto," said the fat old dame, "you *are* a caution!"

Sidney Blackpool saw that Otto's bag was now loaded on an electric golf cart by the putting green. The cart was canary yellow, as was the owner's golf bag. There was a radio in the cart, an electric fan pointed toward the driver, and a small television set. There was an ice chest behind the driver's seat, which the detective figured didn't contain soda pop. There were two yellow cups on the putting green containing a brown concoction. Otto hadn't been letting the desert heat parch him.

"Otto, could I see you a minute?" Sidney Blackpool called.

"Hold that putt, Fiona," Otto said, waggling his finger. "This is my business partner, Sidney Blackpool. Sidney, meet Fiona Grout."

"Charmed, I'm sure," the old dame said to Sidney Blackpool, who smiled and nodded.

"I see you're having a few giggles," Sidney Blackpool said.

Otto's eyes were already glassy and he blew 80-proof Jamaican rum in his partner's face when he whispered, "Sidney, I got one! She's a widow. Lives in Thunderbird Heights, for chrissake. Knows Lucille Ball! Don't take me away from this."

"Otto, I missed it!" Fiona tittered. "You have a chance at me!"

"Gimme a break, Sidney," Otto pleaded. "I'm on a roll!"

"I got a great idea," Sidney Blackpool said. "I'm going back to the hotel and call Palm Springs P.D. See if Terry Kinsale's registered again for a hotel job. I'll call Harlan Penrod too and see if he found out anything. I gotta be back here tonight for a date with Harry Bright's ex."

"Yeah? You're amazing," said Otto, looking anxiously over his shoulder at Fiona who had waddled over to the cart for another mai tai. "You mean I can stay here and play around? I mean . . . play a *round?*"

"Sure. Can you get back to the hotel when you're finished?"

"I'll cab it back," he said. "Unless old Fiona wants to gimme a lift. She's got a new Jaguar she's just *dying* to show me!"

"My, you *are* the one, Otto," Sidney Blackpool said.

"See you later, Sidney," said Otto. "If I'm a little late don't wait up."

Then he turned and hurried back to Fiona who said, "Otto. It's time for you to have another drinky poo!"

"Well, I never!" Otto cried. "I guess I *did* drink mine all gone!"

The last thing Sidney Blackpool heard him say was to a putt that was rolling fifteen feet

328

by the cup, thereby losing for him whatever were the stakes. "Come home, punkin!" Otto called to the errant golf ball. "Daddy forgives you!"

"Oh, Otto, you *are* a caution!" Fiona giggled, whacking him so hard on the shoulder that he spilled mai tai down his sweater.

When Sidney Blackpool got back to the hotel there was a message at the front desk from Harlan Penrod. He went straight to a pay phone in the lobby and dialed the number but got a recorded message saying, "Hellooo. This is the Watson residence. Your call will be returned as soon as possible."

He went into the dining room and had a salad, then returned to the room where he lay on the bed and resisted the temptation to call room service for a drink. It was only three o'clock, much too early. He called Palm Springs P.D. and spoke to the detective lieutenant, getting a negative on Terry Kinsale.

When the lieutenant asked him what it was about, Sidney Blackpool lied and said, "Doing a favor for the Watsons. This Kinsale kid left something at their house."

He was getting drowsy when the phone rang. When he answered, Harlan Penrod said, "It's me!"

"Yeah, Harlan, what's up?"

"You'll never guess. I found Terry!"

"You did?" His feet hit the floor and he was

sitting. "Where is he?"

"I don't know where he is at the moment, but I know where he'll be tonight. At Poppa's Place. It's a gay bar on the highway in Cathedral City."

"How do ya know?"

"Well, I found two bars where he hangs around and I told a fib. All in the line of duty, of course. Told the bartenders that a friend of Terry's was leaving Palm Springs for good and wanted Terry to have his Rolex as a memento. I said somebody'd meet Terry at six o'clock at Poppa's Place."

"Won't that sound a little unbelievable? An *unnamed* friend?"

"I learned that Terry has *lots* of friends, and believe me, he wouldn't know the names of *half* of them. He'll go for it, the little slut."

"You do very good work, Harlan," Sidney Blackpool said. "I'm proud a you. If it turns out Terry's our boy, I'm gonna recommend that Mister Watson give the reward money to *you*.

There was silence on the line for a moment, and then Harlan Penrod said, "I didn't do this for a reward."

"I know you didn't, but . . ."

"The Watsons've been very good to me. I have a job here for as long as I want, and at my age that's a lucky break."

"I know, but . . ."

"I wouldn't want a reward for something like

330

this," Harlan Penrod said. "I'm doing this for Mister and Mrs. Watson. And for Jack."

"Okay, Harlan," Sidney Blackpool said. "Anyway, I'll let you know what happens."

The detective hung up and, three o'clock or not, called room service and ordered a double. Then he ran a hot bath and hoped that a soak and a Scotch would help him unwind. He decided to leave a message at the Thunderbird pro shop telling Otto to meet him in front of the clubhouse at 5:30 sharp. They'd stake out Poppa's Place and if they got their man they'd make an evening of it. In case the kid didn't take the bait, Sidney Blackpool was already going to be dressed in jacket and tie and would proceed to the dinner date with Trish Decker.

He realized that the singer on the radio sounded like Ted Lewis.

"I can't save a dollar, I ain't got a cent.
"But she wouldn't holler, she'd live in a
    tent.
"I got a woman that's crazy for me, she's
    funny that way."

Harry Bright. Poor dumb son of a bitch. He wondered where Trish Bright had met Herbert Decker. He'd bet it was while she was still a dutiful cop's wife. He knew all about cop wives and greener pastures. In fact, Trish Decker reminded him of his ex-wife, Lorie. The coloring, the refined profile, the lopsided

331

sardonic smile. And the sad eyes.

Trish Decker had sad eyes all right, but she'd never live in a tent, not *that* girl. He vaguely realized that he was starting to feel sorry for a suspect in a murder case. He was about to examine that bit of silliness when there was a knock at the door and a voice said, "Room service."

The Johnnie Walker Black and a hot bath made him forget just about everything for two hours. He dozed without dreaming and was startled to see that the sun was already behind the mountain when he awoke.

Otto Stringer was starting to see two tees, two balls and two Fionas and *that* was a whole lot of flesh. They were nearly on the back nine. It was so late in the afternoon that nobody pushed them. They'd already let five foursomes and another twosome play through and they'd stopped keeping score when each of them figured to top 160. Which Otto said he couldn't face, but which Fiona said was her average round.

After a quart and a half of mai tais, Fiona's blouse was sticky with brown rum and fruit juice. The more she drank, the harder she'd whack Otto's right shoulder when he said something funny. And by now *everything* was funny.

It was clear to Otto that this incipient romance might go somewhere and he decided that when he finally got the fat old doll in bed, he was going to show her his freaking shoulder, which was turning purple from all the slugging, and explain that he couldn't go around feeling like he'd spent fifteen rounds trying to slip punches with Marvelous Marvin Hagler. But he'd cross that bridge when he came to it, as now he crossed the actual bridge over the fairway to the ninth tee where Lucille Ball lived. He sniffed the grapefruit and tangerine trees and Fiona promised to introduce him to Lucy and to Ginger Rogers.

"Lots a bucks around here," Fiona said, as he pumped her for information that would permit him to estimate her wealth. "A house in Thunderbird Cove sold in only four months for one million bucks profit. The owner of the San Diego Padres lives there."

"That's a tidy sum." Otto Stringer was exceedingly blasé.

"Not excessive considering the property," Fiona said, belching wetly.

"I wouldn't say so, no," Otto agreed, hoping he didn't run over a Mexican gardener. He'd almost hit two already. If they gave sobriety tests for golf-cart driving, he'd be in the slam before Fiona could think it was a caution.

"Fiona," Otto said, as she was putting on number eight, a pretty three par protected by a lake with a tiny island containing three palms surrounded by red azaleas. "Is your house rather . . . sumptuous? Or do you prefer a more simple arrangement?"

"I got a big one, Otto," Fiona said, doing better than she had on the seventh green where she six-putted. One of the earpieces on her glasses was now hanging loose and she was squinting at him through only one lens. "Look at my blouse!" she cried. "I seen tablecloths at an Irish wake cleaner'n this!"

The second batch of her homemade mai tais was stronger than the first. Otto hit a ball off the tee toward a home near the thirteenth green, causing a nice young fellow in shorts and a golf shirt to jump up from his patio chair and rush toward Otto as the detective staggered out of the cart to chase the shot. The young man kicked the ball out onto the fairway saying, "There you go, sir."

"Thanks," Otto said, and shanked it the other way with his three wood.

"You get a free drop," Fiona belched. "Anytime you get near the house you get a free drop."

"Why?"

"Can't go too close. That kid's a Secret Service agent."

"Is that where *he* lives?"

"Yup," Fiona said, looking like she might fall asleep before they got back.

"I can't believe it!" Otto cried, and he stopped the cart on the fairway to watch some people come out the back door of the unimpressive fairway home.

"Fiona!" Otto whispered, and now he was whacking *her* on the arm, jarring her out of a stupor. "It's him! No, it ain't! Yes, it is!"

"Does he look like Herman Munster?" Fiona Grout mumbled, her glasses once again askew on her face.

"Yeah. He just tripped over the garden hose. It's *him!*"

Otto was not so drunk that he could forget a thousand past mistakes he'd made in this condition. He didn't want to risk losing his chance with Fiona. He was just sober enough to know that in this lifetime he was never going to have another shot at the sweepstakes.

Otto was plotting his strategy as well as he could, and trying to keep from smacking his fairway shot into ball-grabbing palm trees when, near number fifteen, Fiona said, "We got bass in these little lakes, Otto. You like to fish?"

"Oh, yes, Fiona," Otto said ardently. "I'm quite a fisherman."

"I got the bait for those suckers on my *wall*," she said. "I bought a Peruvian tapestry from one of our bigtime desert interior decorators, and you know what? It was full of moths!"

"I had a tapestry like that once," Otto said. He remembered buying it for thirteen bucks in Tijuana. It was black velvet with a naked redhead in a sombrero painted across it. "I never had no luck with tapestries."

"Well, my moths turned to *worms* before I knew they were there. Now I got maggots!"

"Ugh!" Otto belched. "You should *not* have maggots on a tapestry, Fiona."

"If my husband was alive he'd deal with that little pansy decorator," she said. "He'd have two black eyes."

"Mauve or puce," Otto said. "Not black. It ain't becoming."

Then it occurred to him. He had it: an opening. "You *need* a husband, Fiona." Otto fondled his driver preparatory to destroying the tee on number fifteen.

"I know, Otto," she sighed, opening the ice chest to demolish the last of the mai tais. "It gets lonely."

"Yes!" he sighed even deeper. "We shouldn't be alone at this time a life!"

"Otto!" she said. "You shouldn't talk like that. You're just a *kid*."

Otto Stringer had an inspiration. Though he'd never been a smoker in his life, he took two from her pack, put both of them in his mouth just like Paul Henreid did for Bette Davis in his mother's favorite movie. Then he lit both and took one from his lips, gently inserting it in hers. He said, "I'm not young anymore, Fiona. I'm middle-aged outside but I'm elderly inside. I'm bald and I'm so fat I could breast-feed six Ethiopians. Yet I believe the right woman could light my old embers!"

"Otto, you lit the filter end," she said. "Boy, do these things stink when you light the wrong end."

336

"Here, smoke mine, Fiona," Otto said, quickly jerking the smelly one from her droopy lips and sticking the other one in. "Anyways, Fiona, we *shouldn't* be alone, us two."

"You're up, Otto," Fiona said, adjusting the radio volume. "We don't finish pretty soon, we'll need coal-miner hats."

Otto stalled for time by improvising with Duke Ellington. "It don't mean a thing if you ain't got that swing! Doo-ah doo-ah doo-ah doo-ah . . ." Otto sang it as he staggered around the tee, trying to pull it all together for the 513-yard five par.

Fiona said, "I almost forgot, Otto. Behind you across the water is where Billie Dove lives."

"Who's Billie Dove?"

"Oh, Otto!" Fiona cried. "See, you *are* just a kid. She was a *great* actress of the silent screen. She starred with Douglas Fairbanks!"

"I'm old, Fiona!" he cried. "*Please* don't talk to me like I still gotta sweat out chicken pox!"

He sensed he was losing her. All week he'd felt like his arteries were about to atrophy and now all of a sudden he felt like a snot-nose kid! And thinking of anything but his golf shot, he took a half swing and belted it right on the screws, 230 yards on the fly with a slight draw that took it twenty yards farther.

"I told you you're young, Otto," Fiona said. "You think an old guy can hit a ball like that?"

"Aw shit!" Otto Stringer said, having smacked

the greatest golf shot of his life. "Aw shit, Fiona!"

When they finally played number eighteen, with the sun well behind Mount San Jacinto and the fairway in shadows, they lost five balls between them before reaching the green. A record for a day in which they lost twenty-six balls.

Otto gazed with melancholy at the rows of lacy, cone-shaped trees. He'd even started to love the shingled date palms, and all the other ball-grabbing bastards he'd faced that day, now that he realized this might be *it*. He had minutes to turn a lifetime of shit into sunshine. The thought of years still to come on the streets of Hollywood made him want to weep.

He turned up the radio when at last he parked beside the green. Fiona lurched unsteadily toward her ninth shot, which was twenty yards left. Otto began to sing along with a George Gershwin classic coming from the radio. He composed his own lyrics as he went, looking wistfully at Fiona who whacked a chip shot over *everything*, saying, "Aw screw it!," as her ball hit the concrete and took off in the general direction of Malibu, causing her to say, "Good-bye and godspeed, you lil sumbitch."

"The way you wear your haaaat!" Otto sang it from the heart, and Fiona adjusted her lid, which was now resting across her nose from the force of that monster swing.

Then he sang, "The way you wreck that

teeeeeeee!" And that was true enough. The eighteenth tee, after Fiona was through with all her mulligans, looked like it was nuked.

"Oh, Otto!" Fiona cried. "I don't think I ever enjoyed a round of golf more. You gonna putt out?"

Otto stopped singing and said, "I can't, Fiona. That out a bounds approach shot did it. I ain't got no balls left."

"I don't know about *that*, Otto." She winked and his heart leaped! He still had a chance!

"You little dickens!" he said. "Hey, let's have a drink in the bar! You can't go home yet."

"Okay, one for the fairway," she said. "I just live across the golf course."

"I'd *love* to see your home!" Otto said. "I ain't scared to deal with a wall full a worms. You need a man around the house, is what you need."

It was nearly dark when they got back to the pro shop where Otto was handed the phone message from Sidney Blackpool. He decided that in the event he could keep this romance aflame it would probably be on a golf course. He had a vague plan of playing again tomorrow so he said to the pro, "Gimme another dozen balls, will ya? I don't care what brand. Make them orange. Easier to spot in the water."

He was the same pro who'd sold Otto a dozen before starting this round. The pro put the balls on the counter, saying, "Would you like these to go, or would you like to lose them here?"

On their way to the bar, Otto said, "I don't think that guy was so funny, Fiona."

"They just don't understand how hurtful this game can be to people like us," Fiona said soothingly. "Forget it, Otto."

There was some barroom music coming from the oldies radio station. Carmen Miranda was singing, "Chica chica chic! Chica chica chic!" and Fiona Grout paused in the foyer and did as frisky a samba as could be expected from someone so fat, old, and drunk.

"You and me're *ages* apart, Otto," she said sadly.

"I know that singer!" Otto cried. "Lemme think. She's the one with all the fruit salad! Apples and bananas and coconuts used to sprout outta her skull! I know *all* that old stuff, Fiona!"

They both ordered mai tais and were eyed by a dubious barman who would never have served this pair of de-tox candidates in a public bar outside the club.

Fiona was sucking noisily on her drink even before Otto got his. There were three men sitting farther down the bar telling jokes that were interfering with Otto's game plan. He couldn't understand why the three men sounded so irritating, but they did. In fact, they were making him so mad that he'd forgotten three brilliantly conceived double entendres that he was going to use on Fiona to get her hot.

All he could think of to say was, "Fiona, let's have a date tonight, just you'n me."

"A date? Otto, I can't possibly!"

"Let's play golf tomorrow then," he said in desperation.

"Tomorrow?" She put her mai tai down on the bar, but forgot to take the straw out of her mouth as she said, "I'm playing with another couple tomorrow. And with my fiancé."

"*Your fiancé!*" They couldn't have heard him in Mineral Springs, but only because of a wind storm.

"Yes, Otto, I'm engaged. I'm getting married in December and we're honeymooning in the Bahamas at his son's home. I'll meet his grandchildren for Christmas."

"Fiona!" Otto couldn't believe it.

"Otherwise I'd be glad to date you tonight, Otto. You're lotsa fun! I'd like you to play golf with my fiancé and me. His name's Wilbur. You'd like him."

Otto Stringer could only stare at his mai tai while Fiona resumed her slurping, blissfully unaware that a ship passing in the night had just gotten torpedoed, leaving nothing but an oil slick.

The jokesters were still at it. One of them was Otto's age and the other two were in their fifties. They'd just told a Jew joke about the difference between a Jewish princess and Jell-O is that Jell-O moves when you eat it. Then they told the one about crossing a Mexican and a Mormon and getting a garage full of stolen groceries, and were into the second spook joke about the black sky divers in Texas being called skeet.

And that reminded one of them that something funny had recently occurred.

"Wait'll you hear this," he said. "We had an *African* gentleman try to apply for membership in the club. Because he was quite well known he actually thought he could make it."

"Who was it," Otto said boozily. "Gary Player?"

"What?" the jokester said, looking toward Otto.

"They mean a colored applicant," Fiona whispered to Otto.

"Oh, is *that* what they mean?" Otto said, looking about as surly as Beavertail Bigelow always looked.

"You mean somebody that uses a chicken bone for a teething ring? One a *those*, Fiona?"

"Sorry if we offended you," the man said. "I thought we were among friends here."

"Offend me?" Otto said belligerently. "I ain't a kike or a beaner or a nigger. I sure ain't a *member*." Then he was feeling so unaccountably mad that he lied and said, "Tell you what I am though. I'm a *Democrat*. And I think Ronald Reagan's so old he thought Alzheimer was a secretary of state. And during the Mondale debate he almost reminisced about old Jane

Wyman movies. And he'll balance the budget when Jesse Jackson goes squirrel shooting with the National Rifle Association and Jane Fonda joins the Daughters of the American Revolution."

The three jokesters mumbled something to each other, finished their drinks and were preparing to leave, when Fiona turned to Otto and said, "What's *wrong* with you? Why'd you say that?"

"I don't know, Fiona," he said truthfully. "It was the worst thing I could think of to say around here. I ain't even a Democrat! I think I was trying to pick a fight!"

"Rum makes people crazy," Fiona said, slurping on the empty glass with the straw. "You better go home, Otto. It was nice meeting you though. I had fun."

"I *am* acting crazy!" he said. "I tell those same jokes all the time but they *sound* so different in a place like this!"

"Lots a people here earned their own money," Fiona informed him. "People got a right to play golf with who they want."

"They got a right, but their right ain't *right*," Otto said.

"You're drunk, Otto. You don't make sense."

"Maybe I oughtta go home," he said.

"You got *that* right," she said, sounding like a cop.

"Well, I sure enjoyed my day," Otto said, kissing the old doll on the cheek. "You *are* a caution, Fiona."

Sidney Blackpool was already waiting in front of the clubhouse by the time Otto emerged, trudging dejectedly to the bag drop.

"You look like Arnold Palmer when he took the eleven in the L.A. Open," Sidney Blackpool said. "What happened besides you getting blitzed? Jesus, what've you been drinking? Your sweater's a brown argyle. It was solid yellow when you started the day."

"You ever try to drive a golf cart and drink two quarts a mai tais with somebody that throws more jabs than Larry Holmes?"

"Why so glum? You sick from the booze?"

"I dunno, Sidney. Back in Hollywood I'm too old. Here I'm too young. There I'm a Republican. Here I'm a Democrat. There I dream a all the things you can buy with money. Here we find out some guys in our squad room couldn't buy in if they *did* have money."

"You okay?"

"Soon as you get that job with Watson maybe you'n me can play sometime on his corporate membership. But you ain't gonna get certain members of our Griffith Park Saturday morning boys' club on the course."

"How bombed *are* you?" Sidney Blackpool asked. "What happened in there?"

"And they're all cops. So they *are* my kind!"

"I guess you'll tell me what's wrong in your own good time."

344

"All I can say is, I wanna go home to Hollywood where life don't make no sense at all, but at least you *expect* it."

Chapter 15

PATSY

They walked into Poppa's Place only ten minutes before Terry Kinsale was to have been there at 6:00 P.M. It was already very dark in the desert.

The happy-hour-well drinks were about the cheapest in this part of the valley and were poured by three bartenders who hardly had time to scoop up the tips. It was the noisy, intensely raucous crowd often found in busy gay bars. Sidney Blackpool made a quick head count and guessed there were two hundred men drinking. It was standing room only.

"We'll have to split up, Otto," he said. "No point even trying to get a drink in this mob."

"I had enough," Otto said morosely.

"Think you can recognize him from the picture?"

"I don't know if I could recognize my ex-wife," Otto said. "The second one. I know I couldn't recognize the first one."

"Wish we could get you some coffee."

"I need the Schick Shadel Hospital," Otto said.

The detectives managed to find space in the

346

center of the dark saloon, and each began scanning the crowd. It was a pub crowd, an eclectic mix of professional, businessman and working stiff, with a few marines and bikers mixed in. And there were lots of young blonds, most of whom wouldn't accommodate them by turning for a full face look. A cheering group caused Otto to slouch over to a table where seven men were literally sitting on each other's laps. There was a race in progress. The entries in the race were little plastic windup toys that hopped from one end of the table to the other. All the entries were realistic plastic penises. Each one wore the markings and colors of the owner. Blue ribbons, paper valentines, tiny photos of a lover, all adorned the jolly peckers.

"Well, at least *this* reminds me a Hollywood," Otto said to Sidney Blackpool. "Now if I see Sirhan Sirhan and a William Morris agent arm in arm with the Hillside Stranglers, and they're all talking a development deal, I'll *know* I'm home."

A man in his seventies with a mournful face and sagging jowls stared hopefully at a lad with an amused smile who leaned against the wall. The young man was dressed in an oversized street-urchin tunic and winked at the elderly man who mouthed the words of the song coming from the Palm Springs station. It was Marlene Dietrich singing "Falling in Love Again" from *The Blue Angel*.

"He even looks like Dietrich," Sidney Blackpool observed.

"Her voice is probably a lot deeper," Otto whispered. "This ain't gonna work cause I'm about to faint. And if I faint I'm scared I might wake up at the Honeymoon Motel in a slave bracelet and a tutu. They got more fruits around here than an English boarding school."

"We gotta give it an hour," Sidney Blackpool said. "This could be the break."

"I know, I know," Otto said. "I'm just getting all these bad feelings about this whole case. This ain't a regular investigation. Something very weird's going on and it ain't just in this saloon."

"You feel it too," Sidney Blackpool said. And that surprised him. Otto was not the lost father of a lost son. Otto was just a twice-divorced, sixteen-year cop suffering from mid-life crisis and police burnout. Otto was just a run-of-the-mill big-city detective.

They waited for an hour and were about to leave when Otto said, "Sidney!" grabbing his partner like a beat cop grabs a drunk. "It's *him!*"

The young man was into the Calvin Klein, Santa Monica Boulevard, chic marine, gay fantasy look. That is, his white cotton T-shirt was not bought at Penney's. The jeans were not Levi Strauss. The leather flying jacket was not U.S. Air Force issue. His haircut resembled a marine buzz but with decorator highlights. Both cops immediately looked behind him for the buyer of the fantasy duds, but the young man was alone.

The kid obviously didn't know whom he was to meet, and kept himself prominently in view near the center of the barroom so that the emissary of the forgotten sugar daddy with the Rolex could spot him.

Terry Kinsale looked at his non-Rolex, then glanced nervously about the bar. Sidney Blackpool walked up behind him and said, "Hi, Terry. It's me, Sid."

"Sid?" He had taffy-colored hair and tight little ears. He was taller than the detectives and looked as fit as a tennis pro. It would be very hard for two over-the-hill cops to handle this kid in this environment, and both knew it.

"Phil asked me to give you the Rolex, Terry."

"Have we met?" the kid asked, studying Sidney Blackpool.

"You don't remember, Terry?" the detective said. "That hurts a little bit."

"I'm sorry. Maybe I *should* remember but . . ."

"You were with Phil when I met you at his house in Palm Springs."

"Phil . . ." Terry Kinsale needed lots of help with this one. He looked hopefully at Sidney Blackpool.

"This is my friend, Otto," the detective said, as his partner shouldered through a mob of newcomers who were pressing close enough to crack ribs.

"Hi, Terry," Otto said. "I heard all about you. Wait'll you see the Rolex. Sidney, let's get outta here unless the oxygen masks are gonna drop real soon. I can hardly breathe."

"Okay. Let's go, Terry."

"To where?" the kid asked, but he followed them. "Where's the watch?"

"At Phil's. He lives over near the tennis club. Don't you remember?"

"Is he there?"

"Phil got married," Otto said.

"To a girl?"

"Yeah," Otto said. "That Phil's a caution. He won't be able to see you no more, but he *did* want you to have something to remember him by."

"Sure, I think I remember Phil now!" the kid said, knocking himself on the side of the head. "Sorry I forgot. Tell the truth, I just got myself cleaned up. I was pretty heavy into drugs the past year."

"Booze is bad enough, I can tell you," Otto said, sincerely.

The young man looked disappointed upon seeing Sidney Blackpool's Toyota. Phil and the Rolex apparently made him expect a richer emissary with new prospects.

Otto squeezed into the backseat, allowing Terry Kinsale to sit in front. Sidney Blackpool drove toward Palm Springs, not knowing exactly where the police department was, except that it was close to the airport.

When the detective followed an airport road sign the kid said, "Hey, this ain't the way to the tennis club! You're going the wrong way!"

Otto reached over the front seat with his police badge in his left hand. With his right, he began a pat down. "Just relax, boy," he said. "We're Los Angeles police officers and we wanna talk to you."

"Police! Hey, wait a minute!"

"Freeze, or you're going to sleep for a while," Otto said, getting a loose choke hold around Terry Kinsale, while Sidney Blackpool speeded up the car to discourage thoughts of jumping.

Sidney Blackpool helped pat him down with his right hand, driving with his left.

"What's this about?" Terry Kinsale said. "What's this about?"

Sidney Blackpool found the police station easily enough. He pulled into the parking lot and stopped, turning off the engine and lights.

Otto said, "You have the right to remain silent. Anything you say can and will be used against . . ."

"Hey, I don't *care* about that!" the kid yelled. "I wanna know what you think I did!"

"Quiet down, son," Sidney Blackpool said. "We'll tell you all that in a few minutes."

Otto took his arm from Terry Kinsale's neck and continued the rights advisement with his hand on the door lock. Terry Kinsale slumped dejectedly.

He responded to all the required questions

about constitutional rights and lawyers, and then he said, "I got nothing to hide, sir. I just wanna get this over with, whatever it is. In fact, I was gonna come in here to the police station to register as a hotel worker. I just got a job as a bellman. I don't do drugs no more and I got a new apartment and a new roommate. I got nothing to hide."

"Let's go inside, Sidney," Otto said.

"Just a few questions first," Sidney Blackpool said. "Let's talk for a minute. Tell us, Terry, when did you first meet Jack Watson?"

"Is this about Jack? Wow!" the kid said. "I thought maybe somebody I did dope with last year was, you know, a narc or something. That's what I thought this was about. Like, maybe some old deal where I sold a couple joints to some guy?"

The kid was so relieved that he looked happy, which made both cops very unhappy.

"I shoulda called the police about Jack soon as I heard he was killed. But it ain't a crime that I didn't. I didn't know *anything* about his death. I was more shocked than anybody."

"Where'd you meet him?" Otto asked.

"At a disco."

"A gay disco?"

"A straight disco. I ain't gay."

"Of course not," Otto said.

"No, really. I needed money last year. I did what I had to do to make money. But I ain't gay."

"Okay, so you met Jack. How'd it happen?"

"Just talking at the bar. About which girls looked good, and like that. He was my age. Nice guy. College type. He drove me home that night. We became friends."

"Did he do drugs with you?" Otto asked.

"He wasn't a druggie. Maybe smoked a little grass."

"How about crystal?" Sidney Blackpool asked.

"Not Jack. I did crystal, I admit. Snorted it. I didn't shoot it."

"Where'd you get it?"

"Used to know this biker up in Mineral Springs. Name a Bigfoot. I called him when I wanted crystal."

"How long did you know Jack?"

"About six months. Till he died. I was shocked, and that's no lie."

"How often did you see him?"

"About two, three weekends a month."

"Every time he came to Palm Springs?"

"I guess so."

"Did you ever sleep at his house?"

"No."

"Did he ever sleep at your house?"

"Not all night. No."

"Boy, I got a headache," Otto said. "And I'm about to puke all over your pretty jacket. And I'm also about to book you for *murder* and let the Palm Springs cops sort it out. Now don't fuck with us! You and Jack

353

were lovers, right?"

"Not lovers. I'm not gay."

"You had . . . experiences together," Sidney Blackpool said, double-teaming him with the Mutt and Jeff routine.

"I guess so," the kid said.

"Did he talk about his fiancée?"

"He didn't wanna get married. His family was pushing him. His father's a very strong guy, he told me."

"How much did Jack like you?" Otto asked.

The kid hesitated for a second and stopped looking at his hands and turned to Sidney Blackpool, saying, "Lots *more* than I liked him. Man, I was running wild at that time. Jack was a serious guy. He had so many problems with his dad and his wedding plans that . . . I could see Jack and me could never go nowhere. It'd just be a lotta trouble for me, and I didn't wanna, you know, tangle with his dad. But he . . . Jack liked me a *lot*. He was always calling me from college." Then the kid stifled a sob and said, "And I liked him too. Jack was a good friend. I'd never hurt him."

"Tell us about the night Jack was killed," Sidney Blackpool said.

"About the night he was killed?"

"Son, I'm feeling more dangerous than an Arab with a truck full a dynamite," Otto said in the kid's ear. "My . . . patience is *gone*. You were in his Porsche that night!"

"You know about that?" the kid said, and

this time he *did* sob. "That's why I left Palm Springs! I was scared something like this'd happen. I was in his car but *he* wasn't. I don't know what happened to him out in that canyon."

"Why'd you have Jack's car?"

"I lied to him. He told me his housekeeper was outta town that night. He wanted me to spend the night with him."

"Keep going, Terry," Sidney Blackpool urged.

"I went over there to his house and told him I had to pick up my sister at the airport. I told him she came into town like all of a sudden and I needed to borrow his car. I said I'd take her to a hotel and come back and sleep . . . and, you know, spend the night at his house. He gave me the keys to the Porsche. Told me he'd be waiting. I never saw him again."

"Then what'd *you* do?" Otto asked.

"Well . . ."

"Go on, Terry," Sidney Blackpool said gently.

"I wanted to show off the car to somebody."

"Who's that?"

"To some guy I knew. He was in town on a two-day pass. Some marine I'd met in a . . . gay bar. I liked him better than anyone. He was my best friend. You know what? Now all I can remember is his name was Ken. That's what crystal does to you when you use as much as I did in those days."

"So what'd you and Ken do?"

"We went to score some meth. I called Bigfoot but got no answer. So I went ahead and drove on up there to his house in Solitaire Canyon. We got there just when he was coming home from somewheres and he said he didn't have no crystal. But he goes, 'You guys sit in your car down at the end a the gravel road and wait.' But pretty soon this *other* biker comes up. This huge black guy. He had a shotgun! He told us if we didn't get out he was gonna kill us and feed us to his dogs. We went *real* fast."

"Keep going. You're doing just right," Otto said.

"I can't go no further. That's it. I drove Ken back to my place and I took the car to Jack's. He wasn't home so I parked it in front and put the keys in his bedroom."

"Now how the hell did you manage that?" Otto asked.

"I had the house keys on his key ring. In fact he told me that, you know, when I came back I should just come right in and . . ."

"And what?"

"And like . . . get ready for bed because he'd be . . . already in bed. Only he wasn't *there*. And then I looked in the garage and his dad's car was gone. That Rolls he always said he hated. I figured he was out looking for me."

"Think very carefully," Sidney Blackpool said. "Did Jack know you sometimes bought meth up there in Solitaire Canyon?"

"I don't have to think about it. He knew because he went up there with me the second time I scored. He drove me up in his Porsche."

"I thought you said he wasn't a doper."

"He wasn't! But I begged him to drive me. I told him if he took me just once and loaned me the money for the crystal, like, I'd go to a de-tox center and clean up and never do it no more. Just like every doper says."

"And that was how long before he died?"

"Maybe three weeks."

"Did he know you *hadn't* cleaned up?" Sidney Blackpool asked.

"He knew but he didn't wanna know. He pretended to believe me. It was *all* make-believe, the way we were with each other. Just make-believe."

"Wait a minute," Otto said.

"Sir?"

"Nothing. Go ahead with the story," Otto said.

"That's the end a my story. I walked from the Watson house in Las Palmas to the gay bar where I left Ken. And we spent the night together. I read about Jack a couple days later."

"And what'd you think?"

"I thought he must a went looking for me in the Rolls and maybe some biker shot him and drove his car off the canyon. They all have guns. They're all crazy cranked-out animals!"

"And yet you didn't call the Palm Springs police?" Otto asked.

"They started investigating the Cobras soon as the kidnapping stuff blew over! And they said on television a few days after Jack died that the F.B.I. was getting outta the case and the bikers were the best bet. What more could *I* tell them?"

"You coulda told them about the guy you scored from. About Bigfoot. Maybe he went to Bigfoot's looking for you and got wasted. You coulda told them *that*," Otto said.

"I was scared! I didn't wanna get mixed up in a murder with the Cobras or anybody else!"

"How about the reward?"

"What reward?"

"You didn't know Mister Watson posted a reward?"

"When?"

"About a week after the body was found. After the F.B.I. pulled out."

"I was gone then. I went to Miami Beach for a couple months and worked in a hotel. Then I came back to California and got a job in La Jolla. I didn't hear. How much?"

"Fifty grand," Otto said.

"Fifty . . . let's go!" the kid cried.

"Where?"

"Let's go inside! I wanna make a statement! I want my name down in the police file! If it's Bigfoot, I deserve the reward! Let's *go!*"

Otto Stringer sat back in the seat and held his throbbing head. Sidney Blackpool just lit a cigarette and stared out the side window at the police parking lot. Terry Kinsale jumped out of the Toyota, anxious to get on the money list. He had lost his fear of Cobras and homicide cops.

"Come here, Terry," Sidney Blackpool said. "What time was it when you were up in that canyon, where the big black biker scared you off?"

"I don't know. That was over a year ago."

"Try to think," Sidney Blackpool said wearily. "What time did you say your sister's plane was coming in when you lied to Jack?"

"Ten o'clock. I remember saying ten o'clock."

"So you got the car at what time then?"

"Maybe nine-fifteen."

"And you cruised the boulevard and you went to the gay bar and found your marine. How much time did that take?"

"Maybe an hour and a half."

"What'd you and the marine do then?"

"We sat in the parking lot for a little bit. We decided to score the crystal. I called Bigfoot and didn't get no answer so . . ."

"How long did that take?"

"Fifteen minutes maybe."

"Then what?"

"Then we drove to Mineral Springs."

"So you got to Mineral Springs about midnight or later?"

"I guess so."

"You didn't happen to see a burning Rolls-Royce anywhere off to the left of the canyon when you drove up the hill?"

"You kidding?"

"Okay. So sometime after you left the canyon, Jack Watson was up there looking for you?"

"Maybe."

"Get back in the car, Terry. I'll drive you home."

"I wanna go inside! I wanna make my statement and . . ."

"I'll pass it on tomorrow," Sidney Blackpool said. "Bigfoot didn't shoot anybody. He was with a very good alibi witness about that time."

"Who's that?"

"He was with the big black biker."

"Maybe they *both* did it!"

"The black guy reported *you* to the police a few days after the car was found. You're pointing at each other. Now get in the car and I'll take you home."

The young man walked dejectedly to the Toyota, got in and slammed the door. "I want that reward if those bikers got anything to do with it!" he said. "I wanna start a new life!"

"Don't we all," Sidney Blackpool said, starting his engine.

They dropped Terry Kinsale and then drove straight to the hotel to drop Otto who said he hadn't felt so bad since his second wife got the house and the car.

"Don't wake me when you come in, Sidney," Otto said. "Even if it turns out Harry Bright's ex-wife is the killer and her accomplice is Fiona Grout. Which I might believe right now. This place is even loonier than Hollywood."

"It's this case," Sidney Blackpool said. "This case makes no sense on *any* level."

"He didn't shoot *himself*, Sidney," Otto said. "He mighta been real heartsick about his boyfriend two-timing him, but he didn't shoot himself. You saw the angle a that bullet in the report. And he was right-handed. Forget it if you wanna try'n prove he shot himself."

"I know," Sidney Blackpool said. "That leaves us with Coy Brickman and Harry Bright."

"Sure. Or maybe it was a hitchhiker he picked up when he couldn't find Terry. And maybe the hitchhiker turned out to be Mister Goodbar Junior, and *he* shot the kid and dumped the car up there and . . . I don't know, Sidney, I gotta go to bed. Lemme outta here."

"I'll be awful late by the time I get to Thunderbird," Sidney Blackpool said. "I better think up a story. See you in the morning."

As Otto was walking away, he turned suddenly and yelled, "Sidney! Wait a minute. I almost forgot. I got an idea when the kid was telling us about Jack Watson. Maybe this is a nutty idea but . . ."

"Let's hear it."

"Terry said that him and Jack pretended things about each other. That their relationship was make-believe."

"Yeah?"

"When the Mineral Springs cop was into heat exhaustion he thought the song was 'Pretend.' Now he decides it was 'I Believe.' I was thinking, you take 'pretend' — like, the *idea* of pretend — and then you put it with the 'believe.' . . . Anyways, maybe a delirious guy mightta heard that other old song."

" 'Make Believe'!"

"Yeah."

"Otto, I told you you'd make a first-rate corpse cop!"

"Maybe we can play the song tomorrow. But on second thought I don't know if it means anything anyways."

"I don't know either, but it's the best thing I've heard all day."

"I'm real happy you're happy. Good night, Sidney."

"Sleep well, Otto."

He didn't get to Thunderbird Country Club until after 9:00 P.M. He stopped at the kiosk and said, "I'm Sam Benton. Having dinner with Mrs. Decker. Did she clear me?"

The guard took his name on a clipboard and said, "Yes, sir. Have a good dinner."

He parked and went straight to the dining room. "Mrs. Decker?" the hostess said. "She said she'd be waiting in the bar. That was some time ago."

Next he went to the bar where the barman

said, "Yes, I know Mrs. Decker. She was here for over an hour. Sorry, sir."

Five minutes later he was driving the streets of Thunderbird Country Club. Her car registration had not said Thunderbird Cove or Thunderbird Heights so he figured the street must be around the golf course. There weren't many streets and he found hers at 9:15 P.M. Two hours after the dinner date, he was ringing her bell, hoping that there wasn't a maid or housekeeper at home.

The door opened. She was a little surprised and quite drunk. "I haven't been stood up in a while. The sure sign I'm losing my grip. How'd you find my house?"

"I asked at the gate."

"They're not supposed to give the street address without calling."

"I'm persuasive. Please, can I come in?"

"Just till I hear your excuse. I need a laugh."

"I took a nap. I didn't have a wake-up call because I didn't think I could possibly sleep more than an hour. It's this desert air. I'm mortified."

"That's not a fun story. That sounds too much like the truth. Well, maybe next time. Now I guess I should ask the strange man to say good night."

"I'm not strange. I've known you for years."

"We *met* years ago."

"Please. A drink. I feel miserable."

"One for Highway One eleven," she said,

opening the door wide, taking two unsteady steps. "I was wearing my new leather bolero suit for you," she said. "Now you caught me in my jam-jams."

They weren't exactly jam-jams. It was a platinum nightgown and peignoir made in Italy and sold exclusively in Beverly Hills. It was ankle length and scalloped at the bottom and at the scooped neckline. It wasn't enough to be wearing when one entertained strangers, but she didn't seem to care. He figured he wasn't the first man she'd encountered like this when her husband was away. Maybe not even the first this week.

The interior looked like a decorator package, desert style. All secondary colors, with lots of desert pastels, and glass-framed graphics chosen not by subject but to enhance the hues in fabric, carpets and wallpaper. The kind of package they'll drop in for about $100,000. Not distinguished, but acceptable for a second home. They were all second or third or fifth homes for entertaining and easy living. One member of a desert course, a European industrialist, had thirty-one residences, each named, they said, for a Baskin-Robbins ice-cream flavor.

"Help yourself," she said, waving in the direction of the wet bar before she wobbled to the sofa where her vodka awaited, a whole decanter of it.

He didn't find any Johnnie Walker Black, but there was plenty of Cutty Sark. He poured four fingers, hesitated, poured in another shot and dropped in one ice cube.

"This isn't amateur hour, I see," she said.

"Haven't had a drink all day."

"Gonna catch up all at once, huh?"

She was slurring by now and weaved even while seated on the sofa. He wasn't going to be catching up. Not with her. Not tonight.

"Can't tell you how sorry I am about dinner," he said.

"You've already told me. You did me a favor. I have to lose a few pounds."

"Not by my reckoning," he said, hitting at the Cutty very hard. He had to get a little drunk for this, but not *too* drunk.

"So what'll we talk about? The old days at South Bay? You ever work Northern? That's where I wanted Harry to work. But it was too fancy for him. La Jolla and all that. Called it a silk-stocking job. Of course, Harry was *not* a silk-stocking guy."

She drank to that, then started to put the glass down, but took another drink.

"How'd you ever get out here in the desert?" he asked, thinking he should turn down the music. It was the Palm Springs oldie station.

"It's where my husband wants to be. In the winter anyway. The air's good for arthritis."

"Oh, yes," he said, and realized he was gulping. Mustn't gulp.

"Bet you're wondering," she said, grinning over her vodka tumbler.

"What?"

"How old he is. He's twenty-nine years older than I am. And I'll be goddamned if I'll tell you how old *that* is."

"You're old like Lee Remick's old," he said.

"Wonder who does *her* cosmetic surgery. Mine's done by the same guy who did our illustrious neighbor, Betty Ford."

The obsession with age made Sidney Blackpool up his guess. She was maybe forty-five. Since he felt sixty he wondered how old *she* felt.

"So what else can we talk about?" She missed the onyx ashtray with her cigarette.

"It's hard for me to really remember all that much about Harry," Sidney Blackpool said. "When you leave the job it's amazing how fast you forget."

"I've noticed too."

"Did you meet your present husband in San Diego?"

She nodded. "Shopping in Fashion Valley. Not that a cop's wife could buy anything very fashionable. With Herb it was love at first sight. I sighted his Maserati and fell in love."

Her eyes snapped like a whip. The look had so much defiance in it he figured she might be just about as guilt-ridden in her life as he was in his.

"How many years ago was that? Twelve? I was working Southern then, but I didn't know Harry got a divorce. Guess he didn't bitch about things like most cops. Like I did when I got my divorce."

"Harry wouldn't," she said. "He's not that kind of man. Pour me another one, will you? Just a touch."

He took that as an offer to move to her sofa, so he did. His "touch" turned out to be a triple shot before she said, "That's enough."

She missed the ashtray again and he stepped on an ember as he handed her the fresh drink.

"Sometime I'll burn myself to death if I don't die of lung cancer," she said, looking as though she didn't give a damn one way or the other.

"You never see Harry at all?" Sidney Blackpool was absolutely astonished to see that his own glass was empty. He went to the bar and poured another big one to steady his hands.

"Not now. And never without Herb. Not since the day I walked out of our house in Chula Vista. I left Harry a note with all the platitudes that don't explain anything. I gave him primary custody of Danny because Herb was too old for an adolescent boy. But I saw Danny on all the holidays and a month every summer. I took Danny to Europe once. Why, I even took Danny . . ." She stopped, sighed, took a big gulp of 100-proof vodka and said, "I haven't seen Harry at all since we buried our son."

He was keeping his eyes riveted on his Scotch while she talked. He had a technique for interrogating drunks. If the drunk was talking freely, he never, but *never* did anything to interrupt the flow. And with a drunk, even eye contact could result in a change of mood that might dry her flow like a desert wind.

"I was thinking of visiting Harry," Sidney Blackpool began tentatively. "I mean, you said he was in a rest home. Can you tell me . . ."

"Desert Star Nursing Home," she said. "Down by Indio. I wanted to have him put in a better hospital. My husband was naturally distressed by that, so I dropped it. But I send them money so Harry can have proper care. Herb doesn't know."

"I see. Well, maybe it's not such a bad place."

"It is," she said. "I was there today."

"You were?" Sidney Blackpool said. "I thought you haven't seen Harry in years."

"I haven't. I keep track of him by calling his old friend. You might know him. Coy Brickman? He worked for San Diego P.D. with Harry. Did you know Coy?"

"Coy?" Sidney Blackpool said. "He's out here too? I'l be damned. I lost track a him five, six years ago."

Now he looked up and saw she'd wiped away a few tears. No eyeliner went with it. Those fantastic eyelashes were all hers. Irises the color of apricot jam and lashes you could hang your Christmas lights on.

"Harry got Coy a job at Mineral Springs P.D.," she said. "Now that Harry's . . . in the condition he's in, Coy's been a godsend. I don't know what I'd do without him."

"So you went to the nursing home today? Why?"

"Coy said he wanted me to meet him there to give me a report on Harry's prognosis. Which isn't good."

"Coy always was a strange guy," Sidney Blackpool said, keeping his eyes on the Scotch. "He could've told you what you needed to know on the phone."

"He wanted something of Harry's. He asked me to bring a cassette that Harry sent me."

"A cassette?" Now he stopped looking at the Scotch.

"Of Harry singing." She smiled then. "You might've heard Harry sing at one of the Christmas parties? He embarrassed me to tears sometimes." She showed him that lopsided grin but the tears were welling once more. "Harry sent me a cassette about two years ago. Then he wrote and apologized profusely. Said he was drunk when he sent it and hoped I wasn't offended. And hoped my husband wasn't offended."

The detective said, "Trish, you've got me curious. What'd old Harry sing about on the tape?"

"Oh, God!" she said. "Just all the old songs he loved so much. He played and sang eight or ten of his favorites. My God!"

Now he was getting tense. She was even

drunker than he'd thought. The tears might gush. He could lose it all with one big ballooning drunken sob.

"So old Harry's still singing? I remember he used to play an instrument. Let's see . . ."

"He used to play a guitar when . . . when we were *young*," she said. "Or rather, he knew a few chords. He played a ukulele on that cassette."

"Wonder what Coy wanted with the cassette?" Sidney Blackpool mused.

"Said he wanted to make a copy for himself. Said he'd return it in a week. Now can we stop talking about Harry? I'm starting to get sleepy and . . ."

"I'm sorry," he said. "And I'm sorry you gave it to him. The cassette. I was just gonna ask you if I could hear it. For old times."

"I don't think I can do that."

"You uh, *didn't* give it to Coy then?"

"Told him I threw it away. I had it with me but decided I couldn't let him hear it. Harry made it for *me*. It was personal. It was as close as Harry dared come to a final love letter."

And that did it. She spilled her drink and began to sob. It started out quietly, but very soon her shoulders were shaking. Finally, she threw herself down on the sofa and wept. Sidney Blackpool drank his Scotch and watched. Then he got up and went to the bathroom where he found a box of tissues. He came back to the sofa and gave her a handful. He patted her back while she tried to settle.

"My God, I'm drunk!" she said. "How the fuck do I let myself get . . ."

"Easy, Trish," he said, rubbing her back and shoulders. "It's okay. It's perfectly okay."

She sat up and wiped her eyes, but he didn't stop caressing her body.

"I'm getting sleepy," she said.

"Sure you are." He was now positive that she'd had *lots* of male visitors in her time. The only difference was that the others didn't talk about Harry Bright and make her cry.

But he wasn't positive he could manage it. He'd almost lost interest in sex after Tommy died. Line of duty, he thought sardonically. Black Sid screws over Harry Bright every which way.

He leaned over and kissed her. He ran his hand inside the dressing gown. It was so easy that he became *less* sure he could manage it. He thought of his ex-wife, Lorie. Whatever she was, no matter how much he came to despise her, she could always arouse his passion, every kind of passion, mostly destructive. This one was enough like her in some ways, except that she was vulnerable. But now Lorie might be more vulnerable. Maybe now that Tommy was gone, Lorie was like this woman.

He carried her to bed. Without a word he stripped off his clothes and removed her dressing gown. Her skin was pearly, not young, not old. He made believe she was Lorie all

371

through it. She wept all through it. He hoped that she didn't hate him. He kissed her and caressed her before and after, and he tried not to feel like the miserable son of a bitch he was.

Afterward, he was on his side caressing her. Her back was to him now. He became aware of the radio when she said, "That song always makes me think of Harry."

"The way your smile just beams,
"The way you sing off-key,
"The way you haunt my dreams,
"No, no, they can't take that away from me."

"Harry took the job in Mineral Springs after Danny died," she said. "Danny was just beginning at Cal. Danny was a smart boy. And he had a football scholarship."

"Yes." Sidney Blackpool kept caressing her. "Yes."

"I knew Harry took the job in Mineral Springs so he could at least live close to me. Even though he could never . . . never hope to see me. I knew he had some crazy hope that . . . that someday I might walk away from . . . from all *this*. Harry was such a goddamn fool!" she sobbed.

"Yes," Sidney Blackpool said.

"After . . . after we buried our son, I never saw Harry again. There was no need to. That life was . . . it was irrevocable. Do you know what that means? Irrevocable. Do you know how long it takes to understand that word?"

"Yes," Sidney Blackpool said. "Yes."

"And then last March Coy Brickman called and told me about Harry's stroke. And later he called again and told me there was a heart attack. And from time to time he calls to update Harry's condition. And through all this I never went to see Harry. Not once. Because after Danny died it was . . . irrevocable. And . . . one day I asked Coy, I asked *why* he kept calling me even though I never went to see Harry. And he said because he knew Harry would *want* him to. And . . . and he said he hoped I would *never* see Harry, not the way he is now. He said he knew that Harry wouldn't want me to. He said that . . ."

She sobbed again. He wondered if it was the song. Fred Astaire sang, " 'It's so easy to remember, but so hard to forget.' "

"You remember," she said, "how . . . how he was. Such a big strong happy . . ."

"Hush," Sidney Blackpool said. "Hush, now. Try to sleep, Trish."

"That's not my name," she said, and they were the last words she ever spoke to Sidney Blackpool. "That's what *we* call me now. Herb and all my . . . present friends. When Harry Bright was my man, I was Patsy. I was just plain old Patsy Bright."

"Hush now, Patsy Bright," he said, still caressing her shoulders and neck and back.

She was ready then, and slid into a deep

vodka slumber. He didn't even have to creep or tiptoe. He got out of bed, dressed quickly, and started searching for it: the cassette. She wouldn't keep it by the stereo, not where her husband might find it. It'd be hers, her personal connection to Harry Bright, and to the son she'd left back there.

He rummaged through her drawers and through her walk-in closet containing at least fifty pairs of shoes. He went back to the living room and located the state-of-the-art sound system concealed in a cabinet near the bar. There was a mix of albums and cassettes, all commercially labeled. There was no homemade cassette that she might have left by the machine when her husband was out of town. Then he thought of it: the car.

Sidney Blackpool went through the kitchen and out to the attached garage. He found a four-door Chrysler and her Mercedes 450 SL. Herb had obviously outgrown the Maserati. He opened the passenger door of the Mercedes and then the glove box. It was full of cassettes, all commercially labeled except for one. He slipped that cassette into his pocket and went back inside, turning out all the lights. He locked the front door when he left.

His hands trembled as he inserted it into his car cassette player. He started the engine, punched the play button, and while he drove away he listened to Harry Bright.

O. A. Jones was wrong. Harry Bright didn't

sound like Rudy Vallee. His voice was reedier, more quivering, more of a tenor. But he sang in a similar style. And with the ukulele accompaniment, he sounded like an old-time singer. Harry Bright sang "Where or When." After that he sang "I'll Be Seeing You."

For his last number, Harry Bright cleared his throat and struck a false chord before beginning. Then he strummed until he found the correct one and sang "We'll Be Together Again."

Sidney Blackpool thought of Trish Decker, née Patsy Bright, weeping in her bed. Harry Bright sang, " 'I'll find you in the morning sun and when the night is new, I'll be looking at the moon but I'll be seeing you.' "

It was the end of the medley. He advanced the spool. He punched the play button again but there was nothing. He reversed the cassette. There was nothing at all on the other side. Harry Bright had not recorded "Make Believe." Not on this cassette.

He reversed it and replayed Harry Bright's songs. Harry Bright had dedicated one number on that cassette. His speaking voice sounded an octave lower than his singing voice. Harry Bright said, "This song's for Patsy." Then he strummed an introduction and began "I'll Be Seeing You."

While Harry Bright sang, Sidney Blackpool again thought of Patsy Bright. Until the chorus when Harry Bright sang,

"A park across the way, the children's
carousel,
"The chestnut tree, the wishing well."

Then Sidney Blackpool thought about the
boy he'd never seen. He thought about Danny
Bright. Then he thought of both Patsy Bright
and Danny when Harry Bright sang the last
chorus:

"I'll find you in the morning sun and when
the night is new,
"I'll be looking at the moon but I'll be
seeing you."

Sidney Blackpool found himself searching for
the rage. He *wanted* the fury. It was always so
easy to find it. In fact, it was often impossible
to avoid. Now where was it when he needed it?
He found himself starting to cry and couldn't
say for whom. He got himself under control
just prior to arriving at the hotel.

Chapter 16

ENCHANTED COTTAGE

It was the most fitful night's sleep yet. He didn't think he'd dreamed because he didn't think he'd been asleep long enough. Sidney Blackpool got up at dawn, exhausted. He was too nauseated to eat but managed three cups of coffee from room service. He called Mineral Springs P.D. and disguised his voice when Anemic Annie answered. He reached Officer O. A. Jones just before the surfer cop was to hit the bricks. The detective said: "This is Blackpool. Go to a music store or call a radio station. Listen to an old song called 'Make Believe.' Do it for me today. And don't mention it to a soul. I'll be in touch."

As usual, Otto slept until called. When he'd had his shower and shave he came into the sitting room and said, "Sidney, I don't think I'm up to another day on the links. It's too hard on my head. Except for where Fiona beat on me, my body feels okay, but my brain's all bruised. I was picking fights yesterday. I ain't country-club material."

"We aren't playing golf today."

"I suppose we're going to Mineral Springs."

"Uh-huh," Sidney Blackpool said. "We've run outta rope and nobody's hanged himself. I figure today we have a private talk with Paco Pedroza and maybe with Coy Brickman."

"And also Palm Springs P.D. to let them in on our fun-filled week?"

"Maybe we'll even go visit Sergeant Harry Bright. Let's see what shape he's really in."

"How'd you do with his wife?"

"His *ex*-wife. I got a cassette of Harry Bright playing a uke and singing old songs."

"And?"

" 'Make Believe' 's not on it. There must be another one. Coy Brickman called her and asked to borrow it. We're making him nervous. He's starting to worry that O. A. Jones might get it right. We're getting to him, Otto."

"And Harry Bright?"

"He's gotta be in on it somehow. One a those two sergeants returned to the burning car."

"In on what?"

"I don't *know* what. They killed him. Or one a them did and the other's an accessory. Or the whole damn town's in on it. I just don't know."

"But why?"

"I don't *know*. Maybe today we'll find out."

"Can I have breakfast first?"

"Eat a big one. This's gotta be the last workday, one way or the other. We're outta rope."

"Thank God," Otto said. "I wanna lay by the pool just one afternoon and then I wanna go home. I'm getting so crazy I'm starting to miss all the Ewoks on Hollywood Boulevard."

"I really don't see any reason why we can't go for that today," Sidney Blackpool said.

"Lay out by the pool? Soak in the spa?"

"Let's do it," Sidney Blackpool said. "Tell you the truth, I gotta relax and think. I've been needing a drink in my hand every step a the way and that's no good."

"Did you lay his wife, Sidney?" Otto asked. "Harry Bright's wife?"

"His *ex*-wife."

"That answers it."

"What difference does it make one way or the other?"

"I dunno, Sidney," Otto said. "This whole case stinks like a burnt corpse. I just wish you wouldn't a laid Harry Bright's wife."

"*Ex*-wife, goddamnit!"

"Let's go swimming," Otto said.

It wasn't such a bad day. All in all, it was probably the best of their desert vacation. Sidney Blackpool slept on a poolside lounge chair, and when the sun got too hot he moved under an umbrella and slept some more. Otto got a mild sunburn but enjoyed himself enormously by doing belly flops and squeaking like a porpoise, which tickled a couple of divorced telephone operators from Van Nuys. He thought they were cute, and didn't even care that they weren't rich. In fact, he bought them drinks, and made a tentative date with both of them for 8:00 P.M. in the hotel dining room.

Otto was starting to get his head straightened out. The mountains never looked more beautiful to him. The sky was dappled by hairy white clouds that seemed to skim the peak over the tram as they scudded by in the desert breeze. The Shadow Mountains shimmered in sparkling light. Against his better judgment, he introduced the telephone operators to piña coladas and mai tais, and bought them lunch at poolside. He was hoping that his partner might sleep away the entire afternoon.

At 3:00 P.M. Sidney Blackpool awakened, swam a few lengths of the hotel pool, looked toward Otto and started for the room.

"That's my business partner, girls," Otto said.

"You won't stand us up tonight, will ya, Otto?" the older one asked.

"If I don't show up tonight, it may be somebody's murdered me," said Otto, and the girls giggled like hell and sucked on the piña colada.

At 4:00 P.M. they were halfway to Mineral Springs. "What'd Chief Pedroza say about this meeting?" Otto asked, breaking the silence.

"Nothing. Just okay."

"What'd he say when you said it was confidential and private?"

"Same answer."

"What'd *you* say when he said he'd like to meet us down in the oasis picnic ground? Did you ask if we shoud bring the potata salad?"

"I said okay. Just okay. This is a small town. He knows we been nosing around. He might be getting a feeling that we're onto something. He might even be getting a feeling that Coy Brickman's acting nervous for some reason or other."

"He might even be getting nervous himself, Sidney," Otto said. "Whatever's going on *he* might be part of."

"I thought a that," Sidney Blackpool said. "We're *all* getting nervous."

"We're a long way from Hollywood, Sidney. In lots a ways. We're gonna meet a desert cop out in a lonely picnic ground after dark which makes it only a little bit less risky than a picnic in Central Park. And maybe he knows a whole lot about Jack Watson's death. And we ain't so much as got a slingshot between us and nobody in the whole fucking world knows we're there. We could be the next ones they find in a burned car in Solitaire Canyon. Tell me you thought a all that."

"I thought a all that."

"Tell me why we're meeting him out there."

"He insisted. Said no one would see us."

"Tell me you ain't a bit worried," Otto said. "About Coy Brickman or *somebody* blowing your face off."

How could he tell Otto? He really *wasn't*

381

afraid anymore. Tommy did it. He could do it. How could he tell something like that to Otto? Sidney Blackpool was silent.

"Shit," Otto said, and didn't speak for the remainder of the ride to Mineral Springs.

Paco wasn't there. They parked back beneath the date palms, back where the oasis picnic ground settled in against the foothills and was protected from the wind. The night wind had arrived early. But the wind wasn't moaning yet, only whispering. Somehow the whispering wind seemed more ominous than the moaning wind. They watched dust devils off in the canyon. The desert dervishes would run and twirl, and after a sudden gust, would suddenly change course or explode in a spray of sand when crosscurrents collided. The longer they sat looking for Paco, the longer the shadows became, and the worse this idea seemed: waiting out there for potentially murderous cops. Unarmed.

"We shoulda stopped at a gun store and bought a fucking piece," Otto said. "We shoulda borrowed a gun from Palm Springs P.D. This is like snorkeling in Australia with a pocketful a hamburger!"

"Don't turn your imagination loose," Sidney Blackpool said. "Paco's not a murderer."

"One a his good pals might be. Coy Brickman might just decide to blink for the first time this year. In order to sight down a gun barrel and blow us away."

"He might. But we gotta trust Paco. We gotta trust somebody."

"Why? You never did before."

"It's the only chance to figure it out. This goddamn case! It's our only chance."

"Do you want the job that bad, Sidney? The job with Watson? You wanna get out that bad?"

"I want it more than *anything*," Sidney Blackpool said.

"More than your life, it may turn out," said Otto.

He was thirty minutes late. Shadows advance perceptibly in the desert foothills. A last saber of light slashed across the mountains, and then darkness. He had to use his headlights when he entered the picnic ground. Sidney Blackpool turned his lights on and off again. Paco was driving a Mineral Springs patrol car. He parked beside them and waved them over.

Sidney Blackpool got in the front seat beside Paco. Otto Stringer just stood next to the car on the passenger side, looking at the shotgun in the rack. He couldn't see if Paco was wearing a handgun under his aloha shirt.

"Since you wanted it private, how's this?" Paco Pedroza said. He didn't have the twinkle in his eye, nor the mischief in his voice. Not this time.

"We been doing a lotta work on the Watson case," Sidney Blackpool said. Otto scanned the ridge for a hint of twilight on a gun barrel, but there was almost no light at all.

"This is a real small town," Paco said. "I know you been around the Eleven Ninety-nine, and up in Solitaire Canyon, and over by Shaky Jim's. I even got a rumor you had a little talk with O. A. Jones the other day."

"Did he tell you?"

"No, I didn't ask him. I figured if I oughtta know, he'd tell me. See, I trust my men. All the way."

And this made Otto *very* nervous. Paco didn't sound like the jovial small-town cop. Not at all.

"We haven't known who to trust," Sidney Blackpool said. "I'm sorry if we overstepped our authority."

"You did," Paco said. "If the situation was reversed, I'd a come to you and laid it out."

"But it might involve one a your men. Or more."

"All the more reason to come and tell me about it. I think you owed me that much professional courtesy. But that's another story. Let's hear it now, if you're ready to spill it."

"I could take up a couple hours of your time, Chief," Sidney Blackpool said. "But the bottom line is we traced a rare ukulele found in Solitaire Canyon. Back to Coy Brickman and Harry Bright. Brickman bought it, maybe as a gift for Harry Bright, and Harry Bright recorded songs on cassettes for his own amusement."

"I saw that uke," Paco said. "It was used by Bernice Suggs to smack her old man on the gourd. It really got around, that old uke."

"Coy Brickman didn't know about that, did he?" Otto interjected.

"He wasn't there that day. I never mentioned it."

"That's a relief," Sidney Blackpool said. "Then he doesn't know we're close."

"To what?"

"To proving that Coy Brickman and/or Harry Bright had something to do with murdering Jack Watson."

"And why in the hell would Coy Brickman or Harry Bright wanna kill the Watson kid, can you tell me?" Paco Pedroza had an edge to his voice.

"I don't know, Chief," Sidney Blackpool said. "I'd give a whole lot to work out that one. But I think one or both a your sergeants drove back to the scene of the burned car in Solitaire Canyon just before O. A. Jones was found that day last year. It was Harry Bright that O. A. Jones heard singing. Rather, it was Harry Bright's voice on a car cassette player."

"Well, that's real interesting," Paco said. "But you got a couple problems. For one, Harry Bright was off duty at home that afternoon so he wasn't driving around Solitaire Canyon when that chopper found Jones."

"How do you know that?"

"I personally went over to his mobile home

to borrow his four-wheel-drive pickup. We needed every off-road vehicle we could locate when we were trying to find that frigging surfer cop."

"Did the pickup have a cassette player in it?"

"I think so," Paco said. "Harry liked music. I knew he sang a little. I didn't know Coy bought him a uke, but it don't surprise me."

"What'd you do with Harry Bright's pickup?"

"I had one a my guys use it to drive around the desert and search for the dummy's patrol car."

"Who used the truck?"

Paco lost a little of his impatience and started rubbing his mouth. Then, with his hand still touching his lip, he said, "It *could* a been Coy Brickman. I can't say for sure. I was sending guys all over the frigging place that day. But what's that prove?"

"Now I *know* it was Coy Brickman!" Sidney Blackpool said. "It proves he drove right to the place where the Rolls was buried in the tamarisk trees. He came back and he didn't report a *thing* about the Rolls."

"Maybe he didn't see it."

"He had to've been parked right *there*. I believe O. A. Jones is gonna hear Harry Bright's cassette and say *that's* the voice he heard that day."

"This is evidence of murder?" Paco said.

"Don't need too much evidence in L.A. these days."

"There's more," Sidney Blackpool said. "The Cobra boss, Billy Hightower, he personally told Harry Bright that he saw Jack Watson's good pal, a guy named Terry Kinsale, up in Solitaire Canyon in Watson's Porsche. He was trying to buy some crank the night a the murder. Did Harry Bright ever mention that to you?"

"No."

"He didn't mention it to Palm Springs P.D. either. He didn't mention it to *anybody*. A mental lapse maybe?"

"There has to be an explanation," Paco said. "Maybe he *did* notify somebody at Palm Springs P.D. and they lost the information. We could clear it up if we could talk to Harry Bright." Then Paco chewed on it for a second and said, "Did you run it down? That particular lead?"

"Yeah," Sidney Blackpool said. "It didn't pan out. Terry knows nothing. But the point is, Harry Bright *didn't* pass on the tip. I think Harry Bright wanted them to keep thinking Watson was killed by kidnappers, or bikers, or your everyday opportunist thugs. I don't think Coy Brickman or Harry Bright wanted Palm Springs P.D. to run out of hoodlums and start looking for . . ."

"For what?"

"For your sergeants."

"Why? Why would Coy Brickman or Harry Bright ice that kid? Gimme *some* motive!"

"I don't know."

Paco Pedroza sighed in exasperation and said, "This ain't getting nowhere. So whaddaya want from me now?"

"I wanna play a cassette for O. A. Jones. If it's the singing voice he heard that day, I wanna call Palm Springs P.D. and see how they care to handle the next move."

"Which is?"

"A ballistics test on Coy Brickman's gun. And Harry Bright's. The slug they got from the Watson kid's head wasn't as smashed as it might've been. There's a chance. Just a chance of a make."

"Let's go to the station," Paco said.

"Where's Coy Brickman today?" Otto asked.

"He's working swing shift. He'll be on duty in about forty-five minutes. You can have O. A. Jones right now."

"Let's do it," Sidney Blackpool said.

Anemic Annie knew something was up when Paco came storming in the front door and said, "Annie, call O. A. Jones in here. Code two."

A few minutes later she saw the Hollywood detectives enter, looking every bit as grim as Paco Pedroza. When they entered Paco's office he slammed the door, which was something he did only when he was about to give one of his cops a royal ass chewing. Anemic Annie knew that something was up, all right.

After she reached O. A. Jones on the radio,

the telephone rang. She answered it and told the caller that Sergeant Coy Brickman wouldn't be in for an half hour at least. The caller left a message that she jotted down and tossed in the sergeant's incoming basket. The call was from a pawnbroker.

O. A. Jones didn't look very happy when he entered the chief's office. There was a Sony cassette player sitting on the chief's desk. The young cop got scared, thinking that they wanted to record a statement from him.

Then Sidney Blackpool said, "Sit down. I want you to hear a few songs."

The kid looked relieved, and said, "Is it 'Make Believe'? I heard it. I'm positive that *was* the song. You don't need to . . ."

"We think we have a voice that might sound familiar," Sidney Blackpool said.

"The killer's voice? How . . ."

"Just sit down, son," Sidney Blackpool said. "Let's listen."

Paco punched the play button and the three men watched the young cop. Halfway through the first song, O. A. Jones started to say something, thought better, and sat back. But he didn't relax from that instant. He sat rigid and didn't twitch. Sidney Blackpool knew that he'd recognized his sergeant's voice.

When Harry Bright introduced "I'll Be Seeing You" in his speaking voice, O. A. Jones still didn't move a muscle.

When the last song was played, Sidney

Blackpool said, "Well?"

O. A. Jones looked at the detective. Then at Otto Stringer. He looked at Paco Pedroza, then back to Sidney Blackpool. He said, "I ain't sure."

"What?"

"Sergeant Bright," O. A. Jones said. "I . . . he sings sorta like the guy. I mean, it's old-fashioned, his style and all, but . . ."

"*Could* it be him?"

O. A. Jones looked at the chief of police again, and Paco said, "You gotta tell the truth, boy. This ain't no time for wrongheaded loyalty. But it's gotta be the *absolute* truth."

"Okay, then," O. A. Jones said, facing Sidney Blackpool, who was so tense he was about to come out of the chair.

"It *was* Harry Bright!" the detective said.

"No, I can't say that."

"What?"

"I *can't*, Sarge! I had heatstroke almost. It's been a long time now. I been listening to so many singers and so many songs now, I can't say that."

"What if he was singing 'Make Believe'?" Sidney Blackpool was desperate. "Would *that* make a difference? If I could find a cassette with Harry Bright singing 'Make Believe,' would you be able to say for sure?"

"No, I wouldn't," O. A. Jones said. "I got a good imagination. I can think of Harry Bright's voice doing 'Make Believe.' But I *still* can't say for sure."

"Because he's your sergeant!"

"No, sir," O. A. Jones said. "Because it's too . . . *important*. I gotta be sure beyond a reasonable doubt here. Maybe I gotta be sure *way* past a reasonable doubt before I can say in my heart that I heard Harry Bright's voice out there that day. I just ain't able to say it."

"Goddamn it! You *know* that was Harry Bright!" Sidney Blackpool leaped to his feet.

Paco Pedroza came forward in his chair. Otto Stringer stopped leaning against the wall. O. A. Jones was startled.

"Easy, Sidney," Otto said.

"That'll be all, Jones," said Paco. "You can go back in the field now."

"I'm sorry, Sarge," O. A. Jones said to Sidney Blackpool, who sat back down, pale with rage, gripping the arms of the chair. The young cop couldn't get out fast enough.

When Otto closed the door Paco Pedroza leaned his elbows on his desk and spoke with a trembling voice: "Who do you think you are? You come into my town and try to intimidate my policeman in my station house? Who in the fuck you think you are?"

"Listen, Chief," Otto said. "This case's gotten outta hand. Sidney just . . ."

"This case should be in the hands a Palm Springs P.D.," Paco Pedroza said. "That is, if you guys had some startling new evidence. But so far, all I hear is, you proved Harry Bright can sing. Which I already knew. And that a ukulele Coy probably gave him was found in Solitaire Canyon."

"That *is* a bit unusual, Chief," Otto said, trying to reduce the level of tension in the room.

"It might be to some hotshot gangbusters from the big city, trying to push people around without knowing what the fuck they're talking about. Maybe if you'da asked me, maybe if you'da behaved like *professionals*, I coulda explained all this in the beginning."

Then Sidney Blackpool spoke. The color was back in his face when he said, "Go ahead, Chief. Explain it."

"I knew Harry Bright slept it off in Solitaire Canyon on the graveyard shift, for chrissake," Paco said. "There ain't no secrets in a little town like this. I don't stand for my guys being drunk on duty. Not normally, but . . . well, Harry's gonna be fifty years old next month. I had every intention a dealing with it then. I was gonna take Harry and buy him a gold watch and throw a big party and kiss him on both cheeks. Then I was gonna ask him to retire, effective on his fiftieth birthday when he'd have the pension earned. Except he had the stroke last March."

"What about Solitaire Canyon?" Otto asked quietly.

"It don't surprise me that Harry mighta lost his uke out there some night when he was drunk on duty. Look, he wasn't always a drunk. But . . . well, it gradually got worse. The booze, I mean. I sorta looked the other way with Harry Bright when I woulda fired anybody else. I don't doubt that Harry mighta been out there drunk and singing his heart out like some old coyote. And he mighta put the uke on the roof a the police car, and when he drove off in the morning it probably fell off and got covered by blowing sand. That's a logical explanation."

"And how about the singer O. A. Jones heard?" Sidney Blackpool asked.

"I heard O. A. Jones say he wasn't sure it was Harry Bright's voice. That's what I heard. But to satisfy you I'm gonna bring Coy Brickman in here and we're gonna ask him if he drove Harry Bright's pickup truck into Solitaire Canyon on the afternoon the death car was found."

"I don't expect him to confess to it," Sidney Blackpool said.

"Listen, Blackpool," Paco said, pointing his finger at the detective's face, "I'm gonna go you one better. I'm gonna ask Coy Brickman in your presence to give me his service revolver for a ballistics check. And Harry's too. I know I ain't got no call to do that, but poor Harry don't know what's going on so it can't hurt too much." Then Paco stopped and looked at Otto Stringer and Sidney Blackpool and said, "There'll be something to gain from it when it's over. I'll gain the pleasure a telling you two that my guys ain't killers. Then I'll personally point you to the city limits."

"That's more than fair," Otto said. Then he glanced at Sidney Blackpool, who was staring at the wall. Otto said, "You got every right to be mad, Chief. The way we handled this case."

Paco stood up and paced back and forth behind his chair, and pulled his underwear out of his ass, and mumbled a few times before sitting back down. He was not a man who could sustain anger.

"Okay, okay," he said. "Maybe I'm being a little hardnosed. So listen to me. I wanna tell you a couple things about Harry Bright."

"I'd like to hear them," Otto said, taking an empty chair while Sidney Blackpool lit a cigarette.

"You already know that Harry and Coy worked together at San Diego P.D. years ago," Paco began. "Harry broke Coy in as a young cop. Maybe Harry put his ass on the line once or twice for Coy, you know how that goes. Well, some years back, old Harry's wife got sick and tired a shopping at Fedco or whatever. She was a dynamite blonde and she met a rich guy and it was adios to Harry and to her son, Danny.

"So Harry Bright deals with it as best he can because he's crazy about the broad. And he's always the optimist. And he thinks she ain't really gonna like living at Thunderbird and in Hawaii and doing her Christmas shopping in

Paris. Harry, he looks at Danny and says, this is the thing of value, right here. Patsy'll see it someday and she'll come back to us. That's Harry Bright as he was *then*.

"Well, everybody except Harry knows she ain't coming back. And pretty soon Danny grows up and maybe there's guys that love their kids more than Harry did, but maybe there ain't. And Danny's a good student but he's a great linebacker and he gets a football scholarship and he's off to Cal. Then one day in nineteen seventy-eight, Danny's coming back to San Diego from college because an old pal from his high-school team got hurt in a car wreck and might not pull through. Danny was on the PSA flight that went down with a hundred forty-four people."

Paco Pedroza stopped, stood up behind his chair and looked out the window at the desert night. He stood with his hands behind his back and said, "Sometimes policemen get an extra bad break in life by being at places other people ain't. Harry was where he would never a been able to go if he wasn't a cop. He was gonna meet the plane that morning, and when the news flash came over the radio, Harry Bright was on his way to the crash.

"Harry hung his badge on his civilian shirt and got through all the first roadblocks and was one a the first cops on the scene. That's where Coy Brickman comes in. Because what happened next I never woulda known if Coy hadn't told me. Coy was on duty a couple miles away when the dispatcher started sending units code three to the crash site. It was . . . well . . . unbelievable. After seeing all kinds a things he didn't think was possible, Coy was roaming around wiping black smoke from his face and trying to get hysterical people rounded up and away from the area. Then he spotted two cops he didn't know. They were standing in the middle of what looked like little Hiroshima and laughing. I mean, screaming their heads off.

"Coy goes over to these guys and thinks maybe they're off their nut. He even sees a newsie snap a picture a these weird cops. He asked what's so funny because he needs a chuckle more than anytime in his whole life. They point to this guy over across the street. He's kneeling down looking at something. They say they had to laugh, cry, or throw up.

"Coy goes over to the guy and it's an old patrol partner he ain't seen in a few years. It's Harry Bright. That's when he sees what Harry's examining.

"It was a face. Not a head. Just a face. There were lots a strange things happened with human bodies that day. This was a face only. Laying on the ground like an upside-down dish. Coy Brickman said it was a young face. Looked like a young man, but Coy wasn't sure. He said you'd be amazed how you can't be sure when you remove a face from everything around it.

But it was hardly busted up, that face. Just laying there looking at him."

"Jesus!" Otto said. "It wasn't . . . don't tell us it was . . ."

"We don't know for sure," Paco said, looking at Sidney Blackpool. "Nobody ever asked Harry Bright. Not even Coy Brickman could ever ask Harry Bright *that* question. But it was *somebody's* son, wasn't it? Maybe it really ain't relevant if Harry Bright, with a hundred and forty-four to one shot, found a *certain* face at the crash scene. Maybe the question's just irrelevant. It was *somebody's* face. Somebody's son's face.

"Anyways," Paco sighed, "Harry buried Danny or whatever pieces of a human being they *think* is Danny, and he tries to cope, but he don't have much success. In fact, I bet Harry had lots a notions to kiss the old thirty-eight-caliber crucifix. He couldn't stand the house, the neighborhood, the reminders of all he lost.

"Then Harry heard that Mineral Springs is gonna stop contracting with the county sheriff and form its own police department. He read where I'd been appointed chief and was looking for an experienced sergeant and he called me for an interview.

"Now I look at Harry Bright and I don't see any booze-busted veins in that forty-four-year-old nose, but I waffle about whether I should waive the age requirement and hire this old guy. I check with San Diego P.D. and I find out this is a first-rate street cop and a first-rate supervisor, and you know the two don't always go hand in hand. So I hired Harry Bright and it didn't take me too long to figure out why Harry wanted to finish his police career out here. I learned that his ex-wife lives in Thunderbird, and that the torch he carries for her is big enough for the Olympic games.

"Well, I know people who've lost a lot in this world, but Harry Bright, he lost *everything*. So okay, I looked the other way the past few years when I could see Harry was drinking more and more. I was gonna ask him to retire next month. That's the God's truth."

Paco sat down and stared at his hands. "I didn't like knowing he was getting bombed and sleeping in a police car in Solitaire Canyon, but I played dumb. All my cops knew about it, and they all protected him. Everyone a them, not just Coy Brickman. I *wanted* to come down hard on him when I'd see him all trembly and boozy in the morning. But every time I tried, I thought a that day in San Diego. The man kneeling on the ground with the secret he was gonna take to the grave. A secret that's irrelevant. That face belonged to *somebody's* son and I guess Harry figured that out too.

"Anyways, I excused Harry Bright when I wouldn't excuse nobody else. Now I tell you guys one thing: we're gonna go through with this ballistics check even though there's not one shred a motive for Harry Bright or Coy

Brickman to've murdered that Watson kid. I'll do it, but I can tell you for sure, Coy Brickman and Harry Bright, neither one could ever murder *anybody*."

"He should be coming in soon," Otto said. "How do we get to Harry Bright's mobile home? We have the general location but don't know where the street is."

"Take the main drag two blocks before you get to the oasis picnic ground. Turn left on Jackrabbit Road. Last mobile home at the end a the street. Coy has a key to Harry's place and we keep another at the front desk. The whole department watches after Harry's property."

There was a knock at the door and Anemic Annie came rushing in. "Chief," she said. "There's a sheriff's unit in pursuit on the highway! And one of our units joined in!"

"Who is it?"

"Maynard Rivas! Sounds like they're after a two-eleven suspect from the Seven-Eleven Store!"

"Oh, shit!" Paco said. "Where's O. A. Jones?"

"He's after them!"

"Where's Wingnut?" Paco grabbed his gun from the desk and ran toward the front door of the station house.

"He's off the air!"

"Goddamnit! I'll be back soon as I can! Annie, when Coy comes in, tell him to wait in my office!"

Paco Pedroza was gone before she yelled, "Coy's already on the street! And I can't reach him on the air!"

"Whaddaya mean, he's already on the street?" Sidney Blackpool asked Annie.

"He came in and took his messages and rushed out to his unit. I can't reach him. He's not answering."

As Annie went back to the radio, Sidney Blackpool and Otto looked at each other and walked out of Paco's office. They heard Maynard Rivas break in to broadcast his location as the secondary chase car.

Then Sidney Blackpool said to Annie, "What'd Sergeant Brickman say when he left?"

"Nothing, except to ask me what time the message came in."

"What message?"

"A pawnbroker called to ask if Coy'd been given back the ukulele that the detective had inquired about. He didn't say which detective. I figured it was you."

"Let's hit it, Otto!" Sidney Blackpool yelled, rushing out the front door.

"Loan me a gun!" Otto said to Anemic Annie.

"Are you sure it's okay, Sergeant?" she asked. "You can't join the pursuit in a private car, and . . ."

"Gimme a fucking gun!" Otto bellowed, and the trembling woman quickly unlocked the drawer at the front desk and shoved a .38 Colt four-inch revolver across the counter to Otto Stringer who jammed it in his waistband and ran out of the station.

"We shouldn't be doing this!" Otto said, as he slid into the Toyota.

"We got no choice! He knows we're onto him. He's either getting rid of his gun or Harry Bright's. If it's his gun we can't guess where he might be. If it's Harry Bright's gun we know where that is."

"Brickman might try to shoot us, Sidney!"

"We got no choice. At least, *I* got no choice. Want me to leave you here?"

"I'll back you up," Otto said without enthusiasm.

Sidney Blackpool blew through the red light and was wheeling left on Jackrabbit Road within minutes. He cut his lights and drifted toward the end of the cul-de-sac in total darkness. The street was on the edge of town. There were no sidewalks, no curbs, no sewer lines, and no streetlights.

"Where is it?" Otto asked, barely moving his lips. "Where's Brickman's car?"

There were only six mobile homes on the street and they were all thirty yards apart. Behind them was open desert and a view clear to the foothills. When they parked they heard the coyote packs loping down from the mountains, yapping in ecstasy as they began the night's hunt.

"He's not here yet," Sidney Blackpool said.

"Or he's here and gone."

"No, because he'd wanna find two things: Harry's gun *and* the cassette with Harry's songs. He'd need a little time. I think he's getting rid a *his* gun. I think he'll be coming along here at least to get the cassette. Even if it was his gun and not Harry's that the kid was shot with."

Sidney Blackpool backed in behind a mobile home that looked vacant. At the mouth of the street a dog uttered a halfhearted bark. Anyone would think that the dog was just nervous about the pack of coyotes, as well he should be.

They got out of the Toyota and walked across a grass driveway. The wind gusted and howled, and the coyote voices joined in.

They could see a woman through a kitchen window of a mobile home on the opposite side of the road. The home belonging to Harry Bright was only large enough for one bedroom. There was a telephone line and a cable T.V. hookup coming from a pole at the edge of the property.

"Otto, I'm gonna wait behind the mobile home," Sidney Blackpool whispered. "How about you staying near the car? If he spots me or gets nervous about anything, I'd like you to turn on the headlights and make a lotta noise and run right toward us. I want him to think Paco's with you. I don't want him to know it's just us two. He might fight."

"He might *shoot.*"

"I'm not gonna give him a chance. Soon as he's inside Harry Bright's place, I'm gonna announce our presence and tell him the ball game's over and he might as well come out and talk."

"Wonderful!" Otto said, looking down. "This fucking Colt's not loaded!"

"Paco should be here any minute," Sidney Blackpool said. "I just hope he doesn't pull up at the same time Brickman does, and spook him."

"This is an evil fucking case," Otto said, hefting a flashlight and an empty gun.

A car turned into the dark street and drove to the end of the cul-de-sac. It was not a police car. There were two kids in it. The car made a U-turn and headed back to the main road. The detectives could hear the coyote voices growing faint. That hunt had passed them by.

There were other night sounds: the trill of insects, the hoots and chirps and whoops, and the demented yapping in the desert at night. A shaggy tamarisk tree behind Otto started rattling in the moaning wind and scared the hell out of him. He looked fearfully at the gargoyle shapes behind him in the desert, and up at the glittering gems whirling in the pure black air. He thought of bloated buzzards with ugly naked heads, and of writhing deadly serpents that rattled like the trees.

Sidney Blackpool thought he heard a scrape. At first he believed it was in front of the mobile home. He crept around and looked at the street. Nothing. He was walking back past the door and on impulse gave the knob a turn. It was unlocked!

The idea of it only half registered. His brain needed a second to signal the potential danger. The man in the mobile home didn't need a full second. He was crouched and had been ready to escape for several minutes. He kicked that door the instant Sidney Blackpool turned the knob. The door smashed into the side of the detective's face, jolting him backward. He fought for his feet like a man falling down a flight of stairs. When he landed in the desert garden he didn't even feel the spines of the jumping cholla cactus.

He was aware of saliva turning sour in his throat. Then there were some pulsating flashes. He was aware of Otto running and falling hard and yelping in pain.

"Sidney!" Otto shouted. "Ohhhh, my hands!"

"Otto!" Sidney Blackpool sat up, feeling the stabbing in his face and neck. "Otto, you okay?"

"My hands!" Otto moaned. "I'm in cactus! Goddamn cactus!"

"Me too!" Sidney Blackpool said. "Was it him? Was it Brickman?"

Then they heard the sound of a car engine on the main road as it sped away.

"I dunno, Sidney. He was in dark clothes. *Coulda* been a police uniform. But I dunno.

Ohhh, my fucking hands! I'm *hurting!*"

Both men got to their feet and Sidney Blackpool led the way to the mobile home. The door was hanging open and he reached inside, turning on the light.

"No sense worrying about prints," he groaned. "If Brickman takes care a the place, his prints'd be everywhere anyway."

"Maybe we just walked in on a righteous burglary," Otto said. Then he thought that over and added, "Sure. And maybe you're Robin Hood cause you're carrying a quiverful. Sidney, what're we *doing* in this desert?"

Otto entered the bathroom of the little mobile home. He pulled spines out of his hands and arms and dumped rubbing alcohol over the wounds while Sidney Blackpool ransacked the drawers and closets. He found a wardrobe behind the bedroom near a storage space containing a bicycle and a tire pump. In the wardrobe were six police uniforms with sergeant stripes. He remembered hearing that a desert cop needs six because of summer heat. There was a Sam Browne belt draped over a hook. The Sam Browne held an empty holster.

"Goddamn son of a bitch!" he yelled, kicking the door of the wardrobe closet.

"Okay, so it's gone," Otto said, without being told. "Come in the kitchen and sit. Lemme pull those filthy little needles out."

"See if there's any kind a shoe print on the inside a that door."

405

Otto heaved a sigh, walked to the door and examined it. He came back with his tweezers poised. "Nothing."

"Son of a bitch!" Sidney Blackpool said. "That miserable fucking . . ."

"Hold still!" Otto said, extracting the spines from the side of his partner's neck and face, swabbing the area with the rubbing alcohol. "Maybe we oughtta go down to Eisenhower Hospital and have them take a look. Are these freaking spines poisonous?"

"No, they're just harmless plants," Sidney Blackpool said, so furious he couldn't light a cigarette.

"Calm down," Otto said. "There's nothing you can do. And far as harmless, there ain't *nothing* in this desert that's harmless."

"I shoulda thought about . . ."

"We're outta our element," Otto said calmly. "There's no sense saying what we *shoulda* done. Hold still. I almost got the last a those little bastards."

When he finished, Otto put the tweezers and alcohol away and his partner sat in the kitchen trying to get his rage under control.

"I think we oughtta go home tomorrow," Otto said.

"I think we oughtta book that fucking Brickman for murder!" Sidney Blackpool said.

"We ain't booking nobody," Otto said. "We got some half-baked theories and that's all we got."

"Let's search the place at least."

"For what?"

"The cassette."

Otto leaned over his partner and with his face six inches away, said, "Give . . . it . . . *up!* Don't you hear me? The tape is meaningless now. Jones can't or won't identify Harry Bright's voice. The gun's *gone*. Brickman's onto the whole thing. And we ain't never gonna know what happened. Do you understand that? Can you get it through your head? I'm outta patience, goddamnit!"

"Okay, you're right. The cassette wouldn't make any difference now. You're right. I'm grasping at . . ."

"*Sand*. There ain't even any straws to grasp at in this wasteland. Let's go home."

"It's not the desert's fault," Sidney Blackpool said.

"It ain't nobody's fault, I'm starting to think," Otto Stringer said.

Both men were resigned to failure, but with a policeman's curiosity, each instinctively took a look around the little mobile home. Otto stepped into the tiny living room saying, "Sidney, check this out."

Photographs. Some in photo cubes, some in gilt frames, some in wood frames. Pictures stuck in the corners of larger framed pictures. There were thirty photographs in the little room, some as large as eight by ten. They were on tables; they filled the small bookshelf; they covered the walls. Eighteen were of Danny Bright and twelve were of Patsy Bright. Harry Bright was present in four of the pictures. Otto picked up a framed family portrait when Danny was about ten years old.

"Nice-looking kid," Otto said. "Looks just like her. She hasn't changed much, I'll have to say that. Of course I didn't see her up close."

Sidney Blackpool felt seventy years old. He walked painfully into the living room and sat in Harry Bright's chair.

He took the picture from his partner and said, "Yeah, she's changed. This's Patsy Bright. This isn't Trish Decker. She's changed."

"Harry Bright," Otto said, looking at the beaming cop. It was a shot of him in the tan uniform of the San Diego police. He was holding Danny in his arms and the boy was wearing his father's police hat. Harry Bright was a strapping, healthy-looking man.

"He *looks* like Harry Bright," Otto said. "He even smiles like Harry Bright. Now let's get the fuck *outta* here."

"Brickman rummaged through the cassettes," Sidney Blackpool noted. "I guess he found it. We better report this to Paco Pedroza."

There were several cassettes and records on the floor beside the television set. A cabinet door was open and there was a modest sound system inside. Two small speakers were wired to the wall over the five-foot sofa.

Otto opened another cabinet door above the

408

television and found a video cassette recorder. He turned it on and switched on the television set. Then he punched the play button. It was an old movie. The volume was turned all the way down and Sidney Blackpool stared at a silent movie while Otto went to the telephone and asked the operator for the number of the Mineral Springs police.

The movie was *The Enchanted Cottage*. Sidney Blackpool remembered it vaguely. Robert Young was a soldier whose face had been disfigured by war wounds. Dorothy McGuire was a plain Jane who was neurotically shy. They fell in love and discovered that whenever they entered their little cottage a miracle happened. He was transformed into what he'd been before the war. She was turned into the lovely young woman he saw in her. In short, they were transformed into Robert Young and Dorothy McGuire, two beautiful movie stars. It was a very corny movie. Nevertheless, Sidney Blackpool began watching it with interest. He turned up the volume and even listened to the dialogue.

Otto reached Anemic Annie who said that Paco was at the scene of the pursuit where the sheriff's car and the suspect's car had crashed. Maynard Rivas had been slightly injured. She wasn't expecting Paco back for a while.

Otto took a walk outside, careful to avoid cactus gardens, while Sidney Blackpool continued watching *The Enchanted Cottage*. Eventually, Otto came back inside. He was exhausted.

He looked at his watch and wondered if it would be yet another night of being too late for the hotel dining room. Somehow he wanted just one more dinner in the hotel, and then he was going home to Hollywood whether his partner did or not. But one more meal in the hotel dining room would be very nice. He thought he deserved it.

Otto got himself settled on the sofa while Sidney Blackpool slouched in Harry Bright's easy chair. Otto could see that his partner seemed enthralled with the old movie about people making believe. And people making believe made him think of Harry Bright's song. And thinking of Harry Bright's song made him think of Coy Brickman. And while he was thinking of Coy Brickman he heard footsteps outside the mobile home.

Then the door opened and Otto Stringer said, "I was just thinking about you."

Chapter 17

MAKE BELIEVE

"Paco told me to come get you guys," Coy Brickman said. "He figured you'd be here after Annie told him you borrowed a gun to maybe protect you from coyotes. Night shooting in the desert can be tricky."

"You son of a bitch," Sidney Blackpool said, starting to get out of the easy chair until Otto laid his hand on his partner's shoulder.

Otto switched off the video cassette recorder, and Coy Brickman, pretending he hadn't heard Sidney Blackpool, said, "Watching *The Enchanted Cottage*, huh? That's Harry's favorite movie. Musta seen it a hundred times. I even had to sit through it myself a couple times when Harry was drunk. What happened to your face, Blackpool?"

Sidney Blackpool's jaw was puffy and turning purple from ear to chin. In a swatch, six inches long and an inch wide, were a dozen clotted pin pricks where the barbs had been extracted.

"Sidney fell down," Otto said. "I fell down too. City boys don't belong in the desert."

"I coulda told you that," Coy Brickman said,

staring at Sidney Blackpool with those unblinking gray eyes.

Otto looked at Coy Brickman's shoes, but they were shiny and clean. He'd had time to brush them. His blue uniform pants were also dust free. His thinning auburn hair was freshly combed. In fact, he looked as though he was ready for inspection, which in a sense he was, Otto realized.

"How'd the door get that crack in it?" Coy Brickman asked. "And how'd you guys get in here? Paco give you a key?"

"Don't push, Brickman," Sidney Blackpool said. "Not *too* much."

"What're you talking about." Coy Brickman's question wasn't a question at all. "I was told by Paco that you guys have some cockamamy theory about Harry Bright and me smoking the Watson kid. He says you want a ballistics check on our guns."

Then Coy Brickman scared Otto by whipping his revolver from the holster while staring at Sidney Blackpool. He offered the gun butt first. "Careful, it's loaded," he said.

"Fuck you," Sidney Blackpool said, not touching it.

"You don't want it? Change your mind?"

"You wouldn't happen to know where Harry Bright's gun is?" Otto asked.

"Sure," Coy Brickman said, with what passed for a smile. "It's back here." He walked to the wardrobe, opened it, and said without emo-

412

tion, "It's gone."

"Whaddaya know," Otto said.

"You say you found the place unlocked?"

"We didn't say that," Otto said.

"Well, did you?"

"Yeah," Otto said. "We found the place unlocked."

"Then the gun musta been stolen. I told Paco that Harry's keys shouldn't be kept around the station. Too many people come here. The plumber came a couple times. The cleaning lady comes every two weeks. A window washer came and . . ."

"No telling who left the door unlocked," Otto said.

"That's right," said Coy Brickman. "Looks like nothing else was taken."

Then for the first time Sidney Blackpool spoke to Coy Brickman in other than profanity. He said, "Another thing was taken."

"What's that, Blackpool?" Coy Brickman asked, turning those unblinking eyes on the detective.

"A cassette. With Harry Bright singing some songs. One a them is a song called 'Make Believe.' "

"Yeah," Coy Brickman said. "Paco just told me all about that piece a business. So did O. A. Jones. Saw him a little while ago. You been spinning your wheels all over the desert trying to trace a uke and find a cassette? All you had to do was ask me. I bought that uke

413

for Harry's birthday, and I have the tape. I play it for him from time to time."

"You play it for him?" Otto said.

"Sure. I play him lots a music. Harry loves music. You can't be sure if he can understand it now, but I believe he can. Do you know what an intracerebral stroke can do to a man?"

"Maybe we oughtta *see* what it can do," Sidney Blackpool said. Now he and Coy Brickman were staring at each other with such fury that Otto stepped between and lit his partner's cigarette.

"You wanna *see* Harry Bright?" Coy Brickman said. "Sure. I'll ask Paco if I can go down to the nursing home tonight. I think he won't mind. He'd probably like you to satisfy yourself. I know I would. So we can see you *out* of our little city."

"Just for the record," Otto said, "I don't suppose you were up in Solitaire Canyon the day the Watson car was found."

"Heavens no," Coy Brickman said. "Whatever gave you that idea?"

"And I don't suppose you knew Harry was given a potentially important tip by Billy Hightower a couple days after that?"

"Harry? No, he didn't tell me anything about Billy Hightower."

"I'd like to ask Harry Bright myself," Sidney Blackpool said.

"Well, why don't we go see him then?" said Coy Brickman. "You can ask him anything you want. Now how about you guys answering a question for me."

"And what's that?" Otto asked.

"What prompted all this hard-core sleuthing we been seeing? I mean, this is a Palm Springs case all the way. Most detectives I ever knew were always trying to figure out how to *give* their cases to another jurisdiction, and here you guys are trying to take a case *away* from Palm Springs. Now I just can't help wondering if maybe Victor Watson said he'd like to give you boys that fifty-grand reward if you came up with something. Could that be what's happening here?"

"You answer a hypothetical and I'll answer your hypothetical," Sidney Blackpool said.

"Okay," said Coy Brickman.

"Hypothetically, give me a situation where a guy like Harry Bright could murder a Palm Springs kid when the kid was out where he shouldn't be. What could the kid've seen that'd make a cop murder him?"

"Drinking on duty?"

"Don't fuck with us *too* much, Brickman," Otto said. "You already won but don't fuck with us."

"What's there to *win* around here anyway?" Coy Brickman's face was darkening now. "All I can think of is maybe fifty grand from Daddy Watson if you guys hang something on some poor bastard like Harry Bright."

"Okay," Otto said. "Keep all this hypothet-

415

ical. What *could* the kid've seen in the canyon that'd make Harry Bright smoke him?"

"Absolutely nothing."

"Then, in a hypothetical, why would the kid be murdered?" Otto asked. "Give me something Victor Watson might buy."

"You want a fifty-thousand-dollar story?" Coy Brickman asked. "Is *that* what you want?" The cop sat down on the sofa directly across from Sidney Blackpool and said, "*You* tell me. If that's what you want."

"Yeah, I want a story," Sidney Blackpool said hoarsely. "A story he'd buy for a lot of money."

"Now, that's different," Coy Brickman said, riveting Sidney Blackpool with his gray eyes. "I got lots of imagination. Let's see, how about this: the Watson kid drove daddy's Rolls up the canyon to maybe score some crank. You want another reason, I'm lost. I can't think of another reason for him to be up there."

"So far so good," Otto said.

"It's a treacherous drive up there. Most guys do it on bikes or in off-road vehicles. If you take a wrong turn you end up on the windy side of the canyon. It blows like a hurricane over there and the road narrows to nothing. When you see that, you got a chance to back up and turn around, but it'd be real tricky to do in a big Rolls-Royce. I think it'd be awful easy to slip on over the canyon and fall maybe eighty or a hundred feet down on the rocks by the tamarisk trees. And those trees could hide anything unless someone happened by."

"So far old man Watson might buy *that* much," Otto said.

"Well, for fifty grand I'd have to spin a tall tale," Coy Brickman said. "How about one about this old cop who gets drunk out there in the canyons. Maybe a cop that lives in a place full of photos of what he's lost. Ever know a guy that's lost everything, Blackpool?"

"Let's make this short," Otto said.

"Okay," said Coy Brickman. "Well, you could say there's this old cop who's pretty close to his pension and he's up there in the canyon doing what he does. Getting drunk and playing a uke and singing songs like 'Make Believe' or other oldies. He hears a crashing noise. And then he sees a flash of fire. It shoots up in the air and then settles down when the wind blows it against the rocks.

"Maybe he thinks it's a prospector, or a camper with a blown butane stove. He drops the uke and runs to the trunk of his patrol unit and grabs a fire extinguisher and heads toward that flame back behind the canyon wall, hoping nobody got hurt. Of course, a forty-nine-year-old cop with a skin full of hooch and only months away from a stroke and a heart attack wouldn't be in very good shape to begin with. And by the time he picks his way through the rocks with his flashlight, he's all worn out. Then he comes on it. The wrecked car. It's burning.

"He thought it was only the wind howling at first but he gets close as he can, which is pretty close because the wind's blowing the flames away from him and into the rocky wall. He hears it and knows it's not the wind. Someone's screaming.

"He runs up to the car but it's almost engulfed, and his little fire extinguisher is useless and he sees a young guy pinned underneath. The kid's enveloped in gasoline fire from his waist down and the fire's licking up and the kid sees him and throws out his arms and starts screaming like a child for his daddy. But the wind shifts and the fire keeps licking around and the car's all consumed but the kid won't stop screaming and maybe the face in the fire looks like a face he once found on the ground . . . but that's another story. Anyway, the old drunk, the sick crazy drunk cop, he pulls out his piece and . . ."

Otto Stringer became aware he wasn't breathing when his chest heaved. He looked at his partner who only stared. "Go on, Brickman," Sidney Blackpool said.

"Well, for a fifty-grand fairy tale let's say he fired one, two, three rounds at that doomed boy. Let's say he didn't even know if a slug hit the kid or if the kid passed out. But at least the boy slumped down into the flames and stopped screaming. Then let's say the sick crazy drunk old cop ran back to his unit and tossed the fire extinguisher in and drove off without thinking of his ukulele and went straight to another cop's house and got him out of bed and told him more or less what happened.

"Let's say the other cop thought about it very calmly and made a few decisions. Let's say he took the old drunk home and put him to bed and covered for him with a story that he got sick and had to go home. Let's say the friend thought a whole lot about the old drunk only having a short way to go for his pension. And thought about how then the drunk could live whatever years he had left with a little peace and dignity. Let's say when the friend put the old drunk to bed he even took a look around a room like this. At all the pictures. At a *make-believe* house. Maybe after enough booze and memories and sickness it *did* become an enchanted cottage for the old drunk. Maybe the friend just said, fuck it, this guy's had *enough*."

"So there never *was* a murder in your fifty-grand story!" Otto said, looking at his partner. "That's why you couldn't work it out, Sidney. There never *was* a murder!"

"Not in *my* story," Coy Brickman said. "I don't know how Watson'd like that, but I can't come up with anything more believable for you. Yet even without a murder there *was* a crime of sorts: voluntary manslaughter? Maybe involuntary manslaughter, given all the circumstances. Well, since mercy killing isn't even

419

legal for doctors, the old drunk cop in my story would be in some serious trouble. They just don't give pensions for mercy killing, far as I know. In fact, you can bet the D.A.'d say that if he wasn't drunk, there were other courses of action open to him. So if he didn't get jail time he'd get fired and lose his pension and spend the rest of his living on handouts and eating dog food. That's why his buddy stepped in.

"Anyway, that's how I'd tell it. So the friend cleaned and reloaded the drunk's gun and went back to the canyon the next day as soon as he realized the uke was lost. A uke that could maybe be traced. And he took a peek at the burned car and found two bullet holes in the windshield where the old drunk'd missed. So he knocked the glass out and hoped the drunk hadn't even hit the kid who was torched like a matchstick. The buddy hoped the kid had burned to death. But then the buddy never had the compassion for his fellowman that the drunk had.

"But the old drunk didn't have compassion for himself, and after he got sober he wanted to step right up and tell what happened. Only now the tables were turned. His friend had already covered for him and obliterated evidence of the gunshots. In fact, his friend had aided and abetted, and might be called an accessory if there was a manslaughter rap to face. So the friend persuaded the old drunk that they *had* to keep mum now, for the buddy's sake if not for the drunk's. And that's the way it ended.

"In a way, something happened to their friendship after that. The old drunk, who had more than enough heartbreak in his miserable life, now had a big load of guilt to carry every time he thought of the parents not knowing what really happened to their dead boy. He was always thinking of how the burned corpse was out there in the canyon for two days with the animals.

"So maybe the drunk's buddy, with all those good intentions that lead people straight to hell, had actually *increased* the load the old drunk was already carrying in life. And which was leading straight to a monster headache and a limp right arm and a bed where he ended up diapered and drooling like a baby."

And now Coy Brickman was no longer looking at them with unblinking eyes. He was blinking quite a bit because his eyes were damp.

"That's the story I'd tell for fifty grand. If I wanted fifty grand as bad as you guys must want it. But of course this is all a make-believe story so maybe Watson wouldn't think it was worth fifty cents. Maybe you shouldn't ever tell such a silly story to anyone because you'd sure look dumb trying to prove a single bit of it, wouldn't you?"

"I wouldn't imagine Harry Bright's *missing* gun is ever gonna turn up anywhere, is it?" Otto asked, handing his borrowed gun to Coy Brickman.

"The desert wind doesn't uncover a gun as easy as a ukulele," Coy Brickman said, looking at Sidney Blackpool.

Then the tall sergeant got up and walked to the video cassette recorder. He punched the button and turned on the television. "Watch the end of the movie. I'll be at the station with Paco. I can repeat this fifty-grand make-believe story for him if you want, but why not just tell Paco that you're saying good-bye. Better yet, don't even say good-bye. Just go back to Hollywood where you belong."

"How's *this* make-believe story come out?" Otto asked. *"The Enchanted Cottage,* I mean."

"It comes out real happy," Coy Brickman said. "The young couple get married and probably even have a son, if you like to imagine past the movie ending. Maybe he's just like Danny Bright. The three of them probably live happy ever after. I guess that's the way you'd imagine the story if you started to live a make-believe life."

"Okay, Brickman," Sidney Blackpool said. "You've made a lot a make-believe points here tonight. Now I've just about had enough a you and Patsy Bright and Harry Bright and whatever fantasy he created in this house trailer. I've had enough sad stories about lost kids and lost fathers and everything else. Now there's gonna be no more make-believe. Now I wanna *see* Harry Bright. With my own eyes."

"Let's go. I won't even phone Paco.

He'll understand."

"We'll follow you," Sidney Blackpool said.

"In case you got lost it's . . ."

"We know exactly where it is," Sidney Blackpool said.

There was no fear of losing Coy Brickman's patrol car. He never exceeded the speed limit on the drive toward Indio. Sidney Blackpool chain-smoked. Otto Stringer was getting sick to his stomach but he knew it wasn't the cigarette smoke.

They were on Highway 10 when Otto said, "This is a garbage case, Sidney. You can't turn garbage into gold no matter how you try. I've learned that here. Have you learned that?"

"I think Harry Bright can talk," Sidney Blackpool said. "Or maybe he can at least communicate. That's all it'll take."

"Even if he can, even if he does, I don't wanna be the one to charge him with manslaughter. And I don't wanna throw Coy Brickman in jail."

"I want a way out," Sidney Blackpool said. "I want out the way Watson said it could be. Is it so wrong to want something like that for yourself?"

"It's a garbage case," Otto said. "That's all I know for sure."

There were only a few visitors' cars at the nursing home that time of night. Coy Brickman got out of the patrol car and went in first, saying a few words to the nurse on duty. She nodded and he waved to the two detectives. The nursing home wasn't so bad on the inside. It was seedy but clean, and had one doctor in attendance. The rooms could easily have been tiny motel rooms except that remodeling had joined two rows of rooms with a connecting corridor.

The room was near the far end of the corridor. It was a private room with one bed. There was a lamp on a table beside the bed. Also on the bedside table was a radio with a built-in cassette player. There were I.V.'s nourishing him and oxygen available. Otto looked at the cadaverous old man. Only the feet bulged under the sheet.

"Where's Harry Bright?" Otto asked.

"Take a closer look," Coy Brickman said.

Otto crept closer to the bed to inspect. The face was yellow, with a burst of spidery veins on the nose and cheeks and under the eyes. The eye pouches were yellow-brown like nicotine stains. His hair was wispy and sparse and gray. His fingernails were fungus yellow. Stretched from head to toe he looked to be about six feet three inches. Otto guessed he weighed one hundred pounds, only because of the size of his large bones. The eyes were yellow except for the irises, which were beautiful and blue.

The man stared at the ceiling with his jaw hanging open. There was saliva forming at the corners of his mouth, and his eyes were tearing slightly. He stared as unblinking as Coy Brickman. Otto leaned over the bed to look in those blue eyes for response and saw just the faint twitching of his tongue. He had a strong cleft chin.

The bedsheet fluttered every few seconds with his heartbeats. "That man should be in an intensive-care unit," Otto said.

"I believe he'd rather do his dying here," Coy Brickman said. "I think Harry likes it here."

Sidney Blackpool wouldn't approach the bed. "Is it, Otto?" he said. "Is it him?"

"It's Harry Bright," Otto said. "After life got all through fucking with him."

And then Sidney Blackpool said something that astonished Otto more than anything he'd heard this day. Sidney Blackpool took three steps closer to the bed of the dying man and said, "Brickman, why not tell me where his gun is? If it matches ballistics, that's it. We can write up this investigation to leave you completely out of it, can't we, Otto? I give you my solemn word we can write it up so it looks like you never knew that Harry Bright got drunk and shot the kid after the car crashed. We can tell it just the way it happened and we can prove it, if the ballistics test is positive. Then I'd tell Victor Watson that you deserve the reward for figuring out how the shooting went down and for helping us. Fifty thousand could be *yours*."

Coy Brickman didn't take his eyes from Sidney Blackpool's face when he walked around the bed. He looked below the side rail, then he looked back at the detective and said, "Damn, it's empty."

"What's empty?" Sidney Blackpool asked.

"The catheter bag. I wanted to throw it in your face. From Harry and me." Then he turned to the breathing corpse and said, "Damnit, Harry, why can't you take a pee when I need it?"

"Let's go, Sidney," Otto said. "Let's go home."

"Before you go, I got something you wanted," Coy Brickman said. Then he punched the button on the cassette player and slipped in a cassette he took from the pocket of his uniform pants. He looked at Harry Bright as he pressed the play button. They heard a few off-key chords from the uke and when it was in tune Harry Bright introduced a song again.

Harry Bright's voice said, "This is happy Harry Bright coming to you from the Mineral Springs Palladium out on Jackrabbit Road where I'd like to introduce a tasty tune, a sizzling side, a heavenly hit! It's called 'Make Believe.' And ladies and gentlemen, I'd like to dedicate this number to Patsy."

Otto Stringer turned away and absolutely could not look at the cadaverous figure in the bed as Harry Bright sang:

"We could make believe I love you,
"Only make believe that you love me.
"Others find peace of mind in pretending.
"Couldn't you, couldn't I, couldn't we?"

Sidney Blackpool looked like a sleepwalker. He forced himself to lean over the bed. He studied the corpse that breathed. He leaned over the bed on one side while Coy Brickman stood on the other side watching him. The color drained from Sidney Blackpool's face. He stared into Harry Bright's beautiful blue eyes. Looking for what?

"Make believe our lips are blending
"In a phantom kiss or two or three.
"Might as well make believe I love you
"For to tell the truth, I dooooooooo!"

When it was over, Coy Brickman took the cassette out and reached across the bed, jamming it into Sidney Blackpool's shirt pocket. "There," he said. "You wanted it so bad. Take it."

"Let's go, Sidney," Otto said. "Now. Let's go, *now!*"

As they were walking away, they heard Coy Brickman turning the radio to the Palm Springs station where Fred Astaire was singing "Putting on the Ritz."

"Hey, it's Fred," they heard Coy Brickman say to Harry Bright. "Pipes aren't quite as

427

good as old Harry Bright's, but not so bad for a hoofer."

Otto Stringer took one last glance and saw the tall cop leaning over Harry Bright, gently dabbing the saliva from the strong cleft chin of the dying man.

"The world won't be the same when old Fred's gone, will it, Harry?" Coy Brickman asked Harry Bright, while Fred Astaire sang it as only he could.

Chapter 18

DESIGNS AND DRIFTS

There was no conversation on the ride back to the hotel. When they got to their suite, Otto went into his bedroom and came back with the expense money, throwing it on the coffee table. "Are you going home with me tomorrow?" he asked.

Sidney Blackpool picked up the telephone and said, "I'm calling Victor Watson. I'll do what *he* wants me to do."

When he reached Victor Watson's Bel-Air residence the call was answered by a housekeeper and then Victor Watson came on the line and said, "Sidney? Have you discovered something?"

"Mister Watson," Sidney Blackpool said, "I know how your boy died. But I can never prove anything in a court of law."

Victor Watson merely said, "I'll meet you at my Palm Springs home at three o'clock tomorrow afternoon. Thank you, Sidney. Thank you!"

After Sidney Blackpool hung up, Otto said, "Give him my President McKinleys. Or keep them yourself. I'm catching a bus to L.A. first thing in the morning. I'll pick up my golf clubs when I see you at work on Monday."

"Why don't you stay, Otto? Why go home? What's the point? What're you trying to prove?"

"There's nothing to prove," Otto said. "I don't wanna be there when you tell him about Harry Bright. It might make me feel more putrid than I do now."

"I want that job, Otto," Sidney Blackpool said. "I want a new life. If you can't understand that, I'm sorry."

"I hope you get what you want," Otto Stringer said.

Otto went straight to bed without eating. Sidney Blackpool had no thought of food. He spent the evening planning the best way possible to tell Victor Watson how his son was shot by a drunken cop named Harry Bright in an act of mercy. He hoped he could leave Coy Brickman totally out of the story.

Harry Bright's taped voice was haunting him. There was a time after Tommy Blackpool's death when he *craved* to hear his son's voice once more. But their home movies were without sound. Once he had tried watching a home movie. He never got past the first reel.

At one time in his life he'd foolishly yearned for his son to be more like *him*. Now, if he had a soul he'd give it just for his son to *be*.

It took him two hours and a lot of Johnnie Walker Black before he could fall asleep. Before he did, it came more fiercely than it had in a very long time: the memory of Tommy Blackpool. The last time his father saw him alive.

Sidney Blackpool held his hands over his eyes as he lay in the dark but that wouldn't stop the memory. Nothing would stop it once it started to come. Someday, if he were ever to smoke his .38, it would be to stop it, that memory.

Lorie had come to Sidney Blackpool's house to pick up both children. Tommy was into drugs heavily by then and Sidney Blackpool had found hash in his room and was confronting the boy in front of his ex-wife. During the argument Tommy had cursed both parents, and Sidney Blackpool had exploded. The father grabbed the son by the shirt and said, "You miserable little son of a bitch! You little bastard. I'll *kill* you!" And he'd punched Tommy twice and knocked the boy over the kitchen table, causing Lorie to start screaming when glass shattered and blood from Tommy's nose spattered on the white vinyl floor.

The boy's mother threw herself between father and son and Tommy cried obscenities and ran through the house, his blood dripping on the carpet before he was out the door and gone.

They discovered later that he'd spent the night with a neighborhood friend. The next morning he was truant from school. He was drowned that day by the huge swells while surfing in the cold winter twilight.

After the image of Tommy running bloody through the house finally faded, Sidney Blackpool said, "Oh, Tommy!" It was all he could say. This was *his* secret. Victor Watson had his and Harry Bright had his.

He had the dream that night. In the dream Tommy Blackpool at the age of twelve was watching a football game on television, displaying that special sort of chuckling grin of his. In the dream Sidney Blackpool was still with his wife, Lorie, and he took her aside and made her promise not to tell the wondrous *new* secret: that he had willed Tommy back! At least his essence. But only for them to know.

As always, the dream ended when she said, "Sid, we can enjoy him forever now! But you mustn't tell him he's going to die when he's eighteen! You mustn't tell him!"

"Oh, no! I'll never tell him that!" he said to his wife in the dream. "Because now he loves me. And . . . and now he forgives me. My boy *forgives* me!"

As always, he woke up sobbing, and smothering in his pillow.

For once, his partner was up first. In fact, when Sidney Blackpool dragged himself out of bed with a headache almost bad enough to make *him* fear a stroke, he was surprised to see that Otto Stringer had gone. He looked at his watch and saw it was after nine, the latest he'd

432

slept since arriving. He showered, shaved and stared at his swollen jaw. His face was done in desert pastels. He ate a light breakfast in the suite and vomited it back up almost immediately.

He checked out of the hotel at 1:00 P.M. and walked the boulevards of Palm Springs until 2:30 P.M. Then he drove to the Watson home.

When Harlan Penrod admitted him and saw his damaged face he said, "My gosh! What happened to you? Mister Watson called and said he was coming to meet you. Did you get Terry Kinsale? Is he the one who . . ."

"No, he's not, Harlan," Sidney Blackpool said. "How about getting me some coffee."

"Sure, but tell me who . . ."

"Don't ask me any questions, Harlan. I'll tell it to Mister Watson. Jack was his kid. Ask *him*."

"But . . ."

"Don't ask me a single question."

"Okay. Except how do you like your coffee?"

Victor Watson arrived from Palm Springs Airport by taxi. He wasn't even in the house long enough to shake hands with Sidney Blackpool before he said, "Harlan, take the car down and gas it up, will you?"

"It's full, Mister Watson." Harlan said, "Can I get . . ."

"Go to a movie, Harlan. Come back at six o'clock. Please."

"Sure, Mister Watson," the houseboy said,

433

looking at the grim set of Sidney Blackpool's mouth.

"Look at you, Sidney!" Victor Watson said. "What happened?"

"Cactus," Sidney Blackpool said. "The desert's full a dangers for guys like me."

"Tell all of it, Sid. All of it."

They went into the study and Victor Watson sat behind his desk while the detective sat across the room on a sofa.

Sidney Blackpool told *almost* all of it. There was nothing to gain by naming Coy Brickman. He told Victor Watson about Terry Kinsale, and about his driving Jack Watson's Porsche, and about the gun that was missing and which no doubt was the weapon used to kill Jack during a misguided act of mercy by a sick drunken cop. He protected Coy Brickman by implying that Harry Bright probably disposed of the gun himself.

It was nearly dark when he finished. Victor Watson had asked very few questions during the narrative. He sat staring at Sidney Blackpool and missed not a word. His eye sockets became progressively more hollow in the shadow from desert twilight. He looked even older than Sidney Blackpool remembered him. The detective consumed three glasses of water during the dissertation. He'd never felt more parched. He was slightly dizzy and a bit nauseated, like a diabetic. His jaw ached but he did not want a Johnnie Walker Black. He wanted to end this thing cold sober.

By the time the detective had finished, Victor Watson's eyes were invisible. Sidney Blackpool was staring at empty sockets and could only imagine the granite irises.

Harry Bright had unforgettable eyes. When he'd crept close to his bed he could see them staring in their sockets: beautiful blue eyes. Victor Watson had no eyes at all. Sidney Blackpool looked at his water glass and waited.

When Victor Watson spoke, he said, "I accept full responsibility for the tragic event."

Sidney Blackpool was about to console, to tell him that Jack's death was not his father's fault.

But Victor Watson said, "I should never've brought you into this case. Not *you*, Sidney. I believed we might have a kind of bonding, you and me. I felt, upon hearing about you, that it was . . ."

"An omen!" Sidney Blackpool said.

"Yes. Now I see it was just a mistake. A foolish tragic mistake."

"Whadda you mean, Mister Watson? What mistake?"

"Perhaps my time in psychotherapy is worth something after all," Victor Watson said. "I see myself in you. The way I was. The rage. The confusion. The guilt."

"I don't understand, Mister Watson."

"I know you don't, Sidney. I know. Call it a form of transference, but labels aren't important. You've projected feelings from *your* life, feelings about your own lost son into this investigation. Can't you see that?"

"But Mister Watson . . ."

"It's my fault. It's all my fault. I saw in you a lost father of a lost boy who might succeed where others . . . well, I was right, and being right I was terribly wrong. I'm sorry to have done this to you."

"Please, Mister Watson, I don't understand!" Sidney Blackpool moved to the edge of the sofa but still could not see eyes in the hollow sockets. If only he could read the eyes. An investigator *had* to see the eyes!

"My son Jack," Victor Watson said, "was the finest, brightest, most loving young man you would ever meet."

"I believe that, Mister Watson."

"Our relationship had the normal stresses of fathers and sons, but I think we handled it."

"I believe that," Sidney Blackpool said, and knocked over the empty water glass reaching for a cigarette.

"No one, but *no* one who had ever known Jack Watson could ever under *any* circumstances believe he was homosexual."

"I didn't say . . ."

"And no one, but no one, would ever believe he could be stupid enough . . . insane enough to drive up to that miserable canyon in the dead of night for any reason whatsoever, other than because a criminal held a gun to his head."

Then Victor Watson stood, but his eyes were still in darkness, backlit by the lamp. "A fact that was proved when a bullet was fired into his skull!"

"Please, Mister Watson, please . . ."

Victor Watson sat back down in the chair and said, "I find it all very interesting, what you've told me. It's interesting that there's a cop named Harry Bright who told somebody he shot my son while he was drunk."

"I'll name the somebody, Mister Watson!" Sidney Blackpool cried out. "It's Sergeant Coy Brickman! He told his friend, Sergeant Coy . . ."

"Be quiet, please!" Victor Watson said. "I find it very interesting that an alcoholic cop possibly had a drunken hallucination when he heard about my son being found in the canyon where the cop slept off his drunken tour of duty. It's particularly ironic that the drunk is himself the father of a lost son. That's particularly ironic and very sad. But that's *all* it is . . ."

"But Coy Brickman, Mister Watson! Coy Brickman went to the canyon. He saw . . ."

"Did this Coy Brickman *admit* this to you, Sidney? Will he make a statement to *me?*"

"No, Mister Watson. But I *know* it's true."

"Did he *admit* that to you?"

"He didn't *admit* it, but . . ."

"Will he admit it to anybody?"

"He won't admit it to anyone, Mister Watson.

But I know . . ."

"Sit back and try to be calm, Sidney," Victor Watson said. "Try to understand what I'm saying to you."

"My God," Sidney Blackpool said. "My God!"

"What I've put you through, I'll regret forever. I had no idea how little you'd traveled from the grave of your own son. I tried to use your empathy, but now I've done considerable harm to you."

"My God, Mister Watson! This . . ."

"I believe that Jack had a friendship with this boy, Terry Kinsale. If you say so. But even this boy hasn't claimed that there was anything . . . unwholesome in that friendship. I believe that this boy borrowed Jack's Porsche. I believe he was a narcotics user and that Jack discovered it and didn't approve. I believe in the substance of all the facts you've uncovered. And I'm impressed by your diligence and skill. But what no one who has ever known my son could *ever* believe is that he was some sort of hysterical faggot! Who went trailing after some valet-parking boy up in . . ." Victor Watson stopped and massaged his brow and shook his head. "And everything else you've told me is your theory, your hypothesis, your supposition. Can you substantiate by any independent source any of these . . . *ideas* of yours?"

"My partner, Otto Stringer," Sidney Blackpool said quietly. "He might . . . he *would* agree with my hypothesis."

"I see he's not even here, Sidney. It probably made the poor man uncomfortable to think of coming here and listening to your . . . unfortunate conclusions about a boy you've never known and obviously never will, not in *any* sense."

"Whadda you want from me, Mister Watson?" Sidney Blackpool pleaded.

"Nothing more, Sidney," Victor Watson said. "You're a hell of a detective to've done as much as you did."

"The job, Mister Watson? The job!"

"What job?"

"Director of Security with Watson Industries! I've proved something, haven't I? Even if you think my conclusions are wrong, you admit I'm a good investigator!"

"We have lots of investigators," Victor Watson said. "And we've decided to fill that position with one of our own. It instills organizational loyalty to promote from within. Even your police department always selects the chief from within."

"But this isn't fair, Mister Watson!"

"Sidney, you've been put through a lot by a foolish old man. And I've never felt more like an old man than I do today."

"It's not fair, Mister Watson. This isn't fair!"

"Sidney, of all people, you should know that life isn't fair."

"All right, now listen to me, Mister Watson. This whole case . . . maybe there's an evil design here! You and me and Harry Bright? I thought it was all a fucking accident!"

"What?"

"Everything! But maybe I was wrong! I need more time to think!"

"About what?"

"This case. Maybe there's a kind of design. Right now it's drifting on me. Like sand in the wind!"

Now Victor Watson showed him his eyes. He switched on the desk lamp and removed a checkbook from the drawer. "I want to pay you for your services."

Sidney Blackpool stood up, and came forward like a sleepwalker. "I have most a the expense money here. I can't use it now."

"I want you to keep that and I want to write you a check."

"Not now," Sidney Blackpool threw the envelope on the desk. "Not now."

"Sidney, I think it's urgent that you talk to your police psychiatrist."

"I don't . . ."

"Listen to me please," Victor Watson said "I'll share a secret with you. I hope it helps. Sometimes, Sidney, sometimes, the father of a dead son has to be careful not to turn the awful outrage *against* the boy. Sometimes he might come to feel that the son failed in his *obligation* to survive the father. Don't confuse your

440

torment with mine, Sidney. My son didn't fail me. My son was *murdered*. Now I beg you. Take the money."

Sidney Blackpool stared with eyes as bright as desert gemstone and said, "I can't. It wouldn't do any good now. It's too late."

THE SECRET

It was nearly 10:00 P.M. when Sidney Blackpool found himself approaching Mineral Springs. He'd started out driving aimlessly and suddenly found himself here. He was surprised to be here and yet he wasn't. He was clutching at a shapeless idea. It was just beyond his grasp, a flitting sparkling image. The elusive fireflies would almost alight. Then they'd flutter. It was something very familiar, but kept drifting away.

He drove down the main street and saw Beavertail Bigelow staggering into the Eleven Ninety-nine Club. He proceeded to the other side of town and turned left on Jackrabbit Road. He drove to the end of the cul-de-sac and parked his car. He got out and walked to the door of Harry Bright's mobile home and saw that the broken door had been temporarily nailed shut. He cut his finger on a nail trying to straighten it. Finally, he went to the Toyota and got a screwdriver. He pried the nails loose from the door frame. He jerked it open and entered the mobile home and turned on the light.

Harry Bright's easy chair felt wonderful. He

saw that his finger was bleeding on the arm of the chair and he wiped the blood on his shirt. He looked at the wardrobe closet, at an empty holster that would never be filled, not with the same gun. He had to smile, a crooked smile like the one he'd seen on Patsy Bright. Good thing Harry Bright's gun wasn't there. Good thing.

Then he got up and went into the kitchen and found a fifth of bourbon. It would do. He poured a water glass full of it and went back to the easy chair. He sat and drank and watched the fireflies flitting across his mind.

He got up and went to the video cassette machine. He turned it on and rewound the spool to the beginning. Then he opened the other cabinet door and switched on Harry Bright's modest little sound system. He took the tape that Coy Brickman had shoved in his pocket and slid it into the machine. Then he rewound it. When everything was ready, he switched on the television, but turned the volume all the way down. He punched the play buttons on both machines and went over to Harry Bright's easy chair and made himself comfortable.

While sitting in Harry Bright's chair and drinking Harry Bright's whiskey he watched *The Enchanted Cottage*. Since he knew what was happening he didn't need its sound. Instead, he listened to Harry Bright saying, "This is happy Harry Bright coming to you from the Mineral Springs Palladium out on Jack-rabbit Road . . ."

While Harry Bright sang "Make Believe" and Sidney Blackpool watched *The Enchanted Cottage,* the fireflies in his mind flitted away. The elusive sparkling image took shape. He settled back and felt the way one feels when a fever finally breaks: tired, tingling, yet strangely restful. Pretty soon he felt a kind of peace that scared him and excited him.

The sand had stopped drifting. He wished he could share this with Victor Watson but knew he must tell no one. Not ever. At last he understood. The dream about Tommy Black-pool. Where he could re-create his son. Or the essence of his son.

His heart stalled from the joy of it. Now it was perfectly clear. As clear and pure as the desert sky at dawn. He was so happy he began to weep. Now *he* owned it. It was his and his alone: the merciful magical secret of Harry Bright.